Permanent Position
An Academic Thriller
Sid Stark

I0564423

Newsletter Signup

*Want to stay in touch, hear about new releases and offers, and get a FREE story? Get your copy of the prequel novella **Foreign Exchange** and sign up for my mailing list (but only if you want to!) by scanning the QR code below.*

1

My first day of class was already going badly, and technically it hadn't even started yet.

I had, miraculously, gotten an 11th-hour job offer at the very, very, very end of the previous semester, after my contract at my old college had already ended. A one-semester adjunct position with no possibility of renewal, but hey, a job was a job. I cringed a little inside whenever I thought about how I had gotten the job offer, but I had still taken it, along with the $5,000 "bonus" I'd been offered by the person who had arranged it all. Desperation makes scruples seem silly, and anyway, as he'd pointed out to me, I'd earned it. Besides, I wasn't going to be able to make the move to start the new job he'd gotten for me without it.

So here I was, starting the second week of January by navigating a new town (Charlotte, North Carolina) and a new campus (UNC-Matthews, a satellite of UNC-Charlotte). Which was under construction. In its current form it was more the dream of a campus than an actual campus, but that hadn't stopped the administration from offering classes on it, and, incidentally, taking people's money for them.

My first class of the day, RUSS 1102, started at 10:00am. I had planned to arrive at 9:00. It was now 9:35, and I still was nowhere near Tryon 351, my classroom, and had only a vague idea how to get there.

First I had gotten caught in traffic at the main campus gate. The omnipresent construction was also going on there, narrowing the entrance to one lane. Since this was a commuter campus, the entire student body, as well as all the faculty and staff, had to squeeze through this single lane to get onto campus for morning classes.

Then it had turned out that the main faculty parking lot was blocked off for construction. Since I had paid $200 for a parking pass that gave me access specifically to that lot, I was displeased. But not as displeased as the construction worker who came out and shouted at me in broken Spanglish to get out of the way of the earth-moving equipment that was trying to get through.

I had joined the long line of other commuters cruising hungrily for spaces, and had circled the campus twice before pouncing on a staff parking spot near the sports stadium. I was fairly sure that faculty were not supposed to park in staff parking spots, but it was already 9:30 and I was desperate. Better to ask forgiveness than permission, and all that.

I slid in just ahead of someone in a Chevy Suburban that wouldn't have been able to fit into the space anyway, gathered up my two bags of papers, water, pens, markers (permanent and dry erase), workbooks, textbooks, chalk, a laser pointer, and all the other detritus teachers tend to accumulate, and started hustling across campus to where I hoped Tryon Hall was.

My progress was impeded not only by my two-bag Teacher's Survival Kit and the blister I was rapidly developing on my left heel from my new boots, but by the vast field of mud that lay between me and where I thought my goal was. Probably it was supposed to be a pleasant quad, surrounded by neoclassical buildings and tastefully decorated with flowers and ornamental shrubs, through which sidewalks crossed purposefully, or maybe crisscrossed whimsically, but right now it was just several acres of mud. Abandoned construction equipment stood forlornly off to one side, huddled against the rain.

Oh yes, and it was raining. A cold, soul-sucking rain. I wanted to check my phone to see exactly how many minutes I had left to cross this corner of North Carolina's Great Dismal Swamp, but I was afraid that if I pulled it out, it would get soaked, or maybe slither out of my fingers into the mud, never to return. Then I would be phoneless, and I would have to explain how I'd lost it to Alex, the friend (with benefits?) who had loaned it to me after I had smashed the last one, and he'd probably laugh pretty hard before offering any sympathy, and my first week at my new job would suck even worse than it was already threatening to.

The glorious people's heroes of the Red Army didn't wimp out over a little mud! I told myself sternly. *And what are boots for, anyway?* I started across.

Ten very slippery minutes later, I was on the other side of the mud pit, and only half covered with sticky red clay that was already trying to stain everything I owned. At least I hadn't fallen on my ass. I scraped my boots off as best I could on the little patch of pavement outside the unmarked building I was at least 75% sure was Tryon Hall, and went inside.

Once inside, I saw that yes, I was in Tryon Hall, just on the other side from the entrance I had used when I had scouted it the week before. There was the front desk where all the admins for all of the programs in the entire building were currently housed. I gave a harried wave to a vaguely familiar-looking woman who may have been the one to process my intake paperwork last week. She had her back to me. To be fair, I had come in through the back entrance. Which meant...right is left and left is right...that looks like a stair...if I moved at a brisk jog down that corridor and up to the next floor and along the next corridor, I would be able to come bursting into my RUSS 1102 classroom at 9:59am.

"Hello, everyone!" I said manically as I raced into the classroom, dripping water and red clay everywhere. "Welcome to second-semester Russian!"

"What!" exclaimed someone in the back of the room. "I thought this was Farsi!"

"Isn't this Tryon 351?" I asked.

The students exchanged uneasy glances. "We think so," one of them volunteered. "But they haven't put the room numbers up on all the doors yet."

An exploratory expedition by one of the students sitting in the front led to the information that, as far as he could tell, we were indeed in Tryon 351, although it was a little hard to know because the room next door was a storage closet, so he wasn't sure how it worked into the numbering system.

"I think Farsi is the next room over," he said. "The professor's wearing a hijab, anyway, so it's gotta be Farsi or Arabic."

The confused Farsi student left to investigate that lead, followed by a couple of students who had thought they were there for Spanish.

"Sorry 'bout that," one of them apologized on the way out. "We thought Spanish was on the second floor."

"It is," someone told them. "But the second floor from the ground is the third floor of the building. You gotta go down a level."

"Okay," I said, once the exodus appeared to be over. "Okay. Are we all reasonably sure we're here for the right class? Second-semester Russian?"

The nods from the remaining eleven students were more tentative than I would have liked, like maybe some of them were actually there for Portuguese but hadn't figured it out yet, but I decided we needed to move on. It was already 10:11am and we hadn't even started the class yet.

"Why don't we do a quick round of introductions," I said, emphasizing the 'quick' part.

The student body was much more varied than it had been at my last school. The Liberal State College of New Jersey had been populated almost entirely by 18- to 22-year-olds, most of them white, or white-ish. Most my class at UNC-Matthews was over 25, with three black students, four Hispanic students, and four white students who exuded redneckness with their every movement. Most unusually, there was not a Russian Jew to be found. Most of the students were taking Russian on a whim, and finding it harder going than they had expected. Several expressed an intention of very likely dropping it if this semester turned out to be as hard as the previous one had been.

"I just don't have the time," confessed one woman, full of apology but not quite able to meet my eyes. Everything about her screamed "trailer trash," from her hefty figure to the hunch of her shoulders. "With my daughter and all. I pick her up after work and then I just can't do no more homework. I gotta put being a mom first, you know what I mean?"

The other students all nodded, and launched into explanations of why they had a hard time keeping up with their schoolwork, between their jobs, their families, and all the other things in their lives that took priority over school.

"I understand," I said. "We'll try to make this work for you, okay? If you're having trouble keeping up with the assignments, let me know, and maybe we can figure something out. Now, let's do a little review."

The review revealed that whatever the students had been studying the previous semester, it had included precious little Russian. We worked until everyone more or less remembered how to introduce themselves, and then it was 10:50 and we all had to rush off to our next class, me included. I gathered up my stuff, and, brushing past a woman with a stern-looking hijab and sterner-looking frown, set off down the hall.

"Professor!" A student I was at least 60% sure was named Jason was following me down the hall. "Professor, you got a minute?"

"I have class at 11. Can you walk and talk?" RUS 2102 was in Tryon 447, which involved a brisk climb up to the next floor. My boots were still slick with wet red clay, making me skate as much as walk on the institutional linoleum tiles that covered the floor. At least it wasn't carpet.

"Sure, professor. See, the thing is, I was gonna ask if you could help me."

"Of course I'll be happy to help you if there's something I can do for you."

"See, the thing is, it's my wife."

"Um, okay."

"She's run off back to Belarus."

"Oh." I stopped halfway up the stairs and turned to face him. "Is she Belarusian?"

"Yeah. We met online. But now she's run off. And she's taken our son with her. I need you to help me get him back."

2

"Um..." I said. "I'm, uh, sorry to hear that."

"Yeah. I, like, got her a visa and everything, we got married, had a kid, and then she just up and ran off back to Minsk. Taking our kid with her."

"Did she, uh, say why?"

"She gave a lot of reasons, but it's bullshit! She can't take my kid away from me like that!"

"Uh, yeah," I said. I was hoping that Jason would detach himself from me when I went into 447, which already had half a dozen students in it, but no such luck. He followed me into the classroom, saying loudly, "It's not right! She can't do that! My folks all said I shoulda known better, marrying a foreigner, and turns out they were right!"

"Why don't you send me an email," I said. "Tell me all about it in writing. And then I'll see if I can help you. Maybe I can point you in the direction of people who can help you with this kind of thing."

"No one wants to help! Fathers never get rights in this kind of thing!"

"Uh-huh," I said. "I've got class now, so why don't you send it all to me in an email like I suggested, and then we'll see what we can do."

Jason wanted to hang around and complain about the disgraceful treatment of fathers by the courts, the immigration system, and the world in general, but after the third student pushed him out of the way to get into the classroom, he got the hint and left.

RUSS 2102, fourth-semester Russian, went about the same as RUSS 1102, except that the students were desperately incompetent at a slightly higher level. Most of them were also non-traditional commuter students, going to school part-time in between working and taking care of their families. Most of them had also signed up for Russian more or less on a whim, or because it fit their schedule, or on a dare, and probably should have given it up, but hadn't. Something I should be glad for, because otherwise I would be out of a job. Unemployment was bad. But trying to teach Russian to people for whom it was a fourth priority at best was going to be a trial. Maybe it was a good thing I would only be here for one semester at the longest. Maybe the job market would hold fewer terrors after a couple of months here.

After class, the brightest and keenest of the students, a very good-looking young woman named Shaniqua, came over to ask me if I were Russian.

"Nope," I told her. "As American as you. I'm from Georgia. The state, not the country. But I lived in Russia for several years."

"I've got family in Georgia! Whereabouts are your folks from?"

"Macon," I told her.

"Mine too!"

We spent a few minutes bonding over our shared Macon roots, before Shaniqua went back to her original question, which was how an American had learned to speak Russian so well.

"I've been trying, I really have," she said. "I'd really like to go over there someday. I've got family roots there, actually." She laughed self-consciously. "You wouldn't think it to look at me, right?"

"The African diaspora also reached Russia," I said.

"Yeah, I know, like Pushkin. Do you know who Pushkin is?"

"Yes," I said. "I do."

"Really? That's cool. So anyway, my family was over there later, though. My great-grandfather went over there in the 1920s, when that was, like, a thing, you know? Have you heard of that? How African-Americans went over to the Soviet Union in the 20s and 30s?"

"Like Langston Hughes," I said.

"Right," said Shaniqua, looking startled. Probably she had expected to have to "school" me on the subject. "Anyway, my great-grandfather, he went over there about that time too, and he met a woman, I think she was from...she wasn't Russian; I think she was, like, Ukrainian or something, but similar to Russian; I think she spoke Russian a lot at home...I never met her, but my great-aunty was always talking about her and all the funny things she would cook for them. So I got interested, and I wanted to learn more about her and where she came from, because, that's, like, my heritage too, you know what I'm saying? So that's why I signed up for Russian. I'm getting a degree in accounting, but I thought I'd, like, get a minor or something in Russian if I could, and I'm getting close. But I'd like to go there someday, see where she came from, you know? What do you think: can I get my Russian good enough to go over there? And how do they treat black people over there?"

"Why don't I email you some resources," I said. "For example, there's a blog for minority students studying in Russia."

"Oh, really? So there's lots?"

"Some," I said. "I'll send you some information about it today, all right?"

"Great, thanks, Rowena!" she said. "And maybe you can tell me how your Russian got so good, too."

"Living there helps," I said. "Having a Russian boyfriend helps more."

"You have a Russian boyfriend?" she said, giggling a little at the thought of such a naughty cross-racial romance with a Slavic *Untermensch*.

"I used to. And if you'll excuse me, I really have to get ready for my next class..."

"Sure, and I'll be waiting for your email, Rowena!"

A small part of me wanted to point out that she really should call me "Professor." A larger part of me said that that would be counterproductive. So I told her I would be getting back to her just as soon as I could, and went off to see if I could find my office.

I had found it during my scouting expedition the week before, but parking on the other side of campus, and consequently entering Tryon Hall from the other side, had turned me around. It took me two tries to navigate my way from room 447, where my 2102 class was, to room 419, where my office was. It was on the same floor, which was the fourth floor despite being the third story of the building, but in a suite in a little annex around the corner that took some finding.

Once I got in, it looked just the same as it had when I'd been in it before. Everything was brand-new and barren. There was a phone and a desktop computer on the desk, which were still unconnected to anything. Supposedly I would be able to use both of them, but none of the IT equipment in Tryon Hall had been hooked up and activated yet.

Wifi was at least working, although it was so feeble in this distant corner of the building that I was unable to download any of my emails. With the loss of my smartphone, I couldn't check email on my phone either. I told myself I wouldn't forget about all the emailing I had promised to do, and did a quick prep for my third class.

RUSS 2105, Introduction to Russian Culture, was bigger than both RUSS 1102 and RUSS 2102 put together. It fulfilled the university's Crosscultural Experience general education requirement, and was consequently filled with students who were taking it because they couldn't get into their first-choice class. I spent most of the 50 minutes taking roll and trying to explain to the students where Russia was located geographically and why this was important, something that was hampered by the lack of any kind of a map. Normally I would have pulled up a map on the internet and projected it, but even if I had been able to get a strong enough wifi signal to load an image, the projector wasn't hooked up anyway. I promised the confused students I would try again next time, but for the moment they should take my word that Russia was located in both Europe and Asia, something that was news to them.

Just as everyone was leaving, my laptop, which I had left open in the hopes that it might suddenly pick up enough of a wifi signal for me to check my email, gave a *bloop* noise, telling me that a Skype message had come in.

"Jeez, disrupting class with your message alerts," muttered one of the students on his way out, staring at his phone. I pretended not to hear, and as soon as the last student had filed out, I went over to see what Skype was trying to tell me.

Hey sis, it said. *I can't fucking take another minute here, and I sure as hell can't take another minute with the fam. Can I come crash at your place for a while?*

3

Of course you can always stay with me, I messaged back. *But...*

"Excuse me. Excuse me! This is my classroom."

I looked up. The same woman I'd seen waiting to get into my 1102 classroom, the one with a hijab and a stern expression, was standing over me. I wondered if that was how I would look after another twenty years of grading.

"Oh, sorry! Are you the Farsi instructor?" I asked.

"Arabic," she said stiffly. "Students have study areas in the library, or the lobby downstairs. You shouldn't take up classroom space during class hours."

"I'll just get out of your way. And I'm, um, the new Russian instructor, by the way, not a student."

"That's right, they said they would hire someone," said the woman, not sounding at all apologetic. "You understand that you have to share the classrooms, don't you?"

"I'll just get out of your way," I said, and gathered up my two bags full of things and squeezed out past the incoming students.

I went back to my office, but the wifi was even frailer than it had been earlier, so I decided to pack everything up and schlepp back through the mud and go home and try again there.

I stopped at the front desk by the main entrance on my way out. "Hi," I said. "I'm Rowena. The new Russian instructor."

The student-worker-looking person stared at me in incomprehension.

"I just wanted to, um, check in and let the program know that I'm here and I found all my classrooms and held classes and everything today."

"Right," said the girl. "I'll, um, be sure to tell them. What department was this?"

"It's the Russian program. In the Modern Languages department."

The girl's forehead wrinkled. "I think that's Donna's department. Donna? Donna! There's someone here to see you."

An older and more competent-looking woman stepped out from a kind of booth/cubicle behind the desk. "Yes?" she demanded.

"She says she's here about the Russian program," the girl told her.

"What about the Russian program?" asked Donna, eyeing me with suspicion and more than a hint of dislike, as if she just knew I was about to cause her a major headache.

"I was just checking in to let...you, I guess, know that all the classes went off today without a hitch. Except for wifi. Do you know anything about the wifi here? Is there any chance that the reception might improve?"

Donna's forehead wrinkled up with even more confusion than the girl's had. "Are you a student?" she asked.

"What? Oh, um, no. I'm, um, Rowena Halley. The new Russian instructor."

Donna's forehead wrinkled in a slightly different pattern. "Oh, of course. I processed your I-9 form and your intake paperwork, didn't I? Well, uh, Dr. Halley, that's very, ah, responsible of you to stop and let me know. I'll be sure to pass on the good news to Dr. Whittaker over at the main campus. I'm sure he'll be pleased to hear that, although of course we knew we could count on you."

"Great," I said. "Um, thanks." Brent Whittaker was the chair of the Modern Languages department. We had spoken once during an in-person interview and once during a Skype interview, and exchanged a couple of emails over the terms of the job offer. Since then I had been ignored. Apparently I was considered that trustworthy. Or no one much cared what happened on the UNC-Matthews campus. That was okay. The only thing worse than a complete and total lack of institutional support was micromanaging. They could just keep on ignoring me all semester as far as I was concerned. I gave Donna a bright smile, which elicited a tight grimace in response, and left.

The rain had paused when I stepped outside, so I only had the several acres of red clay to contend with. I tried to scrape it off my boots before getting into my car, but with minimal success. It was nice to be back home in the South and surrounded by familiar things, like red clay. And my clothes were all a faded shade of charcoal, as was the inside of my car, so it wasn't like the stains would show. Too bad about the new boots.

UNC-Matthews was located just outside of 485, the big ring road that ran around the outside of Charlotte and its suburb Matthews. My apartment, which I had gotten not because I could afford it but because it was the least unaffordable apartment I could find on short notice, was in the Arboretum shopping center, across Pineville-Matthews Road from Walmart. For a mere $1000/month (plus pet fees), I had a luxurious 1-bedroom, 1-bathroom place, with easy access to shopping (Walmart), public transport (the bus stop outside of Walmart), and, if I wanted, various megachurches.

Since the vaunted public transport didn't actually run directly from the Arboretum to UNC-Matthews, and neither did any major roads, I had to get on 485, take it to the next exit, get off it, and then fight post-school traffic back all the way home, which meant the better part of half an hour to go less than 5 miles. And I still hadn't dealt with any of the emails I knew had to be piling up in my inbox, let alone done any lesson planning for Friday. And then there were job applications...my shoulders hurt. My shoulders hurt all the time, but now they hurt worse. Maybe hauling my bags back into my apartment would help loosen them up.

4

I t did not. Neither did tripping and almost falling over the pile of boxes by the front door, as my still-wet boots went sliding on the linoleum. Only a half-lunge, half-split combined with a clever martial arts fall kept my laptop from crashing to the ground and shattering into a million pieces.

"Fevronia!" I called, pulling myself up onto my knees and trying to kick off my boots without spreading mud around on the floor. More mud than I had already spread, that was. "Fevronia, I'm home!"

Fevronia did not appear. Fevronia was even less pleased about this move than she had been about the last one. At least the last apartment had had cockroaches and mice for her to chase, and, on several spectacularly gross occasions, catch and eat. This one was just boring, and she still hadn't forgiven me for the 10-hour car ride to get here, especially the part where we got stuck on 95 outside of DC. To be fair, I still hadn't gotten over that either.

I squirmed around until I was sitting on my butt, wriggled out of the two book bags that had gotten twisted in that last maneuver, and pulled off my boots. Then I had to crawl into the kitchen, dig out the paper towels, clean off the red clay that had gotten onto my feet and legs, and go clean it off the entranceway linoleum and—vainly—my boots. Then, finally, I could open up my computer and see what John and the rest of the world wanted from me.

Skype informed me that John had gone offline an hour ago. I repeated my invitation for him to stay with me as long as he wanted, whenever he wanted, but warned him that that would involve sleeping on the living room floor. Then I pulled up my UNC-Matthews email. Jason and Shaniqua had already emailed me with requests for help. I promised myself I would get right on that. I read various administrative emails explaining UNC-Matthews policies to me, and reiterating that I had no benefits and no hope of extending my contract.

Maybe there will be an invitation for an interview in my other inbox! I told myself, shutting down my UNC-Matthews email and opening my personal email account. *Maybe two! Maybe three! According to The Wiki, they thought they were going to start sending out invitations for that job at Trinity soon. And then there's the one in New Mexico. And Portland. There are even some tenure-track jobs still open.*

But my personal inbox was barren of all job-related emails, with not so much as a rejection to console me. I deleted a bunch of ads for penis enlargement devices and Hot Russian Brides, and went back to answering my emails from my other account.

I sent a list of study abroad resources to Shaniqua, and a list of Belarusian contacts to Jason, and sincerely hoped that that would be the end of it with him. Our first encounter had left a bad taste in my mouth, and I wasn't looking forward to having him in my class. Acting as his personal interpreter as he argued with his wife, who I had no doubt was a mail-order gold-digger who had been justified in leaving him once she discovered what a jerk he was, sounded like the kind of headache I could do without.

By the time I was done with that it was after 4. I could plan Friday's lessons, but I'd probably want to save that for Thursday, as a pleasant break from applying for jobs. So I made myself open my job spreadsheet and look at the next application on the list.

This one required a two-page cover letter, a full CV, a statement of teaching philosophy, sample syllabi, copies of recent teaching evaluations, a research statement, a writing sample, and three letters of recommendation. For a two-year visiting position (but with the possibility of renewal for a third year, so that made it okay). Preference given to candidates with valid OPI (Oral Proficiency Interview, a nationally standardized test for speaking ability) certification, and/or the ability to teach all levels of German language and culture as well as Russian.

"Maybe I should just give you my first-born child," I said out loud. "It might be less painful." The job was in—I checked—northern Wisconsin. Who wouldn't want to live in warm and sunny northern Wisconsin? Probably the cost of living was low. Probably if I got that job, I would cry with joy, and cling to it for all three years like a limpet. My parents wouldn't mind me being halfway across the country. At least I could be *in* the country, instead of in Russia like I had been for most of my twenties, and like I had intended to be for most of my life. Best laid plans, and all that.

I opened up the website for *Nezavisimaya Pravda* (*Independent Truth*) without really even meaning to. Dima, my fiancé—*ex*-fiancé, what was wrong with me, he'd broken it off a year ago—wrote for them, mostly war reporting, and even now that we were no longer together, I found myself checking their website at least three times a day. Whether that was for the news or for the jolt to the heart that seeing his name in print gave me was hard to say.

But today there was nothing there other than the usual stories of corruption. Dima's byline was conspicuously absent. I hoped that was because he was busy, and not because he was dead. Surely I would have heard if he'd been killed. It had been less than a month since he'd sent me that one cryptic email, saying he was glad I was still alive and reassuring me that he was, too. Then he'd gone back to covering the war in the Donbass, and there'd been nothing but radio silence from him since. I dug around on the website a little, but came up with nothing since his article from January 1 about the December 31 battle at the Donetsk airport. Presumably he was still there, the moron. Probably in the airport itself. Probably engaged in the actual fighting. On what side was not entirely clear to me. Probably it was not entirely clear to him either.

My phone rang, making me jump and almost drop it as I picked it up and tried to open it. It was a flip phone that didn't flip very well. But beggars can't be choosers.

"Rowena, have you heard?" my mother said before I could say a word. "Have you heard?!"

"Heard what?"

"About the job!"

5

"What job?" I asked.

"Oh, maybe it hasn't even been posted yet! But you know, darling, that I'm friends with Charles, you know, from the clinic, and Charles is also on the board for Crimson College—and guess what!"

"What?" Crimson College was where both my mother and my grandmother had gone. It was a small private college in a small town in Georgia, not that far from where my grandparents still lived in Macon.

"Well, you know they have a good language program for their size, and Charles was just telling me that they're planning to increase their—what did he call them? 'Less Commonly Taught Languages,' I think—their offerings of languages we don't normally teach. And"—her voice rang in triumph—"he says there's going to be a Russian job!"

"Wow," I said, after a long moment of silence. "Really?"

"Yes, darling, really! You mean you haven't seen it yet?"

"Let me check." I opened up my personal email account. And indeed, the most recent email was an announcement of a two-year Visiting Assistant Professor of Russian Language and Culture position at Crimson College.

"It looks good," I said cautiously.

"And darling, you'll be a shoo-in for it, you know you will!"

"There are no shoo-ins," I told her.

"Two generations of alumnae!"

"It can't hurt," I agreed. "I'll certainly apply."

"Of course, if—*when*—you get it, I'll probably be gone, which will be too bad, but you'll still be there when I get back, so that will be fine."

"Gone? Gone where?"

"Oh darling, didn't I tell you? You know I've been planning to do a stint with Doctors Without Borders this year. And it turns out it will be starting very soon. I was just talking to John about it...it's too bad you weren't able to come and see him, darling."

"I know," I said. With the US drawdown in Afghanistan officially concluding at the end of December, John had finally been sent home to Camp Lejeune, months later than we had originally hoped. Since he couldn't or wouldn't take leave, my parents and grandparents had gone out to Jacksonville to see him. But since the start of the semester waits for no man, nor woman either, I hadn't been able to come.

"Of course we all understand, but still...it would have been nice for you to have been there. He's..." My mother's voice dropped. "He's having a hard time, darling. Harder than usual."

"I'm sorry to hear that. I'll try to talk to him, if you think that would help."

"Oh, you know how he is, darling. I'm sure he'll try to push you away, and in very colorful terms, too. But...well, you, um, you have experience dealing with people with these kinds of problems, don't you?"

"Uh-huh. I'll give him a call, or something."

"Please do, darling. And so now I feel bad about leaving for this Doctors Without Borders thing, but John said he wanted me to go ahead and do it, and it's something I've wanted to do my whole life, darling. John knows that, and so he said to go on and do it, he'll be fine. Only I'd feel better if I knew you were watching out for him."

"I'll see what I can do," I said. "And I think doing a stint with Doctors Without Borders is great. What does Dad say?"

"He's looking into coming with me! We might go to Syria, isn't that great?"

"Great," I said. "Really great. I'm sure they'll need you there."

"I know it's a bit risky, darling, but you've never shied away from taking risks yourself, have you?"

"Um," I said. "I guess not. Although I guess pretty soon I'll be the only one who's never been in an active war zone."

"Oh, well...Moscow was close enough, wasn't it?"

"Um," I said. "Not really. I don't think that war zones normally have working metro systems."

"Anyway, darling, I'm *so glad* that John is *finally* back. I'm really hoping it will be his last overseas deployment. He's had more than enough, don't you think? Of course, that's how it is these days. But his twenty years are almost up. Amazing to think about it, isn't it. It's almost time for him to start thinking about retirement. If he could get a place at The Citadel...don't tell your father I said that. But they *do* take alumni, and well, he might as well get something out of it, don't you think? Anyway, he said he was going to contact you—something about needing a place to crash and unwind. He hasn't taken any leave yet, but he said he probably will soon, and he said he'd like to come visit you, especially since you weren't able to come with the rest of us to greet him when he got back."

"He messaged me about it. I'm sure we can work something out."

"Anyway, we won't *all* be in war zones at the same time, darling."

"Just you and Dima," I said, before I could stop myself.

"Oh. Of course. Is he *still* there, darling? Where did you say you *thought* he was? I thought he wasn't, ah, communicating with you anymore."

"Last I heard he was in Donetsk. At the airport."

"Getting ready to fly out?"

"I don't think there are any flights out of that airport anymore, Mom. There's a battle going on there."

"Oh. And has he...contacted you?"

"Not recently."

"Oh. Oh, well...it's probably for the best, darling, really. Make a clean break of it and all. It was never going to work out anyway."

"No," I said. "You're probably right."

"Well, I'll leave you to look at the job posting! Let me know how it goes, darling. Talk soon!" My mother hung up as abruptly as she had called.

I tried to go back to looking at the job posting and making a plan for putting together the very bestest application I could for it, because my mother was right, I had a major advantage and this could very well be my best, maybe my only, shot for gainful employment in my chosen field next year. Most PhDs don't care to live in the South, especially small-town Georgia, so the applicant pool would probably be half the usual size. And having the family connection would suggest to the search committee that I was more likely to like it there than a New Yorker. I couldn't let this miracle of a chance slip away because I was mooning over a man who had sent me away and told me not to come back.

But I couldn't resist taking one last look at the *Nezavisimaya Pravda* website before I went back to application world, just in case. Maybe there would be a breaking story that would prove to me that Dima was still alive. Maybe a miracle would happen, one that would prove to me and my parents that I hadn't wasted years of my life on him.

When I had first announced my relationship with a Russian, my parents had been welcoming. Everyone knows that the best way to learn the local language is to sleep with it. But flings are one thing, and fiancés are another. When I had stayed an extra year, and then moved in with him, and then told my parents that we were engaged, they had been less enthusiastic, although they had come over to meet Dima in person before rendering judgment on him.

Unsurprisingly, the judgment had not been positive. "He's very...intense," my mother had said after their first meeting. "He seems like a very...intense young man."

Which was true. And one of the things he had been very intense about had been me, which is the greatest aphrodisiac in the world. But the intensity of his love for me couldn't compete with the intensity of his love/hate for his motherland. So here I was, struggling to make it in a career I had chosen for him, while he was throwing himself into a war thousands of miles away. The fact that he was reporting on the war rather than fighting in it—as far as I knew, anyway—didn't make it any better. Dima had a drug problem, and his drug of choice was adrenaline, and no woman, not even me, was going to compete with that. So I shouldn't even try. Running after an addict was a recipe for heartbreak and disaster, and I, the child of addiction specialists, should know that.

"I'm going running," I announced to Fevronia. "I've had enough for today. Things will be better tomorrow."

Fevronia didn't answer.

6

The rain had stopped, and it was now 43 degrees and overcast. I pulled on my bright yellow running shoes. My blue ones had been battered into what even I recognized as unusability after I had had to run for my life through the snow last month, and so I had used some of the $5,000 I had gotten out of that little adventure to buy new running shoes, as well as the new boots I'd already ruined. I hadn't bothered with new dress shoes. Let that be an expense of the future, once things really started to warm up, like in March.

Traffic was bumper-to-bumper on Pineville-Matthews Road, so I set off down the sidewalk on my side of it. I tried not to think about all the pollution I must be inhaling. Charlotte was hardly the dirtiest place I'd been. In fact, it must be one of the cleanest places, compared with Moscow or New Jersey. But right now it was almost overwhelmingly overrun with cars.

I turned onto Providence Road and started running in the direction of downtown, several miles away. Hispanic construction and lawn crews on their way home for the evening leaned out their truck windows and whistled and shouted at me as I went past. Good thing I was too fast for them to get more than a word or two out before I flashed by. And it was nice to see that working-class brown men—what we were supposed to be calling them now, it seemed—were definitely not grabbing at male privilege by acting as the shock troops of the patriarchy.

After a couple of miles I was in another neighborhood of apartment buildings, but, judging by the people who were waiting at the bus stop there, ones that were probably more within my budget. Since I was getting a grand total of $9,600 for the entire semester before taxes, $1,000/month was more than I could afford for housing, but I had shown up in Charlotte a week before the semester started with no place to stay other than a hotel I could afford even less than my current apartment, and all my things in a shipping pod that I was paying by the day for.

The frugal thing to do would have been to shop around, see if I could sublet a room or something, get a tolerable roommate who wouldn't steal from me or, worse, disturb me while I was working, but that would have taken time and energy and money that I didn't have, so I had plonked down my deposit on the first apartment I'd found, and here I was. I had used up $2,997.52 of the $5,000 Erik Johnson, the provost who felt himself in my debt, had given me already, paying for the move and the deposit and things like shoes that didn't have holes in them. I wanted to hang onto the other $2,000 for some truly dire emergency, but I was afraid that the truly dire emergency was already here. My car needed work and my credit card only had $359 left on its limit and I needed to submit more applications, which cost money, and payday was three weeks away.

"Lookin' good, hun," one of the men at the bus stop said to me. "You that fast all the time? No wonder that ass is so cute."

I had been planning to turn around and start running back towards home then, but I didn't want to slow down there after that and I didn't want to look like I was running away from him, so I kept running up to the next light, at Alexander Road. I has half-tempted to turn onto Alexander and see where it took me, off into the gathering dark of January. That sounded better than worrying about money and jobs and loneliness and sexual harassment by random strangers who no doubt had plenty of their own problems.

My phone chirped at me. I fished it out of my raincoat pocket and wrestled it open.

"Alex?" I said between pants.

"I hope you're out of breath because you're doing something fun," said Alex.

7

"I'm running."

"Not as much fun as I was hoping for."

"I like running."

"Yeah, yeah, yeah, I know you do. It's why you have such a cute rear end."

"Funny," I said. "That's what the guy at the bus stop just said to me. So now I'm hanging out at the next intersection, waiting for him to get on the bus so I can run home without having to go past him again."

"Shit, Rowena, I'm sorry."

"It's okay. It's different when it's someone you know."

"Yeah, I guess. Are you safe?"

"Define 'safe.' I don't think I'm in imminent danger of being sexually assaulted, if that's what you're asking."

"Well, that's something, at least. Can you get home?"

"Of course. All I have to do is turn around and run home."

"Past someone interested in molesting you."

"I don't think he wants to molest me. Just harass me. And he probably meant it as a compliment. I'm not actually afraid of him; I just don't want him to think that I'm afraid of him, so I didn't turn around where I was planning to in case he thought I was trying to avoid him."

"And you didn't want him to think you were avoiding him because you wanted to prove you were tougher than him, you were afraid he would do something to you, or you didn't want to hurt his feelings?"

"Yes," I said. "D: All of the above. But he's getting on the bus now anyway, so it doesn't matter anymore."

"Are you safe to make it home?"

"What? Yeah, of course. It was just some dude at a bus stop. There have already been at least half a dozen, um, expressions of appreciation for my figure since I set off on this run."

"That doesn't sound very safe," said Alex.

"It's what happens every time I run. Or walk. Haven't you heard? Any woman walking down the sidewalk is fair game."

"Yeah, but...you're in a strange city..."

"I'm in Charlotte!"

"Yeah, that's what I'm saying. A strange city."

"You never used to worry about me running around Franklin Township."

"That's 'cause I didn't know about it. And anyway, Charlotte's a lot bigger, and a lot more..."

"Southern," I finished for him. "You're scared of the South, aren't you?"

"It's not the most civilized place," said Alex.

"I'm from Georgia!!"

"Yeah, but you know what I mean..."

"I'm from Atlanta! The dirty dirty South! Charlotte is..." I looked around at the apartment buildings I was now walking past. They were low-rent, but they were low-rent by Charlotte standards, which meant they were newer and cleaner than nice apartments for twice the price in New Jersey. "Charlotte is very civilized," I said. "Or at least clean and safe. Practically boring. You're just a Yankee snob. Have you ever even *been* to the South?"

"I've been to Miami."

"Miami doesn't count. Miami is basically Havana, with a side of Moscow."

"Okay, then, no."

"Well, don't criticize what you don't know. Come and visit Charlotte—or Atlanta—and *then* you can talk smack about it. Only you won't, because you'll like it so much."

There was a pause at the other end. I could hear Alex choosing his words in the silence. "Would you like me to come visit Charlotte?" he asked finally.

"Yeah, sure." It was now almost full dark, and I was getting cold from just walking in my running gear. Plus, it was a long way back to the apartment. I wanted to hang up and get back to running before my hands went numb, but now was not the moment.

"I could, you know," Alex said tentatively. "Come out and visit you for spring break. It's not like I'll have anything better to do."

"Gee, thanks."

"You know what I mean. Besides, I might want to check up on my phone, see how it's doing."

"The phone is fine."

"Really? It always seemed like a piece of crap phone to me."

"Yeah, but I still really appreciate you lending it to me. And I'll get it back to you soon, I promise."

"Take your time," said Alex. "No rush. And, anyway, I was calling to see how your first day of class went."

"Okay."

"Really?"

"No." I picked up a slow jog to try and stay warm while I filled him in on my earlier misadventures.

"Jesus," he said when I was done. "I'd be outraged, but that would indicate surprise."

"Yeah, I know. What about you?"

"Classes don't start here till next Monday. And I'm on my way back from the interview in Beirut. They have this winter term thing, so they brought me out during that instead of during the regular semester, which was convenient. The only convenient thing about the whole fucking experience, to be honest. I'm actually in Atlanta right now, waiting to catch the connection back to Philly, and I started thinking of you, seeing as how this is your home town and all."

"Say hi to it for me. How did the interview go?"

There was a groan at the other end of the phone, followed by silence.

"That great, huh?" I said.

"My main concern is that I might actually get the job. I feel like I fucked up everything I did, but it kinda seemed like I didn't fuck it up badly enough."

"But it's a tenure-track job, right?

"Yes, God help us all. If I'm offered it, and it's the only offer I get, I won't be able to justify turning it down."

"Do you have any other prospects?"

"Well..."

"Yes?"

"Maybe one," he said slowly.

"Really? That's great! Where?"

"The DLI," Alex said.

"As in *the* DLI? The Defense Language Institute in Monterey, California?"

"Yeah."

"You don't sound as thrilled about it as I would expect. Is it a good job?"

"Yeah," said Alex. "It's a good job. It's just...there's a lot of, you know, complications. I'd be a civilian, but I kinda wouldn't be, you know what I mean? I'd still be sucked back into the military, sort of. And there are people there...anyway, it would be complicated."

"So which would be better? Beirut, or the DLI?"

"I don't know. No, fuck it, I do know. The DLI for sure. I can't...I'm supposed to have a Skype interview with them soonish, although they haven't nailed down a time yet, and...I really don't want to fuck this up, Rowena. But if I don't, and I get the job, I still won't be very fucking happy about it. But enough about that. I didn't call you up to dump all my fucking problems on you. I'm sure you've got enough of your own. How's moving?"

"Moving sucks, but the worst part is over. What about you?"

"I'm still in the process of moving into my room. Yeah, yeah, I know: I'm moving up in the world. I was living in my parents' basement, and now I'm crashing on a friend's couch. Someday I might even have my own studio apartment."

"If you lived in Charlotte, you could afford an apartment," I said before I could stop myself.

"Can you afford yours?"

"No, but it's still cheaper than Philly."

"Everything's cheaper than fucking Philly," said Alex. "What it doesn't cost you in money, it takes by sucking from your soul."

"Really?"

"No, I'm just in a really shitty mood. I fucking hate having to be grateful to that asshole Johnson for my new job, and I especially hate having to be so grateful for such a fucking piece of shit job. If I'm going to worm my way to the top by kissing ass and sucking cock, the top should be a little higher than this, you know what I mean?"

"You saved his daughter's life," I said. "Also, as a feminist scholar and as a heterosexual woman, I feel obligated to point out the problematic nature of your denigration of sucking cock."

Alex laughed into my ear. "If you want it, you shouldn't talk shit about people who do it, is that what you're saying?"

"Pretty much."

"Point taken. Are your teeth chattering?"

"Maybe a little. I can't really run and talk on the phone at the same time."

"Oh, right. Shit, sorry about that. I'll let you go, but let me know how things go, okay? And don't let that Jason guy drag you into anything too shady. That sounds like a big fucking mess and no mistake. And he sounds like a creep."

"Quite possibly," I said. "But he's my creep, so I have to deal with him."

"Yeah, just...be careful, okay, Rowena? I know how you can get sucked into helping people who don't deserve your help."

"Because you've never done the same thing."

"Yeah. Just...I don't know, Rowena, take care of yourself, okay? These assholes are paying you how much?"

"$3,200 per course. So $9,600 for the semester."

"Yeah. Motherfuckers. $9,600 isn't worth taking any risks for. $9,600 isn't even worth getting out of bed for."

"Having $9,600 is a lot better than not having $9,600."

"Yeah. But you know what I mean. Don't go wasting your time doing anything extra for these—I was going to say cocksuckers, but I'll stick with motherfuckers. Don't go running any of those cutesy little extracurricular activities they like to have you do, don't go spending lots of extra time on the students, don't do any of that stuff. Fuck, I wouldn't even write letters of recommendation."

"If I don't, then no one will. And it's not the students' fault."

"Fuck! They're still, what's the phrase I'm searching for—they're still benefiting from your uncompensated labor, or something like that. But you know what I mean. They might not mean to, and they might not even know what they're doing, but they're still fucking doing it."

"Yeah. I know."

"But you sound cold and you need to get home, so I'll stop ranting to you about exploitation and all that shit. Just let me know how things go, okay?"

"Yeah," I said. "You too. Let me know how things go with your new job, okay?"

"You bet your runner's ass I will. I'll be calling you up Monday evening for sure, going on and on about today's students, or something like that."

"I'll be waiting," I said.

"Okay. Take care, okay?"

"You too," I said, and flipped the phone closed with stiff fingers. It rested warmly against my belly when I slipped it into the pocket of my raincoat. Probably it was giving me cancer or something. But it was still nice to feel that little piece of warmth, and know that it came from Alex. Who, unlike certain people I could mention, was around for me and seemed to want to be with me. Which counted for a lot, right? More than almost anything else, in fact.

A pickup with a trailer loaded precariously with ladders slowed down next to me. Three men leaned out the windows and shouted something at me in Spanish. I definitely wasn't going to start running now. The car behind them honked and they sped off. Once they were safely far away, I took off at a hard run towards my new home.

8

It was darker and later than I would have liked when I got back to my apartment. I'd spent well over an hour running when I could have been working. And I only felt a little bit better. But not running would have been worse.

A couple was getting out of a car in the spot next to mine. Both looked tired and unhappy. The woman—"woman" was a strong term; she couldn't have been much over twenty—started to fuss over something in the back seat, and then shouted at the man to help her, which started a short but surly slanging match that resulted in the man loading up an armload of shopping bags and storming up the stairs to the apartment above mine. The woman stiffly retrieved a bulky thing out of the back seat that turned out to be a baby carrier.

"Here," I said. "You need help with the door?"

"Nah, I'm good," she said, not looking at me. "Duane's s'pposed to be helping me anyway. Duane! DUANE!"

The baby, who only looked to be a few hours old, opened up its eyes and started squalling.

"Ah, fuck, Lakeesha, can't you get her to shut up!" the man shouted, not coming down from where he was fiddling with the door at the top of the stairs. He got it open and shoved his way in without coming back to help Lakeesha with the baby, who was now bawling its lungs out.

"Sorry 'bout this," said Lakeesha, looking very tired and not very sorry. "We might be kinda loud. You know how babies is—you got any kids yourself?"

"No," I said. "Is this your first?"

"Yeah." Lakeesha didn't look thrilled at the announcement. "Born this morning."

"Congratulations!"

"Yeah. Duane! DUANE! Where the fuck are you!? I can't carry this baby up them stairs myself!"

There was no response from Duane. "I can help," I offered again.

"Nah, that's okay. Let him get his lazy ass down here and help out for once." Lakeesha started making her way slowly up the stairs, shouting at Duane. The baby tried to keep up by raising the pitch of its screams, but its hours-old lungs were no match for its mother's.

"This should be nice," I told Fevronia as I came into my own apartment. "A new baby. What could be better?" The baby's screams and Duane and Lakeesha's argument filled my apartment as if there were no ceiling between us. Fevronia came creeping out from wherever she had been hiding, looked up at the noise, flattened back her ears, and ran off.

"That's right," I said to her in Russian. "That's the right approach. I should do the same."

The happy sounds of a new little family coming together followed me as I took a shower and made supper. By the time I was done, everyone seemed to have screamed themselves into exhaustion, and something almost like silence reigned. I took advantage of the quiet to open up my email. There was another request from Jason to set up a meeting so that we could talk to his wife. I promised myself I would get to that first thing in the morning, and did a careful read-through of the posting for the Crimson job.

It was the usual: cover letter, CV, statement of teaching philosophy, sample syllabi, evaluations, research statement, writing sample, and three letters of recommendation. I read to the end and groaned: although many jobs gave you a month or so to get your applications in, this one said "Review of applications will begin immediately and will continue until the position is filled." Which meant I needed to get my materials in ASAP, preferably tomorrow morning. Good thing I had no class on Thursdays.

I briefly considered starting the application this evening, but bitter experience had taught me that doing so would not cause me to submit a better application more quickly. Instead I would spend twice as long on it, or make multiple egregious errors, or both. I would be better served by resting and thinking about how I would reword the opening sentences in my cover letter in order to convince the search committee that I was the most perfect of all of their dozens of perfect candidates.

So for the last couple of hours of the evening I found myself surfing the news, pretending that I wasn't looking for Dima or anything that might have anything to do with him, before turning in. Fevronia was still in a snit and refused to get into the bed with me, so I passed yet another night completely alone.

9

I was only awakened twice in the night by the new baby's screaming, so I counted that as a win. Fevronia was less charitable, and expressed her frustration by leaping out from under the bed and sinking her fangs into my calf. Normally she didn't actually bite me, only any male visitors I might have (and there had been precious few of those), but today she was not happy, and wanted to let me know.

I spent a few minutes wallowing in guilt over my inability to provide Fevronia with the situation she deserved. Living indoors all the time and being constantly uprooted from one crappy apartment to the next wasn't fair to her. Good thing I didn't have any kids, since I couldn't even provide properly for a cat.

The baby upstairs started squalling again. On the other hand, an inability to provide properly for a child hadn't stopped Lakeesha and Duane from bringing one into the world.

Frantic screaming accompanied my morning yoga and hapkido forms, and continued to drill into my head as I sorted through my email. Then, promising myself that I would definitely get back to Jason about his request to mediate his marriage into good health and happiness, I sat down to put together the Crimson application.

Since I had most of the required materials ready already, all I really had to do was carefully read through the job announcement and then go through the department and college website, looking for things I could use to show how I was the most enthusiastic, most suitable candidate who had ever walked the earth.

After an hour or so of that fun, I had reworked the key sentences in my cover letter to show the search committee just how wonderful I would be, and how much I wanted the job (but not desperately, of course: desperation was bad). I checked through it and all my other materials one last time, making sure that they were all in the right file format and had the right file names (imagine sending in an application for Crimson that had "Clemson" in the file name. The horror, the horror) and started the tedious process of filling out all the fields in the online application, and uploading all the documents. And then there was the best moment, when I paid $18 for my letters of recommendation to be securely forwarded to the search committee. Sometimes I looked at my credit card statements and started to calculate how much I spent on sending out letters of recommendation, but once my credit card limit had gotten below $500 it had gotten too depressing, so I had, just when I most needed to keep track of my finances, stopped.

Dealing with my documents gave me a good opportunity to contemplate all the ways I was failing as a scholar, and how I hadn't even gotten started on the next article I needed to submit, let alone on putting together a book proposal. I knew I needed to do those things, and I even kind of wanted to do them, but I hadn't. One of the problems with academic work was that the ultimately inconsequential tasks were all parceled up in urgent little packets of time, while the truly consequential tasks tended to have no deadline. So instead of writing and doing research, I was constantly rushing around trying to be prepped and ready for class and in the classroom at exactly the right moment, and answering emails and student questions, and applying for jobs, and all the other things that ate up my time and energy but didn't advance my career or make anyone any happier or wiser.

I told myself once the application had gone through that I would definitely get started on that next article, or even the dreaded book proposal, soon, maybe even this very afternoon. But first I would take a look at my application schedule and see what was next on the agenda. And I would talk to Jason. I already didn't like him, but if I didn't help him, who would? Years of hard work had given me a special and unique skill set, and it would be a shame for it not to be used in order to do good. So instead of doing something that might move me up in the world, I opened Jason's email and, gritting my teeth, told him I'd be happy to help him talk to his wife.

I was hoping that Jason would fail to get back to me and I could go on to planning the next day's lessons in peace, but when I, stupidly, checked my email half an hour later, he had already responded.

thanks for finally getting back to me, his email said. *i really need to set up someone to help me talk to marina arinas sister marinas got her hooks in her wont let her talk to me i know if i can get marina to see sense arina will fall in line but marina doesnt speak english so i need someone who speaks russian to do the talking for me when can we meet*

I resisted the impulse to respond "Never," and emailed back suggesting a consultation during office hours. Jason shot back an email asking if we could meet that evening after work.

Unfortunately, I will be busy then, I replied, not mentioning that I would be busy staying at home avoiding him. *Let's meet before class tomorrow, or during my office hours in the afternoon.*

Jason wrote back complaining that that was inconvenient to him. I suggested that he compose an email explaining in more detail what the problem was and how I might help him, and referred him to the links I had originally sent him, to Belarusian organizations that might be more suited to this task than I was. He sent back an email grousing about how he didn't want to go through strangers and foreign organizations in order to solve a family matter, and how unhappy he was, and how he needed to work as much as possible in order to earn the money he'd need to support his family when he got them back. I told him I understood all of those motivations, and that I'd be happy to talk to him during office hours the next day.

look, he said, after more than an hour of emailing back and forth, *i just really want to set up a skype call with marina this weekend can you do that ill pay how does $30/hour sound*

I hated how much more keen I became to get involved in this for $30 an hour rather than for free. But $30 would buy a lot of lentils. I could live for the better part of a week off of $30.

How about Saturday, if she's available? I wrote back.

can you write her and set it up he asked. *i know she wont talk to me even if i could write in russian her email is marina1980@mail.ru and her skype address is marina1980*

Okay, I answered, despite my returning disinclination to get involved at this new demand. *I'll let you know if/when she responds.*

After that there was no response from Jason, who didn't seem like the kind of guy to give a lot of effusive thanks. Reminding myself that the sooner you went to jail, the sooner you got out, I then spent quite a lot of time crafting an email to Marina. By the time I was done, most of my productive day had gone, and I threw together a hasty lesson plan for my final lesson the next day, and escaped to go running before I could stop myself.

10

I made it onto campus and into my office in a more timely fashion the next day by leaving half an hour earlier. There was still a jam at the main entrance, but I managed to get through it early enough to get one of the precious few parking places left in the small corner of the regular faculty parking lot that was currently not under construction. This gave me time to walk to my office in a more or less normal manner, and on a sidewalk rather than through the mud, too. I even got to run to the bathroom before class.

My triumph was somewhat marred when I looked up out the window after getting out of the stall and discovered that a group of construction workers had set up their scaffolding just above the window. Although the bottom half of the third-floor window was frosted, the top half was clear, and their scaffolding was perfectly positioned to allow them to look straight down through the clear glass into the stalls. One of them caught my eye as I looked up, gave me a huge grin, and said something that, luckily, I couldn't hear or understand.

I pretended to ignore him while I wondered what to do. It probably needed to be reported, but I didn't know to whom. The front desk, where all two of the admins for all the programs for the entire building worked? It had been empty when I had hustled by it five minutes ago. Probably I should tell someone from Facilities Services. I checked the time. 9:45. I wasn't going to have time to find the number for Facilities Services, call them, and explain the problem before I had to go to class. I should probably warn my classes, too. I thought about how this particular bunch of students would respond to my tale of being ogled in the bathroom. That would be it for whatever tenuous authority I had in the classroom for the rest of the semester. They'd be sniggering at the thought of me going to the bathroom, imagining me naked, and blaming me for getting ogled, and maybe also for causing trouble for the workers. I promised myself I'd make an anonymous call to Facilities Services during my break between my second and third classes, and went off to see what RUSS 1102 had in store for me today.

What it had in store for me was more bugging from Jason after class to get in touch with Marina. When I told him as I hustled to my next class that I had emailed her and was waiting for a reply, instead of thanking me, he started pressuring me to email her again.

"We should give her at least twenty-four hours to respond," I said.

"It's already been twenty-four hours, ain't it?!"

"I sent the email yesterday afternoon. It would have been late at night in Minsk."

"And so now it's already evening in Minsk! She's had all day to get back to you, and she ain't done it yet!"

"Well, maybe she's been busy. Maybe she'll get back to me tomorrow. I'll be sure to let you know as soon as she does. She probably wants to talk it over with Arina anyway. *If*, that is, she bothered to read the email at all. She might have deleted it unread, or it might have gone into spam, since it's from a strange email account. And *if* she read it, she might have thought it was a scam. I really think it would make more sense for you to handle this yourself. I don't really understand how I can make things better, and I really don't understand why Marina needs to be involved in this, when she's not your wife, just your wife's sister."

"I told you. I need Marina on my side to convince Arina. That's why I've been studying Russian and all. So I can talk to both of them. And our little boy. Arina said she wanted him to grow up speaking his own language, so I agreed I'd learn Russian and we could talk Russian at home."

"That's wonderful," I said. "Maybe you should...I don't know, start sending him and Arina regular emails or letters or something, telling them about how hard you're working on your Russian, and showing them your progress."

"It won't do no good if she won't listen to me! I gotta make her listen to me! I gotta get my son back! You ain't got no children, right? Then how'd you ever know! I can't live without my son!"

"Well," I said. The students for 2102 were already filling the classroom, and I had gotten tired of talking to Jason before the first word had left his mouth. "Sending Arina regular updates via her sister might not be such a bad idea, then, but it seems like it would be better coming from you rather than from some stranger. I have to go now since my next class is starting, but I'll be sure to let you know as soon as I hear anything back from her."

"You do that," said Jason. He left without saying anything further about payment, or when or if or how much he was going to pay me for taking the trouble to write that email. Under other circumstances I would have been happy to write an email for free. Under my current circumstances, even ten or fifteen dollars would have been a very welcome addition to my weekly budget. But I didn't want to seem like I was desperate, or do anything to give Jason any more of an upper hand than he already thought he had over me, and my next class really was about to start, so I let him go.

11

My other two classes went off without incident, although my students' lack of aptitude was even more apparent than it had been on the first day, especially in 2102. The Hispanic students were all bilingual in English and Spanish, but that was less of an advantage than they thought it was. Most of the non-Hispanic students had studied Spanish in high school, but failed to learn it. Now Russian was turning out to be four times harder than Spanish, and they were too hopelessly confused to even understand why what they were saying was wrong. Much of class was taken up with excuses about why they hadn't done the homework from the previous class. Most of the excuses were legitimate. But they still meant that the students had failed to learn the material.

"I don't see how people who get to be professors do it," said Helena, after explaining that she hadn't done the homework because her toddler had gotten sick and she'd had to babysit for her sister's kids as well. "How they find the time."

"You really want to know?" I asked.

Everyone nodded, looking vastly more interested in this than in our review of the prepositional case. I had the feeling that professors were strange, exotic creatures to them. Maybe they had never talked to any of their professors like people before, or heard anything about their lives.

"You have to make it a priority," I told them.

"Yeah, but I got all kindsa more important things I gotta take care of every day, you know what I'm sayin'?" argued Jamal. "I got mouths to feed, sh—stuff like that."

Most of the other students were nodding in fervent agreement.

"I know," I said. "I'm not saying that you're wrong to make that your priority. But if you want to do well in school, or get good at anything difficult like Russian, that has to be one of your top priorities. You only have so much time and energy, so you can only get good at so many things. You have to choose. And if you want to get good at this, that's what you have to choose."

I tried to say it kindly, but most of the students still looked unhappy. Although students in the Russian program were by default some of the best and brightest of whatever institution they were in, that was relative. Most of my students here obviously didn't enjoy studying for the sake of studying, and were just jumping through hoops in order to get a degree that would in some way propel them to a life of greater material comfort. Undergoing further deprivation and struggle in lives that had already had more than their fair share of it held little appeal, and doing so in order to further some kind of abstract life of the mind, even less so. I could understand that. I could sympathize with that. But it still meant that they were going to fail at the thing that I was supposed to be teaching them.

"Just do the best you can," I concluded. "If you have to wait for the weekend to get your homework done, so be it. Just try not to let it get too far ahead of you."

There was some apologetic grumbling from the ones who had to work over the weekend, and we finished up the class with the half-spoken understanding that they would try as best they could, which wouldn't be very good, and I would be lenient when it came time to grade.

Afterwards, Shaniqua, who was the only one in the class to have actually done the homework, came up to talk to me some more about going abroad in the summer.

"I asked my grandmother," she told me. "She said she thinks her mother, my great-grandmother, was Ukrainian. She's digging through her old papers, searching for anything that might tell us more. If we find something, can we show it to you?"

"Sure, of course."

"And now I'm looking into going to Ukraine for the summer."

"That sounds like a great idea."

"The rest of my family doesn't want me to go. They say"—she shed her neutral American accent, and took on an uneducated "black" accent—"'black girls don't do stuff like that.'"

"Some do," I said encouragingly.

"Oh, I know, I know. But what do you think? Is it safe?"

"Well," I said. "There is a war going on there now. So it depends on what part of the country you go to, and what you mean by 'safe.'"

"Yeah, I suppose you're right, but I meant, would it be safe for me?"

"Anywhere is dangerous. But I've spent a lot of time in the former Soviet Union, and most of it was at least as safe as most places in the US."

"Yeah, but you're not *black*." The expression of gentle superiority that Shaniqua wore most of the time sharpened as she prepared, no doubt, to "school" me once again. I tried to summon up all my best teaching mentality and strength of mind. So far, two days into the semester, I liked Shaniqua the best of all my students, and she certainly was one of the few with any spark of talent and fire, but she seemed determined to fulfill the stereotype of the sassy, obstreperous black woman, type 2.0 ("woke" version). Probably because she thought she could get away with it with me. This meant dealing with her was almost as exhausting as dealing with a man, what with the constant one-upmanship and struggle for dominance. And it was obvious that Shaniqua was used to being the smartest person in the room, and also that she'd never been in rooms with lots of other smart people in them. Hopefully one day she'd get the chance. So I needed to prepare her for the experience, and that included helping her keep her arrogance and her assumption of superiority under control. A certain amount of arrogance was a good servant, especially for a woman, but a very poor master.

"Most of my African-American friends and colleagues found that, while they were used to thinking that the most important aspect of their identity was the African part, when they got to the former Soviet Union, it turned out that the American part was at least as important," I said.

Shaniqua looked startled.

"You'll be a representative of America first and foremost while you're there," I told her. "That's the thing people are going to see first. And sure, your race will matter too. But not in the same way it does here. It will probably be a very different experience for you. Many people find it a refreshing change, to be honest, because when you do encounter racism—which you will—it's normally completely out in the open, which means you can fight it."

Now Shaniqua was looking thoughtful. "I guess...I guess I never really thought of myself as American first, and black second," she said. "That'll be different."

"Yeah," I said. "Not necessarily comfortable, but different."

"So were people unfriendly to you, then?"

"Mostly people were more friendly and welcoming than you can possibly imagine. Sometimes they weren't. Sometimes they screamed at me, or threw things at me, or pulled guns on me—but that had more to do with my boyfriend than me."

"Oh, that's right! He's Russian, right?"

"That's right."

"So they didn't approve of him getting involved with an American?"

"Among other things," I said. "But don't let that stop you from getting a Russian boyfriend if the spirit moves you."

Shaniqua laughed at such a naughty thought, and promised that if the spirit moved her to hook up with a handsome Russian or Ukrainian man, she would definitely follow.

12

After spending a while trying to explain again to my 2105 class that "Eurasian" meant a combination of both "European" and "Asian," I called it a Friday and went home.

Even though it wasn't rush hour yet, I got caught in heavy traffic on both 485 and when trying to turn onto Pineville-Matthews Road. The extra time in my car gave me the opportunity to appreciate how feeble the heater was. It had never been great, and this winter it had gotten even worse. Charlotte was generally warm enough that it had been okay so far, but a cold front was supposed to move in over the weekend, and already I could feel the chill despite turning the heater on full blast. No doubt it needed expensive repairs. I tried to pull through a light, and almost stalled out when I shifted into second gear. As usual. Probably I needed a transmission rebuild or something. Probably I needed to just buy a new car. If only my job that required a car in order to get to it actually paid enough to afford a car. But that was clearly a utopian ideal that could never be achieved.

When I pulled up to my apartment, Lakeesha was getting out of her car, baby in tow. She looked exhausted. When I waved, she gave me a suspicious stare and a very half-hearted wave in return.

"Hey," I said, when I saw that she had bags full of disposable diapers as well as the baby. "You need a hand with that?"

"I got it."

"I don't mind. It looks like you've got your hands full enough already."

"Yeah, well...okay."

"How's it going?" I asked, nodding at the baby.

"Okay."

"How are *you* doing?"

Lakeesha shrugged. "You know how it is."

I nodded sympathetically. That seemed to be enough to get the floodgates to burst, and Lakeesha started telling me everything she must have wanted to pour out to a friendly ear.

"All she do is shit and scream," she said. "And Duane don't do shit either to help out. He didn't want her, you know. He keeps tryin' to get me to say she ain't his. But she is. He was in prison last year, see, and then she happened right after he got out. So he keeps sayin' she must not be his, I musta gotten her offa someone else. Only I didn't. He's tryin' to do the right thing, though, or at least his momma is makin' him do the right thing. She's the first grandchild for both my momma and his. They weren't too happy when they found out she was comin', but once they come 'round to the idea, they got real happy. They're tryin' to help out as best they can, too, but it's tough, you know? Like, I'm gonna have to go back to work next week."

"Yikes," I said. "That's very soon."

"Yeah, I know. And I don't wanna leave her. But Duane can't get good work since he got outta prison. Well, he couldn't get good work before he got into prison, either. But now it's real tough. He's got a part-time job workin' construction, which is like, real heavy labor, you know what I'm sayin'? He comes home from it all beat to pieces every time. And he's got, like, some side stuff goin', but it's not enough for all of us, 'specially the way she goes through diapers. I never thought a baby could make that much of a mess. And diapers is expensive, too. And there's the hostipal bill. I don't know what we're gonna do about that. Duane's momma said maybe she could chip in some, and my grandmama said she maybe could too, but they got their own problems, and don't wanna help us out too much, they say we gotta stand on our own two feet. They keep talkin' 'bout how I'm a grown-ass woman now and I gotta start actin' like one. Only it's hard when you ain't got no money and gotta keep askin' your family for handouts."

"Yeah," I said. "I know."

Some of Lakeesha's original suspiciousness returned. "How's someone like you know 'bout that?"

"Because," I said, trying to smile like it was funny, even though it wasn't, "I have to keep relying on other people's handouts too."

"Really? Whatcha do for a livin', anyway?"

"I teach. At UNC-Matthews."

"So, you're, like, a professor?"

"Yep."

Lakeesha gave me another look of deep suspicion. "I thought professors made good money."

"Alas, no. Many of us don't make good money at all. Most of the time, it's more a hobby for rich men's wives than anything else. Or at least it should be. Unfortunately, a lot of us don't have rich husbands."

Lakeesha took a moment to translate what I'd just said, and then shook her head. "Seems like smart people should know better."

"Academic ability and money-making smarts rarely go hand-in-hand."

"Yeah, a lot of smart folks is dumb as rocks when it comes to a lot of stuff," said Lakeesha, cheering up at the thought of the stupidity of smart people. "'Course"—her superiority ebbed back out of her—"I can't say I'm much better, can I? I mean, look at me, broke as a promise and with a kid at twenty-two. Least I waited till I wasn't a teenager no more, though. Lot of my friends got knocked up when they was fifteen, sixteen—even fourteen. 'Course, their mommas helped 'em out a lot more'n mine is willin' to help me out, what with me bein' a grown-ass woman and all."

"Being a grown-ass woman is a mixed blessing," I agreed.

Lakeesha snorted. "You're tellin' me. So anyways, I still got my job at Walmart—I think—and I'm gonna start back up with that next week. It's only three days a week, so me and Duane should be able to work somethin' out so's there's always someone home with the baby, but I don't know how I'm gonna make it through a whole shift. I'm tryin' to breastfeed her, 'cause they say that's better, you know, and it's sure as hell cheaper'n buyin' that crap they try to sell you, but that means I'm gonna have to pump durin' my shift. I talked to my supervisor, and she said I'm gonna have to do it in the restroom. I don't wanna pump milk for my baby in the restroom, but it's the only place, so I guess that's what I'm gonna do. And my body's still all tore up from the birth. I might have to wear some diapers or somethin' myself so I don't wet myself while I'm standin' at the cash register."

"Gosh," I said. "That sounds awful. But you've got to do what you've got to do."

"Yeah," said Lakeesha. "I ain't got much choice, anyhow. And they say it's all gonna be worthwhile someday." She gave the baby a sideways look of doubt.

"I'm sure you'll look back on all of this and be glad, someday," I said. I hoped my assurance didn't sound completely fake. "And she's certainly very cute. What's her name?"

"Nevaeh." Lakeesha's face scrunched up defensively. "You're gonna tell me it's a trashy name, ain't you?"

"My name's Rowena," I told her. "I would never criticize another girl for having a fancy name."

Lakeesha perked up. "Rowena's a nice name. Maybe I'll use it for my next one."

"You're planning on having another one, then?"

She shrugged. "No, but you know how it is. It's gonna happen; might as well be prepared. You don't got any, right?"

"No."

"How'd you do that?"

"Um...birth control?"

"Yeah. Condoms don't always work though, and a lotta guys won't wear 'em."

"That is true." Lecturing her on how she needed to stand up for herself and not sleep with men who were too selfish to practice safe sex would probably be counterproductive. "There's always IUDs or the pill," I said.

"I don't got health insurance."

"Oh. Yeah, that's a problem, all right." Lecturing her on how paying out of pocket for an IUD would still be several orders of magnitude cheaper than having an unwanted child would probably also be counterproductive. Telling her that when I had been her age, I had saved up my pennies and bought birth control on my own dime wouldn't be much better. And while I hadn't had an unwanted pregnancy with a man I wasn't married to, as I got older and older, my childless state seemed less and less like something to brag about, and more like something to mourn.

For a moment I wondered what it would have been like, if I had gotten pregnant as soon as Dima and I had gotten together. Probably Dima would have insisted on marrying me, and his mother would have insisted that I move in with her and let her take care of the baby. Probably we would have quarreled and fought and made each other and the child very unhappy. Probably Dima would have ended up picking fights and running off to war zones anyway, and I would still be alone, only with a child to take care of. Now I was just alone, and I didn't know which was worse. I thought about saying all that to Lakeesha, and telling her that maybe she was the smart one, the lucky one. Luckily, Nevaeh woke up and started to scream before I got the words out.

"Sorry 'bout this." Lakeesha made a face. "I can't seem to get her to stop screamin.' Everyone's been tellin' me you gotta let 'em scream, and also that by my second one I'll have it all figured out. But I ain't got my second one yet, and I know these walls here don't block shit."

"It's okay," I said. "I know you can't help it. And...you know, most of the time I'm busy, but if you need help on Tuesdays and Thursdays, I might be around." *Why?!* I shouted at myself. *Why did you just make that offer?! You have more than enough of your own problems!!!!*

"Thanks," said Lakeesha. By her expression she seemed to doubt the sincerity of my offer, or maybe just my baby-caring skills. Both were legitimate concerns. She shivered. "You feel that wind? It's gonna be a cold one this weekend! I better get the both of us inside."

"Yeah," I said. "Stay warm!"

"You too!" An extra-cold gust hit us, and we both rushed inside.

13

My evening was spent submitting another job application. January 15 was a popular application deadline, so I had a bit of a pile-up in my application schedule right now. At least I had decided not to bother with even trying to fit in any conferences in the spring. The Southern Slavic conference was in March, and in a perfect world I would be putting together a panel proposal for it right now, but since no one held interviews there, I had decided against it. It was in Kentucky, so it would have been cheap and easy to get to, but not cheap and easy enough.

January was also the time to start putting together proposals for the big national conferences next winter, so as my last order of business for the evening I fired off emails to various friends from grad school to see if anyone had a brilliant idea that I could glom onto. Putting together a simple paper proposal was easy enough, so I was hoping that someone else had a panel topic that I could fit into with minimal effort on my part. How I would pay to go to either of the conferences should I be accepted was another question entirely.

My last email check before bedtime brought me multiple replies from friends who would all *love* to be on a panel at either the ASEEES (the Association for Slavic, East European and Eurasian Studies) or AATSEEL (the American Association of Teachers of Slavic and East European Languages) conferences next winter, and were hoping that I had some brilliant concept that they could join in on. I promised to try to come up with a panel topic—scratch that, at least two panel topics, since we had enough people for at least two panels—that would unite all our disparate paper topics into one harmonious and unified whole that would change the face of Slavic studies, or at least give us a leg up on the job market.

Coming up with ideas was one of my better skills, if I said so myself, so I spent a while lying awake that night mulling over panel topics and coming up with at least six or seven brilliant ones that, unfortunately, would take way more time and energy than I had available in order to implement. This kept me up later than usual, so I was extra unhappy to be awakened out of a nightmare about freezing to death by Nevaeh's piercing wails.

My nightmare was explained by the intense chill in my bedroom. A dementor attack? No, just the promised cold front penetrating my apartment, whose heat insulation was even poorer than its soundproofing.

I tried turning up the thermostat. The sad trickle of lukewarm air that came out of the heating vent was more a mockery of my efforts than anything. I had an extra blanket somewhere. But since I didn't remember unpacking it, that somewhere was probably in one of the unopened boxes stacked up against the wall. Going through all of them at two in the morning seemed unbearable. It wasn't *that* cold. It was barely supposed to dip below freezing tonight. In Russia I wouldn't have considered that "cold." In Russia I would have had heating and proper blankets and warm clothes. Well, I still had the warm clothes, and some of them had already been unpacked. I bundled myself up in two sweatshirts and a knitted hat, and tried to go back to sleep.

A good portion of the rest of the night was spent listening to Lakeesha and Duane argue over how best to keep Nevaeh warm. Judging by her unhappy screams, nothing they tried was working. I wondered how we were all going to survive the next night, when it was supposed to drop down into the teens. Well, it would be Saturday. I would have all of Sunday to catch up on my sleep before going into class on Monday anyway.

I reminded myself of this happy thought as I dragged my way blearily out of bed the next morning, tiptoeing around to avoid waking Nevaeh, who had finally fallen back to sleep at around five. I tried to warm up with some super-quiet asanas and forms, and, when that failed to help, I forced myself to go out for a run.

The run, followed by an almost-warm-enough shower, did warm me up enough that I was able to concentrate on the first pressing order of business for the day: email.

And it was a good thing I was mentally and physically prepared for it, because I could tell by running my eye over the subject lines in my email inbox that I was in for a rough morning. Apparently lots of people had been busy Friday night, and not in a fun way. I wondered about people who sent out work emails on a Friday night. Then I remembered I was that kind of person myself. Then I realized I was stalling. *The sooner you go to jail, the sooner you get out*, I reminded myself, and plunged in.

The middle of January was not only a popular due date for applications, it was also a popular time for the first round of rejections from the fall applications to go out. The first email I opened was a rejection from one of the postdocs I'd applied for in October. I hadn't even made the first round cut. The email was politely worded and was full of generically encouraging phrases about my promise as a scholar, etc., etc., but it was still a rejection. Good thing I hadn't been counting on that impossible-to-get postdoc anyway.

The next email that I made myself open was from a three-year VAP (Visiting Assistant Professor) position that I had applied for. I knew it would be competitive, but I had been holding onto a slim hope for it since it was in the Midwest. But nope, once again, I hadn't even made the first cut.

While I was on this roll of rejections, I checked The Wiki and saw that yep, interview invitations had gone out for the one tenure-track job I had also been thinking of as an outside chance, since it was in Alabama. But nope, I hadn't made the first cut there either.

I spent a while thinking about how the people I most wanted to impress, that is to say, search committees, would be actively happier if I didn't exist. I knew from listening to the complaints of my more senior colleagues that reading through the dozens or even hundreds of applications was a tedious process that took up hours and hours of their time, and was normally punished rather than compensated by their universities, since time spent reading job applications was time not spent doing research. Conducting the interviews was a hassle, and sending out the rejections was soul-destroying, which was probably one of the reasons why so many jobs didn't bother anymore—the committee chair didn't have the backbone for it. The reason all these invitations and rejections had gone out in the middle of a Friday night was because it was being handled by a faculty member who didn't have the time management skills to do it during work hours, and probably cursed every minute they had to spend on the process anyway. My application was just one in a long line of awful burdens that they would rather not shoulder. And if I *were* to be successful and get a tenure-track job, that person would be me. *I* would be the one cursing the day all these job candidates had ever been born.

I will never be like that! I promised myself, but I also knew that words were cheap. People at my stage of their careers dreamed of nothing else but getting a tenure-track job, let alone tenure, but that was a prize of very dubious value. Tenure broke most people and left them as little better than the pathetic shells of their former selves...I really needed to stop moping and get on with checking the rest of my email.

And I was rewarded, sort of, because right at the top of my inbox was an email from Alaska. It took me a beat to remember that I had applied for a one-year visiting position with possibility of renewal there. Not really my first choice of jobs, so the rejection wouldn't be so painful. Or so I told myself as I opened the email.

Rejection might not have been painful, but the shock of excitement and dread that went through me when I saw it was an invitation to interview for the position certainly was. I stared at the screen for the better part of a minute, trying to figure out what it was I was actually reading. Then I pulled myself together enough to reply that I would be *delighted* to interview for the position at their convenience.

The search committee chair emailed back almost instantaneously with a list of possible times. It was nice to see that people started their work day bright and early on Saturday mornings there, since it was 7:00am in Alaska. If I got the job, would I be expected to spend my Saturday mornings doing committee work? Very likely. One of the few pluses of my current position was an utter lack, as far as I could tell, of service work. No committees, no cutesy extracurricular activities. The students here were too busy for them. Maybe the students in Alaska would be too. Maybe it wouldn't be so bad. Maybe I would love Alaska and spend the rest of my life there. Probably not. Probably I would go through a miserable, high-stress, soul-crushing interview, only to be rejected yet again.

Stop it! I told myself, and went back to my email. It was a morning for exciting communications. As I had been sitting there wallowing in self-pity, another email had popped up in my inbox. It was from the elusive Marina.

14

*H*ello, it said.

I don't know what this Jason has told you, but he spoiled my sister's life. Why is he bothering her again? I told her to stay away from him. Has he told you what he did to her? She wanted to move to America so much that she agreed to marry an American she met online. Then, the little idiot, she got a child off him. But after what he did to her I convinced her to come home where she belongs. Americans are complete assholes! I told her not to marry him, and now she knows I was right.

But the boy misses his father. Children are silly like that. He keeps asking to go "home," and says his home is America, not Belarus. I feel sorry for him. We can talk on Skype, you and I, and then I'll decide what to tell Arina, and she can decide what to tell the boy.

With respect,

Marina

I bit back a groan. Marina sounded like your typical post-Soviet pain in the ass, but her story had the ring of truth to it. I disliked

Jason already, so it was easy to see him as an abusive husband. On the other hand, I shouldn't jump to conclusions. No doubt all my male friends and relatives would tell me that everyone always jumped to the conclusion that the man was the bad guy. Of course, often he was.

I gnawed on a fingernail, and then made myself stop. Whatever else, Arina was in Belarus, with an ocean and most of a continent between her and Jason. No matter what the circumstances of their separation, maybe it would be a good thing for her son to be able to talk to his father. I wrote back to Marina saying that I completely understood her point of view, didn't like Jason much myself, but was just passing on the message, and I would be happy to Skype with her at her convenience and hear her and her sister's side of the story.

Sitting still had made me chilled again, so I tried some vigorous asanas before going on to work on some more job applications. Given that it had taken her more than a day to respond to the first email, I had assumed that Marina wouldn't bother getting back to me for another day or two. But when I sat back down at the computer, she had sent me a message saying that she was available now if I wanted to Skype with her.

Part of me wanted to say no. The whole thing had "quagmire" written all over it, and talking to Marina was likely to be unpleasant. She was sure to see me as an American and a representative of the loathsome Jason, and rightly so. Getting more deeply involved in this was only going to cost me a lot of time and aggravation, for very little gain. I should prioritize my own self-interest first.

I closed Marina's email and opened the email with the application requirements for the next position on my job spreadsheet. Close reading of the instructions told me that it required a teaching portfolio that included a statement of teaching philosophy, a list of all courses taught and all pedagogical training undergone, three sample syllabi (a beginning language course, an advanced language course taught in Russian, and a culture/

literature/special topics course taught in English), and a summary of my latest teaching evaluations, with metrics and representative student statements. All this should be compiled into one PDF with a table of contents on the first page.

Beating my head against the table would not make things better. I had most of those materials already, but pulling them all together into one coherent document, and wrestling with auto-formatting's tendency to turn everything into an outline except actual outlines, would take the rest of the morning, maybe the rest of the day. For a job I almost certainly wasn't going to get, and probably didn't want even if I did, since it was in Canada. I closed that email, opened Marina's, and told her I'd be happy to Skype with her any time this weekend she was free.

She was free right now, it turned out. Five minutes later Skype was making its *bloop-bla-bloop* noises, with that awful jangling ringing in the background. I used to find that sound exciting, even erotic. For years it had meant that I was about to talk to Dima. But after more than a year of no Dima, just fruitless job interviews, now it meant I was going to talk to someone I didn't want to talk to, about things I didn't want to talk about.

Marina, when the screen revealed her face, was probably about my age, but with deep lines from smoking and discontent already bracketing her nose and mouth. She had stick-straight ash blonde hair, big, slightly slanted gray eyes, and wide thin pale lips against her thin pale face. So, your typical Belarusian. She was a lot less friendly than your typical Belarusian, though. Belarusians were supposed to be the most cheerful and friendly of the East Slavs, and in my experience that was generally true. Marina, however, looked like she wanted to leap through the screen and claw me with her long, bright-red nails.

"You speak Russian?" she said as soon as the call started. "Good. I don't speak English. Arina speaks a little, but I'm not going to let her speak with you until I know who you are. You said you are an American professor. Why are you helping this Jason?"

I explained that Jason was my student, and had asked for my help, and I had agreed to help him since he didn't seem to have anyone else. I left out the part about the money.

"This Jason is a viper!" said Marina. "You see: he made you trust him just like he made Arina trust him. Even now I don't trust her with him. That's why I wanted to talk to you: I knew that if she heard from him, she would soften towards him. But she and Maks are sledding at the park right now, so we are safe."

"Maks is her son?" I asked.

"Yes." Marina's face softened. "A good boy. His father is a piece of foreign trash, but our Arina's son is still a good boy. That's why he needs to stay here, where his family can take care of him."

"I agree," I said.

"You do? Then why are you helping this Jason?"

"Because he asked for my help. And you said yourself that the boy misses his father."

"True." Marina took out a pack of cigarettes and began fiddling with it, her bright red nails toying with the cellophane, obviously itching to break into it. "I promised Arina I wouldn't smoke around Maks," she said, smiling a little, her face simultaneously tender and guilty. "Or in the apartment while they were living with us. I don't have any of my own children. Do you?"

"No."

"Of course not. You have to choose: scholarship or children, right? I'm a philologist too. Far Eastern languages." Her nails tore open the cellophane around the pack of cigarettes, seemingly on their own. She stopped talking and stared down at them in dismay.

"That's very interesting," I said. "A very important subject."

"True. But it was Arina who had the real talent. Central Asian languages...her teachers begged her with tears in their eyes to go to grad school. But she didn't want to stay here in Belarus, not even in Minsk. Even Moscow wasn't good enough for her. She wanted to go to the West, to America. She"—Marina looked around furtively—"she, well, you know, politics...she didn't like..."—her voice dropped to a whisper—"she was even studying Belarusian! And now she's trying to teach it to Maks!"

"I see," I said. And I did. Speaking Belarusian, as opposed to Russian, was a sign of the anti-Lukashenko opposition.

"But Maks won't speak it. He won't even speak Russian with her. He only speaks English. Of course, his Russian is funny. He learned it just from hearing Arina talk, so he speaks like a girl. He only knows the feminine endings for things, and uses them when he's talking about himself. He gets mad when we correct him. We thought he'd learn after a few months here, but he doesn't like to play with the other kids much, and it's only women at home; just me, Arina, and our mother. So he's not learning how to speak like a boy, and he doesn't want to." Marina exhaled deeply through her nostrils. "He's going to get the shit beaten out of him if he doesn't quit that before he starts school."

"Probably," I agreed.

"How about Jason?" asked Marina. "How's his Russian now?"

"He's working on it," I said diplomatically.

"Arina always said he was dumb as a stump."

"Well...Russian is very difficult for English-speakers..."

"Not for you. You're not Russian, right? You have that funny name. Funny first and last name. Roe-eenna Kha-lli." She sounded it out carefully. "What is it? Central Asian? It sounds like the name of a harem girl in *The Fountain of Bakhchisarai*. Where'd you learn Russian?"

"Moscow," I said.

"Yes, of course. You have an almost perfect Moscow accent. Not like me. I try, but...well. What about Jason's English? What's his English like?"

"He has the local accent," I said, still speaking diplomatically.

"I get it." Marina nodded sagely. "The local accent isn't the prestige accent, right?"

"No, it's not," I agreed.

"Well. We knew what he was when Arina agreed to marry him. Well, I did. I told her he was just a provincial blockhead, if not worse. Turns out he was worse." Marina's fingers, working on their own, opened the pack and pulled out a cigarette, which they twirled unconsciously as she spoke. "He could be worse," she admitted grudgingly. "In fact, she might have married worse staying here. You know what they say: You beat the one you love. Did you ever have a Russian boyfriend?"

"Yes."

"Did he hit you?"

"No."

"Hmmmph." Marina sniffed dismissively. "You just didn't live with him long enough, then."

"Maybe." The placating syllables stuck in my throat. Dima had done a lot of bad things, but he'd never raised a hand against me—which did indeed make him a rarity in Russia. "So Jason used to hit Arina?" I asked.

Marina shrugged tightly. "Sometimes. It was nothing, really. He never hurt her badly, not so that she had to go the hospital or anything. Not even worth complaining about. But he used to"—she flinched, spooked by some noise I couldn't hear, and looked around furtively—"he used to threaten to take Maks away. Send her away and keep the boy. Hitting her would have been less cruel. Arina can't live without Maks. But Jason didn't want her anymore, just the boy. Especially after...well, you know how it is: she had to find a friend in that situation, didn't she? Someone to protect her, someone with connections. She still doesn't have American citizenship; you know how slow these things are. But Maks does, because he was born there. That's how it works, right?"

"In theory," I said.

"And in practice, too, in Maks's case. I've seen his passport. Jason was threatening to have Arina deported and keep Maks for himself, so...Arina saw her chance, and she took it. She would do anything to keep Maks. And so"—Marina's lips tightened into a hard pale line—"would I."

"I understand completely," I said. "And I don't want to help Jason take Maks away, I promise. I'm just passing on a message."

"I know. I can tell by your face: you're a kind person. You wouldn't have anything to do with scum like Jason. Well, except in a professional sense. And Maks does miss him." Marina flinched again at a sound I couldn't hear. "They're coming up the stairs," she said. "I have to go. You seem nice. I'll talk to Arina, and maybe she'll want to talk to you. And if she likes you, maybe she'll let Jason talk to Maks. But only if you're there."

"Well..." That sounded like a conversation I could skip without regrets.

"He needs a woman there to make him behave," Marina said sternly. "That's my final condition! Only if you're there." She looked over her shoulder. "I have to go now." She cut off the connection before I could say goodbye.

15

The rest of the day was spent emailing with Jason over the fact that Marina had Skyped with me—he wanted a blow-by-blow account of our conversation, and expressed his frustration at length when I just reiterated that we had spoken and would speak again soon—and wrestling with the teaching portfolio for the Canada job while trying to stay warm. By the time I got the application submitted, my nose was running nonstop from the cold, and I was seriously doubting the wisdom of moving to Canada. But maybe Canada would be better. Maybe in Canada they had heating that actually worked. In fact, I was sure that in Canada they had heating that actually worked. There just wasn't much point down here in the South, like there wasn't much point having air conditioning up in the Frozen North. On the rare occasions when it was necessary, you sucked it up and got through it somehow.

It was a cold evening and a colder night. I ended up putting my Moscow coat over the top of my blankets for extra warmth. Fevronia, who normally hid under the bed at night despite all my attempts to get her to come cuddle with me, even deigned to get under the covers with me. She only bit me twice; more, I thought, as a sign of disapproval for the way Nevaeh was crying and Duane and Lakeesha were screaming at each other than as a sign of her anger with me.

When I got up, the weather forecast said it was a chilly 13 degrees outside. Getting back into bed and spending the rest of the day under the covers wrapped in all my Russia clothes sounded like a good plan. But I really needed food. What I really needed to do was get in the car and go in search of a dollar store. The shopping center across the street from me was too high-toned for a dollar store. Even the Walmart there was too pricey for me. But the roads were icy, and my car didn't like to start when the weather got below freezing, and driving around would burn gas, and hence gas money, I didn't have. Better to walk to the store and spend an extra $10 on groceries than to drive somewhere. And unlike everyone else in Charlotte, I had the clothes for this kind of weather. It would be a shame not to put them to good use after hauling them around with me. I should just bite the bullet and get it over with.

I pulled on my Moscow coat, which was a knee-length quilted thing that was basically a sack with sleeves, wrapped a scarf around my face, and pulled the coat's hood up over my knitted hat. Fevronia looked at me suspiciously.

"Don't worry," I told her. "It's not actually that cold. I've just been well trained to wrap up warmly."

Fevronia scuttled off to hide under the bed. I pulled on my boots and headed out into the frigid air.

Pineville-Matthews Road was almost empty for a change, as was the shopping center parking lot. The lack of customers did not stop those who were there from looking out their truck windows to check me out, and the fact that I was swaddled in a kind of cold-weather burka did not stop someone who was probably young enough to be my son from pulling up beside me, sticking his head out the window, and asking if I had a boyfriend.

"Yes," I said, trying to smile through the heavy scarf. "Sorry."

"He the one who wrapped you up like that?" Someone should have wrapped up my pursuer a little, since his dark brown skin was turning a kind of sickly blue-gray in the cold.

"Yes," I said, with what I hoped was another conciliatory smile.

"Sure wish it'd been me!" He looked like he wanted to say more, but his teeth were starting to chatter, so he pulled his head back in the window and roared off with a blast of exhaust.

Three members of a construction crew were huddled up together on the bench outside the grocery store. Good to see that construction never stopped, not for Sunday, not for sub-freezing weather. Or maybe their wives had just kicked them out of the house. They, too, found my completely concealed form to be intoxicating, and commented on it at length in Spanish as I went by. Which was not unusual. In my experience, the only way to garner more attention for my appearance than going around in running clothes was to go around in something that hid my figure entirely. This quilted sack of a coat never failed to earn me more whistles and stares than a swimsuit, and the fact that here it was exotic only made it more exciting.

$37.63 and three more propositions later, I was back home. Why, I asked myself as I put the food—mainly lentils—away, was I trying to support myself alone and moping over men who were hundreds or thousands of miles away? Look at all the admirers I had! Admittedly, some were pretty down on their own luck, but construction and lawn work were clearly big business here in Charlotte. From what I knew and from what some of my students had let drop, a decent construction worker could pull down $50-60,000 a year here or most other places, no problem. Maybe I should be responding to some of those catcalls. I could get myself a solvent, employable, and portable husband, one who could find work anywhere, and who might appreciate a wife with an American passport. Learning Spanish well enough to argue with my in-laws would be a snap. With all that money and multiculturalism, I'd be the living embodiment of the American dream. It was a good plan. One that I would consider further once I'd checked my email.

Not for the first time, checking my email caused a sudden swerve in my life plans. Buried in amongst the ads for penis enlargements and Russian mail-order brides was an email from my former student Madison, and an interview (!!!!!!) invitation.

16

The position I was invited to interview for was, once I read the fine print, less exciting than one might hope. A 1-year lectureship in North Dakota. I pulled my Moscow coat, which I had kept on inside the frigid apartment, closer around me as I read the email. 13 degrees was a fine warm day in January in North Dakota. But, like Canada, they probably had better heating. And without employment, I wouldn't be able to heat anything at all. Letterhead with the words "North Dakota" on it was unlikely to help vault me into a prestigious position the following year. But it was better than no letterhead at all. I responded immediately that I would be *delighted* to interview for the position. Then I went on to read Madison's email.

I was pleased, if a bit surprised, to hear from her. After the events of last semester, which had been largely triggered by Madison's decision to blackmail her classmates for a little extra money for cocaine, I thought she might want to hide away from me forever. But I had underestimated her breezy self-possession, it seemed. And since I genuinely liked Madison for all her faults, I was glad to get her email.

> *Hey Professor H!* she wrote. *Hope you're having a fab time. Are you at your new school yet? Too bad you're not still with us! Although I'm not at school this semester either. Still in*

rehab. I know, what a loser, right? But my dad says if I stick it out and stay clean all spring, I can still go to Russia in the summer. Can you write a rec letter for me if I do? And I'm supposed to be writing to everyone I've hurt because of the drugs and apologizing, and thanking everyone who's helped me, so I guess this is sorry and thank you. TTFN! Madison P.S. My dad said he's going to write to you too about things. Hope he doesn't bother you too much! He can be a real pain in the ass, but he's actually been okay this time around. As okay as he can be, anyway. До свидания! See, I haven't forgotten *all* my Russian :) :) :)

I smiled and ground my teeth a little at the same time. As usual with Madison, I didn't know where to start. Congratulate her on sticking with rehab? Try to let her know that this was not how you wrote to professors? And how was I going to write a letter of recommendation for her, anyway? If she needed one, I would probably provide it, since I did genuinely believe that studying abroad would be one of the best things she could do to get an interest in something other than drugs and turn her life around, but how exactly was I going to phrase it? Madison was talented, but she'd barely scraped together a B- in her intermediate Russian class because of her inability to turn in homework and study for vocab quizzes. And she'd helped me out and had that all-important quality, a "good attitude," most of the time, but she'd also almost gotten me killed. And maybe going to Russia would help her decide to stay clean, or maybe she would spend her entire time there drinking vodka and picking up a new, even nastier drug habit. The word on the street was that Krokodil was very, very bad news, but that wasn't stopping people from taking it in large numbers. I'd like to think that Madison would be too smart to get hooked on it, but while I had no doubts about her intelligence, I had grave doubts about her impulse control. But since upper-class suburban New Jersey hadn't been able to keep her safe, maybe she needed to leave it.

Dear Madison I wrote back,

> *How lovely to hear from you! I'm glad that rehab is going well for you, and that you're sticking with it. You're not a loser at all! Far from it. Staying clean is the most important thing you can do. School will always be there when you're ready to come back to it.*
>
> *I hope you do get to go to Russia this summer, and of course I'd be happy to provide a letter of recommendation for you if you need one. Just let me know. And don't hesitate to reach out if you want help keeping up your Russian, or you just need someone to talk to.*
>
> *I haven't heard from your dad, but of course I'd be happy to talk to him. I hope he is doing well.*
>
> *All the best,*
>
> *Professor Halley*

I felt weird about signing myself off as "Professor Halley," especially since I wasn't her professor anymore, but what else was I going to say? "Rowena Halley" was too distant, and I definitely wasn't going to encourage her to call me "Rowena." But "Doctor Halley" seemed awfully formal. So "Professor Halley" it was.

When I'd sent that email off, there was a response from the North Dakota position waiting for me, inviting me to choose an interview time the following week. They hoped I would be available to do the interview at my earliest convenience, they said, because they were hoping to move through the process as expeditiously as possible, so would next Wednesday afternoon suit me for a phone interview?

I wrote back that next Wednesday afternoon would suit me wonderfully. Then I resisted the urge to claw at my face or stress-chew my nails. The interview was great news, because any interview was great news, but on paper at least the North Dakota position was my last choice for any of the jobs I had applied for. The Alaska position actually looked a little better, in that it hinted at the possibility of renewal, while the North Dakota position did not. And I couldn't help but hold out the hope for something better. As a Georgia native and the daughter and granddaughter of alumnae, I *should* be a shoo-in for the Crimson position, because there would be precious few other qualified candidates who would jump at the chance to move to Georgia. And to be honest, it wasn't the world's most attractive position to me either. Crimson was a nice SLAC (Selective Liberal Arts College), but it wasn't a prestigious Research 1 institution. And while I was willing to move back to Georgia for now, I didn't think I wanted to spend the rest of my life there. I wanted to spend the rest of my life...where? Nevaeh started to cry again.

"Why won't she shut the fuck up!" shouted Duane.

"'Cause she's cold, that's why!" Lakeesha shouted back at him.

I pulled my Moscow coat around me more tightly. Wherever I ended up for the rest of my life, I didn't want it to be here.

17

The cold broke during the night, and by the time I set off for class Monday morning, it was back up around freezing. I still wore my Moscow coat onto campus, since my car's heater was practically nonexistent. The coat kept me warm on the drive over, and helped me work up a sweat on the hustle across campus, since the car in front of me got the last spot in the faculty parking lot, and I had to circle around campus until I found a spot half-hidden behind a construction zone. A sign said it was the future home of a green, energy-efficient, handicap-accessible dormitory. I was very happy for its future inhabitants, but less happy about its present existence, since I had to trot around it, trying to keep my two book bags from slipping off my bulky coat shoulders.

Even in the cold weather, builders were already hard at work at 9:15am, although a couple of them managed to take a moment off in order to whistle as I jogged past in my extremely concealing coat, scarf, and hood. I wondered what I looked like under all those layers in their imagination. Probably much more exciting than what I looked like in reality.

I came sliding into my office at 9:30am, only half an hour after I had intended to arrive. Campus wasn't very big compared to what I was used to (the IU campus, where I had done my PhD, was enormous, for example), but since it was a half-finished construction zone with constantly shifting parking access, getting around it took twice as long as I thought it should. Good thing I was already prepared for my first two classes. There was just enough time to organize all my files and check my email before going to my first class. I might even get a little homework graded. There wasn't much to grade, since so many of my students hadn't managed to do the assignments yet.

I was just wriggling out of my coat when there was a knock at the door. It was the Arabic instructor, standing there looking formidable despite being only about five foot two in her boots. She was also completely covered from head to toe, although her scarf was pulled down tightly over her forehead, so that not a spare lock of hair could escape. I tried not to shudder. Wearing her scarf like that could get her into terrible trouble in certain parts of the world. People might take her as an extremist and a terrorist. Because if she wore her scarf like that in those parts of the world, chances were good that she would be an extremist and a terrorist.

"I wanted to ask: will you be late again today?" she said. "Because I need the classroom on time." She looked me up and down as I hung up my coat and her face softened. "You wear the scarf too?"

"What? Oh." I patted my headscarf, which I had put on like any self-respecting Russian woman would on a cold day. Unlike hers, mine allowed a little hair to peek out the front. My Russian friends had shown me how to wrap myself properly in my headscarf in order to keep warm. My Caucasian friends, afraid that my dark hair would cause me to be picked out as a potential suicide bomber, had shown me how to do it in a way that, we hoped, wouldn't cause me to be dragged off and shot. "Um, not exactly," I said.

"You teach Russian, no? I thought perhaps: you are Caucasian. Chechen? Or Central Asian? Muslim? You are wearing the scarf."

"Um, yeah. I mean, no, I'm not Caucasian or Central Asian. I was just...cold. This is how women normally dress there when it's cold. Although many wear scarves for religious reasons as well. You have to wear them in most churches. And I used to work with refugees from Dagestan and Chechnya. So I, um, got used to wearing one." To be honest, I was now sweating heavily under it, and wanted to take it off. But it seemed wrong to do so in front of my new quasi-friend.

"It is good," said the other woman with satisfaction. "It keeps the men respectful, no?"

"Um, yeah." Telling her that in my experience, the more I covered myself up, the more attention I attracted, would only start a pointless argument that I was sure to lose.

"I am Fatima," she said. "I have the next office. Very nice building, no? Nice and new. We each have our own office. Nice. On the old university, I was with six other instructors."

"Yeah," I agreed. "This is better. Even if the building isn't finished."

"Lonely, though, sometimes. You like coffee?"

"Um, yeah, sure."

"On Wednesday I will bring you Arabic coffee. You will like it."

"Wow," I said. "Thanks. That's really nice of you. I'm Rowena, by the way."

"Row-eena." Fatima sounded out the name carefully. "Very exotic name. Are you sure you are not Caucasian? It sounds Caucasian."

I thought about going into a lengthy explanation of the different meanings of the word "Caucasian," and how by the American definition I *was* Caucasian, meaning white, but my ancestors had all come from the completely opposite side of Europe than the actual Caucasus.

"My family is of British descent," I said instead. "Celtic."

Fatima frowned. "Is that like Pakistani? I hear there are lots of Pakistanis in Britain now." She squinted at me. "You don't *look*

Pakistani. From Afghanistan? They often have blue or green eyes, like you."

"I don't think I have any ancestors from Afghanistan," I said. "But you never know."

Fatima nodded in satisfaction. "That is true. I think you must be partly from Afghanistan. That would explain many things. You should investigate."

"That's a good idea," I said, torn between amusement at the thought of investigating my non-existent Afghan heritage, and wondering if maybe I *did* have an Afghan great-grandmother. I mean, my British ancestors did tend to get around, and you never did know.

"Well, I must go now," said Fatima. "Please do not stay late in the classroom, okay? I have lots of students and they do not like to wait. I am glad you are my neighbor, Row-eena. I will bring you Arabic coffee on Wednesday."

"That would be lovely," I said. I waited until Fatima had disappeared down the hall before removing, with a faint feeling of guilt, my headscarf. I checked my phone. 9:45. Just enough time to check my email before heading to class, if the internet gods were favoring me.

They must have installed more routers over the weekend, because the wifi signal was strong and clear in my office when I turned on my laptop. I opened my email, half-expecting to find a message from Marina or from North Dakota or Alaska. But instead I found an email from Madison's father, Provost Johnson.

18

I told myself I should shut down my email without reading it and go to class. I didn't have the time to get caught up in a long email, and what was the point in agitating myself before class? But of course I read the email anyway.

Dear Rowena,

Madison forwarded the kind email you sent her yesterday to me. I wanted to thank you for your continuing support for her. I know she can be difficult and ungrateful, so I wanted to thank you more properly myself. And your offer to write her a letter of recommendation is very much appreciated. I am still debating what to do with her; I might just take her to Russia on a personal tour if she stays clean rather than trying to get her into a program. God alone knows what she'd get up to on her own!

How are you doing? How is the program in Charlotte? Has Brent been supporting you? I know that transitioning to a new department is always challenging, especially with a move on short notice on top of that. And it's such a short-term position. I hope you find a permanent position soon. Of course we'd love to have you back in New Jersey. Meanwhile, have you found a nice place to live? Is there anything you need? Please let me know.

Looking forward to hearing from you, and all the best,

Erik

Telling myself I should have listened to myself when I decided that reading the email would only upset me, I swallowed back the mixture of warmth and nausea it engendered, and went to teach RUSS 1102.

We spent a while going over weather vocab and remarking on how cold it was, which was a review of what they should have learned last week but hadn't. Repetition, as the Russians say, is the mother of learning, so it wasn't surprising that they struggled a bit after only a couple of days of class, but it was evident that almost no one had studied. The pile of homework that was turned in at the end of class was pathetically small, too.

Jason came up to me after class, and, ostentatiously putting down his homework on top of the tiny pile, asked, "Any word from Marina?"

"As I mentioned in my email to you, I did manage to speak with her on Skype over the weekend."

"And there ain't been nothing further?" he demanded. "You ain't tried nothing further?"

I repressed a sigh, and tamped down the mingled irritation and pity that threatened to burst out of my throat into words. Jason was a little guy, barely chin height on me, and wiry. And he wasn't very good-looking. He had the thin hair and rat-like features I associated with a certain kind of hillbilly or cracker, along with the pugnacious don't-take-no-shit attitude, but without any of the good nature and charm. That must have made his life more difficult. And I believed that he missed his son, and needed help. But I also believed that he had been a bad, maybe even abusive, husband to Arina. And he was just generally a pain to be around.

"As I told you, she said she was going to talk to Arina and then get back to me," I said, as calmly as I could. "I'll let you know as soon as she does get back to me."

"Well, that ain't good enough! She needs to get back to me right now!"

"I'm afraid that's not under our control," I said, more firmly than I had intended. Jason gave me a sharp look. I got the sense that, while he wasn't kind or insightful or thoughtful, he wasn't entirely stupid, either. Or at least he had a strong sense for when he was being talked down to.

"I'm building a rapport with Marina," I said, and then cringed inside. "Rapport" was just the kind of word that would come across as condescending. "She's very hesitant to trust me or any other American. It may take some time. But I'll let you know whatever she and Arina decide."

There were other things I could have said, like about our discussion of allowing Jason to Skype with Maks as long as I was present, but I didn't want to get into them yet. The whole thing seemed like sucking quicksand that would drag me down into it, and I didn't want to get any more involved in Jason's life than I already was. I kept hoping that somehow Jason and Arina and Marina would resolve things amongst themselves without mixing me up into their family drama any more than they already had.

"Yeah," said Jason, giving me another sharp look. "That's a good idea. Soften her up, gain her trust. She's such a bitch, you'd never know she and Arina are sisters. Though Arina turned into a real bitch at the end, too. Guess you never know how a marriage is gonna turn out, huh?"

"Um." It was on the tip of my tongue to say that it didn't take a genius to guess that any woman in her right mind was going to run away from Jason. But maybe I was being unnecessarily harsh and judgmental. Probably there were women out there susceptible to his rat-faced charms, and maybe Marina had exaggerated his unkindness to Arina. Sisters were partisan, after all.

Out of the corner of my eye I caught sight of Fatima hovering impatiently at the door. "I'm afraid I have to go now," I said. "The next class is waiting for us to clear out so that they can come in. But I'll let you know if I hear anything further from Marina." I grabbed up my textbook and all the homework and whisked them out of the classroom before Jason could protest, apologizing to Fatima for our tardiness on the way out.

19

RUSS 2102 was the same story as 1102, with most of the students struggling to remember what we had learned the previous week, and very little homework turned in. I was torn between irritation at their slackness, no matter how justified by difficult life circumstances, and gratitude at having less homework to grade, especially since I had an interview to prepare for this week. Ugh. An unpleasant tingle shot through my stomach at the thought, and today was only Monday. Somehow I would have to make it through the rest of the week without freaking out until the interview Wednesday afternoon. And then the Alaska interview was tentatively scheduled for the following Thursday. And I still needed to respond to Erik Johnson's email.

Lesson planning gave me an excuse not to respond to it during my break between 2102 and 2105. After 2105 got out I decided to do all my lesson planning and homework grading for 1102 and 2102 right then, in order to free up Tuesday for interview prep, so that was another good reason to delay answering Erik Johnson's email. Then I had to drive home through traffic that was already heavy even though it wasn't yet 4:00pm, and then I had to go running, and then I had to make supper. Then I had to work on another job application...at which point I decided that responding to the email was the less onerous of the two tasks.

I reread the email over supper, repressing the same mixed feeling of warmth, shame, and offended nausea it had provoked the first time around. Erik Johnson was in some ways a nice person who had helped me out when I needed help. He was also an older man and the father of one of my students—well, former student, but still—and a senior member of the administration of the college where I used to work. So sort of my boss's boss's boss. And he engaged in some semi-criminal activity. And he was, as far as I could tell, attracted to me, and I would be lying if I said there wasn't a spark of mutuality in that attraction. He was an intelligent and good-looking man who liked me, and power was indeed a potent aphrodisiac. Last semester he had made what I had interpreted as a not very veiled invitation for me to take over an unspecified number of the duties of his ex-wife, and this email seemed to me like another not very veiled invitation for the same thing. Or maybe I was completely misreading it? Maybe I had a grossly overinflated opinion of my own charms. Maybe he really was just a responsible senior administrator hoping to retain a talented employee.

Okay, that was ridiculous. Being subtly propositioned for sexual favors by a provost was vastly more likely than a provost wanting to hire me for my professional skills. Not because my professional skills weren't red-hot, because they were, but because the competition was so fierce. TLASC, where Erik Johnson was provost, was just down Route 1 from Princeton, and Columbia and UPenn were not that much farther down the road. He could snap his fingers and a dozen over-qualified Ivy League PhDs would bow down and kiss his overpriced shoes and beg to be allowed to come work for him for starvation wages.

I was sure I was just as good a Russian teacher as most of them, or maybe better, but my state school degree was never going to be as prestigious, and my connections were never going to be as good, and my research probably wasn't going to attract the same kind of attention because I didn't have the same Northeast insider status. Hiring me would not do anything materially to help TLASC climb up the rankings, no matter what had been hinted at that faculty meeting last semester.

So if Erik Johnson was interested in bringing me back to New Jersey, it wasn't for my professional abilities. There were lots of PhDs who could bring glory to the college, but most of them did not possess—I thought modestly—even an iota of good looks and charm. I didn't rate my own good looks and charm so very high in the grand scheme of things, but in academia, the bar was so low that I was a 9, maybe a 10, on that scale. Which was a tool that I should use. I didn't have a string of Ivy League degrees and insider connections, so I needed something else, and this was what I had.

I debated over what to do as I cleaned up after supper. And then I debated over whether or not to contact Alex and ask him what he thought. After all, he did know TLASC better than I did, and since his father had been a dean, he had spent his whole life surrounded by senior university administration. Maybe he would have some kind of special insight. Or maybe he would be hurt and angry and jealous. Maybe I needed to ask him anyway. Maybe it would make both of us feel better if I reached out to him.

Hey, I texted to him. *Just wanted to try out your phone and see if it was still working :) and check in and see how classes went today. Any word on interviews? I got *two* interview invites over the weekend! For 1-year lectureships, one in Alaska, one in North Dakota. And Erik Johnson emailed me today, hinting at wanting to bring me back. Has he approached you with anything similar? Not sure how seriously to take it. Hope you're doing well.*

I fidgeted around for a while after that, hoping that Alex would text right back, but he didn't, so eventually I sat myself down and forced myself to write a short, and, I hoped, polite and encouraging but not too encouraging reply, to Erik Johnson.

Dear Provost Johnson,

Thank you for reaching out to me. No need to thank me for helping Madison; it is my pleasure. I'm glad to hear that she is doing so well, and of course I'll be happy to provide her with a letter of recommendation. As for whether or not she should go to Russia as part of a regular program or under your supervision, I would say you're the better judge than I am. I will be happy to provide any assistance I can as far as choosing programs or making travel plans.

Please do not hesitate to contact me with any further questions, and I hope the semester is starting well for you.

All the best,

Rowena Halley

After three read-throughs and some fingernail gnawing that I tried to hide even from myself, I sent off the email. Then I was so emotionally exhausted that I couldn't bring myself to work on anything else, and went to bed.

20

The next morning I woke up to a string of texts from Alex and a reply from Erik Johnson, along with the knowledge that I needed to dedicate the day to preparing for my North Dakota interview. And prep for Wednesday's 2105 class. I had much more experience teaching language than teaching literature and culture, even though my actual PhD was in literature and culture, not second language acquisition. But grad students taught introductory language classes almost exclusively, and I had also taught upper-level language classes at Indiana's intensive summer program, so I had years of experience teaching the equivalent of 1102, 2102, and beyond, but much less experience teaching the stuff that was actually supposed to be my area of expertise.

This meant I had to spend a lot more time figuring out what it was I actually wanted to teach, and then creating the materials from scratch. Plus, literature/culture classes were, as I had heard from other people and was finding out to be true myself, much more prep-intensive. There was less homework grading, but way more time putting together lectures. So I needed to get on that today, since despite having an office all to myself instead of sharing one with half a dozen other grad students or adjuncts, I couldn't seem to get anything done on campus.

Okay, I had a plan. I would spend the morning prepping for Wednesday's 2105 class by putting together a lecture on the rise and fall of Kievan Rus', and then in the afternoon I would prep for Wednesday's interview. But first I would respond to these troublesome communiques.

Actually, Alex's was not so troublesome. It was only that, just as I had predicted, he was outraged that Erik Johnson had contacted me.

Hey Rowena, sorry for the radio silence, he wrote. *Usual start of semester craziness, including the internet going down. Glad the phone is working out :) Keep it as long as you like. First day of classes was...well, it was the first day of classes. The usual clusterfuck. Lost students, no textbooks, everyone's forgotten every word of Arabic they ever learned; you know the drill. I'm sure it'll be fine by next week, and hey, I've got that sweet, sweet big-boy paycheck to look forward to, right?*

That was followed by a second, separate message:

But I can't believe that fucker Erik Johnson had the—you know what, he can't have any balls, so I won't say that, but the whatever, to write to you and hint about a position. Did he say what kind of a position he had in mind? With me I was always pretty sure it was bent facedown over the desk and taking it up the ass. I'd bet anything the motherfucker has the same thing in mind for you. Literally.

There was then a third message:

Shit, sorry, that was probably uncalled for. Apologies if that was offensively crude. Also, implying that being the receptive partner in that position is degrading is probably sexist and/or homophobic, right? But I wouldn't believe a word that comes out of that smooth motherfucker's mouth. And *only* let him bend you over a desk and fuck you up the ass if that's what you're into.

Followed by a fourth message:

Double shit! I probably shouldn't have written that either. Sorry for the inappropriate late-night ramblings.

Well, if that wasn't a *cri de coeur*, I was blind. What kind of a *cri de coeur* it was I couldn't be sure, but it certainly required a response. I promptly texted back:

Glad you made it through the first day of class okay, although sorry it was so crazy. Thanks for the insights about Erik Johnson. That was my first guess too. And no offense taken :)

P.S. Hope your second day of class goes better. Any more interview news?

P.P.S. That's not, FYI, what I'm generally into.

That taken care of, I moved on to Erik Johnson's email:

Dear Rowena,

*Please, call me Erik! It's sweet that you're so formal and polite—one might even say you have the manners of a Georgia Southern Belle—but I think we're past that, don't you? "Provost Johnson" always sounds like someone else, anyway. Funny how things go, isn't it? I've spent, oh, the better part of twenty-five years trying to get to this point in my life, and now it doesn't feel like it belongs to me. I hope this doesn't happen to you. I was sincere when I told you, the last time we spoke in person, that academia needs more women, women like you, in our corner offices. So I hope that you can achieve that. Anything I can do to help facilitate that, I'll be glad to do. And when you **do** get into that corner office and get that doorplate that says Dean, Provost, President, etc., I hope that you feel a little more like you've earned it than I do. Because you **will** have earned it. When you get it, you **will** deserve it, probably more than the rest of us.*

In the meantime, I wish I could say for certain that we have a position waiting for you back at TLASC, but alas, I cannot. Everything is bogged down in committee, as is always the case. I am hoping to be able to announce firm plans to expand the language openings soon, along with job openings, but that may not be until next year.

*That being said, I was also sincere when I offered you a position watching over Madison. I know it's probably not what either of you would consider ideal (I can hear her screaming at me that she doesn't need a babysitter), but in fact, she **does** need a babysitter. Well, not a babysitter exactly. But she needs **someone**, and apparently that someone isn't me—or her mother. To be honest, we both just seem to make things worse. The only good influence she's come across in the past few years has been you. And I know I might not seem like the best father in the world, and, let's be honest, I'm **not** the best father in the world, but almost losing her last semester made me realize that, fallible as I am, I'm the only father she's got, and she's the only daughter I've got, and I need to do right by her.*

Anyway, what I guess I'm trying to say is that maybe you should be the one to take her to Russia this summer. Do you have any plans to go there already? Will you be leading a program? Taking a personal trip? Would you be interested in being her chaperone while you're there? I'm not going to offend you by telling you I'd make it worth your while, since you've made it clear how you feel about that kind of thing, but obviously I'd make it worth your while.

Think about it, and apologies for such a long rambling late-night letter.

All the best,

Erik

I gnawed on the inside of my lip. Then I gnawed on a fingernail. Then I slapped myself to make myself stop, and went back to gnawing on the inside of my lip. That was *also* a *cri de coeur* of epic proportions, and deserved to be answered in kind. Well, maybe not. I imagined how quickly things could spiral out of control if I poured out my heart to Erik Johnson and explained why I might or might not be going back to Russia next summer, and the whole tortured backstory with Dima. That was just the kind of story to whip the sympathies of a lonely older man into a frenzy, and push things onto a much too intimate footing for my current comfort. But I needed to come up with some kind of a response.

After a couple of hours of creating a lecture, complete with images and video clips, about the rise and fall of Kievan Rus', I had come up with a strategy. I wrote back:

Dear Erik,

No need to apologize. And I guess it makes me feel better to know that I'm not the only one who feels weird about being called by my title :) Although frankly I was hoping it would pass more quickly than you're saying it does.

My plans for the summer and next year are still unfixed. I actually have a couple of interviews for temporary positions coming up in the next week. As for the summer, I don't know yet what I will be doing. I used to spend part of it visiting friends in Russia and part of it teaching at the summer program run by my grad school, but I don't know yet if that's what I'll be doing this summer. If it works out so that we're in the same program or the same city, I would of course be more than happy to keep an eye on Madison. Let me know if you'd like to know more about the programs I've taught at and might teach at again in the future. They might be a good fit for Madison.

All the best,

Rowena

Composing and sending that email was so stressful and exhausting that I decided to take my run right away, instead of trying to prep for Wednesday's interview first. So, telling Fevronia to guard the house with extreme ferocity, I set off, wishing that I could run away from all the intangible complications in my life as easily as I could from my front door.

21

After the run there was a message from Alex waiting for me on the phone:

Glad I haven't manage to offend you—yet. I'm sure it's only a matter of time :) Seriously, take anything that mofo gives you with a grain of salt. Nothing new on the interview front yet. I'll be Skyping with the DLI in a couple of weeks. No doubt that will be painful, and do I even want that job? Who the fuck knows. How are things on your end?

I wrote back:

If you think you can offend me with a few well-chosen expressions, you obviously have never met my brother :) I have an interview this week and one next week for the super-exciting positions in North Dakota and Alaska. I will be sure to update you on how the phone performs :) Good luck with everything!

After I sent it, I wondered if I had been too breezy and impersonal. It didn't take a rocket scientist to realize that Alex was interested in something more than just a casual friendship. Actually, a rocket scientist would probably be oblivious to the clues he was sending out. But a humanist like myself couldn't help but pick up on them. Of course, I'd thought Dima had wanted to be with me too. So much for my humanist/women's intuition on that score. Maybe I should stop fretting over that and get back to prepping for my interview. There I could be certain I would be talking to people who didn't want me.

Despite my good intentions to work hard on my interview prep and not encourage Alex too much when I wasn't sure what either of us wanted, I did in fact engage in a lengthy text-lament with him that evening as I researched the program in North Dakota and came up with ways that I could make it better, or save it from itself and the forces that were inevitably trying to shut down the study of Russian and every other language.

The problem with languages is that they're a skillset that's hard to acquire and requires regular upkeep, Alex texted to me at one point. *You've got to see things from, say, the DoD's point of view. They'd way rather buy a piece of equipment like a plane or whatever than buy a human who requires constant training and retraining. It's just not economical to train lots of people in language and then have them keep their skills sharp. It's like training and keeping a bunch of virtuoso violinists.*

Orchestras do that all the time! I texted back.

Yeah, but they're not supposed to be hardheaded realists. And I bet they have all kinds of funding problems too. Human skills are much less popular to fund than hardware. And with this idolatry of STEM that's currently going on...

Very sexist! I texted. *Someday I should tell you about all the STEM-worshiping that went on at my graduation. Boy did I feel like a third-class citizen. Funny that it all happened *in a language*. They couldn't even elevate STEM and put down the humanities without resorting to a humanities subject. But don't get me started on the sexism inherent in that kind of behavior!*

Lol, too true, Alex replied. *But, I mean, I couldn't even major in just Arabic for my ROTC scholarship and subsequent career path. I had to add a STEM field as well. That's what everyone wants these days.*

Bastards! I texted. *Well, it's done me good to vent. Now maybe I can get on with explaining how I intend to integrate the Russian program with the aeronautics program or the energy engineering program, which seem to be the big things out in North Dakota.*

Have fun! And don't stay up too late stressing over it. Be sure to get some sleep.

You too, I wrote. I was sure as I sent it that we were both thinking of that one night we had spent together, doing nothing but sleeping. But I decided not to bring it up. Better for the moment if we both concentrated on our interviews rather than our love lives, sad as they were.

22

By Wednesday morning the weather had warmed back up into the 50s, so it wasn't the cold that was responsible for the low-level dread I woke up with. No, that was 100% from the knowledge that I had an interview waiting for me that afternoon.

The interview was scheduled for 3:00pm Eastern, which gave me an hour between my last class and it. Plenty of time to do any after-class chatting with students, decompress, make sure all the technology was working properly, and review my materials one more time. Or in other words, plenty of time to work myself into an unbearable state of nerves.

Jason, of course, cornered me after 1102, demanding to know if I'd heard anything more from Marina. I promised him once again that I'd get back to him just as soon as she got back to me. Then Shaniqua wanted to talk more about study abroad after 2102. Then Fatima cornered me in the break between 2102 and 2105 and pressed some Arabic coffee on me.

"It has spices in it," she told me. "Arabic spices. Maybe you will not like it."

She had brought it to me in a delicate coffee service. I wasn't sure that I liked Fatima, but I couldn't fault her for trying to be my friend. I took a sip. "Delicious," I said, more or less truthfully. It was not super-strong, for which I was grateful, and the taste was a mixture of bitter, sour, and exotic spices that were redolent of the Middle East.

A bit of an acquired taste, but I could see how people would acquire it.

"You like it?" She brightened. "Most Americans don't." She frowned at me. "You are not wearing your headscarf today!"

"Um, yeah..."

"Did someone give you trouble over it?"

"Not today. I don't wear it every day," I said, completely truthfully.

She nodded. "Many women choose not to. People can be very unkind about it!"

"True." And I had no doubt that that was true. Certainly I got plenty of hassle when I covered my head and face, although it was entirely sexual in nature. I wondered whether Fatima, whose headscarf screamed "devout Muslim" rather than "Russian woman covering up from the cold," got the same kind of sexual harassment that I did, or if in her case it was all religious harassment. It was not a conversation I felt like starting with her. In either case, we were marking ourselves as targets for sexual objectification, but I doubted she would see it that way. I took another sip of the coffee. "How did you make it?" I asked.

Fatima spent a while explaining to me the intricacies of making Arabic coffee, and insisted on taking my empty cup and washing it herself, in spite of my protests. We seemed to be careening towards friendship, whether I wanted it or not. Which might not be a bad thing. Unlike other places I had worked, where everyone was jammed together cheek-by-jowl and the administration was just a step down the hallway, UNC-Matthews was almost creepily empty. It was nice to have my own office, but it was strange not to have any colleagues to talk to, or even nod to, and there was no dedicated admin person to help me if I had questions. Other than Donna, who was the senior admin for all the programs in Tryon Hall, I didn't even know the names of most of the people who worked at the office down by the entrance. If I were to have a serious administrative problem, I didn't know what I would do. What if I had to call and cancel class at the last minute? I could find the phone numbers, but half the time the front desk wasn't even staffed. If I had to cancel my 10:00am class, there was normally no one there who could put up a note on my classroom door. If, that is, they could even find my classroom door. I could email the students, but some were sure not to get the email in time. Problems, problems...it was time for me to go teach 2105.

The lecture and discussion about Kievan Rus' went reasonably well, or at least the students appreciated my Game of Thrones references. Then class was over, and it was time to do the final prep for the interview.

It was a phone interview, which was the simplest but also in a way the most difficult, since you couldn't see the other people, and had to guess who was who, and how they were reacting. I had Alex's trusty flip phone, with my charger on the ready, since sometimes it lost charge alarmingly fast. I also had my laptop in case we needed to switch to an alternative form of communication, like Skype. Although it sounded like maybe the committee wasn't able to hold a Skype call. I checked my phone connection and my wifi signal, assured myself that everything would be fine, tried to still the too-rapid beating of my heart—drinking Fatima's coffee may have been a big mistake—and started reviewing my notes one last time.

At 2:30, as I was feeling like I couldn't possibly be ready in half an hour, and also like I couldn't possibly bear to look at my notes one more time, someone started running a jackhammer next door.

They'll stop by 3! I told myself. The construction site had been blessedly quiet all day, which I took as a sign of good luck, but it seemed that my luck was running out just when I needed it most.

At 2:45 the jackhammering was still going strong. It almost covered up the loud knocking at my door.

I went to get it, expecting more harassment from Jason, but it was a tall, kindly-faced woman in a hijab.

"Hello!" she said brightly. "I am Naz. The Farsi instructor. This noise is terrible, is it not? Let's go ask them to stop!"

"Um..." I said. "I'm about to have an interview."

"What? Then you must tell them to stop!"

"I don't have time. The interview starts in fifteen minutes."

"You have time! Fifteen minutes is lots of time! Let's go!"

"I really need to stay here," I said.

Naz made a face. "I go then," she said. "Good luck with interview!"

"Um, thanks."

I checked the time when she left. 2:50. Ugh. Another ten minutes. They seemed to stretch on into eternity, and to be much too short at the same time. Like the five minutes until execution in that scene in *The Idiot*. I cringed, remembering my interview for the UNC-Charlotte tenure-track job, the one I hadn't gotten but that had led to getting this job. One of the questions had been what was my favorite Dostoevsky work, and I had said *The Idiot* because it was the only one whose name I could remember in Russian at that high-stress moment. By the look on the one Russian-speaking interviewer's face, that was the answer that had cost me that job.

I still didn't know why she had taken such an exception to *The Idiot*, and since she hadn't contacted me since that day, I probably never would know. And did I even want to know? UNC-Matthew's total disinterest in its faculty was probably a blessing in disguise. I could get on with my business without outside interference. And I should stop comparing myself with Dostoevsky and his characters, or if I did, it should only be to contemplate how fortunate I was. If only I felt more fortunate.

2:55. Did I have time to run to the bathroom one last time? I did not. I should just hold it. Could I hold it? Suddenly I wasn't sure. But

I definitely didn't have time to run to the bathroom. What if they decided to call two minutes early, and I missed them? That would be terrible.

2:57. I checked all my connections again. Sweat was trickling down my sides. I reminded myself that I didn't actually want to move to North Dakota. I wasn't sure what I did want, but schlepping out to North Dakota and spending a year living in poverty there while I hunted for more jobs was not it. But worse than that would be not to have any job at all. My pride rebelled against it on a visceral level, like a kick in the guts.

2:59. 2:59:30. 2:59:45...

23

At 3:01 my phone's ringer put me out of my misery. I grabbed at it and promptly dropped it on the desk. I snatched it up and stared at it in horror. The call was still coming through.

Slowly, carefully, I opened the phone, pressed "Send," and said, with what I hoped was stately, professorial calm, "Hello."

"Doctor Rowena Halley?" said a voice at the other end. It sounded very far away. I'd had connections to Russia that were better than this tinny crackling.

"Yes," I said. And then I had to repeat it when a vigorous burst of jackhammering drowned out my words.

The committee introduced themselves. Since I couldn't see them, I had only a vague impression of two women and two men, none of whom seemed to speak Russian. Half their words were muffled by the bad connection, and the other half were lost in the insistent jackhammering coming from the neighboring building.

I repeated, shouting everything into the phone twice, all my prepared talking points about my commitment to growing the Russian program and fostering student engagement, with specific references to how that could be achieved in North Dakota by emphasizing the importance of Russian for aeronautics and petroleum engineering. I said nothing of my ambivalence about fostering the growth of petroleum engineering. I gushed enthusiastically about how much I would enjoy starting a Russian club and organizing more extracurricular Russian activities. I assured them that I would be *delighted* to live in North Dakota, and said something about how it would feel practically like home after living in Moscow.

"Yes," said the woman leading the interview in a tone that suggested I may have laid it on a bit too thick. For most Americans, Moscow was a remote hinterland, but maybe for someone from North Dakota, remote hinterland took on a new meaning. "Well, that's lovely...what *is* that noise?"

"It's jackhammering," I said. "There's a construction project going on next to my office, and they've been jackhammering away like mad for the past hour."

"Oh! You poor thing." Now the lead interviewer's voice held a tinge of sympathy. "To have someone jackhammering next to you during an interview! And that's not very conducive to work in general. Do they do it often?"

"It's not a very quiet workspace," I confessed.

"Do you work from home much?" asked one of the men, also with something almost like genuine human interest in his voice.

"I do, but my neighbor has a newborn baby, so that's not very quiet either."

"Ah." Everyone sighed sympathetically. "I know how that goes," said the man. "I remember when I was a new faculty member —of course, that was my own baby that was keeping me up. Fun times, fun times. Do you have any kids? Oh wait, we're not supposed to ask that, are we?"

"It's okay," I said. "And no. I don't have any kids. Just a cat."

"That's practically the same," said the woman who was the lead interviewer. Her voice said that she didn't believe that. And neither did I. I was extremely fond of Fevronia, and had already demonstrated my willingness to suffer financial and physical pain for her sake, but our relationship was more that of dysfunctional partners than a mother and child. Plus, I could leave her at home unsupervised without fear of repercussions other than maybe a little vengeful peeing.

"Well, uh, Rowena, it was very interesting talking to you," said the man who had asked about children. "If a little noisy what with all the jackhammering in the background. And you had some, uh, interesting ideas about growing the program. We are interviewing all our candidates this week and next week, and we are hoping to move on to the next stage of the process by the end of the month."

"Yes," said the lead interviewer. "Thanks so much, Rowena, and best of luck. We'll be in touch."

"I'm looking forward to it," I said. I tried to say it bravely, but my voice was drowned out by a final burst of jackhammering.

24

I spent the next couple of days kicking myself over blowing the North Dakota interview, although I couldn't say exactly how I had blown it. Well, I could. The jackhammering had destroyed it. Interview committees only wish you "best of luck" if you've utterly wrecked things, and the jackhammering had been the thing that had wrecked it. As far as I could tell. Maybe it had been something I had said, but I really thought it was the jackhammering. Which was unfair, since I'd had no control over that. Or maybe they just hadn't liked me. Probably they just hadn't liked me. Maybe I'd come across as too desperate. I spent a while texting angstily with Alex over that.

Fuck that, and fuck them, was his advice. *If it wasn't meant to be, it wasn't meant to be. And probably the thing that turned them against you was how overqualified you are.*

I don't think I'm overqualified, I texted back. *I don't think I'm any more qualified than any of the other candidates.*

Trust me, you're way more fucking qualified, Alex texted.

How would you know? You don't even speak Russian, I shot back.

Because, for fuck's sake, you went on a multi-mile footrace through the snow with gun-toting bad guys for a student. I was there, remember?

That doesn't mean I'm a good teacher, I texted back. *And it's not something I can put on my CV.*

First of all, it damn well does mean you're a good teacher, and second of all, that fucker Erik Johnson gave you a letter of recommendation, didn't he? I sure as fuck hope he mentioned it.

I don't know what he mentioned, I said. *I hope he left that part out.*

He still propositioning you?

Not really. Which was true. Erik Johnson and I had exchanged several more circumspect emails, in which I had tentatively agreed to take charge of Madison over the summer if necessary. It would be a kind of one-on-one study abroad tour. It was not clear whether or not Erik Johnson would be accompanying us, or exactly what the arrangements would be. I felt a little sick every time I thought about it, but not sick enough to say no. I needed the cash, and I needed something to occupy my time, and I needed to go back to Moscow.

In my more starkly honest moments of self-reflection, I tried to imagine what it would be like if I ran into Dima after ending up in Erik Johnson's bed. Not good, not good, but I could easily see both those things happening. Because if I needed to sleep my way back to Moscow, that's what I would do. Sober reflection suggested that Dima would not appreciate that. Or maybe he would. He had always been brutally practical when the situation called for it. He had specifically told me on multiple occasions not to be afraid to use sex as a survival tool if that's what was needed.

"Everything is covered by the crown, as Dostoevsky would say," he'd said more than once. Orthodox weddings included standing under a crown, so wedding idioms involved crowns rather than altars. "Once we get married, Innochka, the past won't matter. The important thing is that you get to the crown, not how you got there." But now it seemed that he didn't want to make it to the crown. If I arranged a liaison with another man in order to fund my trip to Russia to find him, the transgression would not be my infidelity, but my fidelity.

But that was all in the hypothetical future. The very real present involved my sense that I had blown the interview for the North Dakota job, so I needed to make sure to ace the interview next week for the Alaska job. There was still no word on the Crimson position. I was trying not to hold out too much hope for it. I would focus on the interviews that I had instead of counting my job-chicks before they'd even been laid.

On Saturday morning, when I had almost given up hope of ever hearing from her again, I got a message from Marina.

Do you still want to talk to Arina? she asked. *She says she will talk to you today if it is just you and me with her.*

I messaged back immediately to say yes, I'd love to talk to her. That was only sort of a lie. In fact, I was inappropriately curious about Arina and her story and how I might help her. It was like being sucked into a real-life soap opera. So a short time later I was listening to Skype's *bloop-bla-bloop* ringtone, waiting to talk to the mysterious Arina.

The video came into focus, showing Marina, still with her harsh facial lines and her bright red nails, this time matched by equally bright red lipstick that did nothing to make her look younger and more attractive. Maybe younger and more attractive was not the look she was going for. Sitting next to her was a woman who looked, well, like her sister, with the same stick-straight ash-blonde hair, wide pale mouth, and slightly slanted big gray eyes set into a face that had Northern European coloring and Central Asian bone structure. So your typical Eastern European.

"Hello?" said the other woman tentatively. She seemed like a younger, softer, more malleable version of Marina. It was easy to see her as the younger sister, the one who had always followed along and been protected, until she decided to strike out on her own. But since she had so little experience at it, she'd made a terrible mistake on her first try. Although maybe it wasn't any worse than any other mistake she would have made in those circumstances. After all, she'd gotten a husband, even if temporarily, a visa, and a son out of the deal. A fair trade, some might say.

"She does look kind of Pashtun, just like you said," Arina whispered to Marina. "Are you Pashtun?" she asked me. "You look Pashtun. Maybe Marina told you: I used to study Central Asian cultures. And Afghanistan. I wanted to be a specialist on Afghanistan before, well...all this."

"She mentioned that," I said. "But no, I'm not Pashtun. I'm of British ethnicity. You know the 'Black Irish'?"

"The Irish are white," said Arina.

"Uh, yeah, but it means, you know, dark hair and light eyes. Like me. Or like the Pashtun."

There was a short but vigorous discussion of whether the Pashtun and the Irish were related, and how that could be, and whether I perhaps secretly had Pashtun heritage, given the lengthy British presence in Afghanistan, before Marina said sharply, "We already discussed this enough last week. It doesn't matter whether she is Pashtun, Irish, or Tanzanian. Besides, she is American. You're American, right? You have American citizenship?"

"I do."

"By birth, or did you get it later?"

"By birth. My family has been in the US for generations."

"So lucky," sighed Arina.

"Yes," I agreed. There was a lot of talk these days about privilege, but most of the people talking seemed oblivious to the biggest privilege of them all, which was being a native-born US citizen. Compared with most of the rest of the world, the most despised American minority was still rolling in a sea of privilege and good fortune.

"That's what I wanted for my Maks," said Arina. "And still want, actually. For him to be a real American. But...I don't know. I thought

I wanted that for him more than anything. But when Jason"—she pronounced it Dzhey-son—"threatened to take him away from me and send me home without him, I realized that more than anything I wanted to keep him with me. Maybe I'm a bad mother."

"I don't think wanting to keep your child makes you a bad mother," I said.

"But if I choose to keep him with me instead of letting him stay in America and be a real American..."

"Doesn't he already have American citizenship?" I asked.

"Yes, of course. He was born there, and his father is a native-born American citizen. He has American citizenship, no question. But I want him to grow up there. But I also want him to grow up with me, and I want him...I missed my home, I'm proud of my homeland, and I want him to know his mother's motherland. I wanted him to know that his mother was from a Hero-City, and her grandparents were partisans who fought the Nazis, and that is part of who he is, too.

"But Dzhey-son didn't want him to know about that. He said it made America look bad, I was always trying to make America look bad. I wasn't! I came to America for a reason. But I can love America and my first motherland too. But Dzhey-son never saw it that way. He didn't want us speaking Russian, let alone Belarusian. We fought and fought about the name Maks. Dzhey-son wanted something strange like Dzhosh-u-ah. Why all these Dzh-names? Dzhey-son, Dzhosh-u-ah, Dzhess-i-kah...why do Americans like this strange sound so much? It's very difficult to pronounce. Although I suppose Serbian has something similar. Well. We fought over everything all the time, in the end. Maks's name, what language we would speak, what we would eat for dinner. And then one day I made vinaigrette—you know vinaigrette? The salad with beets?"

"Yes, of course," I said.

"So one day I made vinaigrette for supper, and Dzhey-son exploded, he started screaming about how I only ever made filthy

Russian food, he grabbed me by the neck and pushed my face down into the salad and then threw me against the wall—I thought I had broken a rib, maybe ruptured a kidney, but I am mostly healed now. Anyway. Husbands...you know how they are. I could have stood it, although I had hoped for something better from an American, but for my son I could have stood it, but then he started screaming at Maks too, he started screaming at Maks to stop speaking Russian, and then he told me that he was going to divorce me and have me deported and keep Maks for himself. So...so I ran away home."

"And you did right," I said.

"You think? I have doubts."

"Do you really want your son to be raised by a man who would do that?" I asked.

"A son needs a father," said Arina firmly.

"Yes, but not one who beats up his mother! That's a terrible example for him."

"Better than no example at all," said Arina. "But I am selfish. I couldn't lose Maks. So...here I am. But Maks cries all the time and asks for his father. It's a punishment for me. One I deserve."

"No you don't," Marina and I said simultaneously.

"What does Dzhey-son say?" asked Arina. "Is he sorry?"

"Um...not as far as I can tell," I told her. "It does seem like he wants Maks, but I don't think he's sorry for how he treated you."

Arina sighed. "Of course not. Why would he be? Well, what do you think? Maks needs to speak with him. Would you be our go-between?"

"Um..." I said. "Do you really need me? Can't you talk to each other without a translator? You were married. For several years."

"Yes, but I don't think we ever actually understood each other even when we thought we were speaking the same language," said Arina. "And it would make me feel better to have another woman there, on his end. He might act better. Please set something up for next weekend."

"Um..." My stomach squirmed at the thought of acting as Jason's representative. "Well..."

"Please, Ro-eenna," said Arina. "Maks needs it!"

"I'll talk to Jason," I said. "Maybe we can set something up. But I hardly think I'm the best person to be doing this."

"You're the only person," said Arina. "So that means you're the best. Can you do it next Saturday? Thank you, Ro-eenna."

We exchanged another round of pleasantries, and agreed that I would try to set something up with Jason, and then, my stomach still squirming in rebellion at what I was getting myself into, I hung up.

25

I relayed Arina's interest in holding a Skype conversation in my presence to Jason that afternoon. Predictably, he responded with an unpunctuated, uncapitalized email demanding an immediate conversation with Arina. My reply that she wanted to do it next Saturday did not go down well, and neither did my insistence on doing it at my office on campus rather than at his or my home. Driving into campus on Saturday morning was not high on my list of things to do, and I wasn't even sure I could get into the building on the weekend, but after Arina's story of Jason's violent outburst over the salad, there was no way that I was going to meet him on either of our home territories.

He kicked up a fuss again after class on Monday. I tried to respond as calmly as possible, and not shrink away from him. The sad thing was that he was at least a head shorter than me, and not excessively muscular. I knew that rage and insanity could give people unexpected strength, but my first thought on seeing him was that I could take him in a one-on-one fight. And Arina seemed like a big strapping girl too. Why hadn't she kicked him in the balls or punched him in the throat when he'd attacked her? Why had she let him treat her like that? Which reminded me, I had another interview to prepare for.

My interview for the Alaska position was scheduled for 11:00am on Thursday, via Skype. After the jackhammer fiasco of the previous week, and my good luck with Skype connections for my talks with Marina and Arina, I decided to try holding this interview at home.

This meant that along with the regular interview prep I also had to prepare my interview space to look as professional as possible. I spent more time than I had to spare cleaning and organizing my living/dining room, which had my only table/work area, and setting everything up so that I had a professional-looking background and I could look into the computer without having the sun either in my eyes or at my back.

I even opened a couple of boxes of books and arranged them on an empty bookshelf that I pulled into just the right position so that interested viewers could see my *Collected Works of Marina Tsvetaeva, Poetry of the Silver Age, The Development of Russian Verse,* and other worthy-looking titles related to my dissertation. Then I agonized over whether that would provoke questions about my plans to revise and publish my dissertation as a book, something I was very behind on. And why was I behind on it? Because all my non-teaching time was taken up with applications and interviews. Probably best not to bring that up. Probably best to have some pat answer about my publication plans, and make it sound better than it was.

Thursday morning found me pacing the floor, looking over my notes. I thought of going for a morning run in order to burn off some of my nerves, but catastrophic scenarios of getting lost, injured, attacked, or run over by a bus, and thus missing the interview, filled my head. Some small rational part of my brain was aware that the tragedy of getting run over by a bus would not be in missing the interview for a crappy job I didn't really want, but that rational part of my brain didn't have a lot of say amongst all the voices in my head right now.

So I did asanas and forms instead, tried to prep for Friday's classes, and then spent the hour between 10:00 and 11:00 looking over my notes on the Alaska program and how to foster town-and-gown outreach between the Russian program and the large Russian population (according to the website) in town.

The *bloop-bla-bloop* of Skype set my nerves all aquiver, as it always did now. The video, when I accepted the call, was not the crisp clear thing it had been during my conversations with Marina and Arina, but grainy and fractured, with a noticeable lag between picture and sound.

"That's okay," said the woman running the interview. "We can just pretend we're interviewing an astronaut calling in from the International Space Station. Are you interested in space exploration, um, Rowena?"

"What kind of a name is Rowena?" the man sitting next to her interrupted before I could answer. "Is that Russian? It sounds kind of Russian."

"No, it's British," said the woman on the other side of him. "Remember? We had a long discussion about whether to bother inviting someone with a British name for an interview. Oops." She turned to me, not sounding apologetic. "You probably shouldn't have heard that. But you must get that a lot. *Are* you British?"

"I mean, my family originally came from the British Isles. But I'm an American."

"Not Russian at all?" asked the woman, sounding disappointed. "We were hoping that at least you would have a Russian mother. You didn't mention it in your materials, but you *did* claim near-native fluency, so we had high hopes that you were at least a heritage speaker."

"No Russian genetic material," I said. "But I did live there for a while."

"How long a while?" asked the woman.

"Five, almost six years, between undergrad and grad school."

"Oh! That's good, then. Where did you live?"

"Moscow."

She made a face. "Hard to get much Russian in Moscow these days, I'd imagine."

"It depends. My job at the time involved a lot of speaking Russian. And I lived for a while with a Russian family."

"Oh! Like a home-stay?"

"Sort of," I said. The committee members all rustled through my application materials and remarked on the fact that yes, I had worked for an NGO in Moscow for the better part of six years, and yes, it said that my job involved interviewing people in Russian, just like I had told them.

"Well," said the fourth member of the committee, who had remained silent so far. Even from one word I could tell he had a strong Russian accent. "Let's test your Russian, shall we?"

"Please, let's," I said, as if nothing could give me greater pleasure.

The man, who introduced himself as Vasily Valeriyevich, and who was the head of the two-person Russian program, grilled me at length about my research, my pedagogical approach, and my personal life. The latter was strictly not allowed, but that never seemed to stop anyone. He was pleased to discover that I had had a Russian fiancé, and even more pleased to discover that we had broken up and I was now single and childless. Since I knew those were major selling points in my favor, I was pleased to tell him that, legality be damned.

By then the other committee members were fidgeting impatiently, so, with reluctance, Vasily Valeriyevich said we should switch back to English so that we could discuss my ideas for supporting and growing the program.

I started trotting out all my thoughts, both my general ones (Petroleum engineering! ROTC! Critical Need Language!) and my specific ones for outreach to the Russian-speaking community around the university. Halfway through, Nevaeh started wailing.

"I thought you said you did not have any children," said Vasily Valeriyevich. His expression when he said the word "children" made it seem like the only way he liked children was well-baked in Baba Yaga's oven.

"It's my neighbor's," I explained.

"Oh! You are at home?"

"Yes. My office on campus is next to a construction zone, so I thought this would be quieter."

I could see all the committee members peering not very surreptitiously as far into the corners of my apartment as their Skype feed would allow them. Some of them, I was sure, were trying to check and see if I were wearing real pants, or just pajama bottoms under my blazer.

"Of course, one of the benefits of this work is that a lot of it can be done at home," said the woman who had first spoken, sounding as if she were forgiving me for some heinous crime. The lag between video and sound made it seem all the more accusing. "It *is* inconvenient when your neighbors have a crying baby, but I suppose you can't really control that—is that a cat?"

"Yes," I admitted. Fevronia had come out from hiding and was rubbing against my calf and crying loudly.

"Oh! Can we see it?"

Against my better judgment, but unable to say no, I leaned down and picked up Fevronia. She promptly bit my hand. I swallowed back a shriek and, hoping any blood was hidden from the camera, held her up so that everyone could see her.

"Oh, how *adorable!*" exclaimed both the women. "She's so fluffy! Is she a special breed?"

"She's a rescue." Blood was now flowing freely from my left hand. I tried to hold Fevronia with my right hand and stop the bleeding by pressing my left hand into my good work trousers. At least they were black. The stain wouldn't show, right?

"How *lovely*! Rescues are the best, aren't they?"

"They are." Fevronia squirmed out of my grasp, drawing blood from my right hand with her claws as she escaped. I tried to wipe off the blood on my other trouser leg without drawing attention to it.

"I just *love* cats." The two women talked for a while longer about their enthusiasm for cats, while the two men stared at them in boredom, and I tried to hide my bleeding hands from the camera.

"Well, Rowena, it's been *lovely* to talk to you," the first woman finally said.

"Yes," echoed Vasily Valeriyevich less enthusiastically. "Very pleasant to meet you, Ro-eenna."

"And you," I said, and repeated it in Russian for good measure. The non-Russian speakers all tittered in appreciation. Vasily Valeriyevich made a sour face. There were some more pleasantries exchanged, and the information that they expected to be able to get back to the candidates in under a month, and then I was free to go bandage up my hands.

26

The cat-inflicted wounds had stopped bleeding and turned into slightly puffy red scratches and punctures by the following morning. I tried to tell myself that Fevronia's interference in the interview had been a good thing. Certainly the two women had been very positively disposed towards her. But was that enough? Or did it just make me seem like a nice person but not a colleague in their eyes? And Vasily Valeriyevich had not seemed impressed at all, and surely he as the head of the Russian program had the deciding vote. And did I really want to move to Alaska, anyway? A brief perusal of my bank balance told me that if they paid enough, then yes, I certainly did. The question of how I would get out there remained open, though.

I stressed about interviews, money, my future, and whether or not I was coming down with blood poisoning all day, barely able to concentrate on my actual classes. Even Jason was less repulsive to me, since I was wrapped up in my own private obsessions. I said something to him about how I would see him the next morning at 10:00am, which was when I had set up the Skype call with Arina, and then drove off in a cloud of anxiety and existential angst.

That did not prevent me from engaging in my afternoon ritual of checking all the job sites, The Wiki, and then *Nezavisimaya Pravda*. I scrolled through the last with only one eye open, thinking about jobs...The sight of Dima's byline caused a physical jolt, like a taser to the heart. I actually clutched at my chest.

He's alive! For a moment the joy was so fierce I could hardly breathe. Then the joy morphed into irritation. He was alive but he couldn't be bothered about the rest of us, e.g., me.

The irritation grew as I read the article. It was an in-depth, eyewitness account of the battle for the Donetsk airport. Judging by what he was reporting, he must have been there in person. On both sides. If he actually witnessed what he was claiming to have witnessed, and one of Dima's more troublesome flaws was terminal honesty, he must have belly-crawled back and forth between the two sides, interviewing them in the midst of the fighting. I wondered how he had convinced them not to shoot him, or maybe torture and execute him as a spy. He had not been entirely successful at avoiding torture, it seemed, since he mentioned receiving "a few insignificant injuries and threats to my life from my Ukrainian brothers before I was able to convince them of my journalistic credentials."

Don't pity him! I ordered myself sternly. *This is what he wanted!*

I read on. He had somehow, maybe by smooth talking, maybe by demonstrating a ridiculously high tolerance for fear and torture, managed to gain an interview with both Dmytro Yarosh, the leader of the Ukrainian paramilitary Right Sector, and Givi, the leader of the DPR (pro-Russian) Somalia Battalion.

"You moron!" I said out loud. I wondered which of those groups hated him more. Dima was mainly Russian, with a side of Jewish, neither of which was likely to endear him to hardcore rightwing Ukrainian nationalists. But he was ferociously critical of most aspects of modern-day Russia, which was unlikely to go down well with hardcore gun-toting Russian nationalists, either. Unless he repented of his oppositionist ways and picked a gun back up and joined them. Which was very possible. I knew that some of his former comrades-in-arms were already in the thick of the fighting.

I scanned the article again. If he had picked up a gun for either side, it wasn't obvious. Given everything Dima believed in, I would have said it was impossible. But given the way he responded to adrenaline and violence, I could easily see him giving in to battle-lust and joining the fray.

You're well rid of him! He would ruin both your lives if you let him! But my words only made me want him more. A piercing pain, like a half-healed injury suddenly torn open again, lanced through me, so fierce and so visceral I wanted to stuff my fist into my mouth and bite down on it to choke back howls of anguish over his absence. Suddenly, everything else in my life seemed not only worthless, but an active hindrance to the one thing I couldn't do without, which was Dima. I wanted to burst out of my apartment and run, run, run all the way across the land, across the ocean, across the war zone, until I was in his arms. But his arms no longer wanted me.

The magnitude of my loss hit me, maybe more sharply than it ever had before. In the first few days and weeks after he had told me to leave and not come back, I had floated along in a sorrow-befuddled daze of denial. Surely he hadn't really meant it. We'd had our ups and downs before—what couple hadn't?—and surely this was just another down, to be followed by an up like sun after rain. And then I'd been plunged back into the final death agonies of finishing up and defending my dissertation, not to mention my futile and exhausting job search. My dissertation committee, with the unerring instinct of the strong ready to destroy the weak, had sensed my anguish and started circling, like sharks after blood. Even my advisor, to whom I'd confessed the outlines of the situation, had been less than sympathetic.

"That's too bad, Innochka," she'd said with a shrug. "I'd hoped we could bring him here as a guest speaker, now that he's gained some notoriety—my colleagues at UNC have been able to bring in all kinds of opposition journalists; Yuliya Latynina, Arkady Babchenko, did you know that? I'm ashamed we're behind them, and this seemed like a great chance to show them that we can bring in interesting speakers too—but he never wanted even to do that, did he? He never would do anything for you, would he? You're better off without him. A husband will only hold you back in your career. Now let's go over your conclusion again. I don't think the committee is going to like what you say on page 235. You should reword it."

So I had by necessity thrown myself into preparing for my defense and chasing those elusive jobs, and in my few minutes of spare time I had adopted Fevronia. That had proven to be surprisingly comforting. Helping others had always been how I made myself feel better. Then I'd had my summer teaching job, and my last-minute move to New Jersey and the job at TLASC, and then the job here. My life had seemed, if not rewarding, then unpleasantly stuffed to the gills with activities. But now, looking at Dima's byline, I was forced to see that all that busywork had just kept me from facing up to my misery.

Stop it! I was sitting doubled over, both arms wrapped around my torso for protection from a pain that no amount of physical armor could save me from. I made myself unclench my body, shut my computer, get up, and go start some water boiling for supper.

The scent of water coming to a boil made me feel sick. How was I even going to eat like this? And tomorrow was another big day. I couldn't wear through my time and energy by moping around and refusing food and behaving like a lovesick Victorian maiden. Lovesick Victorian maidens were a figure of fun, but their heartbreak must have been all too real, just like mine. At least I didn't have to wear a corset. My heartbreak could expand in all directions as much as it wanted. My heartbreak...I ran to the bathroom, afraid I was going to be sick.

Once in the bathroom, though, my whole body was in too much of a spasm to be sick. I couldn't even pee. I gave up trying after a while and splashed some water on my face. When I looked at it in the mirror, it looked the same as it always did, although tireder by the day. But there was no trace of all the immeasurable anguish and despair I could feel welling up inside of me, looking for some outlet and failing to find one. I wondered if this was how I looked when I was interviewing: calm, pleasant, pretty. Probably. Probably I...

"AGH!"

The door from the cabinet under the sink had knocked against my shin. Snakes!!! Was it snakes? Were there snakes in the apartment? Snakes...even in Charlotte, January was a little cold for snakes. The cabinet door pushed against my shin again, followed by a cranky meow. Fevronia had hidden herself in the cabinet and was trying to get out.

"You okay down there?" Lakeesha shouted through the bathroom floor. "You slip and fall or somethin'?"

"Thanks, I'm fine!" I shouted back. "My cat just startled me."

"Well, keep it down, okay? I'm tryin' to get Nevaeh to—" The last word was probably meant to be "sleep," but it was drowned out by the resumption of Nevaeh's piercing cries. I let Fevronia out of the cabinet, jumping to the side to avoid her ill-tempered swipe at me as she darted off.

When I got back to the kitchen, my water was boiling. I made supper with at least 75% of my normal calm, and told myself that I was fine, and I wasn't going to do anything stupid. Then, when I was done eating, I emailed Dima.

27

From: Rowena Halley
    To: Dima Kuznetsov
Subject: Are you okay?
Hello! I saw your article about the airport. Were you injured? Are
you okay?
Inna

Starting the email was a mad impulse, but finishing it and sending it off took the better part of an hour. There were multiple rewrites, ranging from just "Are you okay?" to lengthy explanations of my life circumstances; my future prospects; my feelings about my life, my job, world politics, and us as a couple; and descriptions of Fevronia. Fevronia must have known I was writing about her, because she crept up on me as I was composing that section of that draft of the email, and rubbed her cheek against my calf until she got tired of being ignored, and then bit me.

Once I was done screaming, swearing, and stanching the blood flow, I erased the three-paragraph missive I had been laboring over—I could write reasonably fluently in Russian, but it was still slower going than in English, which made pouring out a year's worth of pent-up thoughts and feelings all the more agonizing—and went for the final 1-line note. Then I sent it off and swore to myself that I would not spend the rest of the evening checking my email every thirty seconds and fretting over the lack of reply. It was the middle of the night in Eastern Ukraine, so no reply could be expected until morning anyway.

This sensible resolution in no way prevented me from going through all the other emails in my inbox. It needed to be done, right? The fact that I would be *right there* for every incoming email was incidental. I was simply demonstrating my commitment and work ethic.

I started by going through my UNC-Matthews inbox, which contained an enthusiastic email from Shaniqua, asking about a potential summer program she had found, and a snippy email from Jason, wanting to know where exactly we would meet tomorrow, as if that were a big mystery.

Both of them addressed me by my first name. In Shaniqua's case I didn't mind at all on a personal level, although on a professional level I wrestled once again over the issue of whether or not I should let her know that the appropriate form of address for her professor in the circles she wanted to move in was "Professor." Early-career academics, women in particular, had a hard time getting the respect we were supposed to be given. But I always felt that insisting, your voice shrill, that you be called "Professor," was counterproductive to getting real respect. Real respect had to be earned. But that was much harder if you didn't "look like a professor," meaning gray-haired, white, and male. Although Lord knows students didn't have a problem making fun of gray-haired white male professors, either.

Anyway, one of the many things in life that Shaniqua apparently hadn't gotten was the training to call her professors "Professor" with the appropriately respectful tone of voice. Upper-middle-class white kids who had gone to the right schools had been trained from birth to show respect without losing their own dignity. Everyone else tended to come across as either obsequious or pushy. And if I tried to train Shaniqua how to do it, I would probably come across as an uppity white bitch trying to put her down. So whatever. In the grand scheme of things, it didn't matter that much anyway. She was smart; if she ever did go to a really good school, she'd pick up the right manners from her new peers quick enough.

Jason, on the other hand, had less rosy prospects ahead of him, even if I didn't strangle him first. He had written:

> *hey rowena im still waiting to hear back from you about where exactly were meeting tomorrow when are you going to let me know campus is really inconvenient your place is probably best*

I gnashed my teeth. Then I thought about how here we had a man separated from his only son, and a boy growing up without his father and in Belarus when he could be growing up with his father in Charlotte, which wasn't the best place in the world but was maybe a little better in some ways than a neo-Soviet authoritarian kleptocracy, and maybe I could help bring them together. Also, there was the chance of earning $30, maybe not even once but several times. It hadn't happened yet but even the possibility of $30, AKA a week's supply of food, was enough to lure me onwards. Or maybe that was the justification I was offering myself for indulging in my addiction to martyrdom.

Dear Jason I wrote,

> *As I explained to you this morning and also in my previous email, we will be meeting in my office, which is Tryon 419. If you have any trouble finding it, please let me know, but it is only one floor above our regular classroom. If it would be easier, we could probably use the classroom instead. Or if that doesn't work, we can try the library. In any case, Tryon Hall will be much more convenient and appropriate than my home. The call is supposed to start at 10:00am our time.*

I intend to arrive around 9:30am in order to get everything set up. You are welcome to arrive any time between then and 10:00am.

Best,

Professor Halley

I felt a little bit like a stuck-up shit for writing like that to him, but not enough to prevent me from sending it.

By then it was well past time for it to be okay to check my personal inbox again, so I did. Nothing. Well, other than a bunch of junk mail and...what was that? It looked suspiciously like an interview invitation. I opened it.

It was, just as I had guessed, an interview invitation. For the Crimson position! (!!!!!!). A faint scream of joy burst out of my mouth before I could prevent it.

I responded immediately saying I would be *delighted* to interview for the position. Then I checked my inbox again. Nothing. I went back to my UNC-Matthews inbox. Another email from Jason.

hey rowena your office is out of my way where do you live maybe its closer

I started to roll my eyes, and then stopped. The pain from sitting staring at a computer screen for too many hours for too many days meant I couldn't even roll my eyes in exasperation at my students. Was nothing sacred? Or was the job search determined to take even this away from me?

Responding right away would only encourage him. I would answer tomorrow. I went back to my personal inbox.

Junk mail, junk mail...the search committee for the Crimson position had already responded to me, with a list of interview times. Apparently I wasn't the only academic answering emails too late at night.

I answered with my top three choices for interview times, and promised myself I would definitely stop dealing with email now. An interview invitation, even for such a crappy job, was such a stroke of luck that nothing was going to top that. I'd just check one last time.

My heart jumped before my eyes recognized what they'd seen. Already, improbably, even though it was 3:00am over there, Dima had responded to me.

Everything's fine, nothing serious). Thanks for reading. Are you still running?

28

I parsed and analyzed that email within an inch of its life, scrutinizing everything from the single close parenthesis, the Russian equivalent of a smiley face (why only one? Most men would use at least two if they really meant it, and most women would use at least three. Why did he stop with one, if he was going to do it at all?), to the verb for "running," which indicated, as I got to teach all my students every semester, repeated round trips or multidirectional, aimless motion. What was he trying to say? Was he asking if I still kept up with my running routine (yes, yes, that was what he was asking me, I knew that perfectly well), or was he asking me if I was running around, running in circles, running with no goal in mind...it was sad. There was a time when I had felt like I knew what Dima was thinking, and could answer anything he said with the comfortable knowledge that he would accept my answer with love, no matter what that answer was, no matter how I tripped up in my words or my thoughts or my feelings. But now I agonized over every single letter in a two-line text.

> *Of course I still read your articles*, I wrote back, unable to stop myself. *And I'm still running too. But it seems like I'm just running in circles. What about you?*

That last line made my stomach clench when I saw it, but I sent it off before I could think better of it. Then I waited for an hour, hoping for another lightning-fast answer. But none came.

There was still no answer the following morning when I got up. I told myself that was only to be expected. Dima had made his lack of desire to have anything to do with me perfectly clear. And that was why he wasn't answering me, not because he'd been killed overnight. Probably.

I spent a while wondering which would be worse for me, personally: the knowledge that he was deliberately avoiding me when I'd made it plain I wanted to forgive him for what he'd done (because sending me away like that was a very big transgression in my book, maybe the worst, definitely worse than infidelity and possibly even worse than physical violence) and reconnect; or if I were to find out that he'd been tragically, heroically killed. Maybe while in the process of composing a lengthy apology to me and a plea to get back together. That sure would be sad, wouldn't it? And then I could cry, and regret all the time we'd wasted, and then I could move on. Whereas as long as he was alive, I was left hanging. Which was a very selfish thought, but it made me see things with more clarity to think it.

There was still no response from him by the time I had to leave to go to campus for the Skype session with Arina and Jason. Boy, was that going to be a barrel of laughs, I could tell. Good thing I was already in such a cheerful mood going into it.

I showed up early, a little after 9:00am, in case there were problems with the connection or getting into the building, and we had to relocate to the classroom or the library. I was aware that there was no good reason for putting this much time and effort into helping Jason, who hadn't even paid me yet, but ingrained habits were hard to shake, so I showed up in plenty of time for troubleshooting.

Tryon Hall was open, though, and the wifi signal appeared to be broadcasting loud and clear. By 9:35 I had everything ready, and was now faced with the prospect of 25 minutes of sitting there twiddling my thumbs and waiting for Jason. 25 minutes wasn't enough time to get anything really useful done, like work on another job application or a paper, but it was too long for me to feel okay about sitting there doing nothing.

I had just started to grade a couple of pieces of homework I had lying around, when Skype told me I had a message. I opened it, expecting it to be something from Marina or Arina, maybe them cancelling at the last minute. But instead it was from John.

Hey sis, it said. *Is that invite for me to come visit still open? What about next month? I have been told I *must* take some leave. They're even threatening quarterdeck if I don't :)*

Sure thing, I messaged back. *Any time, you know that. Only I might not be able to show you such a good time. I'll be busy with work and all. But you're more than welcome to crash on my floor.*

That's all I'll need! John wrote. *I'll make my own fun, you know that :) :) :) .Think you can stand me for a whole two weeks? That's how long I've got off, and I don't have anywhere else to go.*

Of course you can stay with me as long as you like, but surely you've got places you can go. Grandma and Grandpa would love to see you.

Are you fucking kidding me, Ro? Two weeks trapped with them in Macon? Charlotte offers much better hunting grounds :) :) :)

I made a growling noise in the back of my throat. I knew what kind of hunting John was talking about. His favorite targets were leggy, blonde, and had a thin veneer of polish over bone-deep trashiness. Preferably topped off with a tarnished wedding ring. I thought he'd moved past that, but maybe not.

What about—I blanked on the name of the woman he had told me he was seeing in Afghanistan—*that woman you told me about? I thought that was serious.*

Tammy? The private contractor? That ended as soon as I got my orders out.

I'm sorry.

I'm not. I was never anything but a status symbol, a shiny uniform, and a big fat dick to ride anyway. I was never going to pull down the kind of cash she was interested in for her long-term man. She kept nagging me to go private, make some real money, but I've got *some* pride. I'm not ready to turn mercenary yet. So I'm better off without her. Time to move on.

I'm still sorry.

I know you are, Ro, which is I why I want to spend my time off visiting you. I could go hiking or whatever, hit the Grand Canyon or something, but I've already had a multi-month outdoor adventure roughing it in the sand. Well, mostly I was back at the base, so it could have been rougher, but you get what I'm saying. I want bright lights and big city, and I also want to see my family, but I don't want to be trotted off to church three times a week and nagged to death. I figure I'm safe from that with you. Right?

Right, I confirmed. *I promise I won't drag you off to church. And I'll try to keep my nagging under control.*

Yeah, I know you will, Ro. You might have a stick up your ass, but you're not a nag, and for that I appreciate you.

Why thank you. You're so eloquent, as always.

You know it, sweetheart :) Anyway, I'm thinking last week of February, first week of March. I can just drive on over. Hell, I *could* just drive on over any old weekend, but I haven't, have I? I'm such a shit brother. But I've got someone I need to see in Gastonia, so I'll swing by for a couple of hours there, and then come on up to you, probably Saturday. That'd be—oh—Feb 21. How's that suit you? When's your spring break, anyway? You going anywhere?

It's the first week of March. And I'm not planning to go anywhere. I don't have anywhere to go—I thought for a second of Philadelphia and Alex, and then dismissed it—*and I couldn't afford to go anywhere anyway.*

Yeah, I figured as much. It's a shit business you're in, Ro. But we've had this discussion before, so I'll try to rein in my own inner nag...for now. Expect some straight talk from your big brother when I see you in person :)

Oh good! Something to look forward to!

Smartass!

Smarter than you, bro, and you know it!

Fuck, Ro, I don't know whether to shake you, or wipe away a tear of pride :) :) :) Good to know my li'l sis has still got some sass :)

They keep trying to beat it out of me. But they hain't yet.

Hardeeharfuckinghar! You talk like that around your students? "Hain't" my ass!

No. No I do not. I don't have much of an accent at all anymore. I have been assimilated into the prestige culture.

And good for you, Ro. Now you just gotta get 'em to pay you for it. What are you doing this morning?

Actually—I checked the time—*I'm about to do a Skype call between a student and his Belarusian mail-order ex-bride.*

Fuck! Have fun with that. I'll let you go, then. Till next month, okay?

Sounds good. And I hoped it did. John could be...difficult. But he was the only brother I had, so if he wanted to come spend two weeks in Charlotte with me, that's what he'd do.

29

J ason came bursting into my office at 9:58, looking frazzled.

"Shit," he said. "What's with the no parking here? And why's this place so hard to find? Why'd we have to do it here? I don't have time for this shit. We shoulda done it somewhere else like I told you."

"This is my office," I said. "This is where I conduct my professional activities. And I'm doing this as a favor to you."

"But I'm paying you!"

"You haven't paid me yet," I said.

Jason, looking like a woman had never spoken to him in that way before, opened his mouth to argue, but the *bloop-bla-bloop* of an incoming Skype call interrupted him before he could get a word out.

"Arina?" he said, while I was still accepting the call. "Arina, you there? Talk to me, Arina! Is Max there? I wanna see Max!"

"Dzhey-son! Why you yell? You always yell! You scare Maks!"

The call finished connecting. Marina and Arina's kitchen in Minsk came into focus. They were sitting side by side at the table. The top of a small head bobbed in and out of the picture.

"Daddy!" a childish voice said in English. "I wanna see Daddy!"

"Max! Let me see you, kiddo. Pick him up and show him to me, Arina. I wanna see him."

Arina, her mouth in the beginnings of an irked pout, reached down and lifted up Maks, bringing him up into full view. He was a handsome child, who looked a lot like Arina and not very much at all like Jason, fortunately for him.

"Max!" cried Jason. "Hey, buddy! Whatcha up to?"

Maks's face split into a huge grin. He waved at us with both hands, and launched into a lengthy story of everything he'd been doing in Minsk, which mainly involved sledding.

"But I want you here with us, Daddy," he finished. "I want you to take me *katat'sya na sankakh*!"

"I want that too, buddy," said Jason. His face was working like he was going to cry. The genuine emotion in no way diminished his rat-like facial structure and expression. No surprise. After all, rats have feelings too, and probably much purer ones than humans.

"When're you coming to see us, Daddy?" asked Maks.

"Real soon, son, I promise," said Jason. "Your mom and I just have to work some things out."

"Tomorrow?" asked Maks. "Next week?"

"Real soon," repeated Jason. "Now I gotta talk to your mom, okay? Why don't you go with your Aunty Marina to the next room, okay?"

"I don't wanna!"

"I'm not leaving her alone with you," Marina cut in brusquely in Russian.

Jason looked at me for translation.

"Just a second," I said in English. "Arina won't be alone with him," I pointed out in Russian. "I'll be here. And she's safe in Minsk, and he's in Charlotte."

Marina frowned. "You can't trust anything he says," she warned me. "He'll talk her into something stupid! He always does. She can't be trusted with him."

"Please," said Arina. "I'm right here. I can talk to my own husband myself."

"No you can't! When you came home, you still had bruises all over your body from the last time you 'talked.' And you still kept talking about going back to him! Even after you found another...well, anyway. You're too much of a fool to be trusted with him, Arisha. You'll decide to go back to him, and then he'll kill you!"

"He won't kill me!" shouted Arina.

Maks started to cry. "I want my daddy," he said in English.

Jason put his hand over his mouth like he was physically holding back tears. Marina gave him a look of such scorn it was almost palpable, even through the screen.

"Come on, Maks," she said in Russian. "Let's go play. You can talk to your papa again in a bit." She picked Maks up under one arm and walked off with him clamped firmly against her side, like a recalcitrant football.

"Don't worry," said Arina in heavily accented English. "He will come back to say goodbye."

"He better!" Jason had gotten up into a half-crouch and was shaking his finger at the screen. "I swear to God, Arina, if you keep him away from me for another day, I'll..!"

"What?" demanded Arina. Her face was setting into an angry pout that gave it the same harsh lines as her sister's. "You will hit me again? Take him away from me?"

"If I have to! I love that little boy, Arina! I can't live without him! You can't keep him away from me! I'll...I won't let you!"

"How?" demanded Arina. "I have him now! Why must you have him?"

"'Cause I love him! And I'm his father!"

"A bad father," said Arina.

"I was never a bad father to him! I may have...okay, I coulda been better to you, but...you, you...you know what you did! No man's gonna stand something like that! I couldn't help myself! But I'd *never* hurt that little boy, Arina, you know that!"

"I do not know that," said Arina. Her voice was flat and calm now. "My father was angry and mean too, Dzhey-son. He yelled at my mother, every day he yelled at her. Then he hurt her just like you hurt me. Also because of salad. The irony of fate, no? Why do men care so much about salad? It is just salad: beets, pickles...all that. If you want perfect salad, like how you want it, you should make it yourself. Do not hit your wives because they make their own salads, the way they like them. But that is what you did. Just like my father. At first he hit our mother, and then he hit us. How do I know you will not do the same? I think you will do the same. I think first you will hit me because of salad, and then Maks will break something, and you will hit him too. And you will hurt him more, because he is just a little boy. I am strong, but he is just a little boy."

Jason was shaking his head, one hand still pressed over his mouth. "I won't! Arina, I swear to God!"

Arina pursed up her mouth. "How you say in English? 'Talk is cheap.' Talk is cheap, Dzhey-son. Prove it."

Jason took his hand from his mouth, but shrunk down in his seat, his shoulders hunched, till he seemed only half my size. I wished I weren't there witnessing this. "How?" he asked.

"Talk to us. Like Ro-eenna said"—she nodded through the screen at me, bringing unwelcome attention to where I was trying to sit in complete silence off to the side—"talk to us every week. If you will do that and will not be angry and will not make threats, maybe I will believe you."

Rage flashed across Jason's face. "Or what?" he demanded. "I can have Max deported, you know! All I have to do is call the American embassy, and they'll come get him and take him away and you'll never see him again!"

Arina shrugged. "Maybe. Often they do not like to take children away from mothers."

"God *damn* it, Arina!"

"What have you got to lose?" I found myself saying.

Jason gave me a look that was equal parts anger and bewilderment.

"What have you got to lose?" I repeated. "Deportation and custody battles are a messy business, and it could drag on for ages. Why don't you just do what Arina says and start with weekly Skype chats? What have you got to lose? At least this way you'll get to talk to Maks every week, and maybe you can reach an amicable settlement."

Jason's anger and bewilderment deepened, maybe from my tone of voice, maybe from the complicated phrase "amicable settlement."

"What she said," said Arina. "Why you not want to talk to us, Dzhey-son? You will not lose nothing from it."

Jason's mouth worked. I could tell that a lot of his distaste for the proposed arrangement was because other people—women!—were proposing it.

"Perhaps I should leave you two to settle this in privacy," I said.

"No!" said Arina. "I want you! You must—how you say it?" She switched to Russian. "I need someone to witness this," she said. "Marina is right: I can't be trusted not to trust him. And he behaves better with a witness. Please, Ro-eenna: be my witness."

"Um...okay. But I really can't do this every time."

"Oh. Okay." Arina's face fell. "I feel better around him with you there. But maybe Marina...although she hates him..."

The childish wailing that had been the background for the conversation suddenly reached a crescendo. A moment later, Marina came bursting back into the kitchen, Maks still clutched under her arm like a large and squirmy football.

"Here," she said in Russian, thrusting him into Arina's lap. "He keeps whining for his papa. I can't take it anymore."

Arina arranged Maks so that he was sitting upright in her lap, and brushed the tears off his face. "Say hi to your papa," she told him in Russian.

"Hi Daddy!"

"What do you think?" she asked him in Russian. "Would you like to talk to him every week?"

"In English!" Maks said in English. "I'm an American boy! I only want to speak English!"

"'Course you do, son," said Jason. "'Course you do. And I'm gonna get you home real soon, okay?"

Maks frowned. "I want to stay *zdes*," he said. "*Gde* I can go *katat'sya na sankakh*. With Mommy and *Tyotushkoi Marinoi*."

Jason looked like he'd been slapped.

"Talk about it next week," Marina said harshly in Russian. "You've talked enough for today. Talk more next week."

"He's forgetting his English!" exclaimed Jason.

Both Marina and Arina shrugged. "What you expect?" Arina asked in English. "We speak Russian at home. He wants to speak English, but he only hears Russian. And when I speak English with him, he cries and tells me that I speak wrong."

"What if he forgets all his English!"

"That's unlikely," I interjected, still wishing I weren't there. "He's young enough that he'll pick up whatever language is spoken around him with considerable ease for several more years. And if you speak with him every week, as Arina is suggesting, it will help him keep up his English in the meantime."

"Yeah...yeah...I gotta go now, buddy, okay? But I'll talk to you again next week, okay? I promise!"

"Okay." Maks waved at the screen with both hands again. "'Bye, Daddy!"

"'Bye, buddy!" Jason waved at the screen too, and then, clapping his hands over his mouth again, got up and half-ran out of the room.

"Well," said Marina, once he was gone. "I don't see what you see in him, Arina."

"He isn't all bad," said Arina. "He has his good side."

"Yes," said Marina sourly. "His passport." She looked up at me through the screen. "Thank you, Ro-eenna."

"Um, no problem," I said, not very truthfully.

"Can you do the same thing next week?" asked Arina.

"I really don't see why you need me. You'll be talking to him via Skype, so it's not like he can do anything really bad. I think I'll just get in the way."

"Maybe," said Arina and Marina together, with identical tones of skepticism. "We'll talk about it," Arina said, nodding at Marina with her chin. "And we'll let you know what we decide."

"Um, okay," I said. "But I might be busy."

"If I need you and you are busy, we'll find a better time," said Arina.

I ground my teeth a little. This had already taken up three Saturday mornings and a lot of emotional energy, and I had yet to see a dollar of the promised money. "I think you need to learn to talk to him without me," I said. "But of course I'll be happy to help as much as I can," I added, compelled by the look on Arina's face at the thought of talking to her husband on her own. Not that I could blame her. I'd look at least as horrified if Jason were my husband.

"Okay," said Arina. "We'll think about it and talk about it and let you know."

"Okay," I said, promising myself that I would come up with a good excuse not to participate in another of these charming talks when the time came.

"We have to go now," said Arina. "Goodbye, Ro-eenna. Until next time."

"Goodbye," I said, and disconnected the call before she could twist my arm into doing anything any more inconvenient than I had already done.

30

For once my worst expectations went pleasantly unfulfilled. I wasn't paid by Jason, but neither was I sucked into more awkward scenes between him and Arina. He came up to me after class the next week and told me, fidgeting and not looking me in the eye, that he and Arina had agreed to try weekly Skype calls, and that for the moment they didn't need me there to mediate.

"But we might later," he told me. "So I'll let you know, okay?"

I fought a short internal battle over whether or not to bring up the money. I needed it, and he had promised it, but as his professor I couldn't appear either greedy or vulnerable. I was supposed to be above such things as money, or at least have so much of it that I didn't need it from my students. Better not to mention it. Instead I said, "Of course I'm happy to help you in any way I can, but I really think there are more qualified people in this case. Have you considered bringing in a marriage counselor, for example? Surely there are counselors who would work with you on this."

Jason made a face. "They'd just take my money and tell me what a shitty husband I am. They wouldn't help me get Max back."

I bit back the response that Jason *was* a shitty husband, and maybe he needed to hear it until it sank in. "I think a marriage counselor would be much more qualified to help you than me," I said again instead. "I'm really not in a position to solve this kind of problem."

"But you know how *they* are!" he burst out, by "they" obviously meaning Eastern Europeans. "You know how to talk to 'em!"

"And you were married to one," I pointed out. "And still are, technically. And you have a half-Belarusian child. I think you're the expert."

"Max ain't Belarusian! He's American!"

I closed my eyes and prayed for strength. When I reopened them, Fatima was looming meaningfully at the door. "We need to clear out of the classroom now," I said.

"What?"

"It's time for the next class," I said. "We need to clear out so that the next class can come in."

Jason left with ill grace, and came and groused to me about the situation after every class session for the rest of the week, but stopped short of wheedling me into joining him and Arina on their shaky and, if I were being honest, probably doomed efforts at reconciliation. I felt sorry for Maks, who hadn't asked for any of this and was going to be traumatized no matter what, but so far losing his wife and child hadn't made Jason turn over a new leaf and become a more thoughtful, considerate person, so I wasn't sure if there was any hope for him.

Freed from dealing directly with Jason's problems, I was able to get ahead on my job applications, and even start work on an article. That was not a very rewarding occupation, however, so I was glad of the distraction provided by the need to prepare for the Crimson interview, which was finally scheduled as a Skype call for the afternoon of Friday, February 20.

That should have been no problem, since Skype had been working for me just fine, but the battery on my loaner phone from Alex decided that now was a good time to stop taking a charge. Over the course of a couple of weeks it had gone from charging up with sloth-like slowness, to working only when it was plugged into the wall.

I fretted for more than a week over whether or not to get a new phone, since that was not something in my budget, but when I thought of having an interview, especially for a job I actually had a good shot at getting, with no working phone as backup, I broke out into a cold sweat. I shouldn't throw away my future because I was too cheap to buy a new phone, right? I told myself it wasn't because I was too cheap, but just too broke, but I *did* still have some of Erik Johnson's guilt money from last semester stashed away for emergencies. Going into an important interview with no working phone counted as an emergency.

Accordingly, I spent several hours one fine Thursday afternoon—mid-February was already spring in Charlotte, and the daffodils were in full bloom under a warm sun—buying a new smartphone instead of working. Spending both the money and the time made me feel anxious and guilty, but it had to be done. Besides, as a single person I could think of it as my Valentine's Day present to myself.

I repeated that a number of times on my way to the store, while I was standing in the store, and on my way home. Then, when I got home and stood in the middle of my crappy apartment listening to Nevaeh scream, my new phone seemed ridiculously out of place. Surely something so shiny, new, and nice had no place here, or anywhere in my life. Surely I didn't deserve something this pretty and fully functional.

Luckily for me, my guilt over having something new and fully functional was ameliorated somewhat by my difficulties in using the new phone. It took several tries, by which time I was feeling a lot less in awe of it, to send a simple text to Alex telling him that I had gotten a new phone and that he was welcome to have his old phone back whenever he wanted it, although I had to confess about the bad battery.

Fuck, he texted back. *Why didn't you tell me? Now I feel like shit about saddling you with a broken phone.*

It worked when you gave it to me, I wrote.

Yeah, but it was a piece-of-shit phone then and it's only become shittier in the intervening months.

It was the best phone you had, I texted back. *So I appreciate the gesture.*

No, I kept the best phone I had for myself because I'm stupid and thoughtless like that. Do you want me to get it fixed for you?

Don't be silly, I texted him. *I just bought myself a new phone, courtesy of Erik Johnson's desire for expiation as expressed in monetary form. It was something I needed to do anyway. So I really appreciate you loaning me your phone as long as you have, but I'm happy to send it back to you any time you want.*

Yeah...that motherfucker still bothering you?

Erik Johnson? We emailed about Madison's summer plans for a while, but nothing's been definitively decided. I haven't heard from him in a couple of weeks.

And thank fuck for that. You're too good for him, Rowena, so stay far the fuck away from him.

I don't think he's actively dangerous, I texted.

You'd be surprised, Alex texted back. *Well, I suppose he's probably not a rapist or anything like that. But he's damn near as bad as. He uses people and tosses them aside like they're trash. Or maybe I'm just disgruntled and jealous.*

You don't need to be jealous of him, I wrote.

No?

He's got more money and power than we do, true, but I don't know that he's much happier. What does he really have that you don't that matters?

That remains to be seen, Alex texted back. *But I'm glad about the new phone, anyway. Does it have video?*

It should, if I can figure out how to work it.

So we could be chatting face-to-face instead of texting into the faceless ether?

In theory, yes.

Hmmm. I've got to go soon, dammit, but maybe we could try sometime soon? Could be fun. And that way I can really bitch and moan to my heart's content to someone who will nod sympathetically in all the right places.

Any time, I wrote.

Of course, I'd provide the same service to you.

Oh, I have no doubt! So do you want me to ship the old phone back to you?

Why bother? Hang onto it for a while. Maybe there will be a chance for you to give it back to me in person, without spending extra money and time at the post office.

It could happen! I wrote. *If you got a yen to see the fabulous sights of Charlotte, North Carolina, you could work in a side trip to pick up the phone :)*

Is that an invitation? :) Because I'd be down with accepting it.

My heart squeezed and skipped a beat. This long-distance semi-flirtation I'd had going on with Alex since I left New Jersey was nice. Alex was nice. Well, okay, he wasn't nice. He was smart, and intense, and honorable, and responsible, and an abrasive hothead who might or might not be able to avoid throwing away all the advantages he had and sabotaging his career. I wasn't sure whether I wanted to be in a relationship with him, or whether that would be a good idea, or what kind of relationship he had in mind. There were also a lot of practical reasons why getting involved with Alex would be a bad idea, since if we were to become a couple, there was a good chance that one of us would have to give up our career, and there was an excellent chance that that person would be me.

And part of me felt like it still belonged to Dima, and was disinclined to start anything with another man. I had a lot of flaws, and one of them was that I had always been the painfully faithful kind. Doing anything that smacked of cheating in even the tiniest way caused a wave of physical revulsion to wash over me.

But another part of me pointed out that it had been more than a year since Dima had broken off our engagement and told me to leave Russia and not come back. The brief textual interchanges we had had since then had always ended in him uttering some cryptic phrase and disappearing. I *should* move on, and Alex seemed like the best opportunity I had to do so.

It's an invitation if you want it to be! I texted.

I'd like that :) he wrote. *I've got this interview with the DLI hanging over my head—motherfuckers keep rescheduling it—but once that's taken care of, I could celebrate by coming down and visiting you. Maybe for spring break? When *is* your spring break?*

First week of March, I wrote.

Mine too! Okay, let's shoot for then, inshallah, but in any case, I am *definitely* coming down to see you :)

You must really want this phone :)

Among other things :) :)

Looking forward to it :) I texted. And right then, I was.

31

The middle of February was spent putting together a couple of applications for not very promising jobs, working on the article I had promised myself I would submit this semester, and keeping track of all my rejections. Via The Wiki, of course, since most places couldn't be bothered to respond to applications.

It was via The Wiki that I discovered that North Dakota had invited a couple of candidates for a second round of interviewing. I was not one of them. I was not surprised, and under other circumstances I wouldn't have been too displeased, but it did heighten my anxiety about my other prospects. What would I do if, for example, Alaska made me an offer before I had the interview with Crimson?

As is so often the case with worrying, fretting about that turned out to be a pointless waste of energy. By the time my interview with Crimson rolled around, on Friday, February 20th, Alaska had been maintaining complete radio silence with all their candidates for the better part of a month. I was so lucky not to have to fend off all their job offers, or so I tried to tell myself.

John and I had agreed that he would show up on Saturday afternoon, after seeing the person he was supposed to see in Gastonia. This in theory left me all week to prepare myself, with calmness and composure, for the Crimson interview, followed by a relaxing Saturday morning to ready the apartment for John's arrival.

It was a good plan, derailed only by my own frazzled nerves. I had decided to try doing the interview in my office again, since the construction zone had gone quiet over the last week. Ominously quiet, some might be tempted to say, but it still seemed better than trying my luck with Nevaeh, now suffering from severe colic according to Lakeesha, and Fevronia, who had also been in an exceptionally rare mood all week.

Which is how I found myself sitting anxiously in my campus office on a Friday afternoon, watching the clock crawl towards, and then past, 3:30, the time scheduled for the interview.

I started to chew my nails, and then slapped my hand to make myself stop. I tried to review my notes again. No good. I jumped up. Sitting still was intolerable. I was so thirsty...was I going to vomit? No, that wasn't vomit rising in my throat, it was a shriek of pure, unadulterated dread. I bit it back. When the gun-filled event that had caused Dima to break things off with me irrevocably had been happening, I hadn't wanted to scream then. When those mafiosi had come chasing me through the snowy streets in New Jersey last semester, I hadn't wanted to scream. I had wanted to outrun my pursuers, so that I could return and fight back. And I had.

But now I couldn't run, and I couldn't fight. I had to put myself deliberately in harm's way. No, that wasn't the way to think about it at all. I just had to answer a video call. But that was worse, because it meant waiting passively and hoping that everything worked and other people did the right thing.

For example, I had to hope that the computer was working. Why hadn't they called yet? I checked everything again. Was the speaker turned off? Was the app not loaded properly? Was everything set to some kind of mysterious silent mode? Was Skype not working at all? But in that case they would surely call. They had my phone number, didn't they?

I checked my phone. No missed call. Should I leave it on silent? Maybe I should turn the ringtone back on in case they were trying to reach me that way. But if I did, and they did contact me by Skype as we had originally agreed, I would probably in my haste and confusion forget to turn the ringtone on my phone back off, and the one phone call I got per week would be sure to happen right in the middle of the interview. Best to leave it off. At least the office was filled with welcome silence. The persistent jackhammering seemed to have finally stopped.

Skype went *bloop-bla-bloop* just as what sounded like a gunshot went off. I jumped, the shriek I was holding back leaking out around where I was biting my lips closed.

It's a nail gun! I told myself. *It's just a nail gun! Answer the call!* Moving with a calm deliberateness I didn't feel, I hit "Accept call" just as the sound of a nail gun switched to the sound of a power saw.

"Hello!" I realized I was shouting. "Sorry, there's a bit of background noise going on here. Can you hear me?"

A crackly voice said something indecipherable, and then cut out. The video had never switched on. I tried to switch it on at my end, but the call ended.

Aw crap! Now what? I was pretty sure the problem was at their end, not mine. What did I do? Did I try to call them back? Probably best to wait for a moment and let them sort out whatever their problems were. And calling first might seem forward and pushy. As the interviewee I was supposed to sit back and let them dictate the pace. Never one of my best skills, as Dima would no doubt attest...why was I thinking about sex with my ex right now? I looked at the computer clock. Less than a minute had passed. I checked my phone. They hadn't tried to call that way either. I should wait for another minute before trying anything. At least the power saw had gone quiet. For now.

Just when I was thinking maybe I should go ahead and try to call them myself before I gave into temptation and gnawed my fingernails down to the knuckle, my computer emitted another *bloop-bla-bloop* and the screen filled with Skype blue. When I hit "Accept call," a grainy, fuzzy picture appeared.

"Rowena? Rowena, is that you?" A face swam into view on the screen.

"Hi, I'm here!" The power saw chose that moment to let out another ear-splitting screech.

"Goodness, what was that?"

"Oh. Um, there's some construction on campus right now," I said. "I think that's a power saw."

"Oh." The face, which belonged to a middle-aged woman of a certain, very academic, sort, smiled a friendly smile. It almost looked genuine. "I thought maybe someone was practicing the bagpipes."

"Nothing that exciting, I'm afraid." I tried to say it with a smile. I must have succeeded, because the face smiled some more.

"Well, we'll just have to work around it, won't we? I suppose, now that we've got Skype working—*for now*—you must forgive us for our technical difficulties; I'm afraid that computers are not one of our better skills, which is one of the many reasons why we're looking to bring in some bright young scholars such as yourself. Not that we're planning to use you just for your technical know-how, of course!" She laughed. Other people I couldn't see laughed behind her. I tried to laugh along with them.

"Well—can you see me? Us? I can see you—can everyone see Rowena?"

The people I couldn't see all confirmed that they could see me. "I can mainly see the ceiling," I said.

"Oh! Oh dear. Here, let's try this. Is this any better?"

"Um, now I can mainly see the keyboard."

"Goodness, this is challenging! Jessica, do you want to give it a try?"

A hand blotted out everything else on the screen for a moment.

"Now I can see the room," I said.

"Well, that's an improvement I suppose, isn't it? Can we all scooch together, everyone, so that Rowena can see us? I'm afraid, Rowena, that you're our first interviewee, so we really don't have the details down yet."

"It's no problem," I said. "Glad to be of help." But I was fairly sure my words were drowned out by the sound of scooting chairs and another long banshee wail from the power saw.

Once all the chairs had been brought together into the computer's field of vision, I could see that there were five people on the committee. One, the middle-aged woman with the friendly smile, introduced herself as the committee chair, Theresa Mayfield, from French. Jessica was a younger woman, blonde and slightly plump, with an expression that suggested this was her first time on a search committee. She was from German, as was Klaus, an even blonder forty-something man sitting next to her. Then there was Akiko from Japanese, and Vadim, who was from Math but had been brought in because he was a native Russian speaker and could conduct the Russian-language portion of the interview.

"I know this might seem a bit strange to you, Rowena, but since we're a small college, we have to make do with what we can, and work interdisciplinarily much of the time," said Theresa. "As you may have noticed from our website, we have a bit of an unusual structure with the languages, in that we have a Department of Spanish and a Department of Modern Languages, which is, well, everything else."

"Except Latin and Greek," put in Klaus.

"Yes, of course, that's in Classics. Although there is some talk of changing things up a bit soon and creating a Department of Romance Languages, which would include Spanish, French, and

Italian, and a Department of, well, I'm not sure what. There was talk of creating a Department of Critical Need Languages, but where would that put German and Japanese? Or Greek?"

"Gone," said Klaus glumly.

"Oh, surely not! I'm afraid it hasn't been completely worked out yet, but for the *moment* we're all together in the Department of Modern Languages, as you see, although the College *is* very interested in promoting our critical need languages. Especially Arabic and Chinese, but Russian is also a part of that, so...well, that's why we're all here. Shall we start? Is everyone ready to start?"

Things went fairly normally after that. The picture kept breaking up, and there was a lag in the sound for about ten minutes in the middle of the interview, which at least kept them from hearing one last soul-rending wail from the power saw. After that the construction project switched back to nail guns, which made me jump every time but was still an improvement.

After going through the standard "tell me about your research" questions, the committee spent a lot of time quizzing me on why I thought I would be a good fit for a small private liberal arts college, given that my entire career had been at large state institutions. I blathered something about Russian being a small, intimate program no matter where you went, which seemed to please them. My connection with Georgia also seemed to please them. In fact, everything I said seemed to please them, except when Klaus became overcome with dourness, which happened about once every five minutes. Vadim went as far as to compliment me on my Russian, and to say how pleasant it would be to have another decent Russian-speaker on the faculty.

"And I was not expecting that, given your name," he said. "In fact, we almost did not consider you for the position at all because of your name. But you have confounded all expectations. Where did you learn Russian? Not in an American college, I can see that."

"As I may have mentioned"—it was on the first page of my CV, but pointing out that kind of thing was a big no-no—"I also lived in Moscow for several years while doing non-profit work."

"Ah!" said Vadim, Klaus, and Theresa together. Akiko nodded politely. Jessica looked miserable.

"No Russian husband?" Vadim asked with a smile that was only slightly nauseating.

"Alas, no," I said. "Despite my best efforts." I said it with a smile, and everyone laughed. Even me.

"Well, that is all very impressive," said Theresa. "It's been a pleasure, Rowena—what was that?"

"Now that *was* someone practicing the bagpipes," said Klaus. "We are in the same building as Music," he explained. "And our marching band has a bagpipe section. It is raining here today, so they practice inside."

"Well, I think that's our cue to end this conversation, pleasant as it has been," said Theresa. "Rowena, thank you *so* much, and I hope we get to speak again soon."

"So do I," I said, but my words were broken off when she abruptly terminated the call.

32

Having the Crimson interview behind me gave the whole world a nice warm glow, only partly related to the warm sunny late-February weather. I hardly cursed at all when my car stalled out at the intersection of Providence and Pineville-Matthews Road, and remained calm and cheerful when Lakeesha and Duane got into a big fight over whose turn it was to pay for diapers and formula. I also tried to repress my instinctive judgment against them for using formula and disposable diapers. I could hear my mother's voice telling me that at this rate, Nevaeh was going to be as obese as Lakeesha in 20 years. And she couldn't even sit up yet, and she was already wrecking the environment. Although when you don't have your own washing machine, cloth diapers must seem a lot less attractive, and the future of the planet awfully abstract. Speaking of the future of the planet, was this warm sunny weather a little *too* warm and sunny for February? It was 60 degrees outside. I even threw open a window in a vain attempt to get a little ventilation in my stuffy apartment.

Cleaning my tiny apartment the next morning took less than an hour, leaving me with plenty of time to do my asanas and forms and go for a long run, and even get a little work in too, before John came. I knew I needed to get all that done before he showed up. John had a way of filling up whatever space he was in with drama, and my guess was that this time was going to be even worse than usual. Good thing he was my brother, or I'd be tempted to toss him out on his ear. But instead, I waited as patiently as I could—he texted me twice telling me he was running late—for him to arrive.

I saw him pull up through the front window, and opened the door for him before he could get out of the car, not wanting him to knock and wake up Nevaeh, who was, for a change, blessedly silent. When John saw me and started to shout, "Hey Sis!" I held up my finger to my lips to shush him.

"What is it?" he whispered, coming up to the door. "Who're we hiding from? Are we under ambush?" He grinned, but his eyes were serious.

"A baby," I whispered. "Come on in."

John seemed to fill up the entire dinky little apartment when he stepped inside. He was only a couple of inches taller than me, but that was tall enough. And while I was willowy and slender, he was solid all over and broad through the chest and shoulders. He had the same dark hair I did, but his was buzzed short, making the gray that flecked it more evident than the few strands working their way through my shoulder-length hair. His face was more weathered than it had been the last time I'd seen him, with lines from stress and sun exposure showing clearly around his eyes, which were almost the same blue as mine, but tended to look hard rather than wary. Right now they were puffy and red, as if he had been drinking or crying.

"Come here, Sis," he said, pulling me into a one-armed hug. "Christ, it's good to see you. How long's it been? Sorry 'bout missing your graduation. That sucked. I shoulda been there. I know it was a big deal."

"That's okay," I said. "You wouldn't have enjoyed it anyway."

"Too fucking right, but that's not the point."

"Don't worry about it. It wasn't like you were trying to stay away. And I'm glad you could make it now. Here, let me show you the place."

"I think I've already seen all of it," John said, looking around.

"Well...yeah, pretty much. The bathroom's over there. I thought you could set up on the floor here in the living/dining room. My bedroom's through that door. We can switch if you want to sleep on a real bed, or take turns. I know you must be tired."

John held up a sack. "For $34.99 I got a fabulous inflatable queen-sized mattress that I'm sure will be as comfortable as most other beds I've slept on. And I can tell you now that I'm not expecting to spend a lot of nights here anyway."

I could feel my lips pinch together in exactly the way my grandmother's did when she disapproved of something. No doubt when I got to her age my lips would have exactly the same wrinkles hers did because of it.

"You're a big boy," I said, trying and failing to unpinch my lips. "Where you spend the night is up to you. Just remember that I'll be getting up early to go to work."

"I thought you had spring break."

"That's next week. And, um, I might have a guest then."

"Who?" John asked absently, scanning the apartment like he was half-expecting something bad to come leaping out of the cupboards. "Your friend, what's-her-name, Masha?"

"No. It's, um, a guy."

"Not *him*?!" John could rarely bring himself to say Dima's name. He looked down at my right hand, where I had worn the extremely cheap ring Dima had given me. "Your engagement ring's gone."

"I know. I took it off before I started that job last semester. You know, fresh start, all that kind of stuff."

"Did you sell it? Throw it away?"

"No. I carefully put it away in a jewelry box in my underwear drawer."

"Of course you did. At least you're not wearing it anymore. So who's this other guy? Another Russian who will break your heart and throw you away?"

"No. An American, actually."

This made John stop scanning the apartment for whatever dangers he was expecting it to contain, and look me full in the face. "Really?! Like, a boyfriend sort of guy?"

"It's complicated," I said.

"In my experience, it's rarely complicated, Ro, at least not as complicated as women want to make it. Are you sleeping with him?"

"That is currently under discussion," I said.

"Well shit, Ro, tell me about him. I'm all ears. This is the best news I've had all year."

"It's only February."

"Even so," he said with a grin. "It's been a year full of bad news. Is he another nerd like you?"

"Sort of," I said. "He teaches Arabic. And, um, you might not like this part, but..."

"Oh shit," said John. "Let me guess. He's Army?"

"Ex-Navy."

"Could be worse, then. I won't feel bad about asking him to give me a ride, at least."

"I can tell you two will get along famously," I said.

"Yeah, no doubt. So where's this cat I keep hearing so much about?"

"You don't like cats."

"I know. That's why I want to know where she is."

"She's probably hiding in the bathroom, or under the bed. And her name is Fevronia."

"Jesus, Ro, you're as bad as Mom for fancy-panty names."

"Fevronia was a medieval saint. She was supposed to be a magical healer, and very wise. And she's recently become the patron saint of family, love, and faithfulness."

"My point exactly. Also, Jesus Christ. Family, love, and faithfulness, huh?" John looked around again, but Fevronia stayed safely hidden. "Well, I'll meet her when I meet her, along with...what's his name?"

"Alex."

"Great. Can't wait to meet him. So where should I set up?"

We got John set up in the empty corner of the living/dining room where the couch would have gone if I had had one, which I didn't. John inflated the bed and arranged his things on the floor in good humor; he had a lot of flaws, but he wasn't whiny about roughing it.

"Okay, let's go get a beer," he said when he was done. "Let's go get ten beers. Where's good?" He walked over and opened the fridge. "Jesus Christ. What do you even eat, Ro?"

"Lentils," I said. "At 99 cents a pound. Delicious, nutritious, humane, environmentally friendly, and extremely affordable."

"Fuck that. We're going to get some real food. My appetite is finally coming back after all that doxycycline they made us take the entire time we were over there. I need food. *And* beer." He started opening all the cupboard doors. "At least you've got coffee. But not enough. We'll have to stock up on that as well. Because, in case you hadn't guessed, I'm planning to be really fucking hungover the entire time I'm here."

"If you want."

"You sound just like Grandma when she's doing her passive-aggressive thing." John closed the cupboard. The door swung back open, almost hitting him in the face.

"FUCK!" he shouted, slamming it shut so hard it bounced open again, narrowly missing his nose.

"How can you live like this, Ro!" He wasn't exactly shouting, but he wasn't exactly not shouting either. His breath was coming faster than it should have, and a different version of my brother, one who was feral and wild, was staring out of eyes that were almost the same color as mine.

"It's okay," I said gently. "Let's go out, okay, and get you whatever you want. I didn't get much because I figured you'd want to pick it out yourself anyway. And we can go someplace nice tonight if you'd like. We can go check out uptown, if you want. It's supposed to be nice, like a little Manhattan."

"Don't fucking placate me, Ro!"

Nevaeh suddenly started to cry. On top of John's shouting, her wails bored into my brain like a dental drill.

"Shut up, shut up, shut UP!" Duane screamed. "Shut up, God damn it, just SHUT UP!" A door slammed, bounced off the door frame, and slammed again. Angry feet stormed down the stairs next to my door. The crying upstairs died down to a pitiful whimper that sounded sustainable for several hours.

"Do you think he left the baby by itself?" asked John after a minute. His eyes had gone from feral back to serious.

We listened intently for a couple more minutes. No sound of anyone coming to comfort the baby. We exchanged uneasy glances.

"Maybe we should go check on her..." I said slowly.

"Probably," said John. "I'll go. You stay here. Let me take care of it."

"I didn't know you were such an expert on babies."

"I'm not. I just don't want you walking in there in case someone has a gun."

"If someone has a gun with the baby..."

"Then you need to be here to call 911 if someone gets shot."

"Okay. But try not to get shot."

"Yeah, sure. Be right back."

I heard John walk up the stairs and pound on the door. No one answered. He pounded on the door again. Still no answer, other than Nevaeh crying louder.

A car pulled into the lot, its engine sputtering unhealthily. A door creaked shut, too stiff to slam.

"Hey!" shouted Lakeesha. "What you doin' at my door?"

"I was just checking to see if someone was here with the baby," said John.

"You with the police?" demanded Lakeesha, climbing heavily up the stairs. "You from my cousin Ron?"

"No. Just a neighbor. We heard someone shouting, and then he left. We were concerned that the baby was alone."

"He *left*? That asshole left our baby?!?" Lakeesha's heavy tread on the stairs quickened. "Get outta my way!" she demanded.

"Let me know if you need any help with anything," said John. I could hear him step away from the door and start down the stairs. The sound of his footsteps didn't drown out Lakeesha's furious cursing as she struggled with her keys, forced open the door, dragged her groceries inside, and went over to Nevaeh. Even after she shut the door behind her, we could hear her angry outcries at the state of the baby, and the fact that she wouldn't shut up.

"Nice place you've got here," said John, once he was back inside. "Classy. I especially like your neighbors. You sure you don't want a gun?"

"So I could accidentally shoot the baby through the ceiling?"

"Chances of actually hitting it are slim."

"I'd rather not risk it."

"Yeah, whatever. Of course. What are you gonna do, rely on Fevronia the cat to protect you?"

On cue, Fevronia came out from wherever she had been hiding, gave John a jaundiced look, hissed, and fled.

"Yes," I said.

"Your funeral, Ro." John looked around some more. "Let me guess: there's no whiskey in this dump?"

"Not a drop. But there's an ABC store in the shopping center across the street. It'll probably be open for a little while longer."

"Well, what're we waiting for?" John held up his keys and grinned. Both the feral rage and the cold hardness that had peered out from his eyes earlier had receded, covered up by something almost warm. "Put on something nice, and let's go. My treat."

"I can..."

"No you can't. My treat, Ro. It'll do you good to get out of this dump and have some fun for a change."

I thought that my idea of fun was fairly different from John's, but arguing over it would only make both of us unhappy, so, after I convinced him that I was already wearing the nicest clothes I owned, we left to go sample the fabulous delights of Charlotte.

33

John insisted on taking his car, which he drove aggressively, making angry outbursts at drivers he thought were too slow or cutting him off, while cutting off other drivers himself. He steered one-handed, using the other hand to smoke a cigarette down to the nub in the short trip across the street to the shopping center.

He cheered up a little as we were actually picking out groceries, which he insisted on paying for himself, and even more when we made it into the ABC store just in time to get—I winced while he wasn't looking—two bottles of whiskey.

"You want anything?" John gestured around the store. The presence of so much alcohol was making him looser, more expansive. Even his eyes were almost smiling. "What is it you drink, anyway? Vodka? Or something girly?"

The truth was that if I had to drink hard liquor, I preferred it in a way that John would call "girly," meaning diluted with fruit juice. But really I would prefer not to drink hard liquor at all. I had built up a bit of a tolerance while I was in Russia, and kept it up while I was in grad school in order to impress the weaklings who'd never lived in Russia, but that had been one of the few parts of my Russian experience I had been glad to let go. Too bad John didn't feel the same way. The only thing I liked less than getting drunk myself was dealing with drunk men.

"I'm okay," I said.

"Wuss," said John with an affectionate grin. "Come on, Ro, let's go." He took my hand and pulled me out of the store and back to the car in a way that was just short of creepily boyfriend-y. If I made a fuss and made him drop my hand, that would only cause more of a scene, so I let him deposit me into the car in silence.

"Okay, now where?" he asked, throwing himself into the driver's seat and lighting up another cigarette. "Where's good around here?"

"You like Irish pubs, right?"

"I don't hate them," he agreed. "That sounds good."

"There's one uptown that's supposed to be nice. We could go there if you like."

"Let's do it."

"Okay. Would you mind stopping at that ATM up there on the way? I should get some cash if we're going to go out."

"I told you it was my fucking treat, Ro."

"Yeah, but you're my guest, and you just bought all those groceries..."

"It's my treat." John's mouth was pinched in the same thin line mine had been in earlier.

"Okay, well, in that case, thank you. But I need to get a little cash out anyway, just, you know, to have."

"Okay. On one condition."

"Yes?"

"Hand me that bag. Yeah, the one on the back seat."

I got what was definitely not a purse but some kind of a manly, soldier-y sort of a travel case out of the back seat and handed it to John. He opened it up, took out a checkbook, and started to write a check.

"What are you doing?" I asked.

"I'm writing you a fucking check, Ro, what the fuck does it look like I'm doing? I'm paying this month's rent."

"That's very kind of you, but you really don't need to do that."

"Yeah, I do."

"I can pay my own rent."

"No, you can't."

"*And* you're my guest!"

"Yeah, and I'm going to be the guest from hell. Let me make it up to you a little bit."

"You really shouldn't..."

"Take the fucking check, Ro." He pushed the check into my hand, harder than necessary. A muscle was twitching in his right cheek.

"Okay," I said. "I'll accept it on one condition."

"Yeah? What's that?"

"That you take a key to the apartment. I don't want to have to be hanging around waiting to let you in and out at all hours of the night."

The twitch in his cheek turned into something like a smile. "It's a deal."

"Great. And, you know, thank you. I'll just...I'll just deposit it, then, and we can go."

John managed to smoke down most of one cigarette while I was depositing the check, and another one as we made our way through the Saturday evening traffic uptown. I took shallow breaths, the better to avoid asphyxiation from second-hand smoke, and reminded myself that I used to ride around in Moscow's nightmare traffic all the time. Although to be honest, I had generally tried to avoid taking a car. In general, I had taken the metro. Which, aside from the occasional terrorist attack, tended to be pretty calm and safe. Unlike John. Who was lighting up a third cigarette, making it four in the past hour.

"What?" he demanded, looking over at me. "Move it, fucking move it!" he shouted at the driver in front of us, who was being too tentative about pulling out into a complicated intersection involving multiple streets named Queens. "What?" he said again, looking back at me. "Don't give me that look, Ro. You know I smoke."

"I wasn't giving you a look."

"And doesn't what's-his-fuck smoke too?"

"He quit. Well, and then he started up again, while he was, um, in jail."

"Jesus fucking Christ!" I couldn't tell whether the outburst had been prompted by news of Dima's jail time, or the car that cut in front of us. I closed my eyes and sent out a prayer to St. Fevronia. I wasn't a believer, but that didn't stop me from praying at moments like this. I wished I had taken the tiny icon of her I kept on top of my dresser and stuck it in my purse for the journey.

St. Fevronia must have been listening, because we made it to uptown without a car crash or another explosion from John. He even accepted the exorbitant parking prices without comment, and appeared to be in a good mood as we walked down Trade Street to the Irish pub.

He cheered up even further when we ordered, and asked me with every evidence of interest about my classes as he downed his first pint of Guinness. The second mellowed him even more, and by the third he was almost my brother again.

"What do you think?" he asked, once the food had been brought. He nodded over to the bar.

"I think Queens Park Rangers are screwed," I said.

"What?"

"That's what's playing on the TV at the bar," I said. "A football match. And I think Queens Park Rangers are getting relegated."

"Oh, whatever. I was talking about her. The blonde sitting at the corner. What do you think?"

I tried to eye up the blonde woman sitting at the corner of the bar without making it obvious. "I don't know," I said cautiously. "Other than she wears a lot of makeup."

"That's a good sign, don't you think?"

"Um...a good sign for what?"

"That she's looking for a good time." John grinned.

"Possibly. You're not really thinking...?"

"Why not? What else you think I'm planning to do while I'm here on leave?" He wasn't exactly slurring his words, but he was no longer biting them out the way he had earlier, and his whole face was looser. I wished it made me feel better.

"I suppose," I agreed reluctantly. "Although she looks a bit...cheap, for want of a better word."

"Shit, Ro, I just dropped over a thousand big ones on you. The rest of my dates had better be cheap." He laughed. "Don't give me those eyes, Ro! You know I did it 'cause I wanted to. And now I'm about to do this 'cause I want to. How much you wanna bet I'll be able to find someone hot to 'thank me for my service' before we leave this place?"

"I'm not going to bet," I said. "I'm sure you'll win."

"Well, here we go." He winked at me and ambled over to the bar.

I tried to focus on how Hull was beating Queens Park Rangers on the TV instead of how John had—how did he do it?—struck up a conversation with the blonde who I was unable, despite all my feminist training, to see as anything other than cheap.

I got plenty of time to contemplate my own hypocrisy, and watch the second half of the match, while John talked with the blonde. Once the match was over, though, and the waiter had cleared away all the dishes and was asking if I needed anything else with that solicitous manner that meant I'd better vacate the table ASAP, I decided to go over and ask John what he was planning to do for the rest of the evening. I would be small and polite and unthreatening to the cheap blonde as I told John that I would call a cab and go home on my own.

My plan was derailed when someone took my arm just as I was sliding up next to John. I shook off the offending hand, but the motion caught John's attention.

"What the fuck you doing, man!" he demanded, abruptly leaving off his flirtation with Ms. Cheap Peroxide to lean around me and get in the other man's face.

"Sorry, bro, sorry—didn't realize she was your date," slurred the other man. He looked like a banker. Apparently uptown Charlotte was crawling with them, even after the financial meltdown.

"*That's* my date." John nodded at the cheap blonde. "This is my kid sister, asshole! Watch where you're putting your hands."

"It's okay." I smiled conciliatorily at John and at the other man. "No worries. I was just coming to tell you I'm going to catch a cab and go home. You stay here and have fun."

The other woman, whose eyes had narrowed at my approach, was now looking at John like a cat at cream. His outburst had only made her lick her lips in excitement. I sent out another quick prayer to God, St. Fevronia, and anyone else who might be listening, to let me get out of here quick, and to get John back home safely without any assault charges, run-ins with irate husbands, or STDs.

"Like hell," John was saying. "Like hell I'm gonna let you go home in a cab by yourself. Here." He fished out his keys and tossed them to me. "Take my car. I'll make my own way home."

For a moment I wanted to argue, but then I saw the two more empty pints on the bar in front of him, and I decided that me driving his car was vastly preferable to him driving his car, so I nodded politely to the blonde woman, wished them both a good time, and left.

34

John came stumbling in around two in the morning. I might have managed to sleep through that, but a few minutes later, Nevaeh started to scream, and screamed non-stop until four. As far as I could tell, Duane was still gone, which was probably a good thing, but Lakeesha's tearful entreaties to Nevaeh to be quiet were as clear as if she were in the bedroom with me, and her heavy tread on the floor above me was even louder than if she'd been walking on my own floor.

I got up after a couple of hours of fitful sleep, and decided that going for a run would make me feel better. I ran for over an hour, savoring the spring flowers that were now in heavy profusion and the Sunday morning lack of traffic on Pineville-Matthews Road.

When I got back, John was just getting up.

"I was gonna take a shower," he mumbled, his voice sounding like he must have smoked at least ten more cigarettes last night. "But it looks like you need one."

"You go first." The odor of a wild night out was, I decided, more offensive than my sweat from a good honest run.

"You sure?"

"Yes. Go. I'll start coffee."

John trudged into the bathroom. A moment later there was a hoarse shout that, if he ever asked me, was definitely not a feminine shriek.

"God DAMN it!" The bathroom door banged open and John came tripping out, trying to shake Fevronia off of his calf.

"Your fucking cat attacked me! She jumped out from behind the toilet and fucking chomped down on me like a motherfucker!"

Laughing would be very, very wrong. "It's a game she likes to play," I said, keeping my face as still as possible. "Here, let me get her off you." I knelt down on the floor and got Fevronia to transfer her grip from John's calf to my forearm, which she promptly latched onto like a furry fanged limpet.

"She likes to hide and then jump out and get you," I explained. "And she likes to grab you and hang on, but she doesn't normally draw blood. Well, not a lot. It's just a game. Well, sort of a game."

"Jesus fucking Christ!" John was breathing heavily, his eyes dilated. Veins stood out on his neck and forearms. "God damn it to fucking hell!" He made an indeterminate movement with his hands, like he didn't know whether to hit me or hug me. His hands had, I noticed, started to shake.

"Why don't you go take a shower," I said gently. "I'll keep Fevronia from molesting you. And then we can have some coffee."

"Yeah." He took a deep breath. "Yeah. Yeah, that sounds good." He spun around on his heel and stalked back into the bathroom.

When he came out, both his smile and his scent were fresh and clean. Even the sight of Fevronia skulking under the table, and the sound of Nevaeh breaking out into piercing wails, failed to dampen his cheer as he drank two cups of coffee in quick succession and then tore into the bag of bagels he'd gotten last night.

His good humor ended abruptly when he discovered that I didn't have a toaster.

"Why don't you have a fucking toaster, Ro? How can you not have a fucking toaster? I thought you had a fucking toaster!"

"I did when I was living in Bloomington. I found one at the scrap exchange and took it home for a couple of years. But it broke right about the time I was getting ready to move, so I threw it away."

"That was almost a year ago."

"And I've moved twice since then, and will have to move again in a couple of months. Adding to my pile of stuff I have to haul around with me isn't attractive. Plus, I can't afford a toaster."

"How the fuck can you not afford a toaster, Ro! I know they don't pay you shit, but Jesus Christ!" Nevaeh's screaming meant we had to raise our voices in order to be heard. Maybe that's why we were both falling into a shouting argument over a toaster.

"It is what it is," I said, busying myself with the coffee pot so that I wouldn't shout at him or burst into tears.

"How much *do* they pay you, anyway?"

"Not very much," I said.

"Come on, Ro, give me a number."

"It's none of your business." The thought of telling John how little I was making felt icky. It was like confessing to being pressured into providing sexual favors or something. I couldn't help but feel that he would see me as dirty and tainted after he found out, and I also couldn't help but feel that I was somehow at fault. Which I was. I had agreed to all of this of my own free will. Not only that, I had actively pursued it. Well, not this exactly, but a job in this field, yes.

"What is it: six thousand a course? Eighteen thousand for the semester?"

I laughed in spite of myself.

"Fifteen thousand for the semester?"

I laughed again. "No, that's what I made last semester. I've gone down in the world since then."

"Well Jesus Christ, what is it, then?"

"$3,200 per course," I said in a small voice. "So $9,600 for the entire semester. No benefits, no possibility of renewal."

"Jesus Christ." John went silent. "And thank fuck for that," he said after a moment. "If you reupped on a deal like that, I'd come and drag you away by the hair myself, Ro."

"Yeah. But it's $9,600 more than I've got in the pipeline for next semester."

"Fuck." John went silent again. Nevaeh's screams went silent too, thank God.

"How'd we get here, Ro?" he asked, once we had both savored the quiet enough. "I mean, both of us? Because speaking for myself, this was definitely not my Plan A. I mean, it kinda was, but I thought Plan A would be more fun, and involve...fuck, I hate to sound like a sap, but, you know, a hot wife and a kid or two that would go and make me proud at The Citadel when the time came, and definitely not be hippies like Mom and Dad. Plan A didn't involve being an asshole to my only sister and picking up whores at bars. Not once I was in my thirties, anyway."

"Was that woman last night actually a prostitute?"

"She didn't ask for money. She just gave it away for free. Kind of like you, Ro. Shit! I didn't mean it that way. Actually, I kinda did. You've gotta stop giving yourself away for so little, Ro. You're worth more than that."

"Haven't you heard of market forces?" I asked. "I'm getting my agreed-upon value on the free market."

"Fuck that, then. You need to make yourself more valuable, Ro. That needs to be your Plan A, not this shit."

"Yeah," I said. "This was definitely not Plan A."

"Yeah? What was your Plan A?"

"Plan A was to save the world," I said. "Plan B was to marry Dima and raise a beautiful bilingual family in a charming dacha outside of Moscow, which we were going to finance in some way that was definitely not illegal. Becoming a world-renowned professor and making a lasting contribution to scholarship was only ever Plan C."

"So what's this?" asked John.

"I think this is Plan F. Fuck up and fail."

John smiled painfully. "You're supposed to be the smart one, Ro. How'd you end up executing Plan F?"

I shrugged. "I don't know. It just happened."

"Well, stop it! Get back to Plan A. Or even, God help us, Plan B. You know what I think of *him*, but I'd sure as fuck rather see you raising a family than wasting yourself on this shit. And, you know, maybe he would have been a good father."

"Maybe," I said.

"What? Is that doubt? Is Rowena Halley expressing doubt in the virtue of the saintly fucking Dima—what's his last name? I never can remember these fucking exotic names."

"Kuznetsov," I said. "It means 'Smith' in Russian. Being named Dima Kuznetsov is like being named Dave Smith. Not exotic at all."

"If you fucking say so. And I always thought he could do no wrong in your eyes. Be poor as dirt? He was following a higher calling. Get arrested? He was following his conscience and fighting for truth, justice, and the Russian way, or some shit like that. Send you packing after you'd given him the best years of your life? He was acting in your best interest."

"I'd hate to think that those were the best years of my life," I said.

"You know what I fucking mean, Ro. The years you should have been making babies."

"I don't think those years are entirely behind me."

"Yeah, but there aren't that many of them left, are there?"

"Maybe I have a higher calling than making babies."

"Like what? Teaching stupid fuckups who don't give a shit how to say 'Hello, my name is Brittany' for less than minimum wage?"

"There's more to it than that."

"Yeah, whatever. But that's what it boils down to. And none of those Brittanys and Courtneys and Shemekahs and Taylors are going to give a shit about you, not now, not ten years from now, not ever."

"Some of them might," I said.

"Yeah, but most of them won't."

"Okay. Fine. But the truth is that, no matter how much I might have told you that I wanted to get married and have children, I didn't. In fact, I very carefully managed my life to make sure that didn't happen. Getting married isn't hard, and having babies is easier done than said. How many girls do you know like Lakeesha upstairs, who have babies they don't want and didn't intend to have?"

"Too many to count," said John. "They're pretty much a dime a dozen. While *you...*"

"While I didn't. On purpose. I spent a lot of time, money, and effort, not to mention blood, sweat, and tears, on *not* having a baby. Because I didn't want one enough to let it ruin the rest of my life. And as much as I wanted to be married, I didn't want to be married to just any man. I wanted to be married to the right man, or none at all. And that's still true. And besides, Plan B is a selfish plan. The world doesn't need more babies, so the only reason to have one is because you think it will make you, personally, happier. And it sure looks like most people find that having babies doesn't make them happier at all."

"Even so, being alone fucking sucks, Ro. You know it as well as I do. Plan B might be selfish, but at least it still gives you a chance at happiness, which the other plans don't. I'd still say go with Plan B over any of the others. And if you want to make it happen, it's pretty much now or never."

"So, what: you're saying I should have stayed with Dima? He sent me away, John! He sent me away! He said he didn't want to have anything to do with me anymore! You know how you said he chose Putin over me? Well, it's true! When it came right down to it, he chose politics and obsession and adrenaline and all that bad stuff that he couldn't break free of, over me! When it came right down to it, he was the most important thing in my life, but I was the second most important thing in his life! Or not even that. I was down somewhere around thing number five."

"He might not have had a choice, Ro. Or felt like he did."

"Of course he fucking had a choice!"

"Yeah, but...you gotta understand, Ro: this kind of stuff is really tough for men."

"Like's it not really tough for women!"

"Yeah, but it's tougher for guys. You can't understand the kind of pressure guys face over this kind of thing."

I debated the wisdom of pointing out to John that he always got angry and dismissive when I told him that women had a different experience in some things than men, or that there were things that were harder for women than for men. But we'd had this discussion before, and it never ended with him seeing my point of view, or recognizing his own inconsistency in insisting that men had to go through tough things that women couldn't possibly understand, but not the other way around.

Arguing with him about it yet again probably wouldn't make him see the light this time either, and it would just make me angrier than I already was, and remind me of how lopsided our relationship was and how I was always having to be the bigger, more forgiving, man. Certainly Tsvetaeva and Akhmatova had had some harsh things to say about the relative strength of brotherly versus sisterly love. As I recalled, Akhmatova weighted sisterly love as a thousand times more powerful. And sometimes I had to agree. Because whenever I talked to John about relationship stuff, or any kind of problems I was having with men, his number one goal was never to sympathize with me but to make me sympathize with the guy. Even guys he didn't like, like Dima, got more sympathy from him than

I did. It was the same with my dad, although he would no doubt deny it vigorously if I pointed it out to him. In fact, it was the same with most men I knew. Most men I knew had some kind of terror/fantasy of a conspiracy of women, but it was men who seemed to be in cahoots with each other, even if they didn't know it. But telling John all that would only make him deny the truth even harder.

"What do you want to do today?" I asked instead.

"You probably have to prep for classes or something like that, don't you?"

"I prepped for Monday's classes on Friday. But I do have some job apps I should do."

"Anything good?"

"They're all better than this."

"Sounds like fun."

"Sort of." In fact, it felt like my life had become a series of terrible things I had to accomplish as quickly and accurately as possible. I woke up every morning dreading pretty much everything on my to-do list, and went to bed at night glad that they were over. Glad that part of my life was over, never to return. "It needs to be done," I said.

"Okay then. I'll get out of your hair and go...I don't know, find out what there is to do here. Go hiking or something. And I'll take you out to dinner again tonight, and I definitely won't get drunk and pick up cheap women until after you're in bed, okay?"

"It's a deal," I said.

35

John was as good as his word, disappearing for most of the day and allowing me to submit another job application in peace. And when he returned from, he announced, trail running on Crowders Mountain, and took me out to dinner again, he was his most easy-going self. Even his cursing sounded good-natured.

He continued to keep his cool when we got back and found Duane walking Nevaeh around the parking lot, trying and failing to quiet her piercing screams.

"Sorry 'bout all the ruckus," said Duane. His eyes looked like two deep bruises from tiredness, and maybe from Lakeesha punching him in the face, which seemed all too likely. His hair, which was normally the neatest thing about him, was frizzing out of its braids, some of which were coming undone. "She won't sleep for nothin', and I know she's keepin' everyone else up too, but there ain't nothin' I can do 'bout it."

"It's okay," said John. There was still no flash of temper in him at all. "We all know how babies can be. And they say it's all worthwhile, in the end. Being a father will turn your life around, give you something you've never had before."

"Shit," said Duane. "They keep tellin' me that bein' a father's gonna change my life, but it ain't happened yet. I keep waitin', and the only difference I see is I ain't sleepin'. The way they kept talkin', you'd think angels'd come down, singin' in a choir and all, when your baby gets born, but that ain't what happened at all. All that happened was Lakeesha screamed and cussed for twelve hours straight, damn near broke my hand squeezin' it, and then out popped this little mouse"—he give Nevaeh a look of mingled tenderness and resentment—"who don't hardly look like me nor anyone else, and she started screamin' and cryin' all the time, when she's not shittin' up her diapers, that is, and it's just as shitty as it sounds, and I ain't changed a bit. I'm still the same person I always was, just cranky and mean as hell 'cause I ain't sleepin.'"

"Yeah." John smiled. "That's the way it is, sometimes, with the things that matter the most. They don't seem like much fun at all when you're going through them. It's only afterwards that you appreciate them."

"It's gonna have to be a long damn time afterwards for me to appreciate this," said Duane.

"Duane! DU-AAAAANE! Get up here!" Lakeesha stuck her head out the door and shouted. Nevaeh, who had almost fallen silent, started shrieking again.

"What the fuck you shoutin' for, woman?!" Duane yelled.

"I need you to get your ass to the store and get more diapers! I done tol' you twice, and you still ain't done it!"

Duane made a face.

"We'll let you go," said John. "That sounds like an important mission. We wouldn't want to hold you back."

"Important mission, my ass," muttered Duane, but he took Nevaeh upstairs and, a few minutes later, set off on foot towards the shopping center. Nevaeh continued to scream through the ceiling.

"Gosh," I said. "It's times like this that I'm particularly sorry to have passed on the joys of motherhood."

"You'd be a better mother than that, Ro, you know that. And you sure as hell wouldn't be such a bitch to your husband. And you wouldn't want to because you'd have a better husband, anyway."

"That's not fair to Lakeesha and Duane. I'm sure they're doing the best they can."

"Yeah, that's the scariest thing. The best they can do is shit. Your best would be much better."

"Maybe. My baby would still cry, though. And I might"—I shuddered, only partly joking—"become one of those parents who thinks their parenthood is more important than anyone else's anything."

"My, my. Is that bitterness I detect? You're not about to break your oath and complain about your sisters in solidarity, are you?"

"I didn't say they were all women."

"No, but I'd bet my car that most of them are."

"Well...yeah. But mainly because fathers can get away with a lot more irresponsibility."

"Fathers have lots of responsibility," said John, starting to heat up at this sign of my lack of sympathy for the heavy plight of men.

"Yeah," I said. "But somehow it's mothers who end up being the ones to take time off work and inconvenience others in order to go take care of their kids when they're sick or something. And I understand why they do that, and I'm willing to do my part to help out—but I end up pulling a lot of their weight on top of my own, it seems. It's always assumed that what they're doing outside of work is so much more important than what I'm doing. *And* that I can never understand their feelings and experience what they experience, as if parental love is some completely different thing from every other human emotion. As if love for other family members, or a spouse, or a friend, or a pet, or a comrade, or your country, or any of those things, doesn't count at all. I've had people telling me my whole life how being a parent will turn your life around and make you a better person, but none of them seem to be better people from it. It's like Duane just said: you're still the same person you always were, just more sleep-deprived. They say being a parent makes you a less selfish person, but as far as I can tell, parental love is the most selfish of all. And I don't want to have to become a parent to be a good person. I want to be a good person all on my own."

"Yeah," said John. "Well, I don't think you've got anything to worry about there, Ro. I think you're a pretty good person all on your own, already. Too good, some of us might say. After all, you're making the rest of us look bad. Thank God you've got just enough sanctimoniousness to keep you from becoming completely fucking unbearable."

"Jeez," I said. "Thanks for the sympathetic ear, and the vote of confidence."

"You better take what you can get, 'cause this is as good as it gets from me, babe. Speaking of which, I'm going back out. Don't wait up for me."

"Do I even want to ask where you'll be going and what you'll be doing?"

"No. You don't, Ro. You stay here and think saintly thoughts, and I'll go out and make sure that the world still needs people like you."

"I suppose that's a deal," I said doubtfully.

"It's the best deal you're gonna get. And Ro?"

"Yes?"

"Wish me luck." He grinned, but his smile didn't reach his eyes.

36

John came in at one in the morning, waking me up mere minutes, it seemed, after Nevaeh had finally gone quiet and I'd managed to fall asleep. Since it was Monday morning, AKA a workday, I felt no compunction about waking him up at 6:00am when I got up to go for a run. Well, hardly any compunction.

I was still convincing myself I felt no compunction about disturbing his rest as I got dressed to leave for campus. Especially given how grumpy he was in the morning. So I wasn't too worried when he suddenly shouted, "Ah fuck!"

"What is it?" I called from the bedroom.

"There's some gross shit...it's vomit! Ro, your cat has barfed all over the kitchen! And...fuck, what IS that?!"

I came running into the kitchen. Fevronia strolled over, and in a fit of unusual friendliness, rubbed her ears against my calf as I examined the pool of vomit on the kitchen floor.

"I think it's a worm," I said.

"It's still moving!"

"It's a live worm."

"Jesus! I've seen some gross, fucked-up shit, but..."

"Give me a paper towel," I said. John continued to go on and on about how gross it was while I cleaned up the vomit, including the worm in its death throes, and put everything in the trash.

"I guess you need to go to the vet," I said to Fevronia when I was done. "You're probably due for your shots and stuff anyway. She was vaccinated, dewormed, the whole nine yards, when I got her from the shelter," I explained to John. "But that was over a year ago now. I knew she was due to have it done again, but I kept putting it off, hoping that money would come showering out of the sky and make it more affordable. And at our last place she kept catching mice. Which was nice, but she probably picked up worms from it."

"Well, it's your lucky day, baby, because—"

"You've already showered me with money," I said.

"And I can keep on making it rain, babe, if that's what you need."

"Ew. Please. Save it for your, um, romantic companions."

"I don't have romantic companions, Ro," said John. "Just married women looking for adventure."

"I was trying to put an elegant spin on it. And while I appreciate all your generosity, I can pay for my own cat's vet visits."

"You just said you couldn't."

"Yeah, but since you forced me to take this month's rent from you, I can. I've just been too lazy to do anything about it."

John inhaled deeply in exasperation, and then broke into a gagging fit. The odor of cat vomit was still strong in the airless kitchen.

"Fuck, you could weaponize that shit," he said when he could talk again. "One sniff of that and the enemy would drop in their fucking tracks. I think it's worse than when they teargassed us in basic."

"For crying out loud," I said. "It's just a little vomit. Actually, more like regurgitation, if I understand correctly."

"With a live fucking worm in it!"

"The worm didn't actually smell. And the rest was just lightly digested cat food. Kind of like ceviche. You know, fish marinated in acid. If we'd left it, she'd probably have re-eaten it after an hour or two."

"Jesus Christ, Ro! Now I'm never going to be able to eat fucking ceviche ever again!"

"I didn't know you liked ceviche."

"I don't. But it impresses the hell out of the ladies when you order it."

"You're a Marine. Your uniform is enough to get every woman who comes your way to fall into your bed, as you like to remind everyone around you at least once an hour. I don't see the need to force-feed yourself raw fish on top of that. Stick out your chest, firm your jaw, and declare you don't eat that wussy shit."

"Nothing wussy, only pussy," said John, with a wicked grin.

"You're a poet and you don't know it!"

"Maybe I should start advertising that as well. Might get me a better class of married lady."

"Or even unmarried ladies," I said. "You could branch out."

"Nah. Married ladies are better."

"Why? Because there's no future with them?"

"Yep, got it in one."

"You know, you keep going on at me about how I need to make a family, blah blah blah. Maybe you need to turn a little of that on yourself. Make that your Plan A, like you said you wanted."

John's face closed up. "Maybe when I retire," he said.

"That might be leaving it a little late."

"I mean from the service. Which won't be very long from now at all."

"Yeah, but why wait? Why not start looking now? You know, start training yourself to seek out desirable and eligible partners, instead of...you know."

"I don't think so."

"But..."

"Leave it, Ro."

"You won't leave it when it's me. Why should I leave it for you?"

"I said fucking leave it, Ro!"

Fevronia, who had been following me around like a puppy as I had been cleaning up the vomit, maybe because she was seeing me as in loco parentis, maybe because she was hoping to snatch a mouthful of vomit before I disposed of it, stopped rubbing on me to give John an evil look and hiss at him.

"And you too! Fucking leave it, you goddamn hell-cat!" John made as if to swat at Fevronia.

"Don't!" I shouted, just as Fevronia sank her fangs into his hand. He shouted and tried to shake her off, which only made her dig in deeper.

"Stop it! Stop it!" I told him.

"Get your fucking cat off of me!"

"Stay still!" I disengaged Fevronia from John's hand, a process made much more difficult than it should have been by his swearing and struggling. When I finally managed it, Fevronia hissed at him and, with another look of supreme evil, ran off to hide under the bed.

"You should take that fucking cat to the pound, Ro! Before she kills us all!"

"She doesn't normally attack me. Only people who piss her off. Well, okay, she's been attacking me a lot recently, but she has a reason to be in a mood. She has worms, remember? She must feel awful. She'll probably become much more reasonable just as soon as she's dewormed."

"That's no fucking excuse! She's a fucking maniac!"

Don't shout at him! "But she's mine," I said, as calmly as I could manage. "She's the only person I've got who's always there for me, and always mine."

"That's really fucking pathetic, Ro!"

Do NOT respond in kind! "Let's get you cleaned up," I said, instead of all the things I was really thinking. "I've got some Band-Aids and stuff in the bathroom. Let's get you cleaned up and bandaged before you get blood on your clothes."

"I got it." John looked down at the drops of blood welling out of the fleshy pad below his thumb. "Just a fucking flesh wound anyway. Your stuff in the medicine cabinet?"

"Yep."

"Okay. I'll go take care of it. And, Ro?" He punched me lightly in the shoulder. "Nice attack dog you got there." He grinned, his rage dissipating like it had never been. "Now that I think about it, you should keep her. No one's gonna fuck with you while she's around to protect you."

"Yeah." I thought about saying that cats rarely made good guard dogs, but that seemed like just asking to reignite the argument, so I smiled and said, "You're right," instead.

37

I got Fevronia to a vet on Tuesday, and even managed to get the dewormer down her afterwards. She spent most of Tuesday and Wednesday in a huge snit, and then on Wednesday evening suddenly cheered up and stopped attacking us.

This was good, because John continued to pick plenty of fights on his own. Something was eating him, and in true John fashion, he was doing his best to spread the misery around as much as possible. He groused about my job, about my apartment, about my prospects or lack thereof, about the women he picked up every night, and every other thing he could think of to grouse about. By Friday afternoon I went so far as to suggest that if he hated it that much here with me, he should go home.

"Fuck no," he said. "I got told not to come back till I got my attitude under control."

"Did they offer, I don't know, counseling?" I asked.

He gave me a look that could have etched glass. "Of *course* they offered me fucking counseling, Ro. This is America. You can't take two steps without tripping over a goddamn therapist. They offered me counseling, drugs, whatever I wanted. But none of that'll do a goddamn bit of good if you've got real problems, and you and I both know it."

"Um, well...that seems a bit harsh, given what Mom and Dad do."

"Yeah, and we've both seen firsthand what a fucking waste of time it is, too!"

"I don't want to agree with you, but I kind of do," I said. "But you're being a real pain in the ass, John. You need to get it together."

"That's easy for you to say!"

"I know," I agreed. "But you still need to get it together."

"Fine. As long as 'getting it together' means getting it together with some hot chick who wants to admire my tattoos."

"Fine," I said. "Whatever works. Just don't bring it home to my place."

"Fuck no, I wouldn't do that. Whaddya think cheap motels are for?"

I resisted the impulse to respond to that, and also turned down John's invitation to join him on his nightly prowl. Although I was half-tempted to go along with him in order to act as his designated driver, I doubted it would actually do much good. I just had to hope that he would spend long enough with his chosen companion for the evening to sober up before he drove home.

I was cheered up some after John left by a text from Alex, who had been incommunicado for the past week. I had half-assumed he wanted to back out of our tentative plan to get together during spring break, and hadn't wanted to harass him about it.

Sorry about the radio silence this week, he wrote. *I've just had a lot on my plate, and I didn't want to interfere with you visiting with your brother.*

No problem, I wrote back. *Interfere away :) How's your week been?*

Great news! Well, sort of. The DLI interview is *over*!!! God, what a bunch of motherfuckers. They kept me hanging for more than a month. But we got it done this afternoon. And just in time for spring break :) Any exciting plans?

Work. Trying not to commit homicide and/or suicide. The usual.

That much fun, huh?

There's just a lot of tedious work that has to be done, and with my brother here...well, you know brothers.

I'm an only child. So no. But that's okay. Sounds like I haven't missed much.

You've missed a lot. Just not all of it is good. Anyway, he's my brother, so that's that. So are you on break next week too?

Yeah. And I was thinking...

Yeah?

I was thinking I could drive down and stay for a few days, like we talked about, he texted. *If you want.*

Yeah, I texted back. *I'd like that.*

Really?

Yes, really. I'd like to see you. And I could show you the fabulous sights of Charlotte!

Of course I'd be happy to see any sights you cared to show me. But don't feel like you have to go out of your way to entertain me. I just want to see you.

I'll be busy some of the time with work and stuff, I texted back. *Even though it's spring break. You know how it is. But we could still have a good time.*

Yeah. And, uh...

Yes? I texted, after waiting for him to finish his sentence and getting nothing.

This is sort of awkward, but I want you to know that I don't, uh, have any expectations, okay? I mean, there's a way I'd like this visit to go, but you shouldn't feel obliged.

I appreciate that, I texted. *Let's just see how things go, okay? But now I'm curious. How *would* you like this visit to go? :)*

Haha. I mean, I hope I've made it clear in a non-creepy way that I'd be into some sexy good times. But I'll be coming down to see you, you know, not to, how shall I put this...

Cum?

Hahaha :) :) But yeah.

Let's just see how things go, I repeated. *But I should warn you, there's not a lot of space here, so you're either going to have to sleep with me, or with John.*

I would strongly prefer one over the other, he texted back. *But it's up to you. And, you know, if it's just, um, Platonic, that would be okay too. I mean, not ideal, from my point of view, but you know you can trust me to be a gentleman, right, even if we're all cuddled up together in the same bed? We've done that before and it was okay, right?*

I know, I texted. *Let's just see how things go, and how John is behaving when you get here. Having my big brother in the next room might be a problem.*

Yeah, major mood killer, lol.

And he's being kind of difficult. More difficult than usual. Honestly, I'm glad he's here with me instead of our parents. I know they were disappointed to miss his leave, but to be honest, I'm glad they're not seeing him like this.

I'm sorry. Is he being a pain?

Mostly he's in pain. Which means yes, he's being a pain. A lot of drinking and stuff.

Shit. Do you think he's dangerous?

I hope not. But I should warn you that a certain amount of your visit might be taken up with wrangling John and dealing with his feelings and behavior.

Maybe I can talk to him. You know, as someone who's gone through it myself.

He's gone through it himself too. But this time it seems worse.

Yeah. I can try to talk to him, even if he is a stupid jarhead :) No offense :) :)

None taken.

And I mean, I was really fucked up after I got back from Iraq. Angry at everyone, especially myself. I'm lucky anyone who knew me back then will still speak with me.

That must have been difficult, I texted cautiously. Alex never talked much about his service, other than to say that knowing about it tended to make people take him as something he wasn't.

Mostly my own fault. Of course, the whole thing was mostly my own fault. But when I got back and got out of the service, I wanted to burn my uniform, did I tell you that?

No. You must have had a very difficult time.

S'okay. Other people had much worse times. Especially the Iraqi people we were "liberating."

It was a difficult thing for everyone.

It was what it was. And when I got back and got out, I took my uniform out to my parents' backyard and started a fire in our firepit. Because of course we're the kind of folks who have a poncy outdoor firepit in our backyard. So no pity! So I started up a fire, and my dad came out and saw I had my uniform all laid out next to it, and he was like, "What the hell are you doing, son?" So I told him I was going to burn my fucking uniform, and what I couldn't burn, I was going to smash with a hammer.

What did he say? I texted, when it became apparent that another message was not immediately forthcoming.

Ha. He put his arm around my shoulders, and said, "I'd hold off on that, son, if I were you. Someday you might want to have kept it. Someday you might be proud of it."

I thought he disapproved.

Yeah, me too. I said as much.

And what did he say?

He said—fuck, why is this so hard even to write?—he said that *he* was proud of me, no matter what, and that if I didn't want to keep the *uniform for me, I should keep it for him. He said he'd keep it and give it to his grandson when the time came, if I didn't want to.*

That was kind of him.

Nah, he wasn't doing it to be kind. Well, maybe he was. He just really wanted to be proud of me for *something*, and even though he gave me the silent treatment for most of my actual service, once I got back and got out he wanted to have the bragging rights that went along with being the father of a vet. Also he wanted to remind me that he was waiting for grandsons. Not that that stopped him from trying to screw up every relationship I might have with a woman.

Ouch.

Yeah. Why the fuck are we talking about him anyway? Or any of this. We were supposed to be planning how I was going to come down to see you and hang out with you and maybe, if the stars align and the gods are kind, have sexy good times. I've got some grading I should finish up before I head out. So does me arriving Monday afternoon/evening work for you? Then we can...do whatever we're going to do and I can spend a couple of days there wrangling John or whatever you need done, and we can, like, play it by ear or something.

It sounds good. And...

Yes?

I hope the gods are kind!

He sent a string of smile emojis in response. The last one had a heart in it. This cheered me up so much I went to bed without my usual late-night walk of anxiety through the job postings and news feeds. Maybe that was why I slept so well, and had pleasant dreams.

38

The next morning I woke up to the sight of John passed out, still dressed, on top of his covers, and a one-line email from Dima. *They killed Nemtsov.*

I screamed a little bit. John came bolting up off his bed, cursing and stumbling as he tried to run over to me.

"What the fuck?" he shouted. "What the fuck is happening?"

"It's okay," I told him. I tried to speak soothingly. "Well, it isn't, but we're not in danger."

"You coulda fooled me!"

I tore my eyes away from the screen in order to focus on John. He had broken out in a fresh fear-sweat on top of last night's sex-sweat, and looked even more like hell than usual.

"Go take a shower," I told him.

"You sure? You sure you're okay?"

"Go take a shower," I repeated.

As soon as John disappeared into the bathroom, I started checking all the major news outlets. Every one had as their leading article the story of the assassination of Russian opposition politician Boris Nemtsov, gunned down Friday night outside the Kremlin.

I hadn't actually known Nemtsov, at least not very well, but I cried a little bit nonetheless. Then I emailed Dima back.

John came out of the shower, looking slightly less like death warmed over, just after I hit "Send."

"What the fuck happened, babe?" he asked as soon as he saw me.

I turned the computer screen so that he could see it. He read through the BBC's article, a muscle jumping in his jaw.

"You know this guy?" he asked when he was done.

"No. Not really. It's just...it's just so awful. For someone that important to be gunned down like that. And, I mean, if they can get Nemtsov, they can get *anybody*."

"I don't know who the fuck 'they' are, but you think they're coming after you, Ro?"

"No. I don't think so." I laughed, but it came out more like a sob. "Not as long as I'm here. I'm not worth chasing all the way to the US. I don't think. No, don't look at me like that! I'm not that important. No one's going to be bothered tracking me all the way to the US and dealing with all that hassle, even if they *could* get in, which they probably couldn't. I'm safe as long as I'm here."

"This why *he* sent you away?" John asked. A muscle was still jumping in his jaw.

"Um...sort of?"

"What the *fuck* happened last year, Ro? What the *fuck* happened in Moscow?"

"You know. The usual."

"No. Do not give me that shit. Something more than 'the usual' must have happened last time you were there, if even that complete *fucking* lunatic, and I say this as someone who knows it takes one to know one, got scared. So what *the fuck* happened?"

"Dima got beaten up in the fall," I said in a small voice. "Pretty badly. He was lucky he didn't end up with a plate in his head, like Oleg Kashin. That was the plan, apparently. The guys who beat up him—they kept saying 'Let's Kashinate him' as they kicked him. But Dima was lucky."

"Who the fuck is this Oleg what's-his-fuck?"

"Another journalist."

"Of course it's another fucking journalist. Getting the shit kicked out of you is just another day on the job if you're a Russian journalist. So, what? You decided you didn't want to deal with that?"

"No! Of course not! But then...but then..."

"But then what?" John grabbed my wrist, too hard. "Then what, Ro? Did they beat you up too?"

"No. They just...they just...they just grabbed me."

John squeezed my wrist even harder. "And?" he demanded.

"And then they drove me to Gorky Park, and made me get out and walk to where they had set up a meeting with Dima, and they...they put a gun to my head, and they told him he had to stop working on the story about them and leave Russia. They were going to keep me until he sent them a picture of himself in Kiev."

"And then what?"

"And then we managed to run away. They got shot, and we didn't. But they were very serious people, John. They're probably still hunting for him. And I don't even want to think about what they'd do to me, if they caught me again."

"Jesus. FUCKING. *CHRIST*. Are you fucking kidding me? And you didn't tell anyone? You didn't go to the US Embassy and tell them someone kidnapped an American citizen?"

"They would have just told me to go home."

"Too fucking right they would have. So, what: you decided to keep it a secret? You didn't tell Mom and Dad? You didn't tell *me*?"

"What could you have done?" I said.

"I could have told you to get your ass the fuck back home, that's what I could have done."

"That's what I did anyway. After Dima broke off the engagement, and told me to leave and never come back."

"And good for him, too. Jesus, Ro! You damn near got killed! Because of *him*!"

"I know! But I knew all along that that was part of the deal!"

"Well, it's a shitty fucking deal, Ro! You're better off out of it! And if you don't see that, then you're a fucking moron! Think about...Jesus *fucking* Christ, Ro, think about what that would do to the rest of us, if you got yourself killed over there! Just think for one tiny second what that would do to the family if that happened!"

"I think I have a pretty good idea," I said. "Seeing as how that's something we worry about with *you* all the time."

"I'm not...that's fucking different, Ro, and you know it!"

"No," I said. "No, I don't. And if you'll excuse me, it looks like I have email to answer."

John inhaled so sharply the lines around his mouth and nose went white. "Fine," he said. "Fine. Be that way. I'll take your word that you're safe here. But just answer me one question: do you have any idea who these motherfuckers are? The ones who—I cannot *believe* I am fucking saying this—put a gun to your head and threatened to pull the trigger?"

"They were wearing ski masks. But we know who they were working for. There was a Russian oil company and a Chechen oil company who were engaged in a, shall we say, hostile merger, and we got caught in the middle."

"Of *course* the fucking Chechens were involved!"

"Most Chechens aren't bad," I said. "Most Chechens are victims of terrible repression."

"Yeah, yeah, yeah, spare me the fucking sermon, Ro. Victims make the worst terrorists, and you and I both know it." John looked over at my computer screen. "Looks like *he's* already gotten back to you. You gonna answer that?"

"Yes," I said. "Right away."

"I fucking thought so," said John, and stalked off to make coffee.

39

I'm okay, Dima had emailed me back. *I'm still in Ukraine, so I'm safe. "Safe"—how do you say it in English: lol? LOL, then. I wanted to come back for the march*—Nemtsov had been organizing a protest march—*but I got talked out of it. I was told it would only cause more trouble for me to be there. Apparently my native city doesn't love me anymore.*

It was the longest message I'd gotten from him in more than a year. I had to respond.

I'm glad you're safe. Please, stay safe. Where are you now? Still in the war zone?

By the time John had finished making coffee, Dima had written back.

*Still in the war zone, yes. Still unable to return to Moscow, even for something like this, or so they tell me. My editors and Mama all keep telling me to stay **away**, so that's what I'm doing. And you should too, Inna. Stay in America, where you're safe.*

Didn't I tell you I almost got shot here? I wrote back furiously. *America isn't the safe place you think it is. And...I miss you.* Tears threatened to come spilling out of my eyes as I typed those words. I looked up to see if John had noticed, but he was pouring himself another cup of coffee. *If I'm going to be poor and in danger, I'd rather it were with you than by myself,* I finished, and hit "Send" before I could think better of it.

By the time John had come back to the table, fresh cup of coffee in hand, a reply had already hit my inbox. Dima must have been typing as furiously as I was.

If where you are in America is dangerous, then find a safer place, silly, he wrote. *And don't talk nonsense: of course it isn't as dangerous as it is here. It's not as dangerous because I'm not there. You **need** to stay away from me, Inna. And you don't need to be by yourself. I'm sure you can find yourself ten men, all twice as good as me, in the blink of an eye.*

I don't want ten men, all twice as good as you! I wrote back. *You seem to think that*—I blanked on the Russian word for "disposable" and quickly improvised—*I could just throw you away and buy myself a new man at the store! But you're not an old shoe I can throw away when you get worn out or go out of fashion. You're a person, even if you don't see that.* Then I burst into tears.

"Jesus Christ," John muttered under his breath. Then he set down his coffee cup and came over and put his arm around my shoulders. "He's not worth it, Ro," he said. "None of them are. Not this guy who was killed, not this guy who's yanking you around like this—none of them. Just walk away."

"I can't," I said.

"Yeah, I know you can't. Which is why I'm glad *he* can. Shit, is that another email from him already?"

It was. I disengaged from John and opened it.

Stay away, Inna, it said. *And don't worry about me. I'll be fine. This old shoe isn't quite worn out yet. But you need something nicer and more fashionable, so go to the store and pick something out. Something handsome and rich. Or handsome and young, or handsome and clever. Do whatever you want, as long as you stay away from me. I shouldn't have written to you. I just went a little crazy when I heard the news. But I've sobered up, and I won't be writing to you again. For the love of Christ, don't write back. Goodbye.*

After that I cried some more. John tried to comfort me, which made me acutely aware that the person I would have gone to first for comfort was the one who was currently hurting me. For so long my first instinct whenever I was sad or mad or had anything I wanted to tell someone had been to go tell Dima. But now, when I was really in pain and needed a friend, he not only wasn't there, he was the one who was causing my pain.

I said as much to John when he made me tell him what Dima had written. When he heard it, all the lines stood out whitely in his face again, and for a moment I thought he was going to smash the coffee cup, or maybe the computer. Which would have made a shitty morning even shittier.

"So are you going to do what he says?" he asked, when he had unclenched his jaw enough to speak.

"I guess. Sort of. I can't force him to take me back. But I also can't just run to the store and pick up a replacement for him, either."

"No. Not really. But you've got this guy coming on Monday, right? What about him? No, wait!" He threw up his hands. "Don't look at me like that! I'm not saying you're whoring around, or looking for a cheap substitute, or anything like that. I'm just saying, it's been more a than a year since you and Dima called it off"—"Since Dima called it off without consulting me," I interjected—"yeah, since he called it off and sent you packing, *which was the right decision*, if you ask me. How long ago was that, anyway?"

"Fourteen months," I said. "But who's counting?"

"So it's been more than a year since you've seen him—have you even talked to him on the phone since then?"

"No," I admitted. "Just a couple of emails. Today's exchange was the longest we've had since, you know, it ended."

"So you are *definitely* not with him, and haven't been in over a year. So now you're doing the smart thing, and finding, not a replacement, but someone else, someone better."

John moved so that he was looking me right in the eyes, both hands on my shoulders. "I won't say I know what you're going through, because honestly I've never cared for any woman a thousandth of a percent of how much you obviously cared about *him*. And maybe that's a good thing. It's made you do a lot of stupid things, Ro, and it'll continue making you do stupid things unless you stop it. So stop it. Now. Stop moping about fuckface off in Russia, come out and have fun with me today, and then spend tomorrow sobering up and getting pretty for this new guy, who I'm prepared to like just because he's an American, even if he was—what did you say? Not Army, right?"

"No." I laughed a watery laugh. "Navy. But just for a few years. I don't think he enjoyed it very much, or took much pride in it."

"Jesus, who would? Thank Christ he got out before it fucked him up entirely. So you pull yourself together and get dressed and get ready to spend the day out with me, and if you do that, I promise I'll be nice to this guy."

"Really?" I asked. "You'll really be nice to him?"

John grinned. "No," he said. "But I'll be less of a dick to him than I could be. Now get up and get dressed, Ro. First I'm taking you trail running, and then I'm taking you drinking, and when I'm done with you, you'll be too wiped out and shitfaced to care about men at all."

"If you say so," I said. "But I have work to do..."

"No." John hauled me upright from my chair. "It's the first Saturday of spring break, or have you forgotten? No work, only partying. Come on, Halley! Do I have to send you to quarterdeck? Get those sneakers on! Now, Halley, now!"

While I couldn't be happy about everything that had just happened, John seemed more cheerful and more together than he had since he'd arrived, so I told myself I should be grateful for that as he hustled me into running clothes and dragged me off for what he promised would be a "puke-inducing" run up and down Crowders Mountain.

40

The run up Crowders Mountain and back was not, as it turned out, puke-inducing. At least not for me. It was a near thing for John.

"Fuck," he said when we got back to the bottom. He stopped and rested his hands on his knees, gasping for breath and spitting copiously on the ground. "Jesus Christ, Ro. When did you get so fit?"

"I've been running for a while, you know that."

"Yeah, but like, wussy little jogs around the block. This time you damn near kicked my ass."

"I've had a lot of pent-up nervous energy to burn off," I said.

"Yeah, I can really fucking tell." He straightened up with a groan. "Ah shit! I think I'm gonna puke. Nope, wait for it, wait for it...I'm good." He grinned. "And if you ever tell any of my buddies you outran me, I'll kick your ass."

"I never get to meet any of your buddies. So no danger there."

"Too fucking right you don't. I'd never trust any of them with my kid sister. Okay, in the car. Time for Phase II of the operation."

"What's Phase II?" I asked.

"We're going to go out and get shitfaced. I'm not even going to pick anyone up tonight, 'cause I'm gonna be spending it with you, making sure you don't wuss out and stay sober. Unless you pick someone up yourself. Nah." He thought about it for a second as he got in the car. "Nah," he said again. "You're not gonna pick anyone up. I wouldn't even have to stop you, would I?"

"Probably not," I agreed.

"You know, most of my buddies who have kid sisters, the worst they have to worry about is them slutting around. But you'd never do anything like that, would you? You have to go and get into the big kinds of trouble, instead of the little kinds of trouble that most girls get into."

"Yep," I said.

"Welp." He sighed. "I guess I'm stuck with you, aren't I? Come on. I hope you're prepared to show off your drinking skills, Ro."

To John's disgust, I stopped showing off my drinking skills that evening at around beer three, and took an Uber ride home, leaving him to go hunting for sex partners on his own after I assured him that I was fine, I could go home on my own, and I wasn't going to do anything stupid. *Unlike you*, I thought but did not say. John gave me a narrow look, though, like maybe he knew what I was thinking.

The run and the evening out left me tired enough that I did fall asleep that night instead of staying up fretting, and, unlike John, woke up the next morning without a hangover. He tried to get me to go out and do the same thing all over again. I agreed to the run, as long as it was in a park in town rather than up and down the mountain again, but not the going out drinking.

"I don't like drinking that much," I told him. "Drinking makes me sad."

John refused to believe that, but accepted the alternate argument that I couldn't go out drinking late that night because I needed to be fresh and pretty when Alex arrived. I in fact had little intention of making any kind of special effort to be fresh and pretty for Alex, which, since we had shared an adjunct office for a semester, seemed like a complete waste of time, but to John that seemed like a perfectly good reason.

All the running, combined with the moderate amount of drinking, not to mention arguing with John, meant that by Monday morning I was more or less back to normal, at least on the outside. I had not written back to Dima, and he hadn't written back to me. I had spent whatever part of the weekend John had left free for me reading about Nemtsov's murder, until John caught me at it and closed my laptop.

"Stop it, Ro," he said. "What's it to you? You never really knew this motherfucker, right? And he probably had it coming anyway."

"No one has something like that coming!" I protested.

"You know what I mean. He was cruising for martyrdom. Well, he got it. Don't let you be next. Put all that shit behind you, and focus on the positive, blahdeefuckingblahblah." He grinned, but it didn't reach his eyes. "Maybe I should be a counselor, whaddya think? I think I've got the spiel pretty down fucking pat. I've sure heard it enough times. So now let me unload a little of that shit onto you."

"It can be your new career after you retire from the Corps, like I said," I told him.

"Yeah. So when's this Alex guy showing up?"

I checked my phone. "He just texted me to say he's leaving now. So not till this evening."

"Cool. I'll get out of your hair, okay? Unless you want me to be here when he shows up."

"Of course you're welcome to join us."

"I fucking hope not, Ro."

I rolled my eyes. "You know what I mean!"

"Well, what *I* mean is, should I be here to suss him out, put the fear of God into him, the whole nine yards, or should I get out of the way and let you two crazy kids do whatever the fuck you're gonna do?"

"I don't need protection from him, if that's what you mean."

"You sure about that?"

"Yes, John. I am quite sure of that. If I were not, I would not have invited him to come stay with me."

"'Kay. Fair enough. Just let me know when, and I'll be out of here."

I wrestled with the temptation to ask him to clear out now. "I doubt he'll be in before five, maybe six," I said instead.

"No problem. I'll be long gone by then."

41

True to his word, John cleared out well before Alex arrived, leaving me with the injunction to "Look pretty, Sis. And try to smile."

"Maybe I only frown when you're around," I said.

"You're a poet and you don't know it!"

"Just get out," I told him.

"No problem. Just don't do anything I wouldn't do."

"*Is* there anything you wouldn't do?" I asked.

John appeared to give the question serious thought. "Well, to be honest, I'm pretty damn sure I wouldn't sleep with this guy, so I guess that was bad advice, huh?"

"Just get out!" I repeated. John grinned, not very nicely, and left.

I worried, especially after the wild emotional storms of the weekend, that I would feel awkward when Alex arrived, but in fact, when he showed up at my doorstep, only an hour after he was originally supposed to arrive—"Fucking DC traffic," he explained—I didn't feel awkward at all, not even when he put one arm around me and kissed my cheek.

"Damn," he said when he let me go. "I'd forgotten how good-looking you are."

"I didn't know you thought I was good-looking."

A pained expression crossed Alex's face. "Then you must be blind, Rowena." Then another pained expression crossed his face, maybe from embarrassment, and he took a step back from me, so that I could no longer feel the low-level quiver that always emanated from him, at least when he was next to me. He cleared his throat. "This your place?" he asked, looking around a little too casually.

"Yep. It's not much."

"Are you kidding me? You should see the shithole I live in. This is great! Oh, hey, and it's your cat. What's her name again?"

"Fevronia," I said, as Fevronia came up and, in a surprising display of friendliness, sniffed Alex's leg and rubbed against it.

"She seems to like me more than she did the first time we met."

"Yeah. She'd been getting crankier and crankier, actually, till last week when I realized she had worms and took her to the vet. Now she's a regular love bug."

"Really?"

"No," I said. "Touch her at your peril. But she's stopped jumping out and attacking people for the moment."

"Well, that's good. So, um...are you starving? I'm starving. I hate to be the guest who shows up and demands food, but I didn't eat the whole drive, what with getting caught in DC and all, and now I'm ravenous. Can I, like, take you out to dinner or something?"

"Um," I said. "Sure. I mean, I feel that as your hostess I should provide you with food, but..."

"No buts. Dinner it is," he said firmly, sounding relieved to have a plan that didn't involve us being alone together in the apartment. "Oh, and what about your brother? Isn't he here?"

"He cleared out," I said.

"What, for good?"

"No, just for the evening. He offered to stay around and threaten you, and when I said no, he left in a huff."

"Jeez. Sounds like a real charmer. Dammit! I guess I shouldn't say that about your brother, huh?"

"It's okay," I said. "I'm sure you two will get along famously when you meet. But maybe it would be better if that meeting were put off for a bit. Let's go have supper."

Over supper Alex filled me in on his new job and all the trials and tribulations involved in being the son of a former dean at the university.

"Shit," he said, after the third story about someone who had asked him if he was following in his father's footsteps. "I'm sorry. I'm just gabbing on about myself all the time, aren't I? Feel free to smack me and make me shut up."

"It's okay. I don't want to smack you. It's nice to hear this. It's nice to talk to someone else in the business." And it was. The lack of supervision I had at UNC-Matthews was pleasant, but after years of being jammed together in a small office with other grad students and then adjuncts, being completely on my own like I was now was lonely sometimes. I'd forgotten how nice it was to complain with a fellow sufferer. I'd also forgotten, although I didn't blurt it out in the same way he had, how good-looking Alex was.

Actually, I'd never thought of him as good-looking before, not really, but seen in this light, he was. Or rather, he had an intelligent face and a body that he kept fit. And his golden-brown hair and stubbly beard glinted in the restaurant lights in interesting ways. And he smiled whenever he looked at me, and he was always looking at me. Sitting there talking to him, I could feel a big chunk of the anguish of the weekend slip back under the surface of my mind, and something happy and hopeful bloom in its place.

We spent the better part of two hours eating and chatting, and when we came back from supper, John was still nowhere to be found.

"It's for the best," I told Alex. "He's not very good company right now."

"Like I said, I'd be happy to talk to him if it would help," said Alex.

"Thanks. I'd like for that to happen—but don't think you should have to put up with him for my sake."

"I'll be happy to put up with him for your sake, Rowena. And for his. Like I told you, I was a real pain in the ass when I came back too."

"This isn't the first time for him. But it's the worst time. Something's eating at him, and I don't know what it is. But he'll tell me when he tells me, and nagging him about it prematurely isn't going to solve anything."

"Yeah. It rarely does. So tell me about this job you interviewed for."

"I already told you pretty much everything interesting. Any interview prospects for you?"

He grimaced. "Other than the DLI thing, you mean?"

"Yeah. That's great!"

"An interview is not the same as a job, as we both know all too well."

"Yeah, but still! An interview is better than no interview. And it seems like you must have a good shot at it."

Alex shrugged. "Maybe. And on paper it's a good opportunity. Long-term contract, full benefits—the whole nine yards, the thing we've been chasing and chasing. Although, alas, the rumors that you get to assign pushups to underperforming students are greatly exaggerated."

"Dammit. I've always wanted there to be at least one shining, beautiful place where that could happen."

"Yeah." We both spent a moment in misty-eyed contemplation of what it would be like to be able to make our worst screw-ups and loudmouths do pushups until they puked. In theory I abhorred such things. In practice, the temptation to say it would be for their own good was strong.

"Anyway," said Alex. "I know it's a good chance, and if I get it, I'll probably make myself take it. But, it's, you know, pretty far away from home, and there are some downsides too."

"Such as?"

"Just"—he shook his head—"shit that maybe shouldn't bother me but does. People that shouldn't bother me, but do."

"Do you know someone there?"

"Yeah. But whatever." He straightened up from where he had been leaning against the counter. Even from where I was standing on the other side of the sink, I could see and feel the barely contained energy that always seemed to fill him. "So," he said. "What do you want to do for the rest of this evening, since your brother isn't here to start fights and cause trouble?"

"You remember how I told you I hoped the gods would be kind?"

He went still. "Yeah."

"Are you still interested?"

"Ye"—he cleared his throat. "Yes, I am. Very interested."

I stepped up to him and took his hand. It tightened convulsively around mine, warm and strong and alive and very much present and eager to be with me. "Come here, then," I said.

42

Afterwards, I lay with my head on his chest while his hands stroked my hair gently, as if they couldn't quite believe they had the right to be there. The high-strung vibrations that emanated from him most of the time had temporarily stilled, and he seemed relaxed in a way he rarely did, almost a different person.

"That really happened?" he said after a while. "I didn't imagine it, did I?"

"What do you think happened?" I asked.

"I mean, we just, like, had really hot sex, and you were really into it, and came twice, and...all that. That really happened, right?"

"Either that, or we had a shared hallucination."

"Either way, it was good, right?"

"It was," I said. Alex had been, just as I had guessed he might be, an eager and attentive lover, quick to follow my lead and respond to my desires. "I think it was the best first time I ever had," I told him honestly.

"Really?" I could feel him smiling into my hair. "That's fucking great. And for me too. And best second time too. I think we've really got something, Rowena."

"Yeah," I said. "I'll be right back."

"You okay?"

"Yeah. I just have to run to the bathroom." I slid out of his arms and ran off into the bathroom, hoping he took my haste as a sign of my eagerness to return to him, not my eagerness to escape him.

I shut the door behind me and sat down on the wobbly toilet, my face in my hands. Was I crying? Maybe a little. Alex didn't deserve that. He hadn't done anything wrong. It wasn't his fault that he wasn't Dima. It wasn't his fault that he was in some ways a better lover and probably a better man than Dima. My first time with Dima certainly hadn't involved a feeling of safety and love, along with two intense orgasms. I had been too nervous and uncertain about what I wanted back then, and Dima had required a lot of training to reach the point where he could give it to me. But that wasn't his fault either. Neither of them had ever deliberately set out to make me feel bad. But they both had anyway.

I got up and looked in the mirror. I looked sexually sated, and the marks from Alex's beard were still bright pink on my pale skin. But there was no hiding the fact that my eyes looked teary and sad.

"I'm just going to take a quick shower," I called.

"Take your time," Alex called back.

When I got out of the shower, I looked and felt calmer. It was the first year AD—After Dima—I reminded myself, and a new era meant new things. I had nothing to regret, and certainly nothing to feel guilty about. I dried myself off in a more cheerful frame of mind, and only shrieked a little when Fevronia suddenly popped out from where she'd been hiding under the sink.

"You okay in there?" Alex shouted.

"Just a surprise cat attack," I shouted back. "No harm done." I scratched Fevronia's back. Instead of clawing at me like she used to, she arched her back and purred. Even she seemed to like Alex.

"Tell me," I said as I came out of the bathroom, still stark naked. Good thing John hadn't come back while we'd been occupied. Although his entrances tended not to be silent. Even focused on sex and showering, I was unlikely to have missed him. "How extensive is your skill set?"

"In this area of expertise? Extensive enough, I hope." He flashed me a smile, his teeth bright white against his beard and the darkness of the room. "You certainly haven't seen most of it yet, babe."

"Care to do another demonstration?"

He held out his arms. "Come here," he said.

43

John came stumbling in during the middle of the night, but I ignored it, and only came out of the bedroom in the morning, at my usual time. Alex was still sleeping. John was passed out on his air mattress. I tried to make coffee for all three of us as quietly as possible, hoping to let them sleep and delay the moment of confrontation. John had promised to be nice to Alex, but as he said, his "nice" was only marginally less dickish than usual.

Alex came padding out in his boxers as I was finishing with the coffee. He caught sight of John, and did an immediate about-face back into the room, emerging a couple of minutes later fully dressed.

"I was going to bring the coffee into the bedroom for you," I whispered. "You drink it, don't you?"

"Are you fucking kidding me? I mainline it like a junky."

"Do you want sugar? Non-dairy creamer?"

"Fuck no. Why adulterate that sweet, black, addictive goodness?"

"Here you go, then." I handed him coffee in the least chipped of my mugs. He ran his fingers over mine, and accepted it with a smile.

"So should we sneak back into the bedroom?" he whispered. "Leave the sleeping dragon to lie, and all that? Not that I'm running away from him, you understand. I just don't want you to have to deal with a scene."

"I appreciate it. Yeah, let's...Oh, morning, John."

"Fuck, why are we all up so fucking early?" John said hoarsely, sitting up and knuckling his eyes. He looked at his phone. "Jesus Christ, it's not even seven. I only got"—he did a quick but hazy mental calculation—"five hours of rack time. Better than average, actually."

"Good for you," I said. "I hope you had a good time."

"Good enough. Found yet another woman who was willing to 'thank me for my service,' went back to her place for a while." He grinned nastily.

"Did you happen to catch her name?" I asked, trying to make my voice as non-judgmental as possible.

"Chlamydia," Alex whispered into my ear. "Gonorrhea."

John must have heard, because he gave him a very sour look. "Is this him?" he asked.

"Um, yeah. Alex, this is my brother, John. John, this is Alex. My, uh, friend."

"Fuck buddy, you mean," said John, and threw off the blankets and stalked into the bathroom. He was still in just his boxers, and he didn't bother to put anything else on, even after he came out of the bathroom and sat down at the table.

"Is that coffee?" he demanded.

"It is. I made some for you. Aren't you cold?"

"What?"

"You're not dressed. Aren't you cold?"

"Nah. I'm not a chilly girly-girl like you, Ro."

"Okay, then."

John took a long drink of coffee. I could almost see it reviving him, chasing out last night's hangover and bad sex and whatever other unfun things he had been up to, and returning him to what I thought of as his old self. "So you're the infamous Alex," he said, when he had drained half the mug. "Welcome to North Cack."

Alex gave me an inquiring look.

"North Cackalacky," I explained. "North Carolina. As opposed to South Cack."

"Okay," said Alex. "I'm not sure I'm cool enough to use those terms in casual speech myself, but I'm glad to be able to add them to my passive vocabulary."

"He always talk like this?" John demanded.

"Fuck no, man," said Alex. "Only when I'm pissed off."

John grinned, and tried to hide it by taking another long swallow of coffee. "I've heard a lot about you," he said when he was done.

"I'm very flattered to hear that," said Alex.

"Ro said you were in the service." John eyed Alex up and down, looking for flaws. "Navy." He made a face. "So what should I call you, sailor? What rank did you reach before you fucked off back to the safety of the civvy world?"

"If you want to call me by my title, you can call me Dr. Miller," said Alex evenly. "Or if you want to be my friend, you can call me Alex. Your choice."

John snorted into his cup, and finished off the rest of his coffee before pouring himself the last of the pot.

"You've got to get a bigger coffeemaker, Ro, I keep telling you," he said, as he started another batch.

"This one is normally more than enough for me." I bit my lip in order not to start an argument with him at 6:30 in the morning. Neither of us had gotten enough sleep last night, although—I thought smugly—I was sure I had passed my night more pleasantly *and* virtuously than he had, and at least he was making his own coffee, instead of demanding that I make it for him. And it was coffee he'd bought us with his money, too.

"Yeah, but if *he*"—John nodded at Alex—"is going to be coming down here all the time, you're going to need a bigger one."

"Okay," I said. It seemed the better choice than explaining to John all the reasons why I couldn't afford to buy another coffeemaker, especially one that would take up more space and be more difficult to haul around. I was still scarred by the toaster contretemps.

"So are you gonna be here all the time?" John asked Alex.

"Maybe," said Alex. "Some of the time, at least. I teach at Temple, so..." The rest of his sentence was drowned out by John's snort of contempt.

"Couldn't you find someone more local, Ro?" John demanded. "Instead of someone who lives three states away?"

I took a deep breath. The smell of freshly brewing coffee was soothing, and conveniently covered up the fact that neither John nor Alex had showered since they'd last had sex, and John was hungover. "Pennsylvania isn't that far away," I said. "And who knows where we'll both be next semester, anyway."

"Yeah. Who fucking knows." John glowered at the brewing coffee, and then turned to look at us. "Long-distance relationships are hard," he said, his voice sounding reasonable, almost sympathetic. "Take it from me, I know. There's always something—or someone—there to take away your focus, get you to stray off and do stuff you shouldn't, break the other person's heart, generally act like a prize shit. And it's hard to keep a relationship going when you're not in the same bed every night."

"There are still things you can do," I said.

"Like what—sext each other's brain's out?" said John.

"Sexting is good," I said. "It builds vocabulary and, done properly, can help develop a sophisticated literary language of feminine desire, something that is sorely lacking in both classical and modern letters. And then of course there's always video."

John and Alex both choked on their coffee. After a manful struggle, Alex managed to swallow most of his down, but John had to go run and spit his out in the sink.

"Fuck, Ro, you *are* a dark horse," he said, once he could talk again. "Jesus Christ. You sure you're up for this, Miller?"

Alex was rubbing his hand over his face. His eyes were bright and his shoulders were shaking with suppressed laughter as he said, with the formal enthusiasm of someone at a job interview, "I would be delighted to participate in the development of a sophisticated literary language of feminine desire. And my vocabulary could always use more building. I would be sure to study very hard. No doubt assimilation would be rapid, and I could move from passive to active use after a very short period of instruction."

I laughed. John shook his head. "This is your idea of dirty talk, isn't it?" he said. "Jesus! And you're doing it right in front of me, too!"

"You did ask," I pointed out. "Questions should be answered; otherwise, how will you learn?"

John put his cup down in the sink. "I have to go," he said. "I can't handle the level of kink in this place anymore. Let me know when it's safe to come back."

44

John went off for a run, and when he came back, he showered and dressed with hardly any snide comments at all, and announced that he had to go to Gastonia and was going to be out for the day, but that he'd be back to take us to dinner in the evening.

"So drag yourselves out of the sack, get showered, and be ready at eighteen hundred hours sharp," he ordered.

Alex gave John a look like he couldn't quite believe him, and then looked over at me questioningly.

"At least he's not threatening to send us to quarterdeck," I said.

"No point when you're just going to fuck each other's brains out all day anyway," said John, and left, shutting the door with a slam, before either of us could respond.

"He *is* a little tightly wound," said Alex. "I thought I was bad, but Jesus fucking Christ. Has he always been like this?"

"He's always been what folks back home would call 'a real piece o' work.' Or in other words, a royal pain in the ass. But this time is worse. He's out of our hair for the moment, though."

"So, um..." Alex eyed me thoughtfully. "Although I appreciate his suggestion for our choice of activity for the day, I honestly don't know that I'm up—pun intended—for ten hours of it nonstop. You gotta let stuff rest and regain sensation, you know what I'm saying?"

"I do," I said. "And I have to check email and get some work done anyway."

"Thank fuck. I do too, but I didn't want to be a jerk and say so."

"Thanks for letting me be the jerk, then."

Alex laughed at that, and then we set up his computer across my small, somewhat wobbly table from mine, so that we each had our own work area. It was, we agreed, more convenient and spacious than the adjunct warehouse back at TLASC, and the wifi was better, too. Nevaeh's intermittent wailing was a little distracting, but, Alex said, much better than his current office mate, who liked to describe her job search woes in exquisite detail every day.

"It's not that I don't feel her pain," said Alex. "It's just that I spend enough time worrying about that shit on my own time. When I'm in that dust trap—I don't think the bookshelves have been dusted since the Civil War, or maybe the Revolution—I just want to get my homework graded and get the hell out of there."

"I know what you mean."

"So what's your current setup like?" he asked. "Can we go on a field trip and check it out?"

"I think campus is closed for active shooter training right now," I said. "But if you really want to, we can at some point, sure. It's just not that exciting. It's basically a half-empty construction zone, through which a small number of faculty and students wander, perpetually in search of an open parking lot and dry pathways through the mud. Sometimes power saws and concrete cutters wail like lost souls in torment, punctuated by the sound of nail guns putting them out of their misery."

"Jeez, sounds charming. Students any good?"

"Some of them could be, if they didn't have a thousand other priorities that come ahead of school. A couple have real promise. My student Shaniqua, for example, has just decided to go ahead and apply for a summer program in Ukraine."

"Isn't there a war going on there?"

"The program is in a different part of the country. Hundreds of miles away from the front."

"Gosh," said Alex. "*Hundreds* of miles away from the front. So no problem, then."

"It'll do her good to go somewhere where major political events are unfolding right before her eyes. And besides, she's got family from the area. I know, I know, not what you were expecting to hear about someone named Shaniqua, but it's true. Her great-grandfather went over to the Soviet Union in the twenties, which was totally a thing for people trying to escape the Jim Crow laws. Too bad they ended up in something even worse. But he made it out alive and brought back a Ukrainian bride. So anyway, I guess I should go ahead and write her letter of recommendation. It's not my favorite activity, but it needs to be done, and the sooner you go to jail, the sooner you get out."

"Yeah," said Alex. "I remember you saying that. Nice expression. As it happens, I've got three letters of recommendation to write too. Good thing they pay us so much, right?"

"Yeah," I said. "I mean, it's not so bad once you get in a rhythm—oh crap!"

"What?!"

"It's Jason! And he wants to meet with me! This week! Argh!"

"What Jason?"

"Remember the guy I told you about at the beginning of the semester, who wants me to help him get back together with his Belarusian mail order bride?" I filled Alex in on the latest developments in the Jason-and-Arina story.

"And now he says he's arranged a couples counseling session via Skype, but he wants me there to translate if necessary. Tomorrow. At least it's at the therapist's office, and not here. He keeps pressuring me to meet with him here."

"Have you agreed?"

"No! Ugh! I never let students into my home, especially ones with a known history of violence against women!"

"And thank fuck for that. So are you going to do it?"

"Probably," I said. "Not for Jason, but for Arina. And for Maks."

"I think it's a bad idea," said Alex.

"Of course it's a bad idea. But if I don't help them, who will?"

"I don't know. Maybe someone they'll actually cough up the cash to pay for?"

"Yeah...he says Arina is insisting I be there. She doesn't trust anyone else."

"Then Arina is a good judge of character. Which is nice for her. But is it the right thing to do for you?"

"Look at it this way: If I do it, I'll probably be annoyed with them. But if I don't do it, I'll definitely be annoyed with myself."

"Fair enough," said Alex, in a tone that suggested he did not, in fact, consider it fair.

"I'm sorry. I didn't mean to abandon you when you've come all the way down here."

"This'll be, what, an hour? Plus getting there and back? So two hours, tops?"

"Should be, yeah."

"I'm a big boy, Rowena. I think I can I can take care of myself for a couple of hours, even if I'd rather be spending them with you. But"—he shut his laptop—"if you're going to abandon me tomorrow, maybe we need to make hay while the sun shines today, so to speak. Those letters of recommendation able to keep for a couple of hours?"

"A couple of hours?" I shut my laptop too. "That's ambitious."

"What can I say. I've always been an overachiever."

"That sounds like something that needs to be put to the test," I said.

45

Alex and I managed to put several things to the test, and then shower (more things may have been put to the test in the shower), dress, and settle back into work by the time John showed up at five.

"You two crazy kids decent?" he asked, cautiously opening the front door and poking his head in. "Ready for dinner?"

"It's only seventeen hundred hours," I pointed out. "And I'm still working on this recommendation. Give me a minute."

"No problem. Gives me time to pre-game with a beer before spending all evening with you."

"You don't have to spend all evening with us," I pointed out. "It was entirely your idea. Feel free to go out on your own—or stay in on your own, for that matter."

"Stay in?" said John, coming all the way into the apartment and making a beeline for the fridge. "Who do you think I am, Ro? You?"

"No," I said. "You are *definitely* not me. Now leave me in peace for a minute. I'm having a hard time getting this form to work." Shaniqua's letter of recommendation was really an electronic form that I had to fill out and then email to the program. Convenient, except for the formatting. I was supposed to rank Shaniqua's motivation, responsibility, academic ability, and cultural sensitivity as compared with her peers. Was she in the Top 1%, Top 10%, or Top 25%? Or—although of course I could never put down something so damaging to her chances—merely in the top 50%? I was supposed to put an "X" next to the appropriate line, but the Xs kept jumping down to the next line.

John cracked open a beer and offered one to Alex, who had just sent off his second recommendation and called it a day, saying that the third would have to wait till tomorrow.

"Thanks man, I'm good," said Alex. "Why don't you let me take a look at it, Rowena? I'm supposed to be good at this computer stuff. Hell, I *am* good at this computer stuff."

"What, really?" asked John. "How did that happen?" He took a long pull from his beer. Even from across the kitchen, I could see the tense set of his shoulders. His eyes were red and puffy, like he'd been drinking or crying or caught in a dust storm.

"I went to school," said Alex. "They made me learn stuff. Very mean of them. But every now and then it comes in handy. Try revealing the formatting and see what it tells us, Rowena—yeah, now highlight that bit and delete it. Now try again."

"It worked! Yes!" I kissed Alex on the cheek. John made a gagging noise from behind his beer.

"My alma mater will be so proud," said Alex.

"Hey—where *did* you go to school, anyway?" demanded John, taking another long pull of beer.

"I did my undergrad at UPenn," said Alex. "Double major in Computer Science and Near Eastern Languages and Civilizations, if you must know. I'd be happy to provide you a copy of my current CV if it would make you feel better. Along with three letters of recommendation, and, hell, my discharge papers. Honorable, in case you were wondering."

"Isn't UPenn a fancy school?" said John.

Alex grimaced. "Maybe a little."

"So where'd you get your PhD, then? Another fancy school?"

"Maybe."

"What does 'maybe' mean? Where'd you get it? Yale or some shit like that?"

Alex made a face. "Harvard," he finally said in a low voice. "A joint PhD in History and Middle Eastern Studies from Harvard. I can show you the diploma and the crimson robes to prove that as well, if you want."

"Well, shit. What's a snob like you doing with my sister?"

"I get that she's slumming," said Alex. "But I'm hoping she'll be willing to overlook my bad choice of educational institutions. My only defense is that my dad insisted. And they gave me money for most of it."

"Most of it?" demanded John, more aggressively than the question warranted. Maybe this hadn't been his first beer of the day. I tried to finish up with the form as quickly as possible in order to break up the argument I could sense brewing.

"They guarantee you funding for five years," explained Alex. "The program takes six. It's a nice little racket for the student loan companies."

"So now you're broke *and* in debt, and with no guarantee you'll have a steady job in the future," John stated.

"That pretty much sums up the situation, yes."

"Jesus Christ!" John's face was going redder than just one beer warranted. "What kind of idiot *are* you? How could you let yourself be suckered into something like that?!"

Alex shrugged. "It seemed like a good idea at the time, and Harvard was *thrilled* to provide funding for an Iraq vet. I'm sure they thought they were going to get to educate me in the ways of the liberal intellectual elite." He snorted. "They were fucking disappointed there; I'd been indoctrinated into their ways since before I could talk. But my dad was thrilled too, and it seemed marginally better than anything else I had going for me at the time, and everyone was telling me that the demand for Arabic instructors was sky-high and was only going to get higher, and I was stupid enough to believe them."

"Harvard." John shook his head. "He's not just a Yankee, Ro, he's a *Harvard* Yankee."

"We all have our flaws," I said.

"Well, at least he's not Russian. At least he's one step up from your previous...whatever you want to call him. *That* shitheel."

"Maybe I shouldn't be here for this conversation," said Alex.

"No, I think you fucking should," said John. "The other guy was never around to hear this, so I want to make sure that you do."

"I really don't think this is appropriate," I said. Lucky for me I had to concentrate on composing the email accompanying the recommendation form, or otherwise I'd be pissed. Couldn't John stop himself from being an ass for one day? No, no he couldn't.

"So, what: you'd rather get treated like crap all over again, is that it, Ro?" John waved his beer at me expansively. His second beer. How did he stay so trim? All that running, probably, and sleeping around burns up a lot of calories too. "You let one guy treat you like shit and walk away from you and you liked it so much, you thought you'd go back for seconds?"

"I'm not going to treat Rowena like shit," said Alex evenly. "And I'm not going to call her names, either, unlike *some* people."

"Oh, give him a fucking medal!" John slammed his beer bottle down on the counter hard enough to make me jump.

"I think the neighbors can hear you," I said. I double-checked the email. I sure hoped there weren't any egregious errors, because I was too angry to notice them if there were. I pressed "Send" before I could get any more distracted.

"Well, maybe they'll learn something," said John. "They sure aren't shy about sharing their family problems with us, so maybe we can share ours with them. Only unlike them you don't have a family, do you, Ro?"

"I would have said I did, but now I'm starting to wonder."

"I mean your own family," said John. I guess my glare-of-death had bounced right off him, repelled by an impenetrable shield of alcohol. "A husband. Kids. You know."

"That's not the only kind of family."

"But it's the most important kind! That's what you said! Or have you forgotten?"

"I haven't forgotten," I said. "But things can change."

"Can they? *Can* they?" John turned to Alex and took a step towards him. "Is that what you're here for? Is that what you're ready to give her? Or are you just another loser wasting her time?"

Alex was still standing next to me. His hand, which had been on the back of my chair, came around to rest on the top of my back. It was barely touching me, but I could feel the tension in it. He moved a half-step closer to me, and slightly in front, as if shielding me from John. "Rowena and I haven't discussed that yet," he said calmly. "Maybe we will someday, but that's our business."

"It's my fucking business too! She's my sister!" John turned back to look at me, his face right up in my face. His eyes were even puffier and more bloodshot up close, and he smelled of cheap beer.

"You told me that that's what you wanted, Ro! More than anything! I asked you why you were throwing yourself away on...*him,* when you could have had a good career, a *great* career, back here in the States, if only you didn't load yourself down with a foreign husband and a foreign mother-in-law and bunch of foreign children, and you said that's what you wanted! You said family was the most important thing for you, that making your own family was more important to you than any career could be! It's what you wanted most in the world, and you'd sacrifice some—what were your words? 'Cold, selfish, pointless career'—to get that! Only what happened? He kicked you out on your ass, and now you've got no husband, no children, and a 'cold, selfish, pointless career' that takes up everything you've got and doesn't even pay well! Well, what I want to know is—is *he*"—he jabbed his finger at Alex—"just another vampire who's going to suck up the last few years you've got to start a family, and then kick you to the curb too? Is he just another parasite, like your last lover and your job and your cat and everything else in your life?"

"Fevronia isn't a parasite," I said.

"No, she's just wormy," said John, leaning back against the counter. I tried to laugh. Alex's hand relaxed against my back.

"Why don't we have some supper," I said.

John wrinkled his nose. His flash of rage was melting away like it had never been, and now he seemed just like my joking, goofy, silly older brother. "Not if it's going to be tofu or lentils or some shit like that," he said. "Let's go out to dinner. Like I said, I'm buying. It's the least I can do to show you I'm not a parasite either."

"You're not a parasite," I said. "None of you are parasites."

"No, but our jobs are," said John. "He"—he nodded at Alex—"might not mean to be a parasite, but how long are you here for, man?"

"Three more days."

"And then you're going to go back to—where? Philly?"

"Philly," confirmed Alex.

"And you're going to stay there for the next two months, because neither of you make enough money to fly back and forth, and it's too long to make the drive every weekend, and that's two more months you won't be getting any closer to making any kind of a decision about your relationship, and that'll be two more months that you, Ro, won't be getting pregnant—how many more months do you think you have? And then you'll both be working over the summer, too, probably in different programs in different states, and then it'll be fall again and the next semester'll be here and you'll still be in some are-we-aren't-we long-distance relationship, five hundred miles apart and too fucking frazzled to think it through. That's if you both still have jobs by the fall. Maybe one of you won't, and maybe that'd be a good thing—but let's say that happens. Let's say Ro doesn't get a job for the fall. Can she move in with you? Can you support her? I don't fucking think so. I think she'll just be your piece on the side, no matter what happens, because no matter what, you'll be fucking married to your faithless whore of a job."

"Or maybe I'll be her piece on the side," said Alex.

"Yeah, for the same fucking reason! Because you're both committed to something that just sees you as a piece of meat to chew up and spit out."

"It could be worse," said Alex. "We could be Marines."

For an instant I thought John was going to throw a punch at Alex, and maybe at me as well, but then he laughed and said, "Too fucking right," and said he felt like Mexican for supper, no arguing, and the moment was past.

46

After his outburst, John was well-behaved for the whole dinner, almost good company. He even suggested that he and Alex go rock climbing together the next morning. What he was like for his second shift of fun and good times that evening, I didn't know and didn't want to know.

"Has he been doing this every night?" Alex asked when we left the restaurant together, leaving John behind. "Staying out and drinking?"

"And picking up a different woman every night, too," I said. "He specializes in blondes. Preferably married."

Alex wrinkled his nose. "I've never understood the attraction of married women," he said. "You know you're just going to get your heart stomped on, and maybe your balls as well. Plus, you're going to break someone else's heart too. If not hers, then her husband's. Either way, you're going to feel like a real shitheel by the end of it, and rightly so."

"I think you've just put your finger on the crux of the attraction."

"Yeah. Your brother is really fucked in the head, Rowena."

"I know. But there's only so much I can do about it."

"Yeah," said Alex. "So you're going to come riding in on your white horse and save someone else's marriage, instead. Shit! I didn't mean that."

"Yeah you did," I said. "And you're right, too. So let's get home so that I can go to bed in time to get up early for my 9:00am couples counseling session."

"Better you than me," said Alex. "Although sounds like there might be a little therapy in this rock climbing session too. But I'd still rather be doing that than dealing with those fuckheads you've gotten mixed up with."

I was heartily agreeing with him when I showed up at 8:45 the next morning at the strip mall where the counselor had her office. I told myself as I surveyed the dingy surroundings not to be so judgmental, and that perfectly decent, respectable people could be working out of strip malls. After all, I was hardly rolling in cash myself, was I? The only reason I worked somewhere more aesthetically pleasing was because my employer put their money into beautifying the campus grounds instead of paying me a living wage.

The inside of the building was even less inspiring than the outside. Dirt-gray carpeting smelled faintly but unmistakably of mold, and the potted plants and cheap artwork couldn't quite hide all the stains on the walls. The receptionist looked like she would have been more at home sitting on a sagging porch in front of a rusty house trailer rather than working the desk at a professional office. When I smiled at her and told her what I was there for, she got flustered, and then she got angry. The counselor had to come out and explain the deal herself before I was allowed back into the therapy room.

The counselor, who introduced herself as Patty, was friendlier than her receptionist. She had a soft Charlotte accent, a warm smile, and a good hundred pounds of extra weight that her cheap suit did little to hide. When I caught myself guessing the price of her clothes, I reminded myself that I also wore cheap suits, and was therefore in no position to judge. Who could afford to buy decent suits, anyway?

I had to concentrate on holding my attitude of non-judgment when Jason came bursting in, five minutes late and in a grouchy temper. We then spent several painful minutes setting up the Skype feed, and a couple more minutes on a blaming match between Jason and Arina.

Patty, in a demonstration of at least a modicum of skill in the couples counseling department, broke up the blaming match before it could devolve into shouting and tears, and suggested that we move right into the main business of talking about why we were there.

"Well, we know why Rowena's here," said Jason, giving me an annoyed look, as if he hadn't asked me there specifically, and as if I weren't doing him a large favor by showing up to this sure-to-be-awkward session in the middle of spring break.

"Yes, of course, but I meant you and—Arina, did you say it was?" Patty struggled to pronounce the name, trying and failing to roll the "R."

"Yes. Arina." Even over the computer, Arina sounded miffed, maybe at being forced into this, maybe at having her name butchered.

"Since Jason has initiated this session, perhaps Jason would care to start," said Patty, her face taking on a look that I, as professionally nice person myself, recognized as a mask to hide her growing desire to give them both a well-deserved smack on the ear.

"I told you!" Jason crossed his arms like a defiant toddler. "I want Max back!"

"Of course you do," said Patty smoothly. "And you're doing the right thing by starting this attempt at a reconciliation. Arina, how about you?"

"Maks misses his father," said Arina.

"And you, Arina?" asked Patty.

Arina shrugged. "I wanted a husband. But maybe not this husband."

After that things went downhill. I had not been prone to migraines in a long time, but I could feel the beginnings of a bad one growing as I sat there listening to Jason and Arina bicker. The problem was that they were not particularly compatible, and Jason was a selfish and occasionally abusive jerk. But now they had a kid, and the kid wanted both his parents, and both of them wanted to do what was best for the kid. Even Jason. Well, as long as it didn't involve becoming a better person, or even apologizing. There was a lot of talk about how it was all Arina's fault, both for running back to Minsk and, as far as I could tell, having some kind of affair while she was still here in Charlotte, and how cruel it was, and how Jason was going to take Maks away from her, and so on and so forth. Fortunately I was only called on to translate a couple of times. Mostly I just sat to the side and wished I weren't there.

"Well," said Patty when the fifty very long minutes were up. "I think this has been very productive, don't you? Shall we say same time next week?"

"I have class," said Jason. "With *her*." He nodded at me as if I were the cause of all his problems.

"Well," said Patty, smiling a false bright smile. "Some other time, then? If you need to check your schedules, you can always phone and make an appointment at a time that works for you." She shepherded us out of the office as quickly as possible.

"That was crap," said Jason when we were out in the parking lot.

"You can't expect a miracle after one session," I said.

"Yeah? You have a lot of experience with counseling?"

"No. I was just expressing a common-sense opinion. Something like a separation in your marriage isn't going to be fixed in one fifty-minute session. And a counselor can't be the wizard who waves the magic wand and makes everything better, any more than a teacher can just pour their knowledge straight from their brain into yours. No matter what, most of it has to come from you. Especially the will and the hard work. Maybe you don't need to see a marriage counselor, but you need to do *something* if you want to fix your problems. And this is a structured way of doing something."

"I don't see why it has to be so difficult," said Jason. He was crossing his arms over his chest like a defiant toddler again. "This stuff should be easy, you know what I'm saying?"

"Why?" My voice was taking on that sharp edge it got with people who were getting on my last nerve. Normally I could repress it, but even a professionally nice person like me had her limits. And Jason, at the end of the day, was a student, and maybe needed to hear some hard truths from his teacher. "Why should it be easy?"

"Well..." Jason looked like he'd never asked himself that question before. "'Cause that's what it's for, ain't it? To make you feel better about yourself? Help you out when times are hard?"

"Among other things. But most people find being in a relationship hard."

Jason's eyes lit up, like he'd found a weakness in me that he was looking to exploit. "Did you?"

"All relationships are hard." I thought about mentioning John. Some might say a brother was the most important man in your life, more important than a lover or a husband or anyone like that. But getting along with them sure could be difficult sometimes. Maybe I should say so to Jason. I looked at his rat-like face, full of craftiness without wisdom. Nah.

"All relationships are hard," I repeated instead. "Well, I have to go now." I made to get into my car.

"Wait!"

I froze. Had Jason remembered that he had promised to pay me for my time and trouble?

"I don't wanna set up another waste-of-time session here, but I do wanna talk to Arina some more. Can you sit in with us again?"

"I don't see why you need me," I said. "She speaks a fair amount of English, and you speak a little Russian. You don't need an interpreter."

"Yeah, but we need"—he shuffled his feet and squirmed—"like a ref or something. You think we were bitching at each other back there, you should see us when there ain't no one there to keep us on our best behavior."

"I hardly think it's appropriate," I said. "Since I'm your professor. I think Patty would be much more qualified."

"Yeah, but...I'll ask Arina, okay?"

"I really think Patty would be more qualified," I repeated. "And while I'm happy to help you as much as I can, I don't have an unlimited amount of time to deal with this kind of thing. That's what marriage counselors are for."

"But Arina likes you. She only wants to do it when you're with us! It would be a lot easier if we just set something up, just the three of us! Maybe at your place. That would be easy and cheap."

"I might be able to squeeze in one more session at some point," I said. "But I certainly can't be making a regular thing out of it. Like I said, that's what marriage counselors are for. And I don't think it would be appropriate at all to meet at my house."

Jason opened his mouth to argue, but I told him I had to go and got in the car and drove away before he could say anything.

47

Jason had come to the counseling session in a beaten-up Ford Ranger that used to be white. I thought I had made a quick getaway and escaped him, but I caught sight of a beaten-up Ford Ranger at two different intersections on my way home, including the light at Providence and Pineville-Matthews Road. Was that little creep following me? That would turn this into a much messier situation.

I wondered what would happen if I had to report one of my students for stalking me. Who would I even report it to? What would anyone do about it? Nothing, that's what. It would just be a massive hassle that would ruin my last couple of months here in Charlotte. Besides, it could be a coincidence. He could be driving to the shopping center across the street, or it could be a completely different beaten-up Ford Ranger that used to be white. They were not exactly in short supply. I decided there was no point in borrowing trouble, and that instead of fretting, I should go grocery shopping. With both John and Alex in the apartment, we were going through coffee at a stunning rate. Occasionally food was consumed as well.

When I pulled up to my apartment, John and Alex were standing outside my door, smoking. As soon as I got out of the car, Alex dropped his cigarette on the ground and stubbed it out with his foot.

"You didn't see that," he said.

"I'm glad to see you two getting on so well," I said. "Did you have a good time rock climbing?"

"Turns out Miller and I were both in Iraq at the same time," said John. "Of course Miller here was sitting in a closet in a boat somewhere, but I guess it still counts."

Alex looked like he wanted to say something harsh, but then he looked at me and swallowed down whatever reply was bubbling up inside of him.

"I'm sure you were both very heroic," I said. "Anyone care to heroically help me unload groceries from the car? I'm not sure I can lift all this coffee."

"I'll come," said Alex. "Since it looks like Halley still hasn't finished his cigarette. And I'd hate for a Marine to have to break a sweat, do some heavy lifting."

John grinned and stubbed out his cigarette too. I wondered if he would clean up all the butts that were now littering the entrance to my apartment. Probably, but he'd grouse and complain about it a lot first. Since he seemed more relaxed than he'd been since he'd shown up, I didn't want to break the mood. Maybe Alex would do it with better grace.

They unloaded the car and carried the groceries into the apartment, bickering amicably about rock climbing, smoking, and other bad habits.

"I used to smoke like a chimney," Alex admitted. "I quit when I got out of the service. I wanted to go clean from all that bad shit, you know what I'm saying? And I was clean for a little while, but, damn, grad school...then I quit again when I defended. Or so I told myself. I had a smoke before my defense and another after, and I told myself that was it, I was done. But I still sneak a smoke sometimes. There's nothing like it for your nerves."

"Yeah, man, I hear what you're saying. Though I bet Ro never smoked in grad school, did you?"

"You got me," I confessed. "I never smoked even when I lived in Russia."

"Nah, 'course not. Why would you do something normal and healthy like smoking?" John grinned as he said it, and punched me in the shoulder to show he was being friendly. Since it was a friendly punch, it only knocked me to the side instead of all the way to the floor.

"Jesus, Halley! Watch it! You okay, Rowena?" Alex had one arm steadying me and the other in front of me, in a kind of shielding position.

"I'm fine," I said. "It was nothing."

"Nothing! He almost knocked you down!"

"It wouldn't be the first time," I said.

"Jesus Christ!"

"Although the last time was when he was twelve and I was eight," I went on. "As I recall, Dad got pretty pissed with him, read him the riot act. He never did it again."

"Yeah. Sorry 'bout that, Ro. Both for that time and for this time." John gave me an awkward smile. "I thought you were sturdier than that. Thought I taught you better self-defense than that."

"I'm fine," I said. "I know you were just playing around. I just wasn't expecting a sparring match. It's okay," I told Alex. "It's fine. Nothing bad happened."

"But it could have." Alex was still standing between me and John. His normal "fuck this" attitude had turned into something much quieter and angrier. I could only see his face from the side, but whatever John was seeing head-on made him put up his hands and take a step back.

"Chill, man," he said. "I said I was sorry, didn't I? And it was just a little playing around."

"Punching a woman so hard she almost falls down is not my idea of 'playing around,'" said Alex.

"Jesus Christ! I thought you served in 2004, not 1904. It's an integrated service now, haven't you heard? We punch women all the time these days."

"That's different and you know it is."

"Hey," I said. "Hey, you two! Hey! Enough. I'm sure we can all agree that there's a clear difference between healthy sparring and beating the crap out of someone, no matter who they are or what the relationship is. Now, if you'll excuse me, I have work to do."

John rolled his eyes. That let the mood break, and in a minute Alex and I were set up with our computers at the table, while John lounged on his air mattress and checked his phone.

"Whaddya think?" he asked, interrupting my and Alex's complaints about the dozens of meaningless emails clogging our multiple inboxes. "This chick wants to get together with me. For a second time. Which isn't really my style. I don't like to give my one-night-stands a second go-round. Except for this Iraqi prostitute. I ever tell you about that?"

"No, and please don't," I said.

"Nah, nah, see, it's not like what you're thinking. She was really sweet, she came up to me and was all like, "Aw, you poor boy, you want some love, don't you? Well let me give it to you.' Sweet, like I said. So I let her give it to me that night, and again the next day."

"John Ivanhoe Elladan Halley, prostitution is a disgusting form of human trafficking!"

"And how the fuck would you know, Ro?"

"Because I used to work with trafficking victims!"

"Well, it's not all trafficking."

"Yeah, but...you were invading her country!"

"For fuck's sake, Ro...and it's not like sailor boy over here is any better. Are you, sailor boy? Although maybe not. What'd they used to call guys in the navy? Doughboys, wasn't it? Probably 'cause your dicks are like dough. You couldn't get it up enough to need a prostitute."

"As an officer and a gentleman, I considered paying for sex to be beneath me," said Alex, shooting his cuffs one at a time with ostentatious little flicks. "Besides, I never had to, unlike some poor pathetic jarhead. And can we go back to the subject of your full name?"

"John Ivanhoe Elladan Halley," I supplied helpfully. "The John part he gave to himself when he turned eighteen. The Ivanhoe Elladan part was given to him at birth."

"Ivanhoe—like Sir Walter Scott's Ivanhoe? And Elladan, like Elrohir and Elladan? Elrond Half-Elven's sons?"

"First of all, fuck you for knowing that," said John. "You're even sadder than I thought. Second of all, ask Rowena what her middle name is."

Alex looked at me expectantly.

"Arwen," I said. "Mom and Dad were very into *Ivanhoe* and *The Lord of the Rings*."

"I can see. And now I feel even more uncool than before. My middle name is James. Clearly my parents were lacking in imagination."

"That's okay," said John. "We forgive you. Anyway, I don't normally do second times, but this blonde chick was pretty fucking hot the first time around. Whaddya say, Miller: worth a second shot?"

"Gosh," Alex said. "Maybe you should try it, Halley. You might find that by the second time you'll have improved your technique enough to actually satisfy your partner. Not all the way, of course. But it might be enough to get her to agree to a third time, and by then you might have a chance. There's this thing called the female orgasm that you might actually get to experience, with enough practice."

"Fuck you, Miller," said John, but he said it amiably. "But you got a point. Maybe by the second time *she'll* have figured out a few things herself. Though she seemed pretty experienced already, you know what I'm saying?"

"What a fucking surprise," said Alex.

"Ah crap!"

Both men looked at me sharply.

"It's nothing," I said. "It's just that Jason has *already* started sending me emails harassing me about doing another session with him and Arina. He wants to set something up for tomorrow." I groaned. "And he keeps wanting to do it here, for some reason."

"Don't let him come here," Alex and John said together.

"Of course not. Although I think he might have followed me home. Or at least I saw a truck that looked like his when I was coming home this morning."

"Are you fucking *serious*!" said Alex.

"And you're only fucking telling us now?!" said John.

"It might not have been him. And he could have been going shopping, just like me. There's no reason to think he's actually stalking me."

"There's no reason to think he's not," said John.

"I hate to agree with Halley here on anything, but he's got a point," said Alex.

"So: what?" I asked. "What am I going to do? Go to the police and say I may have seen someone I know at a large and popular shopping center?"

"I hate to agree with you on this, but you've got a point too," said Alex. "But I still don't like it."

"Well, I'm certainly not going to let him come here. He wants to meet tomorrow. I'll suggest my campus office—no, wait, campus is still closed. I think they've finished up the active shooter drills, but now they're doing some big piece of construction and they've shut everything down. I'll suggest a coffee shop."

"Are you *fucking serious*!?!?" said Alex. "You're not really going to meet with him again, are you?"

"Well, I'll have to meet with him three times a week for the next two months no matter what. And making a big deal out of it seems counterproductive. So what I was going to do was suggest meeting with him one last time, and then insisting that he find someone else to act as the babysitter for his Skype sessions with his wife."

"I don't like it," said Alex.

"I do," said John. "Set up a meeting with him tomorrow, Ro, and let me have a little talk with him beforehand. Or afterwards. Or both. Miller can come along as backup if he likes. He's not exactly what you'd call an imposing presence, but sounds like this Jason shithead isn't either."

"I don't think threatening him would be productive either," I said. "Or entirely legal."

"I'm not going to do anything illegal," said John. "Just put the fear of God in him."

"I hate to say it, but I like this plan," said Alex.

"Fine," I said. "But we're going to do it with finesse, okay? No overt threats. You'll both come along with me and just...be a presence. Maybe Alex can sit in on the session, or something. We'll come up with a reason for you to be there. And John can just drink coffee in the background."

"With finesse," said Alex, his lips quirked in a smile at the thought.

"Hell yeah," said John. "I'll finesse the shit out of the situation. So whaddya think: should I give Hot Chick a second chance?"

"Repetition *is* the mother of learning," I told him.

48

True to his word, John went out that evening in order to hook up with the blonde he had decided to grace with a second appearance. Lucky, lucky her. Alex and I stayed in. Which was, we agreed, much more fun than whatever sad thing John was getting himself into. Plus, we were fresh and ready to go the next morning, whereas John was hungover and miserable, just like he'd been every morning since he'd gotten to Charlotte.

"You're doing this to yourself," I pointed out to him as he rested his head, groaning, on the table.

"I know. I guess I'm like Gary Allan."

"What, you get off on the pain?"

John lifted his head up off the table and made a cocking-and-shooting motion with his finger. "Bingo. And congrats for getting that piece of Regular Heartland America pop culture, Ro. I didn't know you had it in you."

"I spent six years living in Indiana. I feel very immersed in Regular Heartland America."

"Fair point." John took a big sip of coffee and went back to resting his head on the table and groaning.

When it was time to go meet with Jason, though, he stopped groaning and outlined a plan of action that, he made clear, he expected me and Alex to follow.

"No," I said. "Why would you come and talk to Jason one-on-one? That's ridiculous. And it will undermine my authority. *I'm* the professor here. I need to be the one who runs everything. You can come in with me and sit down with me until he shows up, and I'll introduce you, and then you have to leave."

"What if he's there first?"

"Then you'll come up to the table with me and I'll introduce you, and you'll leave. To go browse *Guns & Ammo* or something nearby."

"I don't read *Guns & Ammo*."

"You do when you're acting as my unspoken threat."

John gave me a look of incredulity, which morphed into a pleased grin. "Sometimes I can actually believe you're my sister, Ro."

"I think anyone who takes one look at us would guess that. Everyone ready? Let's go."

There was a short argument in the parking lot over whose car(s) we would take, which ended in all three of us piling into John's car, which was, as he very correctly said, the only one that could be trusted to get us all to the bookstore coffeeshop that I had chosen as our meeting point. I had picked one in the Cotswolds shopping center, which was in a different part of town from the Arboretum, in the hopes of keeping Jason farther away from where I actually lived.

Letting John drive had seemed like a good way to keep the peace, but since he smoked furiously the whole time while cursing out the other drivers at the top of his no doubt rapidly blackening lungs, I regretted my weakness of character the entire way across town. Even Alex looked a little shaken as he climbed out of the back seat once we arrived at our destination.

"Does he always drive like that?" he whispered to me.

"He's always been a fast driver, but this kind of road rage is a new thing."

"Any chance of him letting me drive on the way back?"

"I sincerely doubt it."

"Yeah, me too. Wishful thinking. Okay, are we ready? Everyone got their game faces on?"

"I think you're seriously overestimating the problem here," I said, but I let John and Alex flank me as we stepped into the store, and escort me over to where Jason was already sitting at a table, sipping coffee and looking annoyed.

"Who're they?" he demanded as we came up to the table.

"Hi, Jason. These are some guests I have visiting over the break. My brother, John."

John leaned over and shook Jason's unenthusiastic hand. I could tell from Jason's expression that he'd done it a little harder than necessary, and that John's attempts at looming were working.

"And my friend, Alex. Doctor Miller, actually: he's also a professor."

"You teach Russian too?" Jason demanded.

"Arabic," said Alex, shaking Jason's hand slightly less aggressively than John, but putting on his best I-am-a-professor-and-you-will-respect-me face. I could only see it from the side, but Jason, who got it full-on, shrank back a little in his seat.

"They gonna sit in on us?" Jason asked me. He was trying to look tough, but like yesterday, mainly he looked like a defiant toddler. "'Cause I don't think Arina'd like that."

"No, of course not. They just thought they'd come and browse while we talk. I don't get to see them very often. Actually, this is the first time John and I have gotten to spend any time together in over a year. He's just back from a long deployment in Afghanistan with the Marines."

Out of the corner of my eye I saw John's lips quirk. He mouthed, "Finesse," before turning away to hide his smile.

"So of course we want to maximize the amount of time we spend together now. Who knows when he'll be deployed again? It could happen at any time, you know. So they're just going to browse, read magazines, you know, while we talk." I turned to John and Alex. "I'll come get you when I'm ready," I told them. "I don't think it'll take that long, do you, Jason?"

"Who knows what Arina'll wanna say," Jason said sulkily. "Could take ages."

"I fucking well hope not," said John. "I've got places to be this afternoon. See you in a bit, okay?" He patted my shoulder, nodded in a not-very-friendly manner at Jason, and ambled over to the magazine racks.

"I'll just be over there too," said Alex. "Nice to meet you, Jason. Professor Halley has told me a lot about her students. You're in good hands with her." He also nodded without a lot of warmth, and strode off after John.

"They always like that?" demanded Jason.

"Pretty much, yes. Are you ready to call Arina? Do you have a list of things you want to discuss with her, like Patty suggested?"

"That woman! She wanted to turn this into such a chore. I don't want this to be a chore. Talking to my wife shouldn't be a chore, you know what I mean?"

"Like I said, sometimes relationships can be a lot of work. Shall we get started?"

Jason hadn't brought a list of discussion topics, but Arina had, and she insisted on going through each one of them in detail. This task was not made easier by Jason's unwillingness to cooperate, even though he had been the one to request the meeting.

Getting through everything took the better part of an hour, by which time John and Alex were both circling closer and closer to our table, talking loudly and looking meaningfully at their phones. Finally, after John had already come over once to say that we really needed to get going, Arina agreed that they had talked through everything they could realistically talk through in one session.

"And, because you were so patient, next time I will let you speak with Maks," she said.

"Really?" Jason's face lit up. Then he shut it down again. "You should! I've been more than patient with you, and all you do is make more demands on me!" He turned to me. "Tomorrow work for you?"

"What? I really think you don't need me here for this," I said.

"Sure I do! Don't we, Arina?"

Arina frowned through the screen. "It is better when you are with us," she said.

"If you need a third person to sit in on your sessions, then I really think you should have your therapist do it."

"But..." began Jason.

"I am hardly qualified for this, and besides, it's quite difficult for me to find the time," I said firmly. "I think if you want to move forward, you should work through your therapist rather than having me as your babysitter."

"But..." said Jason again.

"I'm sorry, but I really think you should talk to your therapist about this rather than me. She will be able to help you much more than I can. She's the professional, while I'm just doing this as a favor in my spare time. And I'm not going to have a lot of spare time in the second half of the semester, I'm afraid. It will be much easier for you to arrange things without having to work through me."

"Yeah, but..."

"She doesn't want to work with us anymore, Dzhey-son," said Arina. "And why would she? Thank you, Ro-eenna, for your help," she added formally, in Russian. "Perhaps I will write to you again if I have any questions, but you are right: you have done all you can for us. Dzhey-son and I must work this out for ourselves."

"You're welcome to write to me whenever you want to," I answered in Russian. "But I think you're right: this is something between the two of you. Or maybe with your therapist."

"Of course," she said in English. "Goodbye, Ro-eenna. Goodbye, Dzhey-son." Arina cut off the connection.

"You can't just leave us like that!" said Jason. I wasn't sure if he was talking to me or her. Probably both.

"I have no doubt you'll be able to work things out between you," I said, with much more confidence than I felt.

"Why? We sure as hell ain't managed to yet."

"Yes, well..." I could feel myself softening towards him. "I know you've had your difficulties, but you *do* need to learn how to talk to each other without me around, don't you? I can't be your babysitter forever, after all. Why don't you try a few times without me, see how it goes."

"And then you'll help us if we need it?"

"Maybe." John, who was standing directly in my line of sight, only a couple of tables away, rolled his eyes and slapped his forehead in theatric irritation. "But I doubt you'll need it," I continued encouragingly. "I bet that after a few sessions, you'll realize it's much less awkward without a third person there anyway."

Jason looked like he wanted to argue against that some more, but I stood up and said I had to go before he could get the words out.

"Have a great rest of your break," I said, and left, John and Alex flanking me again. Both of them turned back to give Jason a hard look on the way out the door.

"Sorry that took so long," I told them as we got into the car. "They have a lot of problems."

"Yeah," said John. "But they're not your problems, Ro. And don't let them become your problems, either. You got plenty of your own."

"True," I agreed. "Lunch?"

"Sure," said John. He started up the car, and pulled out of the lot with a chirp of rubber. Which did us little good, since we were immediately stopped at a long red light.

"I think that's Jason two cars behind us," I said as we waited.

"What? Is that motherfucker following us?"

"Probably he's just waiting at the light, same as us."

"Yeah, well, we're going somewhere on the other side of town for lunch, just to be on the safe side."

"Okay," I said.

John gave me a sideways look. "Why the hell are you doing it, anyway, Ro?" he burst out. "It's not like he's suddenly going to become husband of the year."

"Everybody needs a shot at redemption," I said. "Plus, there's a little kid who cries himself to sleep every night because he misses his daddy. Let's not forget about him."

"Yeah, yeah. But seriously? Everyone needs a shot at redemption? Even rat-faced little wifebeating fuckheads?"

"They probably need it more than most," I said.

"It's not like he's going to take it."

"No," I agreed. "Most people don't, in my experience. But it needs to be offered anyway."

"As long as it doesn't get you in trouble, Ro."

"Jason was going to cause me trouble no matter what," I said. "He causes trouble wherever he goes. I was never going to escape it from the moment he registered for my class. But maybe this way my trouble will serve some purpose."

"Yeah. If you say so. I still he think he should be sent to quarterdeck for the rest of his life."

"Yeah, but that's your solution for all problems," I said. "I don't know why. You're an officer, not a drill sergeant."

John grinned. "I can still make quarterdeck happen if I really want to. And there's nothing wrong with it. And who knows? I think a lot of people find redemption there too."

"I'm sure they do. Redemption can be found anywhere, if you're looking for it hard enough."

"Yeah." John went silent for a moment. "I'm going to remember that," he said.

"You've got green," said Alex from the backseat.

John pulled forward too quickly through the intersection, and made a hard turn down a side street with no light. We wound for a while though a subdivision. When we came out on the main road again, Jason's beaten-up Ford Ranger was nowhere to be seen.

49

The next morning I was greeted with a lengthy, poorly-spelled, and unpunctuated email from Jason, saying that he and Arina were going to try to talk on their own a couple of times over the next week, but that he would be sure to get back to me when they needed me. Only it was a lot less polite than that. I wrote back and said I thought them working it out on their own was a good idea.

I was also greeted by an in-depth article by Dima on Nemtsov's murder and its possible connections to the report he had been purportedly planning to release about Russian involvement in the war in the Donbass. I read it through without actually grasping most of the words. Then I read through it again more carefully. I still didn't grasp most of the words. Instead of the article, I kept seeing the phrase "For the love of Christ, don't write back." It had been suppressed by John and Alex's insistent demands for my attention. Which was probably a good thing. But now, with Dima's byline staring me in the face, all I could see or hear or think of was those words, juxtaposed so painfully with other words of his, words that had promised he would always be there for me and I could always count on him and he would never, ever leave me, no matter what.

"I have to go for a run," I said, shutting the computer more firmly than it deserved.

"I'd offer to go with you, but I know you'd kick my ass," said Alex.

"Same here," said John. "No way in hell am I letting you run your nervous energy off on me again. But you sure look like you need it. What'd you read that's got you all worked up? More shit from Jason?"

"Among other things."

"Uh-huh. Did"—John looked swiftly over at Alex, and then back at me—"*he* write you again?"

"No." I stood up. "I'm just going to go out around the neighborhood. I'll be back in an hour or so. Have fun without me, but don't do anything I wouldn't do."

"A run around the neighborhood doesn't look like it's going to do much for you," said John.

"I don't feel like driving anywhere. I'll be back soon. Be good, both of you."

John snorted. Alex watched me with silent concern while I shimmied quickly out of my nightclothes and into my running clothes, but let me go without saying anything. Probably wise.

I started off running much too fast. Then I kept running too fast. I could hear my mother lecturing me about the stress fast running on hard pavement was putting on my knees. It didn't drown out the sound of Dima telling me he would always be there for me, and then telling me to go away and not come back. *For the love of Christ, don't write back. For the love of Christ, don't write back. For the love of Christ, don't write back*...Shit! I needed to stop thinking about it. It was over and done with, and there was nothing I could do about it anyway.

An hour of hard running failed to get it out of my head, though. Maybe what I really needed was company. I let my feet carry me home, still running too fast and hitting the pavement too hard.

50

When I got home, John was gone and Alex was lying on my bed, studying a textbook on advanced Farsi for reading purposes.

"That looks scintillating," I said. I dropped down on the bed next to him.

He shut it with a snap. "It's not."

"So why are you reading it, then?"

"I figured I'd be more competitive if I brushed up on my Farsi."

I put my head on his chest. I felt bad about it, like I was cheating on Dima, but I also wanted the comfort, so I went ahead and did it. I was sweaty and panting, but Alex didn't seem to mind. "How's it going?" I asked.

"Badly. My Farsi's fucking terrible."

"I'm sure it's not that bad."

"It is. It's even worse than my French, and that's saying something."

"I didn't know you spoke French."

"Because I don't. Well, technically I do. And Farsi. Technically I can speak and even teach all three. But my French and my Farsi are a joke. But since one critical need language is not enough, I'm trying to pass myself as off as trilingual—"

"Quadrilingual," I interrupted. "If you count English. Do you have any other hidden talents I should know about?"

He kissed the top of my head. "You bet. I'd be happy to give you an in-depth demonstration of what my tongue can do any time you want. But as far as languages, it's just Arabic, plus a fucking pathetic semblance of French and Farsi."

"That's still pretty good," I said. "I really only have English and Russian. And enough German and French to pass the doctoral reading exams, of course, but that hardly counts. I dabbled a bit in Serbian but never got anywhere with it. I keep thinking I should learn Ukrainian, but so far I haven't."

"Yeah." Alex kissed the top of my head again. "Ukrainian would be useful right about now."

"Yeah."

"So. Want to tell me what the matter is? I take it it's something to do with the guy John refers to as *him*. He filled me in a little, by the way. I hope you don't mind."

"No. I don't mind. It's not like it's a secret."

"Sounds like a mess. A painful mess. Like being sucked down into poisonous quicksand you can never really escape. As it happens, I've got someone kinda like that in my own life. So I sympathize."

"Thanks."

"No problem. What are friends for, after all?"

"Listening to you complain about troublesome exes who can't stay and can't fully leave you, either, apparently."

"Too fucking true." Alex put his textbook down and put both his arms around me, pulling me so that my head was tucked under his chin. "I've gotta leave tomorrow," he said.

"I know."

"I don't want to."

"I don't really want you to either. But if you don't leave tomorrow, you won't be able to teach on Monday, and then the world will come to an end."

"Yeah. Or more likely, my students will cheer, and their parents will complain about not getting their fucking money's worth, and my chair will haul me into the office and lecture me about responsibility and attitude and some shit like that, and I'll blow my stack and do something I regret, and then...I don't know. Where's the downside? I don't see the downside."

"Unemployment," I said.

"Okay, fair point. You know, when it was offered, my new salary seemed like unimaginable wealth. $21,000 for a single semester! But of course it's not. Philly's not cheap, so most of it disappears into rent and all that other shit, till I'm damn near as poor as I was last year. I haven't even gotten my piece-of-shit car fixed up, let alone replaced."

"Maybe something will come through," I said. "Maybe that job in Beirut will work out."

His arms tightened around me. "Do you want me to take the job in Beirut?"

"No, but I don't want you to be broke and desperate the rest of your life either. But there's this thing with the DLI too. Maybe that will work out."

"Yeah," he said.

"You don't sound very enthused about that."

"It beats Beirut. But not by much. Wherever I go, there's gonna be history, problems...you just can't leave yourself the fuck behind, you know?"

"I know."

"And Monterey's pretty damn far away from here too."

"It's still in the same country."

"Yeah, it's got that going for it, but it's not like I could just come over and see you whenever I wanted, is it? If you'd want to see me, that is."

"I would."

His arms tightened around me more, but this time with affection, not tension. "Glad to hear it. But, much as I hate to say it, your fucking brother has a really big point. Long-distance relationships are hard. As you know. And, in case you haven't guessed, I do too."

"I know."

"Yeah. I guess you do." He hesitated. "So...can I ask...about this guy in Russia...?"

"What do you want to know?"

"Whatever would make you feel better to tell me. And, for example, I don't know, did you try to make it work out for a while? Carry on a transatlantic relationship?"

"We did. For six years, the whole time I was in grad school."

"Jesus. How? Why?"

"It wasn't supposed to be that way," I said. "The plan was for us to get married and for him to come live with me in the US while I finished up grad school. Then I'd look for work in the US and Russia, and we'd move wherever I got a job. He could work from anywhere, he said. And his mother would come live with us."

"Jesus Christ, living with your mother-in-law? That sounds like a recipe for a fucking disaster."

"Yeah, I know. But it's the rule in Russia, rather than the exception. And she's a widow, and Dima is her only child, and who else was going to take care of her? And besides, she was always really nice to me. I lived with them for pretty much my whole last year in Russia, and every time I went back while I was in grad school, and it was fine, even in their tiny apartment. Well, as fine as it can be, cohabitating with someone on a fold-out couch in the living room, with his mother just across the wall."

"Sounds awkward as fuck."

"It was okay. You learn how to manage. And everyone takes it for granted there. Although I think it would be better with a bigger house. Anyway, the plan was always for them to come live with me in the US. But it never happened. Every semester something always came up. Either there was no money, or Dima was covering an important story, or Galina Ivanovna—his mother—had something going on at work, or I was studying for comps, or Dima had an important story...it was pretty much always that Dima had an important story, to be honest. Or he was in jail."

"In jail!"

"For political protest, that kind of thing."

"Yeah. Okay. I can see that. But Jesus fucking Christ."

"Yeah. But really, looking back on it, it was always that Dima had an important story, something he couldn't leave. We could have found the money, and I could have managed to study for my comps, and all that, with him around. We could have at least gotten married, since I went back every summer and winter break. But we didn't. We'd email each other almost every day, and Skype each other pretty much every week, and I'd go visit him for every break—but sometimes he wasn't even there for that. Sometimes I'd fly in and two days later he'd fly out, off to cover Abkhazia or South Ossetia or Transnistria or Nagorno-Karabakh or wherever.

"So I'd sit at home with his mother, since I couldn't go out and do things after spending my every last penny on the airfare out there, and we'd drink tea with jam and discuss poetry. She was the one who got me into poetry, actually. She'd always wanted to study philology instead of medicine, and she kept her apartment crammed full of books of poetry, and she'd read it to me every chance she got. She was so thrilled when I decided to write my dissertation about Tsvetaeva. We'd talk about it for hours, and she really helped me develop my thesis and flesh out the details, find obscure poems that supported it, that kind of thing. She should have gotten credit as my advisor, to be honest, not my actual advisor. Anyway, so I'd sit there with her and work on my dissertation and sometimes we'd talk about what a hero Dima was, just like his father, and just as likely to get himself killed."

"Shit."

"Yeah, his dad was killed in Afghanistan when Dima was a baby. He doesn't remember him at all. And Galina Ivanovna never remarried. She said one man was enough, and Dima was sure to be even more trouble than his father. Which was true. Anyway. Anyway, we kept the relationship going almost the whole six years, but we never managed to move it to the next level and get married like we should have, and then one day it was over."

"I'm sorry," said Alex. "Like I said, I know what that's like. It sucks."

"Yeah, it does."

"So are you off long-distance relationships forever now?"

"No," I said. "But I don't think I'd let things drag on like that again. I think I'd insist on coming to some kind of a resolution, one way or another, after a couple of years at the latest."

"Yeah. Me too. I just...I don't know. I don't want to throw this away right now, Rowena."

"Me neither."

"Glad to hear it." He nipped at my ear, making me laugh and squirm out of his arms. "Naughty boy," I said, pushing him back on the bed.

His pupils dilated, making his hazel eyes dark. "Yes, ma'am," he said. "I apologize."

"Apology accepted."

"So what do I have to do to atone for my bad behavior?"

"I believe you said something about wanting to demonstrate your oral proficiency."

"Yes *ma'am*. I would be *delighted* for you to give me an oral proficiency interview."

"Then what are we waiting for?" I said.

51

John managed to be almost civil to Alex that evening, and again the next morning as Alex packed up and got ready to go. He said several times as he was doing it that he wished he could stay for one more day, but he really had to get back and prep for Monday's classes. I said several times that I understood, and that we would stay in touch and visit each other again soon, maybe when the semester ended, maybe earlier.

"Yeah," said Alex. "I guess it's not that long a drive to get down here, is it? I could totally do it in a weekend if I put my mind to it."

"Or you could fucking fly, if you had any money," put in John helpfully.

"Or I could luck out and catch a cheap flight from Philly to Charlotte, even without any money," said Alex.

"Yeah," said John. "And maybe soon you'll be working a real job with the DLI, and be able to fly over from California whenever you feel like it. Or maybe Ro could fly over and stay with you."

"That would be nice, if she wanted to," said Alex. "But let's not count our chickens prematurely. Well." He hoisted his backpack up on his shoulder. "I'm off, then." He kissed my cheek. John made gagging noises in the background.

"You don't have to be here for this," I told John.

"Where else am I going to be? Okay, enough. Get on the road before you lose your nerve, man."

"Yeah, okay, okay." Alex kissed my cheek again and gave me a hug, before walking, even more quickly than his usual quick movements, out the door. He waved at me from the car and again as he was pulling out of the parking lot. Then he was gone.

"So," said John, when I came back inside the apartment. "You gonna mope and cry all day?"

"No," I said. "Are you?"

"Fuck no. Let's go run Crowders again, for old time's sake."

"Only if you're ready to get your ass kicked down to the ground even harder than last time," I said.

"I think you'll find I've got what it takes to kick *your* ass, Ro."

John's bluster all the way to the park notwithstanding, the run ended up being a tie. Although maybe a tie that I finished slightly ahead in. But I didn't say anything about that on the way home, or when we went out again that night. I did remark on John's decision to come back home with me that night, and not try to score one final one-night stand.

"I don't want to show up at work hungover. Plus, I might have to make one final run to Gastonia on my way home, and I wanna be sharp for that."

"What's in Gastonia?" I asked. "A woman? Someone you're considering for the long term?"

I said it with a smile, but John didn't smile back. "Just some people I need to see," he said, and refused to talk about it the rest of the night.

52

John's unusual temperance the night before paid off in unusual good cheer the next morning. He bounced out of bed, downed a large pot of coffee, and told me he needed to head out in order to get home in time to get dinner and get ready for going back to work the next morning.

"And looks like I don't need to stop off in Gastonia on the way, so it'll be a straight shot," he said.

"That's good."

"Yeah. So...thanks for putting up with me, Ro. I mean it. I know I've been kind of a pain in the ass"—"More than 'kind of,'" I put in—"Okay, okay, a giant pain in the ass. An even more giant pain in the ass than usual. What? You think I don't know what a pain in the ass I am? Of course I know. Hell, I *revel* in it. You might say that's what I live for. But even I know sometimes enough is a enough."

"Wow," I said. "Wisdom. Watch out, or you *will* end up working as a life coach by the time you reach your forties."

"Smartass. But seriously, anything comes up, you need anything—just give me a call. I'm only a few hours away."

"Of course," I said. "And same here."

"For now."

"For now," I agreed.

"And I really hope that someday really soon you'll be somewhere not just for now, but for a long time. You *need* to get out of this shitty situation you're in. I've said it before and I'll say it again, Ro: You don't have to do this. You *shouldn't* be doing this. You're smart. Way too smart to be letting people treat you like shit all the time." John had been leaning casually against the kitchen counter, looking almost relaxed, but now he was straightening up, getting angry again, pointing his finger at my face. "No, don't argue, just listen, okay? You had to borrow money from me to pay rent this month, for fuck's sake."

"You offered," I said. "I didn't ask."

"No, but you fucking well should have! And I don't mind, because you're my kid sister and it's not like I've got anyone else to spend my money on, but for Chrissake, Ro, you're almost thirty-five, you have a PhD, and you can't even make rent."

"That's not my fault. Or not just my fault. Lots of people in my situation are in the same boat."

"Yeah, I know, but you know what? That doesn't make it okay. That's not an excuse for letting yourself be used like this. Just walk the fuck away, Ro. Find something else to do. For fuck's sake, marry this Miller guy and go be a housewife."

"I didn't think you liked him. At least not that much."

One side of John's face turned up in a smile. "I'm an asshole, Ro; haven't you noticed? I don't like anyone. Especially some guy who's fucking my little sister. But I'm smart enough to see that he's smart, and kind, and seems to like you pretty well, so if he could pull it together enough to get a decent job that would support you, I'd be all for it."

"That's not entirely under his control," I said. "And *if* we were to get married, which is a lot less likely than you seem to think it is, maybe I'd be the one to pull it off and get a decent job that would support us."

"Maybe. I wouldn't count on it though, and then what's he gonna do anyway? Hang around cooking and cleaning for you?"

"Why would that be worse than me cooking and cleaning for him?"

"Because, for fuck's sake, Ro, you wouldn't be cooking and cleaning for him, you'd be doing it for *you*. You'd be doing it for *you,* Ro, and that family you told me you wanted more than anything else in the world. You told me that Plan A was to save the world, but we both know and we always knew that was never gonna happen. But Plan B was to get married and have kids and be happy. And you know what? That's doable. People who are way stupider than you do it every day."

"Most of them don't seem very happy."

"Yeah, but neither do you, Ro! How happy are you now, huh? Tell me the truth: How happy are you now?"

"Not very happy," I said, my chest tight. "But at least I have the promise of happiness, John. Or not happiness, but something more important."

"What the fuck is more important than happiness?"

"You tell me," I snapped. "After all, you joined the *Marines*. I don't think you did that because you thought it would make you happy."

"Yeah, actually I did, Ro."

"And did it?"

He took a deep breath and turned away from me, leaning his palms against the counter and not looking at me. "Not the way I thought it would," he admitted.

"And yet you're still there. You haven't quit. You're planning to serve out your twenty years, aren't you? Even though they keep sending you to bad places and getting you involved in bad things, and then you come home and drink and chase married women because you can't stand the idea of someone depending on you. What about you, John? What about *your* need to have a family, and all that?"

"This isn't about me, Ro."

"But don't you see? Maybe I feel exactly the same way you do! Maybe I can't quit for the same reason that you can't."

John turned back towards me and looked at me like he'd never seen me before. "That's fucking awful, then, Ro," he said after a moment.

"No worse than anything else. You say I'm not happy, and maybe that's true, but I'll never be happy living just for my own happiness. I have to be devoted to something other than myself. Whether it's a man or a movement, I can't just be stuck in my own selfish self. I have to be giving myself to something. And I'd say the same about you."

"I'm not in the habit of giving myself to men much, Ro," said John. He looked angry, but also as if he were trying not to laugh.

"Not in a sexual way, but what else do you think you're doing? You've spent your entire adult life giving yourself up to something bigger than yourself. Something, I have to point out, that's mainly made by and for men. And you can't stop."

"Yeah," said John. "Yeah. You're right. Yeah."

"And it's eating you up, I can see it! Or something is."

"Yeah," repeated John. "Something...Ro. I don't think I can do this anymore."

"I know," I said.

"No, I mean, I know I've said it before, but...this time it's different. This time I really don't know if I can keep going. Go back and keep going. You know...you know where I was before I came here? Where I had to go before I came here? And go again a few days ago? Did I tell you what the whole thing in Gastonia was about?"

"What?" I asked.

"I was...one of my kids...I know we're supposed to call them 'men,' or, these days, 'servicemembers,' or something like that, but they're really just kids. This one was nineteen. A lot of them are.

Nineteen, and even stupider than I was when I was nineteen, which is saying a lot. This one...he got killed, Ro."

"I'm sorry," I said softly.

"Yeah, and it was his own stupid fault! And mine! But mainly his, even I can see that. Stupid kid! It was the day before we were supposed to leave, the last day before the pullout, and...and he wasn't paying attention and walked into a spinning rotor and...kid hamburger."

"I'm sorry," I said again.

"So I felt like I had to go see his parents. And tell them how sorry I was, blah blah blah, and how he'd died a hero—but he hadn't! It was just a stupid accident! Plus, he was a cocky fuckup who was no great loss, to be honest. He was a pain in my ass the entire time he was under my command, and I was actively scheming to get him transferred as far away from me as possible. But he was their son, and he's gone and he'll never come back to them! And I had to look them in the eyes and tell them that! And then they wanted me to come back and see them again, so I did. But all that sitting around and talking about him we did didn't make him one iota less dead. Thank fuck they said not to come for a third time. And—it was a stupid, senseless, pointless tragedy. We weren't even supposed to be there! We were supposed to be out of there already! It shouldn't have happened, but it did, and it happened on my watch! And it...somehow it seemed to sum up my entire fucking life. Just a stupid, senseless, pointless tragedy. And then I came here, and...and I haven't been able to get sober since, and I can't stop fucking women who don't give a crap about me, and, well...shit. What is wrong with me, Ro?"

"I think you're unhappy," I said. "And rightly so."

"I fucking deserve this for everything I've done, is that what you're saying? I'm a bad person and now I'm getting my just desserts?"

"No," I said. "I don't think you're a bad person, John."

"But you think I do bad things, right?"

"You've done a lot of good, too."

"Yeah? Like what?"

"What about all the kids you've taken under your wing, and helped out when they were in trouble, and taught how to read and write and balance a checkbook, and all the other things that they needed to learn but that no one had ever bothered to teach them before? What about that twenty-year-old who got his girlfriend pregnant, and you arranged for him to get leave, and went to his wedding, and made sure they got the help they needed when the baby was born? What about all those kids you helped get into college, one way or another, and put them on a path to a better life than they ever would have had if they hadn't served with you? What about when your friend Bryson wanted to kill himself after he lost his leg, and you went and sat with him every night for a week, and got in touch with his dad when he wouldn't, and brought them back together? Or this family you've been going to see in Gastonia, even though you don't want to. And what about..."

"Jesus Christ, Ro, you're going to make me sound like a fucking saint, and we both know that's not true. Just look at me!"

"I am. And I know you're not a saint. In fact, like you said, you're the biggest pain in the ass I've ever met."

"Worse than Dima?"

"Even, God help me, worse than Dima in some ways. But you're still my brother, and you've still done good in the world. Even when you were in a really bad spot and it was really hard for you. Like that story you told me about how you stopped them from firing on those villagers in Afghanistan, or the family you helped in Iraq, driving them yourself to the doctor when no one else would, or..."

"Stop it, Ro. I know you're just trying to make me feel better. I know how you feel about what I do."

"There are better things you could be doing, in my opinion. But there are worse things too. Much worse things."

"Well." He took a deep breath. "That's probably the nicest thing you've ever said to me, Ro."

"Jeez. That makes me sound like a really bad person."

"No. It's because you're a good person, Ro. You're a good person, and I know you think a lot of what I do is wrong, so when you say that what I'm doing isn't so bad, that I'm helping people at least some of the time, well, it means a lot more coming from you than from someone else. You know, being your brother is tough. Maybe even tougher than being Mom and Dad's son. You're all such a bunch of fucking saints, so where does that leave me? The only way I can make my mark is by being a sinner. So here I am. But I still want to hear you tell me I'm a good person despite the fact I'm not, so thanks. And jeez, next you're going to tell me even I get a shot at redemption or something, right?"

"Gosh," I said. "Glad to help. And yes. Everyone deserves a shot at redemption, and you more than most."

"Thanks. I really mean that. And you know what, Ro?"

"What?"

"There are worse things you could be doing, too. In fact, if they paid you, I'd be thrilled that this is what you're doing. For a while there I thought you were going to be splashed across the front pages as the next sacrifice to the Putin gods, so you know what? Being poor as fuck is a step up from that."

"I'm glad you think so."

"And seriously, Ro, if you don't get this job you've been telling me about, there are other things you could be doing that would be even better. Like tutoring. One of the women I met here told me how she's bringing in hundreds of dollars a week as a test prep tutor. You could tutor the shit out of overprivileged teenagers, way better than her, since you're not a self-centered slut who has to come up with excuses for why she has to get a different dick in her every night."

"I'm glad to see that you respect your sexual partners."

"If they were worth respecting, they wouldn't be fucking me."

"That's sad."

"Yeah, whatever. You know what I mean. But you could totally get into the tutoring business, move in with Miller, and bring in a nice chunk of change wherever you had to live."

"You seem really fixated on Alex," I said.

"Because I think he's the best thing you've had going for you in the past ten years! Maybe ever! So don't fuck it up, Ro. Don't get so obsessed with what you think you want that you throw away what you really need."

"That," I said, "is good advice, and I wish you would take it for yourself."

He grinned. "Maybe I *should* start charging for it, just like you said. Set up as a life coach after I get out of the Corps. Straight talk and tough love, and I'll send 'em all to quarterdeck if they don't listen?"

"Sounds like a million-dollar idea to me," I said.

"For sure." He punched me lightly in the shoulder. "Well...it's been fun, Ro. Or at least, less sad than it could have been. And really, seriously, call me if you need me, okay? For anything. I can be over in a few hours if you need me."

"Thanks," I said. "Same here. I'm only a couple of hours away. Let me know if you need anything, even if it's just a shoulder to cry on."

"Marines don't cry. But Charlotte is a great place to pick up women, so I might be back sooner than you think." He pushed himself away from the counter. "But I gotta go now Ro, so take care of yourself. Don't let anyone take advantage of you or talk you into doing anything you know is a bad idea, okay?"

"Okay," I said. "As long as you promise to stay away from married women who just want to piss off their husbands and brag to their friends about bagging a Marine. I don't know what you see in them, I really don't. They're just into your uniform."

"Yeah. Sometimes I feel like I could have them fuck my uniform, and we'd both be happier. They don't give a shit about me at all. I'm just a fantasy and a suit of pretty clothes to them."

"Since it's International Women's Day, I have to tell you 'Welcome to being an attractive woman,'" I said before I could stop myself.

He laughed. "I walked right into that one, didn't I? It's not as much fun as I thought it would be."

"So stop."

"I don't know about that, but I'll give it a try. I guess. And I guess you're going to tell me that now I know what it's like to be you, right? I'm getting in touch with my feminine side, or some shit like that?"

"Mary Wollstonecraft would be so proud of you," I said.

"Who the fuck is that?"

"An 18th-century feminist scholar who said that both women and soldiers were defined by their clothes."

"Jesus fuck, Ro, where do you read all this shit?"

"School. I have a PhD, remember? That makes me officially smarter than you."

"I don't know 'bout that."

"Okay, fair enough. But it does mean that I know about people in times past who have gone through the same things we have now, and who've thought about the same things and come up with wisdom that maybe we could apply. So I'm going to use that position of power to tell you that you need to get yourself under control and stop sleeping around with married women. It's only making you unhappy. Besides, if you don't, I'll tell Grandma on you."

He held up his hands in surrender. "Jesus, Ro, pulling out the big guns now? Okay, I promise, I promise. And now I gotta go." He put his arms around me and pulled me into a bear hug, before pushing me roughly away, shouldering his bag in a jaunty swinging motion, and heading out the door. I watched him give me a one-finger salute before starting up his car and driving away.

53

The week after John and Alex left seemed flat and boring. In general I liked living by myself, but the apartment felt empty and my evenings felt long and excessively work-filled without them. Even John. Fevronia continued to be affectionate, but cats and humans provided very different kinds of affection, and the one couldn't replace the other. Tsvetaeva and Akhmatova had harsh things to say about both brotherly and loverly love; how would they weigh it against feline love? Maybe I needed to get a dog. Maybe a dog would provide canine love, which still wouldn't be the same. Maybe John was right and I needed to make an active effort not to spend the rest of my life wandering lonely as a cloud from ill-paying job to ill-paying job.

My sense of discontent was increased when I discovered via The Wiki that someone else had been offered the Alaska job. An inside candidate, to be precise. They had gone to all that trouble and torture when they already had someone there doing the job. There was considerable speculation on The Wiki about whether they had always planned to hire the inside candidate and had just been going through the motions of a competitive search in order to placate whoever it was who demanded that all faculty positions be filled through the facade of a competitive search, or whether they had seriously considered getting rid of the person who'd been working there for years, and bringing in someone more glamorous. None of us, including the inside candidate herself, knew.

The knowledge that both the North Dakota and Alaska jobs had fallen through made me spend the weekend sending out more applications, including applications for jobs that had opened up teaching Russian at Fort Bragg and McChord Air Force Base, as well as a community college in Alabama and a high school in—no!—New Jersey. All of them sounded like nightmares, and Fort Bragg and McChord had already rejected me last year, but whatever. You only get if you ask, and I didn't have anything better lined up for next semester.

The following Monday, though, I got an email from the search committee for the job at Crimson.

Dear Rowena (if I may),

> *Greetings! I hope you are doing well, and your semester is coming to a satisfying conclusion, and without too much stress! As I mentioned during our first meeting, we were considering holding a second round of interviews for the Visiting Assistant Professor of Russian position. After extensive deliberation, the committee has decided to proceed with that plan. However, it will be a bit of an unusual second-round interview! I suppose we all must move with the times. Instead of the more traditional campus interview, we have chosen to move forward with conducting the second-round interviews remotely, an arrangement we hope will be more convenient for everyone.*

> *As you may have already guessed, I am writing to inquire if you are still interested in the position, and to invite you to the next round of interviews. Because there have been some changes in the membership of the search committee, and two of the new committee members are technically on*

leave or research sabbatical this semester, we have decided the simplest way to bring everyone together will be via conference call. Now we just have to hope that the technology gods smile down upon us! In any case, we will have our able IT technician—I suppose that's a bit of a tautology, or at least an infelicitous phrasing, isn't it? But that's what we call them—standing by. All you will have to do is provide us with your phone number. I have been assured that either a land line or a cell line will be equally adequate.

Please let me know regarding your interest and availability at your earliest convenience. I'm afraid our own schedule is a bit tight due to previous commitments on the part of some of our committee members, but I am sure we can find a mutually satisfactory time! Our tentative interview slots are at 11:00am , 12:00pm, or 1:00pm Eastern time the coming Friday.

Looking forward to your response!

Warmly,

Theresa Mayfield

Associate Professor of French

Department of Modern Languages

Crimson College

I punched the air in triumph. Then I groaned. Another interview! When would this torment end? I had obviously made it into the top three, but another round of interviews meant at least another month before I found out either way. The semester here at

UNC-Matthews would be almost over. I supposed it didn't matter, but the idea of finishing up the semester *again* without any kind of firm employment prospects for the following semester was agonizingly grim.

Don't think like that! Think about the positive. This was definitely better than any prospect I'd had so far, after two years on the market. And while another round of interviewing was unappetizing, and phone interviews were the most awkward form of interview, it meant that I didn't have to cancel classes and make a whirlwind trip down to Georgia during the busiest period of the semester.

I wouldn't have to cancel classes *if* I could snag that 12:00pm interview slot, that is. All that talk of the difficulty they'd had in finding mutually compatible times even for a phone interview was ominous. As was having hour-long slots for the interviews. That sounded like requesting a different time would cause inconvenience and headache, which would predispose them against me, so I had damn well better go with the originally offered times and not try to make any waves. And hour-long slots meant...God, what would we even talk about? I could commiserate with Masha, my best friend from grad school, over Skype for hours, and sometimes Sveta and Lena, my other close grad school friends, too, and Dima and I had always found plenty to say...and show...and do...to each other, but talking with interview committees was torture. How in God's good name were we going to fill an entire 60 minutes?

Maybe they're just well-organized and are factoring in time for deliberation and note-taking and technical consultations, I told myself. It was a comforting thought, if not one that I had much reason to believe. But that's what I was going to think so that I didn't freak out any more than I was going to already.

And now I needed to get back to them right away and see if I could claim that 12:00pm spot. I hit "reply" and started to type.

Dear I wrote. Then I stopped. Ah shit! Theresa had called me by my first name, with that super-annoying "if I may" tagged on at the end. I never could tell if people who did that were trying to be approachable and put things on a friendly footing, or if they were trying to intimidate me and put me down. Sometimes it was one, sometimes the other. But now I didn't know what to call her. If she had just written "Dear Rowena," I would have no problem responding in kind. The same with "Dear Doctor Halley." But "Dear Rowena (if I may)"? What kind of terms were we on now?

I spent the better part of five minutes agonizing over that, five minutes that were maybe being spent by the other, more organized and decisive, candidates in responding to their own emails and claiming my coveted noontime interview slot. So I decided "Aw, fuck it," and plunged ahead.

Dear Theresa I wrote (if she took terminal offense from that, the job was probably doomed anyway),

> *Thank you for contacting me. I am still extremely interested in the position, and would be delighted to participate in a second-round interview. Doing things by phone will certainly make it easier for everyone!*

> *The most convenient slot for me of the three you have indicated would be the one at 12:00pm Eastern, as I have class at 11:00am and 1:00pm. However, I am completely at your disposal.*

> *With best wishes* (I couldn't quite bring myself to sign off with "Warmly" to someone I had only met during a Skype interview),

> *Rowena Halley, PhD* (I added the last bit after another couple of minutes of back-and-forthing. "Adjunct

Professor" seemed too demeaning to use as a title but I felt like I should put *something*. So I went with PhD).

I hated the look of that "PhD" there, but every second I wasted worrying about it was a second in which one of the other candidates could be pipping me to the post for that midday interview slot, so I bit my lip, bit my tongue, bit everything that needed biting, choked back my distaste, and hit "Send."

54

Theresa got right back to me to say that the 12:00pm slot was mine if I desired it, so that was easy enough. Maybe a little *too* easy, the part of me that had watched too many movies wanted to say.

Having the interview that Friday meant little time for preparation, but also little time for fretting. And how much more preparation could I really do? Oh God, what were they going to ask me? How on earth could we fill an entire hour talking about things we hadn't talked about before?

It's not about exchanging information, it's about seeing if you like each other, I reminded myself. Job interviews were more like dates than anything else, especially at this stage. Although I had so rarely made it to this stage that I knew that more from hearsay than personal experience. But that's what everyone said. So I needed to brush up on my charm rather than my insider info. But I *also* needed to brush up on my insider info.

And maybe my Russian. It had been months since I'd gotten to spend much time speaking Russian with anyone other than beginning students, and my last session with Arina had made me uncomfortably aware of an increasing inability to speak in sentences longer than three words. With accompanying hand gestures to help my interlocutor puzzle out my meaning. When I had had Dima and my Russian grad school friends to write and talk to every day, I had felt—and been—fluent even after months in the US, but now, when it was just me, Fevronia, and a bunch of people I spent three hours a week teaching how to say, "I have a red suitcase," I could feel my tongue and brain growing rustier by the day.

I spent a while worrying about that on Tuesday as I skimmed through the Crimson website, trying to guess what we might talk about at the interview and what I could research that I hadn't researched already. Then I shut down my computer and drove over to the Matryoshka Market, which I had been told was the premier (and only) market for Eastern European food and other items in Charlotte. I would spend money I didn't have on authentic treats for my students, and would also look for books. Now, three years after my PhD comprehensive exams and a year after my dissertation defense, I felt like I was almost ready to start reading Russian books again, instead of just scrolling through news reports, a sick feeling in the pit of my stomach.

The Matryoshka Market was in a strip mall that was somewhat less nice than the strip malls in my part of town. Its sign was a matryoshka doll with peeling paint. Good thing they weren't playing to stereotypes. The only person there was a Caucasian-looking man sitting behind the counter. He gave me one sharp glance and went back to looking bored.

I strolled around. There was, as promised, a wide selection of candy, waiting to be scooped out of its bins. There was also a haphazard pile of used books on a table by the door. I went over to browse. Maybe I could find something by Ulitskaya. And didn't Prilepin have a new book out? About the first Gulag camp?

I dug around on the table for a while, but failed to find any such gems. Eventually I settled on an extremely battered copy of Danil Koretsky's *Antikiller*. That would certainly expand my vocabulary.

The man at the counter livened up a little when I came up with my book, and even more when I said I wanted to buy large quantities of candy. He told me bits of his life story in Russian with a strong

Armenian accent as I bought a kilo of bulk candy. I hoped the students liked it. I hoped it wasn't so far past its expiration date that it was inedible, or maybe poisonous.

"Come back anytime," the man told me. "We don't get very many pretty women in here, just old Soviet *babushki* who weren't pretty during perestroika, and are even less pretty now. The last pretty woman who used to come in here regularly was Arina, from Minsk." He sighed. "But then she had to go home. Her American husband was causing problems. I offered to sort everything out, but she was afraid the American would cause more trouble."

"Really?" I said. "I think I might know her. With a son, Maks?"

The man brightened. "Cute little boy. Spoke Russian like a girl, though. I tried to teach him to speak Russian like a man, but he wouldn't listen. Kept telling me my accent was wrong. Hah! Of course I have a mountain accent. I'm proud of my Caucasian accent, even if it would get me in trouble back in Moscow these days. Or Minsk, probably. That Arina—she used to turn her nose up at me. Viktor from Armenia wasn't good enough for her! Then she warmed up, got friendlier, as her husband caused more and more trouble. She was worried about him taking the boy and deporting her. And she was right to worry. I told her she wouldn't be the first person that'd happened to. So I helped her get away. And with other things." He grinned at what were obviously warm memories.

"Um...is that so? It sounds like an, um, complicated situation."

"Families are always complicated," he said philosophically. "And I felt bad about taking a boy away from his father. But he was a Yankee, so I didn't feel too bad. Yankees need to have things taken away from them sometimes; it's good for them. Remind them that you can't just spend your life accumulating more stuff than you can ever need. Well. I have...connections, shall we say. Well, you know how it is. I'm Armenian. Of course I have connections. So—what kind of passport do you have?"

"American," I said.

"Is that so? What, you got your citizenship already?"

I smiled and nodded, not bothering to say that I'd gotten my citizenship when I'd been born.

"You must have connections too," the man said, looking at me speculatively.

"Of sorts. But probably not as good as yours."

"Everyone knows I'm the person to come to in Charlotte if you need help with visas, passports, getting in and out of the country...America has so many laws, you know, and these Americans, they try to follow their laws, it can be so annoying sometimes the way they say they don't take bribes—but you can always find someone."

"I'm sure," I said.

"Although in Arina's case it didn't take much. She just had to get a passport for the boy, which wasn't difficult. Well, the only difficult thing was doing it quickly, without her husband finding out. But we did it, and legally, too. More or less. A visa, too. And then she just...picked him up and left. Like I said, I was sorry to see her go, and I felt bad about taking a son away from his father, but that man was never much of a father to him, so I didn't feel too bad."

"Mmmm-hmmm," I said.

"And now—maybe Arina's told you—she's talking about coming back. She sent me an email a couple of days ago saying she wants to come back, maybe, and what should she do about the paperwork."

"She hasn't told me," I said. "Do you think she's serious about it?"

He shrugged. "With Arina who can say? I wouldn't come back to that husband, would you?"

"No," I said.

"No woman in her right mind would. Although"—he grinned again—"she might not be coming back to him. But people will do almost anything for an American passport. Look at me: I used to be a banker. Now I sell old candy by the kilo. But I sell it in America, so I tell myself it's worth the sacrifice."

"Many people think it is," I said politely.

"What about you? Well, you've already got your passport. You could go back if you wanted to. Or maybe not. Do you have any sons?"

"No," I said. "No sons."

"Good. It's okay for little boys, but you know what happens to the older ones, don't you? They say they draft them into the army."

"Yes," I said. "I've heard that. But since I don't have any sons, it's okay. I might go back someday."

"You should go to Armenia," the man told me. "They say it's nice now. And—you married?"

"No."

"Not anymore, right? You got your passport and you got out of there. Good for you. You should go to Armenia and find yourself a real man for your second husband."

"Good idea," I said.

"Mountain men are the best," he told me with a leer.

"So I have heard," I agreed. "Well, thank you very much for all your help, but it's really time for me to go."

"Any time." He gave me another leer. "Come back any time. I'm always ready to help pretty women."

I thanked him for his offer, and left. At least, I told myself, I had proof that my Russian was still good enough to pass as a native speaker under the right circumstances. So that should give me a big boost of confidence going into the interview. If only that would be enough.

·

55

Friday brought the second interview with Crimson. I tried very hard not to think about how this could be a pivotal, defining moment in my life. I tried very hard not to think about how simple, trivial encounters could change the course of your whole life. *For the love of Christ, don't write back*...No! I definitely wasn't going to think about that. I was going to focus on getting through the interview, and accepting the fact that lots of things, including things that directly affected my future happiness and prosperity, were largely out of my hands. But first I had to get through my morning classes.

Everyone seemed distracted and out of sorts during class, making it hard to get into the flow of things and stop worrying. Jason came up after the first class and said that he and Arina had been talking, but that she had said she needed a break from all this interaction, and could I change her mind.

"I'm sorry, but I don't have that kind of control over her," I said, trying to slide out of the room as fast as possible. "And maybe she's right. Sometimes it *is* good to take a break."

"You think so?"

No, I didn't. I thought it sucked, especially when the other person was the one calling for it. "Yes, I said cheerfully. "Now, if you'll excuse me, I have to get to my next class."

Shaniqua grabbed me as I was trying to slither out of my second class.

"Oh, Rowena! Thanks for the letter of recommendation. The program's already gotten back to me, asking for some more information. Can I go over their questions and the materials with you?"

"Sure," I said, sidling as quickly as possible towards the door without actually turning tail and running. "Only I've got an appointment now, so..."

"It'll only take a minute, I'm sure."

"My appointment's right now, so I'm afraid I really have to go. But email me everything, and we can go over it after my last class, or next week."

"When's your last class over?"

"Two," I said, edging out the door.

"I've got class at two."

"Then email me everything and we'll go over it on Monday. Sorry! Gotta go!" I speed-walked down the hall, ignoring Shaniqua's words about "urgent." There was very little in academia that was actually urgent on a Friday afternoon. Except interviews.

Fatima was just coming out of her office as I approached mine. I waved to her and tried to open my door as quickly as possible, hoping she wouldn't stop to say hi.

"Hi!" she said. "How is your week? Are you ready for the weekend? How are your students?"

"All good!" I said with manic brightness. "Now, if you'll excuse me, I've got an appointment." I got the door open and darted through it like a rabbit, closing it in her startled face. I felt bad, but when I checked the time and saw it was 11:58, not that bad.

I set myself up at my desk, phone in front of me, ringer on. 11:59. I riffled through the notes I had left sitting square in the middle of the desk before class this morning. Nothing new jumped out at me to enlighten me. 12:00. Okay, *this was it!* 12:01. Or not. 12:02. Where were they? Was there something wrong with the connection? 12:03.

Was I wrong about the time? What if I'd gotten everything wrong, and already missed the interview? What if...

The phone only rang a long, long, *long* nine minutes after 12:00pm. This time the desire to scream was even stronger than the time before. How could something that posed no physical danger be so terrifying? But it was. And then when the phone rang, I nearly dropped it trying to answer it.

"Hello? Hello, uh, Rowena, is that right? Can you hear me?"

"I can hear you just fine." That was only somewhat a lie. The connection was crackly, and the speaker's voice kept going in and out.

"Oh *good*. We're doing this over conference call, and I'm afraid none of us are very good at this kind of thing. But two of us are here in the room with you—virtually, that is, haha—and two more of us are phoning in from out of state."

"Hello, Rowena!" boomed a man's voice, making me jump. Some crackling noises followed, which I assumed were the other out-of-state interviewer trying to say hello.

"Very nice to speak to you all again," I said.

"Yes, of course...we're not *quite* the same committee you spoke with last time; there are some new members, but some of us old guard are still here," said the interviewer. "Well, I am, at least. You remember me, of course: Theresa Mayfield. I'm afraid that there's just *so much* committee work going on right now, what with the proposal to reorganize the language programs, that, well, the rest of the original committee couldn't make it, and we had to call on some faculty members who are currently on leave. But that's one of the wonderful things about Crimson: we're a very close-knit community, and everyone's always ready to pitch in whenever anyone needs a hand."

"Then I'm very glad to meet—"

"Anyway," she rushed on before I could finish what I was saying. "I know we're running behind—so sorry about that; you know how it is—and I know you have class at one, so let's get started, shall we?"

"Of course," I agreed. There was nothing else to say. It didn't matter that I didn't know who was who of the people I was speaking with. It wasn't like I could see them, or even hear them that well, anyway.

Theresa jumped into a number of the same standard questions that we had gone over last time, asking me about my teaching experience, my research portfolio and plans, my ideas for growing the program...it felt sometimes like I could answer these questions in my sleep. Which was good, because I never felt entirely conscious while I was answering them. I couldn't help but worry as the words floated out of my mouth, seemingly with little connection to either my body or mind, that maybe I had memorized the wrong answers. Maybe the reason I had never gotten a decent job offer was because most of what I said was stupid. Maybe most of it was gibberish! Maybe I was actually speaking in tongues the entire time without realizing it! Maybe...maybe I needed to focus on the matter at hand. We seemed to be coming to the end of the regular questions. This ordeal could be almost over...Theresa had just taken the kind of breath interviewers take when they're about to launch into a new, unexpected topic. I braced myself.

"You're not finding that your language skills are deteriorating with only teaching introductory and intermediate levels this semester?" she asked, with the warm sympathy that was often such a bad sign.

"It *is* a concern," I agreed, infusing my voice with as much warmth and sincerity as I could manage. "But I have been taking the opportunity to keep up my skills by doing some extra reading. I always keep up with the news and other media sources, but now that

I'm no longer dissertating, I've gone back to reading for fun in my spare time."

"That's *wonderful* that you're reading in your spare time in order to keep up your language skills," said Theresa. I could almost feel the condescending pat on the head over the phone connection. "What are you reading right now, if you don't mind me asking?"

What I was reading right now was the battered copy of *Antikiller* that I had picked up at the Matryoshka Market, but I rather wished I weren't, what with all the violence and the soulless sex, and I certainly wasn't going to admit to it. "Post-Soviet fiction," I said instead. My voice didn't sound evasive at all to me.

"How lovely," said Theresa. Apparently my voice hadn't sounded evasive to her either. Or maybe both of us were excellent liars. "You know, I've often wondered about creating a Special Topics course or maybe a First Year Seminar on something *contemporary*, you know? Not that it's my area of expertise at all, but my impression is that Russian always seems so stuck in the classics. Introducing some contemporary works might be just the thing to spice it up, don't you think?"

"Yes, I think that would be a *wonderful* idea," I agreed. "I would be *delighted* to create such a course."

"If you *were* to create such a course, what authors would you include?" she asked.

Shit! The only name I could think of right now was Danil Koretsky. *Don't say Danil Koretsky!* I ordered myself. But at the moment the name DANIL KORETSKY was blotting out the names of literally dozens of other authors who would be more appropriate to mention, and whom I knew much better, some of them personally as well as professionally.

"Well," I began. *Stall for time, stall for time, stall for time until you remember some names!* "Post-Soviet literature has become a very, shall we say, heterogenous field. The relaxation of censorship in the

Yeltsin period, and to a certain extent the early Putin period, along with a turn towards a freer market in publishing, has meant that you now see everything from the traditional 'brick'-style serious historical and philosophical works, to samizdat-style satirical critiques of society, to the pulpiest of pulp genre fiction, all being sold together on tables outside every metro station. I mean, to give one such example, there's the popularity of low-grade thrillers like Danil Koretsky's *Antikiller"—maybe if I say the name, it will be exorcised from my brain!—*"not that I would want to build a course around *that*, fascinating as it is as a cultural phenomenon."

Theresa laughed politely. I found myself laughing along with her, although my laugh sounded more sycophantic and hysterical than polite. *Oh God! I am becoming everything that I hate! And I **still** can't remember any other names! Keep talking, keep talking!*

"Plus the rise of internet publishing has meant a flourishing situation with regard to blogs, independent media, and self-published fictional works, despite the creeping return of censorship in recent years," I said. The authority in my voice was astonishing. It was almost like I actually knew what I was talking about, instead of drowning in a puddle of sweaty fear. "And, in contrast to earlier eras in Russian literature, female authors are really finding their voice. Instead of just the occasional lone savant, like Karolina Pavlova or Anna Akhmatova or, of course, my own Marina Tsvetaeva, it seems like there is a rising collective of female authors with an interest in telling specifically female stories, be they journalists and non-fiction writers, as in the case of Anna Politkovskaya"—*YES, YES, YES! I remembered a name*—"or Yuliya Latynina, who to a certain extent has taken up Politkovskaya's mantle following her assassination—as I just mentioned, I read a lot of news, which I consider to be a very important 'art form,' for want of a better word, in contemporary Russian letters; or fiction, as in Lyudmila Petrushevskaya and her interest in 'female Homers' and the written transmission of the oral storytelling style." *HOLY SHIT WHERE DID THAT COME FROM????? AND WAS IT REALLY PETRUSHEVSKAYA WHO SAID THAT? MAYBE IT WAS ULITSKAYA. OH GOD, IT WAS ULITSKAYA. IT WAS ULITSKAYA, AND NOW I'M ABOUT TO BE CALLED OUT ON IT. AND THEN I'LL BE SUMMARILY REJECTED AND DOOMED TO A LIFE OF FAILURE AND POVERTY. OH GOD, WHY AM I DOING THIS? I SHOULD JUST PACK IT IN AND SEE IF I CAN GET A JOB AS A BARISTA.*

"That does sound extremely interesting," said Theresa. "And you have quite an impressive command of contemporary Russian literature. I have to confess I've never heard of—what did you say her name was? Petrushka?"

"Petrushevskaya," I said, trying not to flinch at being forced to repeat what I was now convinced was the wrong name.

"Petrushevskaya," Theresa repeated, her voice plummy with satisfaction at getting the difficult name out. "Maybe you could create a course specifically focused on contemporary women's writing. I could see that being a big hit, especially if it were cross-listed with WL, um, GB, uh, TQ—Women's and LGBTQ Studies, that is. Wait...I think they've added something to it, but I can't remember what. Was it A? For, I guess, asexual? Or was it P? Darryl, do you remember?"

"Maybe it was D," said a man's voice doubtfully in the background. "For demisexual."

"It could have been S," volunteered the man with the good connection to the conference call. "For sapiosexual."

"What's that?" asked Theresa, temporarily diverted.

"When you're sexually attracted to smart people," explained the good-connection speaker.

"That's a sexual orientation?" exclaimed Theresa. "I wish it had been invented back when I was still in school, then."

There was some hollow laughter from all of us.

"Anyway," continued Theresa, "I don't think that's it. Is it P? For, ah, polysexual?"

"Polyamorous?" suggested the booming-voiced man. He sounded far too pleased at the word for me to be comfortable, especially in the middle of an interview.

The man with the bad connection tried to say something at length, but all I could hear was static.

"I'm sorry, Alan, what was that?" Theresa shouted into the phone, making me jump.

"I think what Alan is trying to say is that we discussed making it P at a faculty meeting last semester, but eventually it was voted to make it A for Asexual," said Darryl from the background. "I just checked."

"Oh!" said Theresa. "So asexual means...what?"

"Math majors," I said before I could help myself. Then I felt bad, but I felt a lot less bad when everyone burst into laughter.

"Math majors need lovin' too," said the booming-voiced man. I tried not to convey any sense of cringing from the lasciviousness in his voice. I had just scored a major point; shouldn't go wasting it with a little squeamishness.

"So what are—what did you call it, Darryl?—demisexuals?" said Theresa.

"I think it's someone who's only sort of interested in sex," said Darryl.

"Oh! Really? So I guess that would be—"

"Engineering majors," said Darryl, just as the loud-voiced man said, "Women."

"Yes," said Theresa, in a way that made me think she cared for the loud-voiced man even less than I did. "Anyway," she continued. "I'm afraid I'm a bit behind the times, but I can't help but notice that what we used to call 'Women's Studies' is now a catch-all for anyone who is sexually...unusual. Makes you think, doesn't it? Especially since most of these other people are men. Anyway, I'm sure we could still find a cross-listed home for a course on Russian women's writing there. Of course, we might not get a lot of male students, but you'd be surprised at how many hetero cis-gender males we *do* get in our WLG, um, BTQ, um, A classes." She sighed. "They *can* be a trifle...outspoken sometimes. I get a fair number of them who sign up for my French literature classes and don't realize they're cross-listed as WGLT—I mean, WLGB, uh, TQA—classes, and, well...but such things make lovely teachable moments, don't you think?"

"I do," I agreed, with all the perky enthusiasm I could muster. "Knowledge is only gained through confrontation with the unknown, and all that."

"Of course, of course." She laughed, only a little bit hysterically. In the background, I could hear only slightly hysterical laughter from the rest of the committee.

"Well, Rowena, I have really enjoyed this, and I could talk to you all day about contemporary women's fiction—and students' reactions to it—but I'm sure you have things to do, so I'll wrap this up. And, just to let you know, we'll be finished with the second-round interviews this week, and the committee will be deliberating the following week, and we hope to present a candidate to the dean's office the week after that, and they normally get back to us with an approval—they almost always approve our selections; it's really just a formality, but formalities must be observed, of course—within a couple of weeks, rarely longer, so we are very much hoping to be able to make an offer within a month, or six weeks at the outside."

"I see," I said, when it became apparent that a response was expected. "That's quite...prompt. And thank you for being so transparent about the process."

"Oh, of *course*. We pride ourselves on our transparency here at Crimson, you know, as well as our close, collegial atmosphere. So thank you again, Rowena, and we will be in touch very soon."

The line went dead before I could respond. Maybe that was a good thing, because my first thought was that "within a month" was a new and unusual definition of "very soon." Although by academic standards, "within a month" *was* very soon.

I wiped off my sweaty palms on my shirt, trying not to press it against the rivulets of fear-sweat running down my stomach and sides, and checked the time. 12:50. I had a whole ten minutes to pull myself and all my stuff together, run to the bathroom, and make it to 2105.

The time crunch didn't prevent me from Googling Petrushevskaya's Wikipedia page while I was walking down the hall, and forcing myself to read it, even though I could hardly bear to look at it through one squinted eye...I was about to find out that I had ruined my entire future...YES, THERE IT WAS! IT WAS PETRUSHEVSKAYA WHO SAID THE THING ABOUT FEMALE HOMERS! I'M SAFE! I'M SAFE!

I broke out in another sweat, this time of joy. And then I remembered that none the interviewers had known who any of these authors were, and didn't speak a word of Russian. I could have attributed that quote to Mirra Lokhvitskaya or Nadezhda Krupskaya or Saint Fevronia herself, and they wouldn't have known the difference.

You're the expert now! I reminded myself. Which was a terrifying thought. Being the expert meant I was even more acutely aware of all the things I didn't know. My God! No wonder the world was going to hell in a handbasket. If *I* was the expert, what did that say about the level of ignorance of all the non-experts? What did that...fortunately, my panic-stricken musings were interrupted by my arrival at my classroom, where I was, inarguably, more of an expert than everyone else.

56

After the interview was over, there was nothing for me to do but go home and wait to hear back from them. And from everyone else I had applied to and who hadn't gotten back to me. It was already the end of March, and I still didn't have anything lined up for next fall.

I did get contacted by the summer program at Indiana, asking me if I'd be available to come back to teach that summer. Which was great, except that I still didn't have any clarification over the Madison situation. I could see lots of reasons why going with Madison and especially her father to Russia would be a bad idea, but I felt it would be rude to make other plans without consulting them. Which meant contacting them. Which I didn't really feel like doing. But with the IU summer program wanting me to make a quick decision, I couldn't put it off. So, biting my lip with distaste the whole time, I fired off a quick email to Erik Johnson, asking how Madison was doing and letting him know that I had another offer for the summer that I was considering taking.

Dear Rowena he wrote back almost immediately,

Thank you for your consideration in contacting me. I am pleased to say that Madison is continuing to do well in her program, and we are seriously pursuing some kind of a trip this summer as a reward. However, her mother has—now that Madison looks like not being in such desperate need of her—asked for a partial reconciliation with the both of us. So we are currently planning to combine the two things, and to take a short trip to Europe, including Russia, together as a family. Frankly, I don't think Madison is completely pleased with this development, but I think it's important for all three of us to try to reconnect. So thank you very much for all the help you've given us, and have stood ready to give, but if you have a job offer for the summer, I would go ahead and take that if I were you. Certainly any place that can snag your services is lucky to have you! Let's keep in touch, since I sincerely hope that one day we can persuade you to come back to NJ.

All the best,

Erik

I laughed over that, in relief at not having to deal with demands that I join them in Russia, and joy in not having to count on Erik Johnson to help me out when he had always been a rather slender reed to lean on, and a little bit of mirth at the idea of attempting a family reconciliation while traveling through Russia. I had never met Madison's mother, but my image of her was of a super-spoiled and self-involved person who would not handle inconvenience well. Not that Erik or Madison were that different. I spared a moment to hope that they were in Moscow or St. Petersburg during the annual water shutoff for maintenance. Boy would that be funny. Then I felt ashamed of that thought, but that didn't stop me from chuckling over it on and off for the next hour.

That taken care of, I wrote back to IU saying, with more truth than normally accompanied the words, that I would be *delighted* to come work for them this summer. Then I spent a while staring at my bank balance and trying to figure out how I was going to afford the trek back there. Especially since I had a six-month lease on my current place, which meant that I was going to be paying double rent in June unless I could find a short-term sublet for the apartment here. And was I even allowed to sublet it? This sent me on a dive into my rental contract. Nope. No subletting.

So that was $1,000, or more than 1/10 my total pre-tax salary for the spring, going down the drain. And I would need to find a place and set up a sublet in Bloomington, put down a deposit, and then make my way over there. Which would mean packing up all my stuff and doing something with it. Every move caused me to pare down on my belongings more and more, but I still had a bed and a table and two chairs and a chest of drawers, not to mention a large collection of books related to my area of expertise, and something had to be done with them. Oh God. Probably the best thing would be to find a furnished apartment in Bloomington, and then put my furniture and so on into storage. Storage wasn't that expensive, right?

This led to another bout of research, which told me that I was probably looking at about $100/month. Probably for lots of people $100/month wasn't that much money. For me it was. *And* I would need to rent a van and find or, more likely since I didn't have any friends in the area, pay helpers in order to load up the furniture. Between the month of rent I wouldn't be able to get out of, and storing my stuff for the summer, I was looking at $1,500-2,000. Plus another $1,000-1,500 for rent for the place in Bloomington over the summer, plus gas and sundry expenses. And let's not forget about groceries. I would get paid for the Indiana job, of course, but I would have to put down my deposit and get myself out there in May, and my first paycheck would only come at the end of June. Good thing even after the new phone and Fevronia's vet visit I still had a little over $1,000 of the money Erik Johnson had given me, or I would be stuck in Charlotte with no way to leave and no way to get to a new job. And they wondered why more people from disadvantaged backgrounds didn't go into academia...

I wrote a long email to Masha, letting her know the situation and asking her to keep an eye out for a good sublet. Then I spent the next several days talking her down from the ledge she was currently teetering on as she prepared for her dissertation defense. Which did very little to calm my already frayed nerves.

57

Masha successfully defended during the last week of March, which caused me to exhale a sigh of relief almost as big as hers. Not that I had doubted her ability to defend, but you never knew what curveball a committee might throw you. In theory it was in their best interest to pass you and get you the heck out of there, and most of the time that was how they operated, but as Dostoevsky had so astutely noted in *Notes from Underground*—now I could remember it, after not thinking to bring it up during my ill-fated interview for the permanent position I hadn't gotten in Charlotte—humans are primarily motivated by willfulness, not self-interest.

That massive hurdle cleared, we both could go back to worrying over our non-existent job prospects. Masha was interviewing for a short-term position at a Catholic school, which she had grave reservations about.

"They're Catholics, not monsters," I said. "You'll be fine as long as you don't bring up the Irish Troubles."

"The what?"

"You know, Northern Ireland?"

"What about it?"

This led to a lengthy digression about Northern Ireland, which Masha, like most Russians, had a hard time understanding, since to her all Westerners were Catholics.

"Don't worry about it," I finally counseled her. "Just try to get the job. And try not to need contraceptives."

"Khakhakha! Khakhakhakha!" We both laughed darkly over the idea of needing contraceptives, since my boyfriend, such as he was, lived three states away, and Masha didn't have one at all. Then we made tentative, and not entirely joking, plans to look into stripping over the summer if we didn't have anything in our actual field lined up for the fall.

"We could probably find work right here in Bloomington," she said hopefully. "It's a big university, with lots of athletes and your weird American fraternities. I'm sure there are plenty of strip clubs here, we just never went to them. But they must be here. We wouldn't even have to move."

"What if some of our former students came and saw us perform?" I asked.

"Tfoo!" We both spat in disgust. Then we speculated on whether former students would tip us extra out of sheer pity.

The first week of April was spent discussing with Masha the pros and cons of various sublets she had found, and trying to brush off Jason's insistence that I sit in on a Skype session with him and Arina again. The second week of April brought an elated message from Masha that she had been offered the Catholic school job—"I'm so grateful, I might convert," she said—and a much less elated message from Alex that he had been offered a 1-year position at the DLI.

It's not the permanent position I originally interviewed for, he texted me. *That went to someone else, of course. And maybe that's a good thing. I don't know how long I really want to be there. But they decided they needed a short-term person as well, so they offered the chance to me. It means moving out to California for one year, which sucks. Both the California part, and the one year part.*

It's still a job! I texted back encouragingly. *At the DLI! Surely that's some great letterhead to use for sending out your applications next year.*

*Oh God. **More** applications? Another year on the market? Kill me now!*

I know how you feel. But what are you going to do?

I don't fucking know, he texted back. *I just don't feel like I can take another year of this shit, but I don't think I could look myself in the face if I gave up. People keep suggesting looking into alt-ac jobs, but they're not exactly a dime a dozen either, are they? It's not like I can just magically snap my fingers and find some other kind of job. I suppose I could go into intelligence, but even if I wanted to, which I don't, those jobs are hard to come by too, and take months or years to get sometimes. Oh God! Oh fuck! Maybe I should become a plumber, what do you think?*

Would you enjoy being a plumber? I asked.

I don't think so. I think I'd hate it. But maybe I'd hate it less than this.

Yeah. I know what you mean. In any case, you've got something lined up for next year, which is great.

Sort of. How do you feel about coming out to CA at some point?

I will if I can afford it, I promised.

Yeah. Well, I might be so desperate for company that I'd spot you the airfare. Shit! I didn't mean it like that. I wouldn't be doing it because I'd be desperate for just any company. I'd be doing it because I wanted to see you.

I know what you meant, I wrote back. *And I appreciate it. What are you doing over the summer? Do you know yet?*

Ugh, don't fucking remind me! I just signed the contract. I'll be teaching at the summer program there in Monterey. Which I'm not very fucking happy about. But it was sweet, sweet cash in my pocket.

Pocket cash is nothing to sneeze at.

No, it isn't. Well, maybe we can get together before, during, or after our summer teaching jobs? What do you think?

I think we should try.

Yeah, me too. Although I hate that your brother was right about how difficult this long-distance thing is.

It wasn't like we didn't already know that.

Too fucking true. What's wrong with us, Rowena? Why can't we find someone closer?

Because we're picky and difficult? Because there aren't very many partners for people like us? I mean, can you really just go into a bar and pick up the first woman who catches your eye? Because I can't. The first man, I mean. But you know what I mean. Most people bore me out of my mind.

Yeah, me too. Well, I guess we're stuck with each other for the moment at least. Pact :) :)?

Pact, I wrote back.

Sweet. That makes me feel better, actually. Like it's one less thing for me to have to worry about right now.

Yeah, me too.

Although I see how it could so easily lead to taking each other for granted and falling into the long-distance pseudo-relationship trap.

Yeah, me too. Pact that we won't do that?

Pact :) :) he wrote.

I still don't know where I'll be in the fall, but maybe you could come down to Charlotte at the end of the semester? And/or visit me in Indiana before the start of the program?

I'll have to check on dates for the latter, but for the former, definitely. Meanwhile, do you want to practice building a sophisticated literary language of feminine desire? :) :)

Absolutely, I texted back.

58

The third week of April was, as I was acutely aware, the one-month mark after the second Crimson interview, which meant that I should hear back from them any day now. Just any day now. I got up on Monday and checked my email. Then I checked The Wiki. Then I checked it many more times than was healthy all day. The same for Tuesday. Still nothing. The only person who seemed to want to have anything to do with me was Jason.

He cornered me after class on Monday, pulling me aside and complaining that Arina still didn't want to talk to him.

"Did she say why?" I asked. "Or give a time when she'd want to start talking to you again?"

"Just a load of bull honky," said Jason. "She's not sure she wants to get back together with me, she's not sure she can trust me, she wants Max to grow up with his family—like I ain't his family!"

"Of course you're his family," I said soothingly. "But he has family there too."

"Not like me!"

"Yes, of course. Now if you'll excuse me, it looks like the next class is waiting to get in."

"What?" Jason looked around in confusion, and continued to look confused as Fatima bustled in and started putting her books and papers on the lectern with ostentatious flair.

"The next class," I repeated. "We need to make way for the next class."

"'Kay. I'm gonna email you about it. Maybe you can talk some sense into her." Jason left before I could argue against that plan.

"That man." Fatima shook her head. "Always keeping you here."

"I know."

"Is he a good student? He doesn't look like a good student."

"No," I said. "He's not a good student. But he does want my help. Although not with schoolwork."

Fatima shook her head again. "He looks like a problem."

"He doesn't just look like a problem, he *is* a problem," I said. "Well, I'll get out of your way."

Jason emailed me after class, and, when I told him I didn't think I could help him solve his marital troubles and he should consider seeing a therapist again, or just giving it a rest until Arina was feeling more in the mood, he emailed me again twice on Tuesday, insisting that only I could help him. So I agreed, with considerable reluctance, to message Arina and see what she had to say.

I messaged Arina on Skype on Tuesday. I got a reply on Wednesday, but from Marina.

Tell Jason to back off, she wrote. *Arina needs to think.*

That's what I told him, I wrote back. *But he doesn't want to hear it.*

*Maybe he **needs** to hear it*, she responded.

I'm sure he does. But that doesn't mean he'll listen.

When do men ever listen?))))

Very rarely, I wrote back. *But maybe if Arina gave him some kind of a time for when she'll get back to him, he'll calm down.* To be honest, I felt just the tiniest bit sorry for Jason. Not because he was a good person, but because I knew all too well what it felt like to be pushed away and cut off by someone you desperately wanted to be with. Not that Jason seemed to care about Arina in the slightest, but he did, in his own way, seem to love Maks, and he had to get through Arina to get to him. I wondered if Dima felt the same kind of irritation towards me that Arina obviously felt for Jason. What an awful thought! To become a thorn in the side of the person you thought loved you more than anyone in the world. It was like we were living through *Anna Karenina* or something. Or maybe *The Kreutzer Sonata*. Tfoo! Hopefully without the murder and suicide. But crazy love/hate could make people do all kinds of bad things.

Thursday I got a message from Arina.

Tell Jason to stop bothering me for now, okay? He made all kinds of threats the last time we talked, and I don't want to talk to him until he's calmed down.

What kind of threats? I wrote back.

The usual kind. He's going to take Maks away from me, he's going to deny me my chance at American citizenship, he's going to kill me...you know how it goes.

That sounds serious.

Very serious! And I was thinking of coming back to Charlotte. Not to Jason, you understand. That's over. To someone else. But then he and Maks could see each other every week.

And you told him this?

Oh, he's known about the other person for ages. It was one of the things that drove us apart. Of course, he cheated first. But yes, I told him the last time we talked that I was thinking about coming back, but to the other person, and he lost his head. So now I don't want anything to do with him, and I don't want Maks to have anything to do with him until he can calm himself down.

Understandable. Do you think he will?

With Jason who knows? Right now I'm mainly worried about the other person. Do you think you could check on him?

Well...I don't know him at all.

He says he thinks he knows you. It's Viktor from the Matryoshka Market. He was surprised to learn you weren't actually from Moscow.

Really?!? Well, um, I suppose I could drop by, but surely a warning coming from you would have more effect.

Yes, but I hate being so far away! I feel like bad things could happen to people who are important to me, or people who are important to me might do bad things, and I'm on the other side of the ocean and can't stop them.

I know that feeling very, very well, I told her. *Very well. I'll check on him. Does he work in the store every day?*

Tuesday through Saturday.

I'll go on Saturday then.

Thank you!!!! I'm sure Viktor will complain about me sending a woman to look after him, but I don't have anyone else, and besides, for some things a woman is better, don't you agree? More subtle, more trustworthy. I knew I could count on you. Now let's hope Jason doesn't do anything stupid before then.

Let's hope not, I agreed. I was unsure how I was going to prevent it or what I was going to do about it if he did, but I promised again that I would go check on Viktor as soon as I could.

59

Still nothing from Crimson, either in my inbox or on The Wiki, on Friday. I slept poorly, a situation not helped by Nevaeh crying half the night, and got up on Saturday so convinced that I was going to find an answer waiting for me, one way or another, that I checked my inboxes and The Wiki three times before I was able to grasp the fact that there was still no news.

Your problem is that you're too dependent on other people, I told myself. *You're desperately waiting for news about a job offer that you have almost zero control over. You're still mooning over Dima's decision to break it off, even though you had no control over that either. And even though you're not really in love with him, you can't help but smile and feel like at least there's something right in this world every time Alex texts you. You need to stop depending on other people so much. There's probably some Buddhist teaching about that or something.*

Brave words, but the problem was that, all brave words aside, I *was* dependent on other people, and in very real, very physical ways. This job offer I had almost no control over could mean the difference between another year, and maybe a whole career, of financial stability instead of precarious poverty.

And while I didn't have very much control over the men in my life, the plain truth was that if I wanted to have love and a family, which I did, then a man was essential. Tsvetaeva had a number of things to say about that. Maybe I should spend a while rereading

Letter to an Amazon, in which she explained why women inevitably went back to the husbands who could provide them with children, instead of staying with their lesbian lovers. Maybe I shouldn't be taking life advice from someone who had ended a turbulently unhappy life by hanging herself. Maybe people like that had the best advice to give of all, since they actually knew what life was like, unlike people who'd had softer rides. Maybe I should stop refreshing my screen, do some asanas and forms, go for a run, and then, if there was still nothing, fulfill my promise to Arina and go check on Viktor from the Matryoshka Market. At least someone would be getting some kind of benefit out of my existence.

Two hours of vigorous exercise later, followed by a hot shower and a short play session with Fevronia, and there was still nothing from Crimson or anyone else of interest. I put on my second-nicest (of three) outfits and set off for the Matryoshka Market.

It looked even more rundown and faded than I remembered. This time a couple of other cars were parked in the parking lot, and a handful of Soviet-looking women were moving slowly around the store, criticizing the goods for sale.

I bypassed them and went straight to the cash register, where Viktor was sitting behind the counter, reading a newspaper in Armenian.

"Akha," he said when he saw me. "The American who is almost a Russian. What is your name, by the way, American? I don't think you told me last time."

"Rowena," I said. "But my Russian-speaking friends normally call me Inna."

"Inna," he repeated. "A good name. How can I help you, Inna?"

"I'm actually here because of Arina," I said.

He stiffened. "Is she okay?"

"Last I talked to her, she was fine. But she's worried about you. She wanted me to come check on you. She's afraid that Jason might...do something."

"Akha." He nodded. "Very possible. That Jason—a real temperamental guy. But not like an Armenian. I don't think he has any mountain honor, like a real man. He's the kind of man who stabs you from behind because he's too scared to come at you from the front."

"You may be right," I said. "Which is why Arina asked me to, well, warn you, and check up on you."

"I am offended," said Viktor, but he was smiling as he said it. "That she would send a woman to protect me! What kind of a man does she think I am?"

"I think she thinks you're a better man than Jason," I said. "But she also said for some things you need a woman's touch."

Viktor nodded. "Very true. But not in matters of honor, I think."

"Well...if there's anything I can do for you, I guess, um, I'll leave you my card? In case you need to call me for, I don't know, help."

Viktor took my card and looked at it with interest. "That is very kind, Inna, one might even say gallant, but I think you should be calling me for help, not the other way around. I'm the man. I'm the one with connections."

"I'm the one who was born in America," I said.

He laughed. "Good point! Very well, Inna. I have my own protection—your American gun laws are so delightfully free and open!—and I'm not so poor and defenseless as you might think. This store is, shall we say, just one of my business ventures, and it suits me to make it not worth noticing. If I need help, I can call on it—or buy it. But I will take your card, and if there is anything I need from you, like the testimony from an American citizen of good repute, I will call you. Now, is there anything you want to buy?"

"Um…" I looked around the store. Everything seemed as old and faded on the inside as on the outside. "That's okay," I said.

"Here." Viktor winked at me. "For being so brave. Some October chocolate. On the house."

60

Monday brought the last week of regular classes. There was still nothing either way from Crimson when I checked my email and The Wiki before heading off to campus. But that was unlikely, I told myself. Probably they were going to send out their letters in the afternoon. Or maybe they'd made an offer to someone who wasn't on The Wiki or didn't want to share that an offer had been made, and that person was taking a while to mull it over, and meanwhile the rest of us were left hanging. Also a plausible scenario. In fact, the most plausible scenario. Probably they *had* made an offer last week, just not to me, and now they were waiting for the official acceptance and the paperwork to go through with their first-choice candidate before informing the rest of us. That must be it.

That thought brought with it the calmness of despair, which got me through my first two classes in a fairly even-keeled state of mind, even when Jason tried to pester me after class and Fatima gave us a death glare for being in her way when she arrived.

I gave into temptation and anxiety and spent the hour between my second and third classes repeatedly checking my inboxes and The Wiki, but the only result was that the calmness of despair left me, and I was in a state of jittery nerves for my third class. Luckily, everyone had learned so little about Russian Civilization over the course of the semester that they couldn't tell how shaky some of my answers to their questions were. To them I was still an oracle of wisdom because

I could spout out the dates of major revolutions and wars without checking Wikipedia.

By Tuesday there was still no news. I told myself I was resigned to my fate. My resignation increased when I received rejections from the two high schools I had applied to. Well, that was okay. American high schools were bad places, and working at them was not a morally good thing to do. Of course, American colleges were also bad places, and working at them was probably not a morally good thing to do either. But I didn't have a lot else going for me, so I should send out more applications instead of finally sending off that article I'd been half-heartedly working on all semester. And I should stop thinking about how this kind of selfish, weak-willed thinking was how the Nazis came to power.

But before I gave myself more fully over to the Dark Side, I had to finalize the details of my short-term move back to Bloomington, which involved going to the bank and wiring the deposit for the sublet that Masha had, after weeks of searching for something slightly less sketchy than most of what was available in Bloomington, found for me. Then I reserved the moving van and storage unit in Charlotte, which left my credit card balance scarily high and my bank account scarily low, and sweet-talked John into coming over for the weekend and helping me move out.

"What about Miller?" he asked, once I got him on my third call that evening. "Or is he too much of a wimp?"

"He's getting ready to move to California. He offered to come down and help me pack up, but I said I really couldn't ask him to do that when he was in the midst of getting ready for a giant cross-country move himself. We're trying to coordinate things so that he can stop off and spend a couple of days in Indiana with me on his way over."

"And this is how you want to spend your life," said John.

"No, but it's how I currently am spending my life. If I could just snap my fingers and make it so that I could have the job and the man of my dreams, and all conveniently located within the same geographical location, I would, but I can't."

"Yeah," said John. "I know you would, Ro. Okay. I'll be there. But you're going to owe me a beer. A lot of beer."

"It's a deal," I said, with more confidence in my beer-buying abilities than they actually deserved. I was going to get paid for April on Thursday. That $1,500 would be enough that I could at least find the change for a 6-pack somewhere. Sure I could. Providing it was the cheapest possible kind.

By Wednesday the reality of next week's final exams was beginning to penetrate the students' brains, and anxiety levels were high. If only they had been higher earlier in the semester, then they could be a little lower now. But I didn't say that, instead promising to post extensive study guides on the class websites. It would give me something to do other than stress about my rapidly onrushing unemployment.

Thursday was spent making and printing the final exams. At home, of course. In theory I had access to a printer somewhere in Tryon Hall, but I had never been able to find it, and no one I had asked had ever shown any desire to tell me where it was. So not only was I working for poverty wages, I was printing off my exams on my own dime, too. At least angsting over that prevented me from angsting over the continued radio silence from Crimson.

Friday, the last day of classes, dawned bright and beautiful. This time of year it was warm but not hot, and the explosion of flowering trees that had started in March was still going strong. And it was May Day. A great day to go for an early-morning run. Even all the comments I received on my appearance from the legions of lawn crews on their way to work failed to put a dent in my mood. Yes, finishing up the semester was always a bittersweet thing, and yes, I didn't have anywhere to go next fall, but on a morning like this it was easy to believe that the adventure was just beginning.

Besides, Alex had hinted that if I needed a place to crash, I could crash with him. Maybe that wouldn't be so bad. Maybe John was right and I should move in with Alex and give up on this career crap. It certainly felt like it had given up on me. But I wasn't going to go down that road right now. I was just going to enjoy the beautiful May Day morning, and the knowledge that in a couple of weeks I would be out of here and back in Bloomington, where most of the streets and many of the people were my friends.

I was still radiating good cheer when I showed up for class that morning. The students in 1102 remarked on it, and suggested it was because I was looking forward to tormenting them with the final.

"Nah, she just wants to leave us," said Jason loudly. He had been sitting huddled in the back all week, looking miserable and refusing to answer questions or participate in class activities. I had suggested that if he felt unwell, he should stay home, but he had insisted he wanted to be there, and had come to all three class sessions, blighting the rest of the students' moods when they were already in a fragile state from the oncoming train of final exams that was rushing towards them.

"It's just a nice day," I said, while the students made semi-sincere comments about how much they would miss me.

After class Jason came up and cornered me by the lectern.

"You gotta help me with Arina," he said.

"Are you sure you should be here?" I asked. "You look terrible. You look like you should be home in bed." His hair appeared to not have been washed all week, patchy bits of beard stood out all over his face like he'd swiped at it randomly with a razor every other day, and his eyes were ringed with dark circles. Pity, revulsion, and irritation warred within me.

"It's all *her* fault! She's still saying she can't trust me! And for a while she was saying she was gonna come back to Charlotte, but then she told me she was gonna be living with another man, with *him*—you know about him? Motherfucker! And I ain't even sorry 'bout saying that about him—she wants to live with *him* because 'they understand each other' and 'he's a real man,' blahblahblah, all that bullshit. But now she's saying she's not even sure she wants to come back to Charlotte at all, and all 'cause of me! She says she can't trust me enough to let Max stay with me or anything like that, so what's the point? She said—"

"Excuse me," said Fatima loudly, coming over to the lectern. "My class is waiting to come in."

"Why don't you go home and lie down or something," I told Jason. "And then I really think you should try going back to your therapist."

"That bitch always takes *her* side!"

Fatima sniffed loudly at Jason's choice of words, and gave him a look that, had he been paying attention to it, would have burnt him to ash.

"Why don't you go home," I told Jason again. "In any case, I have to go."

"Yeah. You ain't gonna help me no more'n anyone else." Jason's shoulders sagged, and he walked off, weaving slightly like he wasn't quite sober.

"That man!" said Fatima. "He needs a wife to straighten him out! Only who would marry him?"

"I know," I said.

"But anyway, Rowena, Naz and I want to invite you to come with us for coffee this afternoon. You know, to celebrate the end of the semester. The new coffee shop in the library is open, now that it's the last week of the semester."

"Um," I said. I didn't actually like Fatima or Naz much, or even know them that well. But they were the closest things to friends I had here in Charlotte. "Sure, I'd love to," I said.

"Wonderful! My last class ends at 2:00pm. I believe yours does as well? And Naz's ends at 3:00pm. So shall we all meet at 3:00pm? At our offices? They're right next to each other."

"Sounds great," I said, with all the enthusiasm for staying late on the last day of class that I could muster.

61

I spent the last class session of 2105 trying to hearten the students up for the final by telling them how much they'd learned over the course of the semester. Which was true. Most of them could now reliably find Eurasia on a map two tries out of three. But I put it a little more encouragingly than that.

Once I got out, I told myself I was going to spend the hour between the end of 2105 and when I was supposed to meet Fatima and Naz getting a good head start on calculating my final grades. I was not going to spend it futilely checking for a response from Crimson. Definitely. I opened up my grading spreadsheet. Well, maybe I'd just check my email really quickly. There might be something important from a student there.

Nope. Nothing from any students, nothing from any jobs, including Crimson. I should calculate the total homework grades for everyone in 1102.

Whew, that was depressing. Hardly anyone had managed to turn in all or even more than half their homework. I needed to check my email again in case there was something there that might cheer me up.

Nothing. I could check it again after I calculated the total quiz grades. Whoa. That was pretty depressing too. It wasn't that my students were stupid, but most of them couldn't manage to study regularly. I needed to check my email again just to clear the taste of those grades.

Still nothing. What time was it? Oh God, only 2:30. I really needed to keep going. Total essay and quiz grades would be easy, and then I would be almost done and it would be almost time to go. Maybe I could just check my email one more time before I dove into it...

"Hello, Rowena!"

I looked up. Shaniqua was standing at the door, beaming.

"I just wanted to let you know!" she said. "I got into the program, *and* I got a scholarship! I'm going to Ukraine for sure now!"

"That's fantastic!" I said. "When do you leave?"

"Not till June, but I'm really excited! I'm about to try to book my ticket right now!" She made a face. "They're really expensive, though."

"That they are," I agreed.

"But I was thinking, maybe we could get together after finals to talk about things I should expect? And I'd just like to talk to you, you know, girl to girl, someday. I feel like you've got a lot you could tell me about."

"Um, sure." I thought about telling Shaniqua that we could never really talk girl-to-girl. I was ten years older than her, and her professor. But she probably didn't have very many people she could talk to about things she was really interested in. She probably didn't have a lot of good female role models. Maybe we could both be friends of a certain sort for each other.

"Sure," I said again. "I'll be leaving in a couple of weeks for my summer job, but we can definitely get together whenever would be good for you before that."

"Great! Oh." She looked over her shoulder. "Hi, Jason."

I peered around her to see out the door. Jason was hovering in the hallway. He looked even more strung out than before, almost vibrating from distress as he stood there.

"Can I help you?" I asked.

"Looks like you're already helping someone else." He scowled at Shaniqua. "Looks like you're busy with someone else."

"Do you have a question about the final?" I asked. "Or your grade?"

"Why the *fuck* would I care about something stupid like that!? She won't *fucking* talk to me! She just told me again she don't wanna have nothing to do with me!"

"I'm very sorry," I said. "But I'm afraid I don't have any control over that. I really think you should contact your therapist if you want help." I felt like a coward, palming him off on someone I didn't really believe could help him, but I also knew I couldn't help him myself. The only person who could help Jason was Jason, and he seemed determined not to do that.

"Oh. Okay. Okay. If that's how you're gonna be. I guess you're too busy helping *her*." He gave Shaniqua another death glare. "'Bye, I guess." He turned on his heel and slouched off, staggering slightly as he turned the corner and disappeared out of sight.

"What's with *him*?" asked Shaniqua. "We were in the same class when we started, but he dropped out. Guess he's started up again. He always was a weirdo, but he's even weirder now than he was last year."

"Yeah," I said. "He's having a tough time, and he thinks I can fix it, but unfortunately I can't. My powers are much more limited than most of my students seem to think they are."

"Yeah." Shaniqua looked thoughtful. "We all think teachers know everything and have all this power, but they don't, do they?"

"Afraid not."

"I guess I should keep that in mind, huh? Since I'm thinking about becoming a professor."

"Really?"

Shaniqua's smile soured at the disbelief in my tone. "You don't think I can?" She wanted to sound combative, but mainly she sounded insecure.

"It's not that you're not smart enough," I said. "You're *definitely* smart enough. I'm sure you'd make a great professor. But there aren't a lot of jobs. You can be the best professor in the world, and you might still not be able to find a job."

"Oh." She looked startled. "Is that why you're leaving? Because UNC-Matthews didn't want to keep you?"

"Uh-huh."

"So where are you going to be working next semester?"

"That," I said, "is an open question."

"Really?"

"Yes, really. I still don't have a job for next semester."

"But you're such a good professor!"

I shrugged. "Like I said, it doesn't matter. If you're serious about grad school, I'd be happy to talk you through the application process, provide you with a letter of recommendation, all that, but I would also encourage you to think very, very hard about going into it."

"Oh." She frowned in contemplation of this unexpected wrinkle in her life plans. "Okay. Thanks. Maybe we can talk about it some more when we get together next week?"

"Sure," I said. "I'd be happy to." And I actually almost meant it.

"Well, I'd better let you go. Oh, hi again, Jason. Did you remember something you needed?"

"Nah." Jason sounded sufficiently cowed by the ice in Shaniqua's voice. "Just checking to see if you were still here. But I guess you're busy. I'll get outta here."

"You do that," Shaniqua told him. She waited until Jason disappeared again, and then said, her lips pursed, "That man sets all my ghetto senses tingling. I'd stay away from him if I were you."

"Believe me, I intend to."

"Well, he's gone now. I've gotta go, but I'll catch up with you next week, okay?"

"Yep," I said. "Looking forward to it. Oh, and here's Fatima and Naz."

"Oh, hi you two! Well, catch you later." Shaniqua left just as Fatima and Naz loomed at the door.

"Come," said Fatima imperiously. "Let's go."

"Sure." I wanted to check my email again, but I was ashamed of doing it in front of Fatima and Naz, so I shut down my computer without checking and followed them to the new coffee shop.

62

The new coffee shop was in the lobby of the new library, which was still under construction. There were no actual books available yet, but there was a coffee shop and an upscale lounge area that was much too cushy and open for studying. Socializing, yes, but not studying.

"Where does anyone study here?" I asked.

"They do not," said Fatima, her brows beetled together under her tight headscarf. It looked uncomfortable. Maybe it helped prevent wrinkles.

"It's true," said Naz, nodding sadly. Both her face and her headscarf were much softer, almost comfortable. Being with them made me feel weird about being bareheaded. Not weird enough to cover my hair, but I could certainly see why women who were surrounded by other women who wore headscarves would start to believe that wearing a headscarf was a good idea.

"Yeah, I suppose," I said. "It's just, most of my students don't seem to have any kind of good study space at home. And it looks like the library doesn't have any kind of good study space either."

"Students do not come to this school to study," said Fatima. "They come to get a degree without working for it."

Naz nodded sadly again. I found myself nodding along sadly too. It was true.

"It seems like everyone here has something better to do than study," I said. "I feel bad for them."

"Yes," said Fatima. "But not too bad. Many people have much bigger problems than our students, and *they* still are able to study. Girls in Pakistan and Afghanistan still are able to study. Americans are just..." She trailed off, unable to come up with the correct description of what Americans were.

"Too busy," put in Naz. "Americans have so much of everything, they don't even know it. Even poor Americans, like our students, have so much of everything. They think they are poor, but they are the richest people who have ever lived. In everything except motivation and time. Everyone is so busy doing nothing that they cannot find the time to do anything."

"Yeah," I said. "So are you going to be here next semester?"

We ordered coffee and spent an hour chatting about our plans for the summer and fall. Both Naz and Fatima were under contract to teach summer school.

"If enough students sign up," Naz said gloomily. "The university requires at least fifteen students to register for a summer course in order to hold it."

"How many do you have now?"

"Thirteen. And the deadline is next week. So it is very possible that I will have no job this summer, and my thirteen students will have no class."

"And the problem with summer school is that then students don't sign up for classes during the regular school year," said Fatima, scowling. "I currently have fifteen students in my summer class, but normally one or two drop. If one or two drop this week or next week, then the class will be canceled. And then those other students will be too angry with the Arabic program to sign up for the language again. Even though it will not be the fault of the Arabic program. But I still do not have a contract for the fall."

"Neither do I," agreed Naz. "They say they want us to come back in the fall, but we do not get our contracts until July or August, and if the classes are not very full by August, they will cancel them and not offer us a contract."

"I have been here for three years, and every semester they have offered me a new contract," said Fatima. "But every semester they wait until the last minute. And they always make it clear that they might not offer me a contract again."

"The same for me," said Naz. "I do not know why I stay!" This led to us comparing notes in misery until we finished our coffee.

"Well," said Fatima. "That was unpleasant. But I am glad we shared our thoughts. I feel less alone now."

Naz and I nodded in agreement.

"But now I should go home," Fatima announced. "I do not want my husband to be waiting for me! You know, I am a career woman. Islam—the Prophet—says that a woman can have a career, providing her husband agrees. It is a very liberal religion, a very powerful religion, for women. So I always try to keep my husband happy with my job. I always make sure I am ready for him when he arrives home."

Naz nodded in agreement. I smiled weakly. I tried to imagine what it would be like to have a husband about whom I would say something like that, and so portentously. Suddenly singlehood seemed more freeing and less intolerably lonely.

"Well, thank you for inviting me for coffee," I said, instead of what I was thinking. "And let's keep in touch, okay?"

"Of course," said Naz and Fatima. I could tell that none of us meant it. None of us had anything in common other than a less commonly taught language and offices next door. But sometimes that was enough to cling to someone.

We walked out of the library and across the torn-up quad towards the parking lot. The warm sunny May Day weather and the blooming flowers and trees made the campus look less like a construction zone, or maybe a war zone, than it had for most of the semester. With more than half the buildings now completed, and a number of sidewalks now walkable, the campus looked new and clean and pretty. I tried to imagine staying here long term. It was almost tolerable as long as I didn't think too hard about the students.

"Now that the semester is over, the parking lot is finally open," said Fatima. It was true. Three-quarters of the faculty parking lot was now available for faculty parking, with only one corner still taken up with construction equipment.

"Maybe it will be completely open by the time the summer session starts," I said encouragingly.

"Maybe," said Fatima, her voice making it clear that she didn't believe it. And rightly so. Faculty parking was not a priority for university administration.

"Who is that man?" asked Naz. "I have seen him before."

Fatima and I looked over to where Jason was coming our way.

"It's one of my students," I said.

"He should not be parking in the faculty parking lot!" said Fatima.

"I think he's looking for me," I said.

"Why?" asked Naz. "What is wrong with him?"

"So much," I said.

Jason drew level with us. He was still vibrating slightly from distress, and he was sweating in the warm afternoon enough to make his hair stick limply to his forehead.

"I saw you come out of the library," he said. "I followed you here."

Naz and Fatima frowned at him. "You should not follow your teacher," Fatima told him sternly. "It is inappropriate."

"I need her help," said Jason. "She's the only one who can get Arina to talk to me!"

"Who is this 'Arina'?" demanded Fatima.

"My wife!"

"Ah." Fatima and Naz nodded in understanding. "And she has left you?"

"Yes!"

"That is bad." Even with her tight headscarf, Fatima's forehead wrinkled sharply. "You should get her back."

"I know!"

"But I do not see why your teacher can help you. I think you have to do it yourself. Go talk to her."

"She won't talk to me!"

"So go make her," said Fatima.

"She's not here! She's in Minsk."

"Minsk?"

"The capital of Belarus," said Naz.

"Ah. I see. She has gone home, yes? Well, that is not good. A wife should be with her husband. But do not bother your teacher about it. She cannot help you." Fatima folded her arms imposingly. Jason looked at her, and then, when she kept her arms folded, at Naz and then at me. I resisted the temptation to fold my arms imposingly as well.

"I think you should go home and get some rest," I told him instead.

"And when Arina still refuses to talk to me tomorrow?!"

"Have you ever apologized?" I asked.

"For what?"

"It doesn't matter," I said. "For anything you've ever done to hurt her. You could try just issuing a blanket apology and a promise to do better in the future."

"I ain't gonna do that!"

"It's worth trying," I said, as Fatima said, "You should not make yourself look weak in front of her. A man should be strong."

I ground my teeth a little. "If you want to issue an apology, I might be able to help you word it if you wanted help."

"I ain't gonna apologize."

"That's your choice, of course."

"But maybe I should, I don't know, let her know I could treat her better," said Jason. "Can I come over to your place? So you can help me."

"Email me," I said. "I'll be much too busy with finals and moving to meet with anyone this week."

"I heard you promising to meet with that Shaniqua chick!"

"That will be later," I said, thinking quickly. "But you want to do this sooner, don't you? Go home and get some rest and, if you still want to do this, send me an email tomorrow and I can help you word it. Maybe you could write it in Russian; that might impress her."

"I don't see why," said Jason. "Since she's already got another man who speaks Russian way better than me. I'll never be able to impress her that way."

Naz and Fatima both inhaled sharply. "She has another man?" demanded Fatima. "That is bad! You must get her back!"

"That's what I've been saying!"

"You should tell him to stay away!" said Fatima.

"You think so?"

"No," I said, just as Fatima said, "Yes."

"Yeah," said Jason thoughtfully. "Yeah. I should tell him to stay away. It's all *his* fault. If it hadn't been for him, she never would have thought to leave me."

"Of course," said Fatima, nodding wisely. "Wives want to be faithful to their husbands. Most wives, anyway. It is when other men interfere that you have problems."

"Yeah," said Jason again. "You're right. Thanks. I'm gonna go tell him to back off. Once he's outta the way, Arina's sure to come back to me, right? I'm the father of her child."

"Then she *has* to come back to you," said Fatima.

"Yeah. She *has* to come back to me. Thanks." Jason spun around and set off towards the student parking lot, almost jogging in his haste to follow Fatima's instruction.

"I'd better go," I said. "I've got to go talk to someone too. Nice meeting with you!" I was already reaching for my phone as I turned away from Fatima and Naz and headed to my car.

63

My fancy expensive new phone was able to bring up the number for the Matryoshka Market. I called it sitting in my car in the parking lot. I could see Fatima and Naz looking back over their shoulders at me as they walked to their cars, wondering why I was just sitting there.

They stood and conferred by their cars, looking back at me. I gave them a little finger wave while waiting for someone to pick up on the other end. It was nice that they were waiting there to make sure I was okay, but they'd already done enough for me, and not in a good way.

The phone rang once...twice...seven times...eight times...I was about to hang up and try again once I got home, when a breathless man's voice barked, "Allo!"

"Allo!" I shouted back. "Viktor?"

"Yes. Who's this?"

"This is Rowena. Do you remember?"

"Of course." His voice warmed and softened. "The American who speaks like a Russian. Arina's friend. What is it?"

"I wanted to warn you. Jason, Arina's husband—he might be coming to you."

"He wants to face me? Man to man?"

"That's what I'm afraid of."

Viktor laughed. "I'm not."

"I think he's really lost his mind. I think you should be afraid of him, since I think he's crazy, and crazy people are dangerous."

Viktor laughed some more. "That man couldn't be dangerous if he tried."

"He seemed in a really bad state when I just talked to him. I wanted to warn you."

"Thank you, Ro-eena the American. You are a very thoughtful and responsible woman. I will watch out for him. And if he comes for me, I will send him away."

"Um," I said. "Okay. Just be careful."

"Carefulness is for women and old men," said Viktor. "And Western foreigners. Thank you for calling me, Ro-eena. I will be fine." He hung up before I could argue with him.

Well, I had done what I could. I imagined calling the police. The only thing they would do would be to laugh in my face. Or if they did do something, it would probably get Viktor in trouble. He would not thank me for pointing the police in his direction.

I debated going over and checking on him in person. I couldn't see that doing any good either. I had already done everything I was able to do. I should just go home and hope for the best. I waved at Fatima and Naz again, started up my car, and drove off.

The warm May Day afternoon relaxed me a little. Until my car stalled out at an intersection. Then it stalled out at the next intersection. Either I wasn't as relaxed as I thought I was, or the transmission was totally failing. Just in time for my drive to Indiana. Oh goody. My illusion of relaxation evaporated.

When I drove into my parking lot, Duane and Lakeesha were standing on the top of their stairs, shouting at each other. As usual, something about diapers. As I parked my car, Duane uttered one final shout, and stormed down the stairs and off in the direction of the shopping center.

"Everything okay?" I called up to Lakeesha.

"It's nothin," she called back. "Just Duane being an asshole, as usual. He'll be back. Or if he ain't, no great loss."

"Um, okay."

When I stepped inside my apartment, Fevronia came trotting up to me, purring. She rubbed her cheeks against both my legs, and then rolled onto her back and tried to get me to rub her belly. She only bit me a little when I caved in and did so.

"How do you feel about moving back to Bloomington?" I asked her. She swiped at me in response. I disengaged from her as gently as possible, and went to start supper.

Lentils cooking—good thing John wasn't here to pour scorn down upon my choice of food—I unpacked my bags and started up my computer. It had been two—no, almost three—hours since I had last checked email. That had been nice and relaxing, but now all my stress came rushing back.

I took some deep breaths. It was already 5:00pm on the last Friday of the semester for most universities. There wasn't going to be anything important. I was just going to do a quick pro forma email check, and then I was going to move on. Maybe I would do something crazy tonight like read for pleasure, or watch a movie online. A movie that had nothing to do with my research. It would be fun.

I opened my UNC-Matthews inbox. Nothing other than a threatening email about the deadline for turning in final grades. I opened my personal inbox. Skimmed through the subject lines. Trash, trash, trash...wait, what was that? Was that an email from Crimson?

It was. With the subject line "Visiting Assistant Professor of Russian Position."

I took a deep breath. That didn't do much for me, so I took another deep breath. It was almost certainly a rejection. I should open it, read it, and get it over with. Sitting around hyperventilating wasn't going to make things any better. I clicked on the email.

Dear Rowena (if I may!),

I am following up regarding your interview for the position of Visiting Assistant Professor of Russian at Crimson College. The search committee was very impressed with your application and your interviews, and we would like to offer you the position. Please respond at your earliest convenience regarding your availability and interest.

Best regards,

Theresa Mayfield

Associate Professor of French

Department of Modern Languages

Crimson College

"YES!!!" I actually jumped out of my chair and screamed. Then I made myself sit back down. Then I burst into tears.

I made myself stop crying as quickly as possible. That was just embarrassing. This wasn't even that good a job, and I was most likely their second choice candidate. And I still didn't know what kind of salary they were offering. Maybe they had offered me the position because I was the daughter and granddaughter of alumnae and they figured they could get me to work for free. But maybe I was being overly pessimistic. And after so much rejection, even the tiniest sliver of acceptance was like manna from heaven.

My fingers trembling, I wrote back:

Dear Theresa,

Thank you for your email. I am still very interested. Could you please send me more information about the details of the position?

Best regards,

Rowena Halley

By the time supper was ready, I had gotten a reply from Theresa.

Dear Rowena,

Please see the details of the offer below. I will be out of town all weekend, but I will be happy to discuss the offer with you further on Monday.

Best,

Theresa

I replied with confirmation that I had received the offer, and started looking it over. The salary was $45,000/year. $45,000/year! What riches! What unimaginable wealth! Plus health insurance! I was going to be rolling, *rolling* in money!

Okay, I needed to play it cool. It had been drilled into me never to accept the initial offer made. I had been lectured at length about how the reason women had lower salaries than men was because we didn't demand more, so negotiating a job offer was not only necessary for my personal financial health, it was a feminist issue. Too bad that all the jobs I'd ever had were not the kind of jobs that could really be negotiated. But I had to make at least a token effort here, for the sake of all womankind.

Over supper I made a list of things I could ask for during the negotiation process. It was a very short list. The only things that seemed both helpful and possible were moving expenses and conference reimbursement. And maybe a higher salary, but that was not going to happen. Should I even bother? It might make them take me more seriously. If I were a man, it would almost certainly make them take me more seriously. But since I was a woman, it was more likely to piss them off and make them think I was greedy and selfish. Maybe I wouldn't even bother. I'd just ask for reimbursement for moving expenses and conference attendance.

Decision made, I showered, put on my sleeping clothes, and lay down in bed, determined to spend at least one evening this semester, now that it was over, watching mindless TV.

Five minutes into the first episode, a furious pounding at the door interrupted me.

"Open the fuck up!" a man shouted. It sounded like Jason.

64

Ugh, ugh, ugh. Or should I be scared? What if Jason had just come from killing Viktor and was here to kill me? I looked down at myself. In that case I was going to die in faded running shorts and a worn-out t-shirt that said "Do YOU go to Russian table?" in Russian. Well, whatever. I got up and went reluctantly over to the door.

"Open the fuck up!" Definitely Jason. I would recognize that whiny voice anywhere, alas.

"Jason?" I called through the door. "What are you doing here?"

"I came to fucking talk to you!"

"What on earth do you want to talk to me about, Jason?"

"I went and talked to that guy!"

"What guy, Jason?"

"That guy at the Matryoshka Market!"

Oh God. "What did you say to him, Jason?" I shouted through the door.

"I told him to stay the fuck away from Arina!"

"And what did he say?"

"He told me to fuck off! He told me Arina was his now, and I wasn't going to get her back!"

"So what did you do then, Jason?"

"Uh...I came here to get you to talk to her."

"Oh. Okay. So you didn't get into a fight with Viktor?"

I could hear shuffling and heavy breathing through the door. "No," said Jason eventually. "I didn't...I thought it'd be better to come have you talk to her."

Well, that was good. He hadn't shot Viktor. At least it sounded like he hadn't. "I can't talk to her right now, Jason," I called through the door. "For one reason, it's the middle of the night in Minsk."

"It's four in the morning in Minsk!"

"Okay," I agreed. "It's four in the morning in Minsk. Most people, including Arina, are still likely to be asleep. We're not going to be able to get ahold of her, even if it would be a good idea, which it isn't. Why don't you go home, Jason. Go have a good night's sleep, calm down, think about it, and then send me an email about what you want to say to her. And I would strongly recommend that you start with an apology."

"I ain't got nothin' to apologize for!"

"It still might make her more amenable to the rest of your words."

Confused silence came through the door. "It might make her more willing to listen to you," I amended.

"I shouldn't have to lie and smooth-talk her in order to get her to listen to me! She's my wife!"

"'Should' and 'shouldn't' are very dangerous words in my experience, especially in relationships," I said through the door. "Or completely powerless. 'I'm sorry,' on the other hand, is powerful. I really think you should give it a try."

"You just said 'should'!"

"Okay. I did. But I'm only going to help you if you go away right now, and email me tomorrow."

"I need this done now!"

"Hey!" Lakeesha had opened her door and was shouting down at Jason. "People are tryin' to sleep here! Babies are tryin' to sleep here! Stop standin' around shoutin' and either get inside or get outta here!"

"Go home, Jason," I said through the door.

"So you ain't gonna help me?!"

"I'll help you tomorrow, Jason. But only if you go away now and email me in the morning."

There was some more shuffling on the other side of the door. Then footsteps walked away. A vehicle door creaked open and slammed closed, and an engine started up and drove away. Only once I could no longer hear it did I open my door and look outside.

No sign of Jason or his truck. Lakeesha was still looking out her door.

"Sorry about that," I called softly. "Hopefully he's gone now."

"What the hell's wrong with that man?" she whisper-shouted back.

"His wife left him, and he thinks I can get her back for him."

Lakeesha snorted. "Men," she said. "Good thing he got his sorry ass out of here. Hope he don't come back."

"Yeah, me too," I said.

We both returned to our own apartments. I locked my door and put on the security chain. I gave both the bolt and the chain a dubious look. Between the two of them they looked like they could slow me down for maybe five-ten seconds if I decided to kick down the door, and I was not an aggressive or experienced door-kicker. Jason didn't seem like one either, but as I had told Viktor, he had crazy-person strength. After a little hemming and hawing, I put one of my two chairs under the door handle. I had no idea how effective it would be, but it would at least be a stumbling block for any intruder, and more importantly, it made me feel better.

I went back to watching my tv show, but every time a door opened or a car drove into the parking lot, I jumped up and ran to the window to see if it was Jason coming back.

By bedtime, the only person I recognized who had returned was Duane. I heard him pound on the door, triggering a round of wails from Nevaeh. He and Lakeesha had a short but vigorous slanging match outside the door, until he revealed he'd brought back diapers from Walmart, which softened her up enough to let him in. Peace and silence reigned.

I turned off my computer and went to bed. I told myself Jason wasn't going to come back. He was crazy but he wasn't that crazy. I reminded myself that I had a job offer. A job offer! For a semi-decent job. A semi-decent job on the complete opposite side of the country from Alex. How much of a problem was that? Not insignificant, I decided. I wasn't sure if I wanted to marry Alex, or if I was even in love with him, but I would rather be near him than far away. It was easy to imagine living with him, making a life with him...we had so much in common, it would be so easy for us to fall into even more of a relationship than we already had.

And like John had said, I didn't have any other prospects. But now he was on his way to California, and I was probably about to move to Georgia. For one year. Neither of these were long-term jobs. We could decide next year that we wanted to live together, and do something about it then. By which time I would be over thirty-five, and Alex would be almost forty. Awfully late to be starting a life and a family together. But it wasn't like I could go back in time and start things any earlier. The only way out was forward. There was no point in agonizing over the past because it was gone and I couldn't go back. I needed to focus on building a life going forward. I started to doze off.

Fevronia, who had been hiding somewhere, came meowing into the bedroom, jumped onto the bed, and walked across my chest. I swatted her away. She hissed and ran off. But now I was all awake again. God! I should be happy. I should be ready to get a good night's sleep in celebration of all this good news and the end of the semester. But instead I felt fidgety and uncomfortable. I turned over. No, that was uncomfortable too. I tried the other side. Not any better. I returned to my original position. I should just lie still until I fell asleep. Even Nevaeh was sleeping. If Nevaeh could sleep, I could sleep. I was dozing off...a vehicle pulled into the parking lot.

It's nothing, I told myself. *Go back to sleep.*

The vehicle door opened creakily and then slammed. Footsteps came towards my unit. Footsteps came right up to my unit. Footsteps went silent in front of my unit.

It's nothing, I told myself again.

The door to my apartment started to jiggle.

65

I froze. What should I do?

Call 911, I told myself. But I didn't. I didn't want the embarrassment of calling 911 if it turned out to be nothing.

The door kept jiggling. Maybe I was going to die because of my fear of embarrassment. Part of me wanted to hide under the covers. Part of me told me to get up and find out what was going on. That was the part that I listened to. I slid out from under the covers, entered 911 on my phone, ready to hit "Send" if necessary, and padded as silently as I could over to the door.

It was still jiggling. It went still for a moment, and then suddenly cracked open. It hit the end of the security chain, stopped for an instant, and then the chain popped off its track and the door swung open more, pushing the chair forward.

"What the hell is going on?" my mouth demanded. The rest of me was in shock. My legs started to back away from the door on their own, while my fingers tried to hit "Send" without my eyes to guide them. My heart was racing like an over-revving engine, and I could feel all the hair on the back of my neck rising. Primal fear responses were telling me to *run, run, run* and also *fight, fight, fight* the terrible intruder.

Just as I got my call to 911 to send, the door swung open a little more, partially impeded by the chair. The person on the other side of the door cursed and tried to shoulder all the way in. He managed to squeeze through the door sideways, and then half-stumbled over the chair. It was Jason. I should kick him, stop him...he straightened up. He was holding a gun.

"What are you doing here, Jason?" I asked. In the background I could hear, very faintly, someone saying "911. What's your emergency?" but I couldn't answer.

"I told you." He finished extricating himself from the door and the chair, and raised his gun. "I need you to get Arina back."

"Okay." I raised my hands to appear as unthreatening as possible. A tiny, tinny voice in my phone was still asking me what my emergency was. Would they figure out what was going on? Figure out where I was? Probably not in time. Surviving the next few minutes was all on me.

The first shock was passing. I felt very clear and smart, and my mouth knew what to say, just like at an interview. "I'll help you get Arina back. I already said I would do that. But there's nothing I can do about it right now. It's six in the morning in Minsk. Arina isn't going to be on Skype. We need to wait until tomorrow. You need to go home, Jason, and we can try again in the morning."

"I can't wait!" The gun was wavering in his hand. His whole body was wavering. I hated how sorry I felt for him. I could imagine what he was feeling so easily. I had felt it myself. I was still feeling it, on bad days. So I knew just how crazy it could make you.

"I know you think you can't wait, Jason, but you can," I said, as gently as I could. I was astonished at how calm and kind I sounded. "You've waited this long; you can wait until tomorrow if you need to. It's such a short time compared with how long you've already waited. Go home, and tomorrow morning will be here before you know it, and you can send a message to Arina."

"But she won't listen!"

"So you can try a different message, one that she's more likely to hear."

"No! I need to make her listen to me now! I need you to message her right now!"

"Okay. Okay. I'll go get my computer." I started backing away again.

"Where are you going?!"

"My computer's in the bedroom. I'm going to get my computer out of the bedroom. Why don't you sit down, Jason, and I'll be right back."

"No. No, I'm not gonna let you get away from me!" He started stalking towards me, paralleling my movement towards the bedroom. Could I dive into the bedroom and slam the door on him? Could I make it under the bed or into the closet before he fired the gun? Would the bed or the closet protect me? More than nothing at all.

I stepped through the bedroom threshold. With my phone-free hand I tried to slam the door shut. Jason got his gun hand into the door, stopping me from closing it completely. I slammed the door on his arm again, making him scream. I could also make him fire the gun accidentally that way. But maybe that was better than letting him fire it on purpose. I slammed the door on his wrist again. Something crunched. He screamed. Then he screamed again.

"Get it *off* me!"

Through the partially-open door I could see how Fevronia had jumped out of hiding and chomped down on his calf. He was dancing around, trying to shake her off.

"Drop the gun!" I shouted through the door.

"Get it the fuck off me!" He tried to kick Fevronia with his free foot and stumbled. The gun went off inches from my face. I yelled in shock and dropped instinctively to the floor, my reptilian hindbrain taking over and sending me scuttling into hiding.

"WHAT THE FUCK!!!" That was from upstairs. Nevaeh started to scream, drowning out everyone else's shrieks. At least she was still alive.

When I had thrown myself on the floor I had stopped holding the door closed. Jason, still with Fevronia clamped onto his calf, bulled through the door, slamming it against my head and knocking the phone out of my hand, making the screen go dark. The impact must have ended the call. Somehow Jason had kept hold of his gun, even though his wrist was already misshapen and swollen.

"Get this fucking cat off me!" he yelled.

With my reptilian hindbrain still in control, I could feel myself curl up in instinctive aversion to being near him or the gun. But another part of me couldn't bear the thought of him being anywhere near Fevronia. That part won.

"Okay," I said. "I'm going to have to come over to you." I slid over next to Jason and disengaged Fevronia from his calf. She swiped at me, hissed at both of us, and disappeared, I hoped into the bathroom and not out the door.

"Call Arina!" Jason demanded. "Call Arina right now!"

"Okay," I said. "Okay. Go...um, go sit down on the bed, and I'll get the computer."

"No! I ain't sitting down!" He waved his gun at me sharply. "Go get your fucking computer!"

"Okay." My reptilian hindbrain was slipping back into my subconscious, ceding control back to the frontal lobes, but with enough adrenaline coursing through my system that I still felt almost superhumanly smart. Unfortunately, all that my superhuman smarts were telling me was that I needed to keep Jason calm until a chance came to overpower him, or help arrived. Relying on others again, dammit.

I scooted on my butt towards where my computer was sitting on the floor next to my bed. I felt a faint pang of shame that a student was seeing how I lived, how I didn't even have a nightstand.

"It's powered down," I said. My voice was so calm, and it sounded low and soothing, like Jean Hagen's when she dubbed herself saying "Nothing can keep us apart" in *Singin' in the Rain*. Why was I thinking of that now? "I'm going to have to boot it back up. It might take a little while. You should sit down."

My unintentional Jean Hagen impression must have worked, because Jason lowered his gun till it was pointing at the floor and said, "Just make the fucking call!"

"Okay," I said. Jason was no longer vibrating with pent-up bloodlust. This was good. Maybe we would all get through this alive. "I'm going to get my computer now."

"Okay." Jason yawned widely, the adrenaline almost visibly draining from his body. "I'll just go sit down on the bed while you're working—what the hell is that?!"

"WHAT THE FUCK IS GOING ON HERE?!?!" Duane came bursting in through the door. He also had a gun in his hand.

66

"Who the fuck are you?!" screamed Jason, leaping up from the bed, gun on the ready, as Duane shouted back, "Put the fuckin' gun down!"

"No! You put the fucking gun down!"

"You fuckin' shot at my little girl! My baby girl!"

"Is she okay?!" I found myself shouting into the mix. "Is Nevaeh okay?!"

"Yeah." Duane nodded. "She didn't get hit. Bullet went right by her cradle. But"—he turned towards Jason, his gun leveled right at his face—"you almost fuckin' shot my baby girl! My baby girl! You coulda killed my baby girl!"

"I didn't mean to," said Jason. "I wouldn't shoot someone's little girl, man. I got a kid of my own. I wouldn't do that."

"But you almost fuckin' did! You coulda killed my baby girl! You didn't meant to, but you almost fuckin' did!" Duane took a step forward and motioned with his gun. For the first time since I'd met him, he looked confident and powerful, like he was in his element and knew what he was doing. My brain, still running at triple speed, spared a moment to regret all that wasted talent. In another life, Duane could have found something legitimate and useful to spend his energy and courage on. He could have become one of John's Marines, or a police officer, or a paramedic, or a firefighter. But instead he had ended up a petty criminal who'd already done jail time by his early twenties.

"Put down the gun," he repeated.

"And what?" demanded Jason. "You gonna call the cops on me? Who you think they gonna believe, me or you? You're the one who's gonna get shot here, you know that. I bet you're an ex-con, ain't you? And you came bursting into some white girl's apartment, waving a gun. That ain't gonna look good when the cops show up."

Duane's eyes flitted back and forth between me and Jason. I could see him trying to gauge the likelihood of those words coming true. I could see myself trying to gauge the same thing. I would tell the police that Duane had shown up to stop Jason, but it was all too likely that they would shoot first and ask questions later, and the person they would shoot was Duane.

"Jason," I said. I pitched my voice just low enough that he would have to concentrate in order to hear me. "Jason, no one needs to get hurt here. No one's been hurt yet, and no one needs to get hurt. Duane has a kid whom he loves just as much as you love Maks. Both of you can just walk away here, and you won't get hurt, and your kids won't get hurt, and you can go back to them."

"But Arina won't let me back! She don't wanna have nothing to do with me! Even if she does come back to Charlotte, she ain't coming back to me! She's gonna go back to her other man!"

"But you'll still be able to see Maks," I said gently. "That's the important thing, right?"

"Yeah." Jason's gun wavered and started to lower. "Yeah. Yeah, I guess you're right."

"Just put down the gun, and walk out of here," I told him. "And then you'll still be able to see Maks. You'll still have a chance to get him back."

"Yeah, I guess...NO!" He whirled around to look at me, his gun now pointing at my face. "NO! You'll call the cops and I'll go to jail and never see him again!"

"Not if you don't shoot anyone," I said. "As long as you don't shoot anyone, you're not in big trouble. A slap on the wrist at worst. Just put down the gun and walk away, and you're not in big trouble."

Duane had been edging closer as I was talking, until he was almost within reach of Jason. He was looking at me meaningfully, trying to tell me something, but my brain, which had been working so fast, couldn't slow down enough to make sense of what he was trying to say.

Duane took another half-step closer. His boot made a soft scrape on the cheap carpeting. Jason gave a small yelp and tried to whirl back around. My brain seemed completely shut down.

My foot shot out on its own from where I was crouched on the floor and caught Jason in the back of the knee. He yelped again as his leg crumpled. My foot lashed out again, this time catching his hand holding the gun as it waved around, trying to help him catch his balance. The gun bounced out of his hand and flew in a gentle arc away from him. My eyes followed it in horror, expecting it to go off when it hit the ground. It flew elegantly through the air, landing with surprising softness on the worn carpet. I flinched. Duane flinched. Jason flinched. But the gun didn't go off. It lay there, gleaming faintly in the illumination from the security light out in the parking lot coming in through the half-open door.

"Don't!" Jason had made an instinctive move towards his gun. Duane stepped up to block him. "Don't even fuckin' think about it, man. Just get the fuck out of here."

Jason looked back and forth between Duane's gun and the gun on the floor.

"Okay," he said. He held up his hands. "Okay, man. I'm outta here." He edged sideways around Duane towards the door. Duane followed him, always keeping his eyes on him and keeping his body between Jason and the gun. But Jason made no move for it. His whole body seemed shrunken and trying to hide as he sidled away from us and out the door. A moment later I heard a vehicle start up.

"Is that him leaving?" My mouth now felt numb and very far away, but the words came out as if I were having no problem speaking at all.

Duane glanced out the window. "It's a beat-up piece-o'-shit Ford Ranger drivin' out the lot."

"That's him," I said.

Duane took in a deep breath and let it out. "Shit," he said. 'You okay?"

"I think so. You okay?"

He took another deep breath. "Think so," he said. "I'm gonna go check on Lakeesha and Nevaeh. Lakeesha's got a cousin who's a cop and she's supposed to be callin' him. I'm gonna go check on that and then I'll be back, okay?"

"You sure you want to come back for that?" I said.

"They sure as hell ain't gonna believe you took him down by your skinny little self." He grinned. "Even though you kinda did. But I'm gonna get dragged into this no matter what."

"Is that gun legal?" I asked.

"Uh." He looked at the gun in his hand like he'd never seen it before. "Uh, maybe not so much."

"Maybe you should get rid of it before the cops get here," I suggested. "We can just tell them you showed up and surprised Jason and he ran away."

"Uh. Yeah. I guess that's what we'll do. I'll be right back, okay?"

"Okay," I said.

67

Duane left, shutting the door behind him as firmly as it could be shut in its battered condition. I pulled myself shakily to my feet and felt around until I found the ceiling light and turned it on. Where was Fevronia? Had she run out the door? Please don't let her have run out the door. I looked under the bed. Oh no. I staggered out of the bedroom, calling her name. Nothing. I searched around the kitchen/dining room. Nope. What was that smeary stuff on the floor? Blood. Why was there blood on the floor? Because my foot was bleeding. I must have cut my foot when I'd kicked the gun out of Jason's hand. I'd need to bandage it before I set off in further search of Fevronia.

I staggered into the bathroom in search of bandages. I caught sight of my face in the mirror over the sink. I looked just the same as I always did. Kind of wild-eyed and disheveled, but the me who had kicked a gun out of a crazy person's hand was the same person she had always been before.

I turned on the shower and stuck my foot under it. It wasn't much of a cut. I could just slap a bandage on it and head on out. I pulled my foot out from under the water and started dabbing the cut dry. Hopefully Fevronia hadn't run too far. Hopefully she was just hiding out somewhere, like behind a box, or, if she'd gotten outside, under my car. Hopefully... "AGH!"

The door to the cabinet under the sink bumped against my back. I slithered around so that I was facing the cabinet, and pulled it open. Fevronia meowed at me from the inside.

"Fevronia!" I held out my arms. To my surprise, she jumped into them.

"You saved me," I told her. "You saved both of us."

Fevronia meowed and wriggled out of my arms. Out of the corner of my eye I saw her dash into the bedroom and hide under the bed. A moment later, there was a loud knock at the door.

It was the police. Namely, it was Lakeesha's cousin and his partner, who came tromping into the apartment, followed rather uncertainly by Duane.

"I'm Ron." Lakeesha's cousin looked like a bigger, more male version of her. "Lakeesha told me what she knew 'bout what's been goin' on here, but she don't know who the guy was. Duane said he run off?"

"He did. His gun's over there on the floor. It was my student, Jason Anderson."

The gun was collected and stowed away. We went over who Jason was, and Ron went off and made a call to have Jason picked up. When he came back, I went through the story of everything that had happened, leaving out the part about Duane also having a gun.

"Uh-huh," said Ron, giving a Duane a sideways look. "I know you, Duane. I ain't gonna believe you came bustin' in here with nothin' but your bare hands."

"He damn near shot my little girl!"

"Sure," said Ron. "Well, I ain't gonna nose around anymore into it—for now. So then this Jason dude run off?"

It took a surprisingly long time to give our statements to Ron's satisfaction. Around the time we were finishing up, a call came in to Ron telling him that Jason had been picked up at his house.

"Didn't even try to run," Ron reported, shaking his head.

"I think he didn't want to do anything to take himself away from his son," I said.

"His son live with him?"

"No, his son's with his mother, in Minsk."

Ron gave me a blank look. "Where the hell's that?"

"Belarus. Eastern Europe. It's where his mother's from."

"Mail-order bride, huh?" asked Ron.

"Something like that."

"Sounds like it's good she went home, then," said Ron. "Okay, just sign here and I think we're done for now. There might be more questions later, depending on what this Jason fellow tells us. Stay out of trouble, Duane."

"Sure," said Duane. He didn't sound like he meant it. Ron gave him a hard look before turning on his heel and leaving.

Duane went upstairs. A moment later Lakeesha came down and knocked on my door.

"I brought you somethin'," she said. She proffered a steaming mug in my direction. "Some tea. It's this special tea I got from this Korean spa. I can't normally afford to go there, but every now and then I do. Anyway. I brought this for you. It's supposed to help you sleep. I just made some for myself and Duane, and I thought you might need it too."

"Thank you." I stepped back and invited her in, but she shook her head.

"I gotta get back to Nevaeh and Duane," she said. "They're both in a state. Well, Nevaeh's cryin' as usual, and Duane's in a state. He's still swearin' up and down about how that guy damn near killed his little girl."

"I'm glad she wasn't hurt," I said.

"I know." She shuddered. "Makes me shake all over to think 'bout it. But the Lord was watchin' over her for sure." She laughed. "My momma always say shit like that, and I never believed her. But after today I do. Sure felt like the Lord was watchin' over all of us, when I watched that bullet tear through the floor and go by my baby's cradle without doin' her any harm. I'll never forget that, not to my dyin' day. I don't know if I'm gonna be a believer in the future, but right now I sure am."

"Sometimes you need something to hold onto."

"For sure. And Duane—I think that was the moment he realized how he felt 'bout Nevaeh. You know, he's done his best, he's tried to stand by us as best he could, do the right thing, but I could tell he never really loved her like a baby should be loved. But when that bullet shot by somethin' changed in him. Maybe he'll be a good father now," Lakeesha finished hopefully.

"Sure," I said. My guess was that he wouldn't. But he might be a less bad father than he would have otherwise. Maybe this near-tragedy would be the turning point for the whole family. Maybe Jason's loss would be Duane's gain.

"Anyway, I better go now," said Lakeesha. "I'll come and check on you again in the morning, okay?" She smiled. "Too bad you're leavin'. Seems like we're finally neighbors now, don't it?"

"Yeah," I said. "And thanks for the tea. I'll wash up the mug and bring it back to you in the morning."

68

I tossed and turned all night, before finally giving in and getting up at sunrise. Too early to go upstairs and return the mug, I decided. My foot still hurt, and I felt too anxious and weird to go for a run.

I did all the asanas and forms I could manage with my cut foot. It was an incredibly minor injury, but it would be messy and annoying to reopen it. Then I sat down at the table with a cup of coffee, and, gritting my teeth, sent Arina a message about what had happened last night. I left out a lot of it, partly out of kindness and partly out of an inability to summon up the necessary vocab in Russian while I was still in this fuzzy, buzzy state. Maybe I needed to read *Antikiller* more closely. But I decided that nothing would be gained by giving Arina all the gory details, so I limited myself to saying only that Jason had come and threatened me with a gun, and that the police had arrested him.

Arina messaged back almost immediately. *I'm not surprised*, she wrote. *That man was always going to do something stupid. What will happen to him now?*

I don't know, I wrote back. *He didn't actually hurt anyone. He'll probably receive a short sentence for threatening with a deadly weapon, or something like that.*

What am I going to tell Maks? she wrote. *He misses his papa so much. That's why I was thinking about moving back to Charlotte. Not to Jason, of course. I couldn't stand to be in the same house as him. I realized that when I thought about it. But Viktor isn't a bad man, and we're both from the "former one-sixth," so we have that in common. I guess Homo sovieticus really is a thing, isn't it? Or was. Viktor and I are the tail end of the last generation to feel an attachment to the "former one-sixth," even if from a certain point of view we were both from colonized countries. Well, it doesn't matter. We'll both be Americans soon. At least I hope so. You say Jason will probably get a short sentence?*

American courts are notoriously unpredictable, I warned her. *He might get nothing at all because he was judged to be temporarily insane due to the loss of his son. Or he might get twenty years because he almost shot a baby. But probably he'll get a short sentence.*

I hope he does. Not for his sake, but for Maks's. Maks needs a father. Maybe Jason will realize that. Maybe this will make him understand how much he loves Maks, and he'll change his ways.

Maybe, I wrote back.

I'll probably move back soon, she continued. *To Viktor. So that Maks can be with Jason. Although I don't like the idea of him visiting Jason in prison. But that's his father's life. He should know about it. And in the meantime I'll ask Viktor if he knows anyone who can help Jason out. A good lawyer or something. Viktor knows lots of people.*

I'm sure. Do you think he'll help Jason?

He will for Maks's sake. He'll help Jason for Maks, just like you did. I know that's why you did it, and I wanted to say: thank you. I know this wasn't the best way you could have been spending your time, but you did it, and I know that you did it for Maks.

Maks has a lot of people who want to help him, I wrote.

He's a lucky boy)))))) Even if his father is about to go to prison. But even that was because of love.

We signed off after that, with vague promises to keep in touch that neither of us really believed. I was about to leave Charlotte, and Arina and I would probably never really be friends without the pressure of outside circumstances pushing us together. But I told her she could call me if she needed help, even so.

After that I sent Alex a short text about what had happened. He called back almost immediately.

"Jesus Christ, are you okay?" he said as soon as I picked up. "I had to call and talk to you in person. Jason *broke into* your apartment? What the fuck happened?"

I gave him a short but reasonably accurate version of the previous night's events.

"Well Jesus fucking Christ," he said when I was done. "I feel terrible that you had to go through that by yourself, but sounds like you handled it a lot better than most of us would—including me. You really roundhouse-kicked the gun right out of his hand?"

"It sounds more impressive than it was," I said.

"Yeah, yeah, that's what they all say. But he's locked up now?"

"He was arrested last night," I confirmed. "I don't know how long they'll hold him."

"Yeah, he could be out on the streets again tomorrow. Look. Why don't you get out of there. Just...I mean, I don't really have a great place to offer you, but I've got a place of sorts, so why don't you and Fevronia just get in the car and come up to Philly. Like, this afternoon."

"I've got exams," I said.

"And that's more important than your life?"

"Tell you what: I'll ask Lakeesha to have her cousin let me know when Jason gets out, and if I'm still here, I'll throw Fevronia in the car and come up then."

"Okay. I'd rather you were out of there now, but I can accept that as a compromise. And if you don't come up here, I'll be coming down to help you pack up and move out, okay? And escort you to Indiana."

"Won't you be busy with your own stuff?"

"Whatever. I want to do this."

"Um. Okay. I don't want to be a bother..."

"You won't be a bother. The only way you can bother me is by not letting me do this."

"Okay. And thank you."

"Yeah, no problem. And stay safe, okay?"

"Yeah," I said. "You too."

After that I felt much calmer and happier. I also felt bad about inconveniencing Alex like that, but I couldn't help but feel glad that he wanted to be inconvenienced for me. Maybe John was right and we were really onto something. Maybe things were about to take a big turn for the better for both of us. Maybe that turn for the better would involve both of us living on the same coast by next year, or even in the same state, or even, maybe, the same house.

Buoyed by that thought, I spent the rest of the day doing a little packing. It was strange not to be working, but my exams were all printed out and ready, and with the offer from Crimson on the table, I didn't feel the need to apply for the visiting lecturer and adjunct jobs that were currently trickling in. I hoped I wouldn't be punished for my optimism, but offer withdrawals at this stage were very rare. I was almost, *almost* home and dry.

Since I had never unpacked half my things, I was able to get quite a lot of packing done on Saturday. Sunday morning I got up full of enthusiasm for finishing as much of the packing as I could before actually vacating the place. I knew that for most people, packing was a horrible chore, and it was for me too, but it was still better than applying for jobs.

I made myself some coffee, opened my email, and started to skim through it. I wasn't expecting anything exciting. The big email from Crimson had already come. But there, in amongst all the junk mail, was an email from Dima. Both the subject line and the body had the same, two-word message:

Forgive me.

The End

*Gosh, what will happen next?!? Find out in **Summer Session,** the next story in the series, which is available on all major retailers.*

*And if you'd like to keep in touch, get regular updates and offers, AND get a free book, you can get your copy of **Foreign Exchange** and sign up for my newsletter (but only if you want to!) by scanning the QR code below.*

About the Author

S id Stark lives a life very similar to her characters', only with more grading and fewer exciting chase scenes. She did once get held up in Heathrow on suspicion of being a Russian criminal traveling on an American passport, though, which was fun. She loves to hear from her readers, and can be reached by email at SidStark@sidstarkauthor.com, at her website at https://sidstarkauthor.com/, on Facebook at https://www.facebook.com/SidStarkAuthor/, and Twitter at @SidStarkAuthor.

Don't miss out!

Visit the website below and you can sign up to receive emails whenever Sid Stark publishes a new book. There's no charge and no obligation.

https://books2read.com/r/B-A-NVEK-QJIFB

BOOKS 2 READ

Connecting independent readers to independent writers.

Also by Sid Stark

Doctor Rowena Halley

Campus Confidential: An Academic Thriller

Permanent Position: An Academic Thriller

Summer Session: An Academic Thriller

Trigger Warning: An Academic Thriller

Honor Court: An Academic Thriller

Total Immersion: An Academic Thriller

Under Review: An Academic Thriller

Doctor Rowena Halley Boxed Sets

The Doctor Rowena Halley Series Books 1-4: Four Dark Comedy Mysteries